CADAN'S BODY WENT STONE-STIFF. "LET'S GO," HE said to me in a low, rapid voice. "This was a mistake."

I started to push my chair back when Ronan spoke again. "I know why you want a Grigori, little lamb. We wolves have big ears. How's the mighty Hammer? Boiling from the inside out, is he?"

Cadan was already standing as I froze and stared at Ronan.

"Ellie." Cadan tried to drag me to my feet, but I sat bolted to the chair.

"Your Guardian's dead," Ronan taunted. "Just as the worthless, self-righteous bastard ought to be."

Cadan swore, but he had no power to stop me as I exploded and the world moved too slowly to keep up with me. My energy detonated and I flipped the table up with my hands. Ronan was on his feet, but I had already leaped airborne, flying over the midair table, my swords shimmering into existence and bursting with angelfire.

The club erupted into chaos.

COURTNEY ALLISON MOULTON

Shadows in the Silence

AN Angelfire NOVEL

 KATHERINE TEGEN BOOKS
An Imprint of HarperCollins Publishers

Katherine Tegen Books is an imprint of HarperCollins Publishers.

Shadows in the Silence

Library of Congress Cataloging-in-Publication Data

Moulton, Courtney Allison, date

Shadows in the silence : an Angelfire novel / Courtney Allison
Moulton. — 1st ed.

    p. cm.

Summary: In the final battle for Heaven and Earth, Ellie, who has
the reincarnated soul of an ancient reaper-slayer, must grapple with
her archangel powers to save herself and all of humanity.

ISBN 978-0-06-200241-9

[1. Reincarnation—Fiction. 2. Soul—Fiction. 3. Angels—Fiction.
4. Monsters—Fiction. 5. Horror stories.] I. Title.

PZ7.M85899Sh 2013   2012005261

[Fic]—dc23   CIP

                                                              AC

Typography by Joel Tippie

13 14 15 16 17   LP/RRDH   10 9 8 7 6 5 4 3 2 1

❖

First paperback edition, 2014

For Leah Clifford,
who gives me courage to go to war

Shadows in the Silence

PART ONE

Hell's Nightmare

1

THE DEMONIC HAD TRIED TO BREAK ME OVER AND over again, but even with my dress drenched in Will's blood, I stayed standing. This night had begun so beautifully and so full of happiness, and it had ended in terror and blood. But this wasn't over yet. Will wasn't dead. The demonic had done this to him, and now only a demonic reaper could save him.

The tip of my sword pointed at Cadan's chest, but he looked more concerned for me than afraid for his life. The others—Ava, Marcus, and Sabina—couldn't help me, but I knew Will's brother could. He was the only person I knew who had met a Grigori, the angels bound to Earth instead of Hell, and the Grigori knew everything about angelic magic and medicine. Will was dying from a reaper's venom, and only the Grigori would know how to heal him. I needed Will by my side to win this war. I couldn't defeat Sammael and Lilith and their demonic legions without him.

Cadan's opalescent gaze was fiery and hard on mine. "Ellie, you can put your sword down. Tell me what happened."

"I wouldn't ask this of you if I knew of another way," I told him. "You're the only person who can help me." I held at swordpoint someone who loved me and asked him to save the life of the one *I* loved. It was so screwed up.

"I told you I'd do anything for you," he said, but I caught the hesitation in his voice. "I keep my promises."

"I don't care what I have to do or how dangerous it is." I sniffed, my hand and sword shaking. "I just have to save him."

"Ellie." He slowly moved toward me, his hand out. His jaw clenched in pain as the angelfire licked up his arm to his rolled-up sleeve. He took my wrist and pushed my arm away before the burn did any permanent damage to his skin. His body was close to me, so close that I wanted to fall into him and be wrapped in his arms, to just be held and cry myself to exhaustion. Will always did that for me. That was no one's job but his.

With a sob, I let my sword vanish, and Cadan exhaled with relief and pulled me into him, his eyes roving over my bloody and tattered dress. His hands fell on my waist and his thumb pressed hard against my skin, testing me, I assumed, for injury. When I didn't flinch from pain, he sighed again.

"This is all Will's blood?" he asked.

I nodded and wiped at the tears on my face. "Merodach brought another reaper with him—Rikken. Will killed him, but not before he was bitten. It's some kind of venom. I don't know."

"I knew Rikken," Cadan said. "A bottom-feeder Bastian scooped up when he discovered what Rikken could do. Bastian collected the unusual ones and ensured they remained loyal for when he would need their abilities."

"The Grigori know everything, right?" I asked shakily. "About angelic medicine and magic? They would know how to save him. They have to!"

"It's likely," Cadan said. "But the Grigori I know is dangerous. Taking you to Antares could do more harm than good. I have a friend who can give us a better lead."

"Antares? The Watcher of the West? *She's* the Grigori you know?"

He nodded tiredly. "She's one of the four elemental Cardinal lords. She's also the Grigori that I—and Will—descend from. Bastian's line."

"But Bastian was demonic," I said, confused. "Only the angelic reapers are descended from the Fallen Grigori angels. The demonic reapers are descended from Sammael and Lilith. That doesn't make any sense."

"Bastian's father was angelic."

"You're joking," I said. "There's no way that Bastian is half-angelic."

"My grandfather was a direct offspring of Antares. This

is a very, *very* well-guarded secret. Antares's blood in our veins makes us more powerful, but our blood isn't as pure as a reaper who's closer to the source like Merodach and Kelaeno. They came directly from Lilith's womb."

"Will killed Kelaeno," I said, defiant of his claim. "And my angelfire scarred Merodach." Those two had monstrous strength, but Will and I had both proved they weren't invincible.

Cadan gave me the smallest of smiles. "You are an archangel and Will is a bit of a freak. You're lucky to have him as your Guardian."

Tears burned my eyes. "But I won't if he dies." I needed Will. I loved him and I couldn't do this without him.

"Ellie, please sit down for just a minute. I'll get you something to drink."

He directed me to the sofa and crossed the living room into the kitchen. Alone, I couldn't help but look around. His apartment was spacious and decorated with a lot of glass and modern artwork. Across the living room was a wall of windows, stretching from floor to ceiling and overlooking a large balcony. Beyond, the city blazed. I was suddenly aware that I was alone in a demonic reaper's home. It was so *normal* here, and that observation surprised me. Had I expected demonic reapers to live in caves or in a hollow tree somewhere? Sometimes they were so . . . human.

Cadan returned with a glass of water. I accepted it, but I could only take one sip before I started to feel ill.

"I'll take you to the place my friend frequents," he said. "He knows a Grigori named Virgil, so we'll look into this lead before we jump to a more dangerous one."

"Then let's go." I shot to my feet. "We're running out of time."

He licked his lips and his gaze passed around the room nervously. "Wait. First, you have to understand that where we're going will be crawling with demonic vir. They'll be everywhere. We can get in and out, nice and clean, *if* we're careful. We can't let anyone know who you are."

"Fine," I agreed. "Anything. Let's just go."

"Do you really understand what I'm saying?" he asked. "Not even you could take on a hundred vir at once."

I stared at him, my glare fierce. "I understand, but we've got to hurry."

"Do you have a change of clothes?"

"What?"

"You need to wear something other than that dress," he said very seriously.

"I don't care what I look like!"

"Where we're going, you don't want to be drenched with the blood of an angelic reaper. That might draw some unwanted attention."

My heart kicked in my chest. Looking down at my dress was a cruel reminder of the horrifying events of the night that had begun so wonderfully. "This is all I have," I said in a small voice.

"Then we have to get you a change of clothes from your house. Come on."

"Okay," I agreed, and followed him without another argument.

Cadan and I drove back to my grandmother's house, where Cadan followed me up the porch steps and Nana burst through the front door, her hand over her mouth.

"It can't be," she breathed, her eyes wide and staring at Cadan and then at my blood-soaked dress. *"Ellie!"*

"Don't freak out," I said carefully. "He's my friend."

"What happened?" she gasped, pulling me close and examining me for injury. "I thought I sensed demonic energy—"

"He didn't do this." I pulled away and walked by her into the house. "This is Cadan. He's here to help me."

"Why?" she cried, staggering against the wall. "What are you doing with a demonic reaper? What's going on?"

"Will is hurt," I said, surprised at the coldness in my voice. I was so emotionally exhausted that now I felt barely anything at all. "We're going to find someone who can save him."

I touched the railing of the stairs and turned back to Cadan. "I'm going to change and be right back. Don't go anywhere."

Then I left the demonic reaper with my grandmother and went into my bedroom. I rummaged through the dresser and pulled out jeans and a T-shirt. The once-beautiful dress was now a pile of bloodied rags at my feet. I resisted the urge to pick it up, smooth out the fabric, and lay it across my bed. I couldn't wait any longer. I had to save Will.

I rushed back downstairs to find that Cadan and my grandmother hadn't moved. She relaxed when she saw me, and Cadan's expression was pleasant, but he seemed a little uncomfortable.

"Cadan was just telling me that he is Will's brother," Nana offered politely.

"Half brother," he corrected.

I brushed past him. "Let's go."

Cadan said nothing and followed me.

"I'll be back," I told my grandmother. "But I don't know when. Don't worry about me. I have to do this."

I looked back at her once to see her nod and smile faintly.

Then we left.

Cadan drove us deep into the city. Detroit was alive as it always was at night, and even inside the car, I could hear cheerful, laughing voices and jazz music pouring from unseen speakers above the sidewalks. Cadan pulled into a parking garage and found an empty spot on the second level. I didn't wait for him and dragged myself out of his car. I stomped toward the stairwell and he caught up to me within a few strides. The heavy steel door slammed shut behind us and echoed off the white, scuffed-up walls. He grabbed my arm and I stared into his face.

"I need your head in the game," he said in a low voice.

"Let go of me," I ordered icily and yanked my arm back.

"Do you remember what I said?"

"*Yes,*" I hissed.

His jaw set. "Keep your eyes down and that snark on a leash. Just go with what I say, okay? And suppress your power to a level dimmer than sleep. Do *not* attract attention or you will get yourself killed. Even if you don't care about yourself, at least stop and remember we're here to save your Guardian's life."

I narrowed my gaze and turned away from him. He was right. I needed to cool off so we could do this successfully. I dimmed my energy as low as I could make it, hoping I could walk among the reapers undetected—as long as none of them recognized my face. The likelihood of that had to be slim. Not many demonic reapers had seen my face and lived another day.

We walked two blocks, venturing farther and farther away from the busy bars and restaurants, onto darker and quieter streets. We passed by a small empty lot with a perimeter of a rusting chain-link fence, and the supernatural pressure hit me. Demonic power oozed from the dark building like fog, tickling across my skin like spider legs, with claws that tore at my lips, trying to shove itself down my throat. I coughed from discomfort and Cadan glanced at me.

"Are you okay?" he asked under his breath.

"Peachy."

"Keep close," he said. "It only gets more dangerous from here."

I patted his shoulder. "Don't be afraid. I'll protect you."

He flashed a little smile. "Remember what I said."

The demonic energy crackling in the air grew stronger and stronger as we turned down an alley and headed toward a metal door beneath a sickly pale fluorescent light fixture. Standing in front of the door was a brawny demonic reaper who seemed completely human on the outside—no horns, wings, or protruding fangs—but his energy crackled the air around me and gave him away.

The bouncer put a hand on my shoulder, stopping me before I could walk by. He was sure to have sensed that I was human and I hoped that was *all* he sensed. I shook him off, aching to *throw* him off, but I bit my lip to quell my temper. Before I could say anything, Cadan stepped forward.

"She's with me," he said.

"Date?" the bouncer asked quizzically, his roving eyes gauging my body.

Cadan took my hand and winked at him. "Dinner."

I squeezed his in return—but not for comfort. I dug my nails into his skin, a warning. His entire arm strained and quivered beneath my strength, and he yanked me closer to him. A warning for *me*. I took a deep breath and remembered that any display of power, even one so small as what I'd just done, would risk exposing what I truly was to the demonic reapers and get us both killed.

He started to lead me by, but the bouncer pressed a palm to Cadan's chest, stopping him.

"I know your face," he said, narrowing his eyes. "You're Cadan. Bastian's son."

Cadan flashed a charming smile filled with bright white teeth. "Guilty."

"Rumor has it you killed Bastian."

His smile darkened. "Not just a rumor."

"Rumor also has it you're not to be trusted."

"Also not just a rumor."

"Makes me think I shouldn't let you in here."

"I'd like to see you try and stop me," Cadan said coolly. "Rumor has it, I killed Bastian."

I squeezed Cadan's hand again, this time gently and for comfort. I wasn't about to let this confrontation turn into a testosterone circus in which I'd have to save his ass.

"Step aside," Cadan ordered.

The bouncer obeyed, at last taking Cadan seriously. Cadan pushed forward, dragging me along behind him, and I glanced back at the bouncer, whose eyes were glued to mine. They flashed red like flames for an instant and went out.

Inside the club, a dusky cobalt light filtered through billowing clouds of cigarette smoke. The walls were draped in black-blue curtains of satin and the sleek, dark tile floor vibrated with the steady, slow, heavy beat of music that was more electronic noise than anything. This place was unlike any club I'd ever imagined. No one was dancing to the music, but reapers—all demonic vir from what I could sense, some gathered in small groups talking, sitting at high tables and in booths, some moving past—glanced at Cadan and me curiously. A female stared into my face and slowed, narrowing her gaze as she approached, but Cadan tugged me close to him and flashed his opal eyes at the other vir as if to establish that I was his, making me extremely uncomfortable. She kept moving. I didn't think she recognized me, but she certainly smelled that I was human, which was very likely to be a rare occurrence here. And she wasn't the only one watching me.

2

CADAN'S LIPS BRUSHED MY EARS. "STAY CLOSE AND don't make eye contact," he whispered just loud enough for me to hear him. "The demonic are competitive, and that one was about to try and take you from me. You'd have to blow your cover to protect yourself."

I took a deep breath. "Where is this friend of yours?"

"Over there."

A few tables from where we stood sat a demonic reaper with scruffy, reddish hair that stuck up in thick tufts. His tangerine-orange eyes widened and brightened and then turned into a scowl when he spotted Cadan.

"I thought you said he was a friend?" I asked him, annoyed.

Cadan took my hand and led me directly to the table. "Most of my friends hate me."

"Surprise, surprise."

The other vir shot to his feet, nearly knocking his chair over as he scrambled up. "The hell are you doing here?" he spit, and his energy prickled defensively.

"Relax, Ronan," Cadan said firmly. "I'm just here to talk."

He gave me a scathing yet hungry look. "With a little meat-bag pet?"

I didn't turn my eyes away from him or show any fear.

"Sit down, Ronan," Cadan ordered. "Otherwise I'll sit you down myself. I need a favor."

Ronan obeyed, but he wasn't pleased about it. "Why would I do any favor for you?"

"Not even for an old friend?"

"You're not my friend!" Ronan snarled, eyes a blaze of vibrant orange. "You took Emelia from me!"

I rolled my eyes at Cadan. "You stole his girlfriend?"

"It's your fault she's dead!" Ronan shouted, hands tightening into fists on the table.

"You *killed* his girlfriend?"

"Ellie," Cadan responded sharply without looking at me.

Ronan ignored me. "I told you I'd rip your face off if I ever saw it again. You and that bitch, Ivar. I'll kill you both."

"Ivar's dead," Cadan replied, his gaze faltering for a heartbeat, his jaw tightening. "I killed her myself."

Ronan stared at him, astonished, and then huffed with

indifference. "Well, it's too late. Emelia's dead and I blame you."

Had Ivar killed this demonic vir, Emelia, for the very reason she'd tried to kill me that night she caught me leaving the library—because of Cadan's fondness?

"I don't have time for—"

Ronan laughed bitterly, cutting Cadan off. "*You.* It's always about *you.* What you want, what you don't have, what you're willing to take. What you don't give two shits about once you have it."

"I couldn't have done anything to protect her," Cadan said, his voice flat. "If I could, I would have."

"Then why now?" Ronan spit. "Why wait eighty years to avenge her? If you loved her, then you'd have killed Ivar decades ago."

"Emelia would have died anyway. She was human, Ronan."

The other vir sat heavily back in his chair and crossed his thick arms over his chest. He shook his head and his mouth turned down in disgust. "You're a cold bastard. Just because she had an expiration date, then it meant nothing for her life to be snuffed out?"

Cadan's hardness broke then, giving away his emotions through his eyes. He leaned over the table and lowered his voice. "*Please*, Ronan. Tomorrow we can fight this out. Tonight I just need your cooperation. It's not for me, it's for her."

Ronan made an ugly noise and his gaze settled on me. "This little thing? A replacement for Emelia? Or have you finally a discovered a taste for human flesh?"

I couldn't hold my tongue anymore. "You talk about me as if I'm a scrap of food and you only insult Emelia's memory by doing so. Was she just a 'meat-bag' to you too?"

Ronan lunged across the table for me, talons sprouting from his fingertips, vicious fangs springing from his gums. My instinct was to lean away from him and call my swords, but before I did either, Cadan was on his feet, reaching over me, and he grabbed Ronan by the throat and shoved him back down into his seat. Yet again, I'd almost just blown my cover, and Cadan reiterated this fact with a frustrated glare in my direction.

He turned back to Ronan. "I'll tear your esophagus right out if you make a move for her again. Are we clear?"

"Like *glass*," Ronan hissed, baring his fangs before they shrunk back into normal-sized teeth.

As Cadan sat down again, I tried not to notice the many pairs of eyes now focused on the three of us. My heart began to thrum harder as my nerves got to me. This plan wasn't going well. I wanted to just get out, but we needed this information. I had to save Will. I had to see this through.

Ronan studied my face and tilted his head curiously. His shoulders rose and fell as he tried to calm his rage, but the more he stared at me, the more anxious he became. "I think I know what's going on. I hear all about you, Cadan, and what you've been up to."

"For the last time, this isn't about me," Cadan replied firmly.

"No, it isn't, is it?" Ronan asked, his lips pulling into an unpleasant grin. "Nobody brings humans in here, and I know you don't reap any more than I do. I know who *she* is."

"You don't know what you're talking about," Cadan said, dismissing Ronan's accusation. "Where's Virgil?"

Ronan's eyes went wide and his head fell back as he laughed. "That confirms it! You want to know where a Grigori is? Your pet isn't who you say she is."

"She's human," Cadan snarled. "Don't do this. I am begging you. I love her, Ronan."

Ronan's dark smile widened. "And you brought her right into the wolves' den. You must be in love with her if you want her dead."

Cadan's body went stone-stiff. "Let's go," he said to me in a low, rapid voice. "This was a mistake."

I started to push my chair back when Ronan spoke again. "I know why you want a Grigori, little lamb. We wolves have big ears. How's the mighty Hammer? Boiling from the inside out, is he?"

Cadan was already standing as I froze and stared at Ronan.

"Ellie." Cadan tried to drag me to my feet, but I sat bolted to the chair.

"Your Guardian's dead," Ronan taunted. "Just as the

worthless, self-righteous bastard ought to be."

Cadan swore, but he had no power to stop me as I exploded and the world moved too slowly to keep up with me. My energy detonated and I flipped the table up with my hands. Ronan was on his feet, but I had already leaped airborne, flying over the midair table, my swords shimmering into existence and bursting with angelfire. One blade slashed down Ronan's chest in a flash of blood and white fire, shredding his shirt and skin. He roared and staggered back, clutching his bleeding chest as I landed.

The club erupted into chaos.

Demonic reapers charged at me from all sides and I unleashed my archangel glory. Cadan took one look at me and ducked for shelter behind the flipped table. Snarling faces and blazing eyes were drowned by the blinding white divine light that was even more deadly than my angelfire. Bodies exploded into flame and ash as my glory swept through the crowd, drenching them in burning light. I lost track of Ronan as I spun and swung my Khopesh swords, the white flames lighting up about a dozen demonic faces—all that was left of the horde after I released my glory. As one blade swept through the neck of a reaper and the second blade buried into the ribcage of another, I had to remind myself that Cadan was out there somewhere, fighting with me. He wasn't Will, who was immune to my angelfire. My weapons were just as deadly to Cadan as they were to my enemies.

I cut through the wall of reapers, my skin splitting against sharp nails, and my ears filled with animalistic screeches and snarls. Hot blood dappled my face and arms, caked my clothing, smeared through my hair. I split a reaper from navel to neck and caught Cadan's eye through the flames. He yanked his sword out of a vir's heart and kicked the body away from him. At his feet was an ever-increasing pile of rubble.

A hand closed around my neck and jerked me around. More hands grabbed my arms, halting my sword strikes, and they yanked the Khopesh swords from my grip. I thrashed against them, but at least three reapers had hold of me— there were just so many bodies, so many that I couldn't focus, couldn't think. I could only move and throw myself around. Gabriel was coming, I could feel that part of me swimming to the surface from black depths. I could see the reflection of my face in the glossy black eyes of the demonic reaper choking me. My own eyes were filling with white as I began to lose myself to my power, but I couldn't let that happen. I tightened my entire body, straining to keep hold of my sanity, to stay here. If I let go, I was sure I could destroy every last one of the reapers in the room—but that included Cadan.

Cadan.

He was there, appearing out of nowhere, slicing the head off one of the reapers holding my right arm. Now that I was partially free, I locked my gaze with the reaper squeezing my throat. I slammed my hand into the weak point on her arm, right into her elbow joint. Bone snapped and she released me as she threw her head back and screamed in pain and rage. I smashed my palm into her face, shattering her nose, driving bone and cartilage so deep into her skull that she turned to stone immediately—dead.

I turned to the last reaper holding my other arm and I buried my knee in his gut, making him double over with a grunt. A shadow fell over both of us and I looked up, gasping, with just enough time to dive to the side as Cadan slashed his sword through the reaper's neck, nearly taking my own off with it. The reaper's grip went slack and he crumbled to stone in front of me.

Demonic energy exploded in my face, sending me flying across the room like a kicked doll. I landed hard on a table, pain shooting up and down my spine, wood cracking under me. I looked up and stared into the face of the vir as she came down through the air. I rolled off the table and hit the floor just as she hit the table, shattering it beneath her weight. I scrambled toward my swords. She tore at me, claws hooking my clothes as my hands found the silver helves. I bounced to my feet and reeled on her. My sword disappeared into her chest, slipping under her rib cage and shredding her heart. She screamed as her body went up in flames, and another demonic presence flashed behind me. I swung my body around with a cry of desperation, my blade sweeping up toward a bare throat—and I stopped, my sword barely an inch from taking off Cadan's head as he locked eyes with me.

I gasped and the angelfire went out. I lowered the Khopesh and he swallowed hard with a deep breath.

"Sorry," I mumbled, embarrassed that I'd nearly just killed him.

"No sweat." He looked around uncomfortably, but we'd destroyed every demonic vir. The female was the last of them—besides Cadan, at least. I took a moment to realize that I had never expected to find myself fighting alongside a demonic reaper. But he'd had my back, very much like Will had always done.

Then I remembered why we'd come here. "Ronan," I groaned, and searched the club in a panic.

I spotted him darting for the door at the same time Cadan did, but he was faster than me. He moved with ultra reaper speed, vanishing from sight and reappearing in Ronan's path. He slammed his palm into Ronan's chest with a rush of demonic strength and sent him soaring through the air. His body crashed through tables and chairs as he hit the floor. Ronan thrashed and was on his feet in moments, but Cadan grabbed his throat, lifted him off his feet, and smashed his back into the floor, shattering tile.

"Stay!" Cadan roared into the other reaper's face.

Ronan loosed an angry groan of pain, squeezing his eyes shut, fangs lengthening in agony, and Cadan backed off, letting me approach. Ronan looked up as I shoved my foot into his throat and poised a flaming Khopesh at his face. Slowly, he raised his hands in defeat.

My chest heaved as I caught my breath. "It's over," I told him. "You're the only one left. There's no one coming to save your ass now." The club was annihilated. Ash and rock littered the floor as if there'd been a landslide. Tables and chairs were shattered, couches shredded, the floor cracked and uprooted. I looked down at Ronan, who didn't dare let his gaze wander from mine.

"You . . . are mighty, Gabriel," Ronan gasped. "I see why he follows you."

I wasn't sure if he meant my Guardian or Cadan. That didn't matter now. "There doesn't have to be any more blood on this floor. Will you help me freely, or do I have to force you?"

"Not all of us are warriors for Hell," the reaper replied carefully. "Some of us just want to live."

I lifted my chin and looked down my nose at the demonic reaper, tapping into Gabriel's fierceness, giving Ronan my best scary archangel face. "You seem to have been deceived by my mortal vessel. Because you are a demonic reaper who does not reap, I am willing to demonstrate the mercy of Heaven instead of turning you to fire and ash. If you wish to live, then you will tell me what you know. Where can I find the Grigori angel known as Virgil?"

"I'm sorry, Gabriel," Ronan said, his gaze faltering for an instant. "But I have bad news. Virgil is dead. He was killed, along with several other Grigori in the past few weeks, presumably by the beast that Bastian unleashed."

"Sammael," I snarled, tasting something bitter on my tongue. "He's wiping out the Grigori."

Ronan nodded. "I've heard that he's trying to take out anything even remotely angelic that may be a threat to him. Once he's strong enough, he'll go after the Cardinals."

"Do you mean the Grigori lords?" I asked. "Of the North, South, East, and West?"

"Yes. The Watchers may be chained to the earth, but they're the closest thing to an archangel's power in this realm—besides you, of course."

Cadan let out a frustrated breath. "He'll go after Antares, the Lord of the West, first, because she's the closest. She's bound to the mountains, up in the Rockies."

I shook my head in disbelief. "Can the Cardinals *be* killed?"

"Anything made by divine power can be unmade by divine power," Ronan spoke up. "All things are limited by the balance."

Which included archangels—and even Sammael himself. Sammael had once been an angel. If he'd been created, then he could be destroyed. That gave me a flicker of hope. We had a chance at saving one of the Grigori lords from Sammael. And once Will was healed, we could take Sammael down for good before he could kill any more of the Watchers.

"Virgil is dead," I repeated, thinking aloud. "Are there any other Grigori nearby, Ronan? Any that could cure a demonic reaper's venom?"

"Again," Ronan replied, his voice small, "I am sorry, but I have nothing that could help you. I wish you luck, truly I do. Sammael can't finish what he's started."

I released Ronan and let my swords disappear while he climbed to his feet. "Cadan." I sighed, turning to my friend. "We have to find Antares before Sammael does. If he kills her first, then there's no way to save Will."

He closed his eyes. "We can find anoth—"

"*No!*" My screech echoed through the empty club, making the two demonic reapers jump and startling even me by its sharpness. I took a deep breath to calm myself, but my lips wouldn't stop trembling. "We have to do this. If you don't want to help me, then I'll find her myself. Sammael has the grimoire and I have no leads on the missing copy Nathaniel made. If Antares gets hostile, then I'll fight her!"

"Ellie," he protested. "Let's spend the rest of the night think—"

"We don't have *time* to sit around and think anymore!" I cried. "The Lord of the West is just a few states away and we can get there in just a few hours. Don't you want to help me? Don't you want to save Will?"

"I don't *care* about him!" Cadan shouted, his fire opal eyes flashing blindingly bright. "I care about *you*! I will help save his life for *you*, because *you* love him. It's all for *you*!"

Tears poured down my cheeks and I buried my face in my hands. Maybe this was too much to ask and it wasn't right using him the way I was. We'd fought at least a dozen demonic vir minutes ago, and he'd even saved my life.

"I'm just hurting you," I whimpered. "I'm sorry."

"The second Will wakes up, he will try to kill me," Cadan said breathlessly. "I will help you save him and I won't stop him when he comes for me."

I stared at him. "I can't let you throw your life away like that."

His gaze matched mine. "And I can't let you throw away yours, either."

I'd completely forgotten that Ronan was still there, that we were still in that club. Cadan didn't make a move to touch me, but he was shaking as if he was fighting himself with everything he had.

"I'm going to find Antares with or without your help," I said at last. "But it'd be a hell of a lot easier *with* your help."

His eyes searched mine and we were again trapped in that fragile silence, balancing on the edge of a cliff, waiting for a gust of wind to blow one of us over into the abyss. "I want to help you. I'll go with you."

"Thank you," I said to him, shaking.

"Antares will know what is needed to heal Will," he said. "She will know everything we need, because she . . . She is the original author of the grimoire."

"*Antares* wrote the grimoire?" I almost shouted.

Cadan nodded, letting his gaze fall.

"Then we have to go to her," I said, my heart lifted. "She knows everything about divine magic. Why didn't you tell me? Why would you try to find another Grigori before her? She's the one we need!"

I was turning wild with hope, and he held my face with his hands to steady me. His eyes drove into mine. "Because Antares won't give up the information willingly. If she doesn't just kill us, then she'll name a price and I don't know what it will be."

My hands smoothed over his and guided them down. "Anything. I would give anything to save him."

He drew in a long breath and let it out just as slowly, his eyes closing for a moment. "Ellie, a Grigori isn't like you, or Michael, or Azrael. They're still Fallen angels. They're trapped here. Earth is their prison. Antares is one of only four Cardinals in the entire world and the most powerful of their kind. They are the Watchers and they are bound to the place where they fell."

I shook my head, not understanding. "What do you mean?"

"I mean," he began, "that Antares fell before time began and she's trapped there. The Cardinal Watchers are practically mad, Ellie. They've been forced to watch the world go by with little to no contact from anyone for so long they have become elemental. And you . . . You're an archangel. You put her there. I don't know what she would do if she saw you."

Did I have the strength, in my human body, to fight her if she attacked me? What sort of price would she demand from me for Will's cure?

"He's right," Ronan said from behind us. "I've heard

stories, but Cadan is the only person I know who's met one of the Lords. You'd be wise to take his advice."

I turned to face him, narrowing my gaze. My hands trembled and I tightened them into fists to hold them steady. "I don't have time to be wise while my Guardian is dying. I have to do whatever I can to save him. Wouldn't you have done the same for Emelia?"

His eyes brightened almost imperceptibly. "If I'd been as crazy as you, she might still be alive."

"Sometimes crazy is a surprisingly successful last resort," I replied. Cadan and I headed for the exit.

"Cadan," Ronan called, and we looked back at him. "If you love her, then let her go. You know you have to."

Cadan's teeth clenched, but he made no move or response to the other vir. I put my hand on his arm and guided him with me.

"Let's go," I said softly. "He doesn't have anything else to say."

He let me lead him from the club and we walked to his car in silence. Too many thoughts ran through my head for conversation, and I assumed the same for him as well. We both knew that I was using him, but he was willing to put his life in danger to help me. I couldn't process what was happening. All I could think about was Will, dying on a kitchen table.

I climbed into the seat, fastened my belt, and leaned back. My eyes fluttered open and shut as Cadan got in the car and turned the ignition. He glanced at me.

"You should try to sleep," he offered, his voice quiet.

I shook my head, fighting to keep my eyes open. "I can't sleep."

And then I did.

3

BEFORE I OPENED MY EYES, I FELT THE COOL MOIST air on my face and it smelled like the sea. The wind was chilly, combing through my hair and pulling at my clothes. I opened my eyes and stared at the ocean in front of me— and the next second I realized in horror that the ocean was hundreds of feet *below* me. Giant waves crashed upon jagged rocks at the foot of the cliff I leaned over. A sharp gasp escaped me and I flailed back, my heart pounding against my rib cage.

I looked around at the rolling, rocky landscape, desperate to know how I'd gotten here—and where *here* was exactly. The sky was dark and gray, the raging sea below even darker and mercilessly hurling itself against the cliff wall. The waves drowned out the cries of the gulls overhead.

"Ellie?"

His voice took hold of my heart and I whirled to meet him, to stare into his face. It had only been a few hours, but I felt like I'd forgotten how green his eyes were. He watched me with a perplexed look, as shocked to see me as I was about everything, but he looked healthy standing there in front of me.

"What are you—?"

I didn't wait for Will to finish before I launched myself into his arms, holding him tightly. Something wasn't right here, I knew that, but it didn't matter. He was here and he was okay. "The last thing I remember is Cadan driving me home. I have no idea how I got here."

He pulled away only just. "Cadan? Why were you with him?"

"He's helping me to save you," I said, twisting my fingers in his sweater. He was warm like always and I wanted to fold myself into him.

Will blinked and looked even more baffled. "Save me? I'm just fine, Ellie."

"You look it right now," I said, still piecing the puzzle together in my head. "But you're sick. I must be dreaming. I must've fallen asleep or something."

"Do you think you're dreaming?" he asked.

I slipped out from his arms and studied the beautiful landscape. The cliffs and sea were familiar, but this particular location was unknown to me. I was certain I'd never been here before. "Where are we? This is Scotland, isn't it?"

He gazed at me fondly. "Yes, the Isle of Skye. This is where I grew up, in the house on the hill. Beyond it is a human village. My mother liked to keep a small distance from them."

Behind him was a small stone house, its chimney smoking gently. I'd never seen his childhood home. There was no way I could have imagined this scene so vividly. "This isn't my dream," I said, turning to Will. "It's yours."

His expression was determined and perhaps a little sad as he accepted this and looked past me and out onto the sea. "I miss this place. It feels good to be back here."

"It's amazingly beautiful," I said, but my gaze was on him instead of the landscape. "Do you dream of it often?"

He frowned some, his brow darkening his eyes. "Not often, but enough so that I'll never forget this place. I dream of many things."

"Memories?"

"Yes," he replied. "Good memories, terrible memories, of things I long for, and of things I fear." At last he looked at me, but his form seemed to mist over, to dematerialize and become solid again, all in an instant. "Beware the serpent," he said in a hollow voice that didn't seem his own. "He comes for you, as he did the giver of life. The venom of God will try to tempt you, Gabriel. You must be vigilant and strong against the incubus."

I caught my breath, staring back at him in surprise. "What?"

Will's form shattered once more before he returned to normal, almost like a glitch in a computer program. "I asked how you're doing. Are you okay?"

"I—I'm fine," I stammered, struggling to gather my senses. "Hanging in there."

I wanted to ask him about what had just happened to him, what he'd said, but I reminded myself that this was a dream and if there was one thing I knew about dreams it was that they didn't make a whole lot of sense. But as I contemplated the cryptic words coming from Will that couldn't possibly belong to him, I began to realize that they made more sense than was first apparent. Was my subconscious taking over here, or was it something entirely else? The serpent, the venom of God . . . that was Sammael, he who tempted Eve, the giver of life, in the guise of a snake. Had the warning meant Sammael, the incubus, would tempt me? He'd have to just try and kill me, because no way would I touch him. But *why* would he try to tempt me? Just because he thought he could, or was there a purpose?

Will touched my cheek, pushing my hair back behind my ear and studying the locks between his fingers as he sometimes did. The gesture was so familiar and comforting that I was able to shove away my stirring fears of Sammael. "Your hair . . . it's like strands of dying embers that flicker with firelight. My fire goddess. I am cold to your heat."

I gave him a little smile. "You're talking like a crazy Martian again."

He smiled back. "You make me crazy."

"Right back at you," I said playfully and kissed his palm before drawing closer to him. I wrapped my arms around his back and he held me tight.

"These are the dreams I wish I always had," he whispered against my hair. "I don't want any more of the other dreams where I lose you. They are nightmares and they are memories."

"Don't think about them," I said, and tightened my grip as if he'd float away. "Concentrate on right now, where I'm here and we're both safe."

"I can't help it." His words were strangled by his shallow breaths. His body tensed against me and I felt his fear so vividly, I could taste it on my tongue like too-ripe citrus. "Your deaths haunt me. I see your face in my nightmares, your blood on the ground and the light dimming in your eyes. The flames flicker out and your embers die."

I drew away from him and stared into his face as my pulse picked up speed with my growing terror. "Will, don't talk like that. We're really not that emo—"

"Every time you fall, I'd gladly take your place," he said hoarsely. "I pray for my own body to lie there, and He never listens. I pray for you to get back up and you don't. I close my eyes, but I hear nothing but my own prayers. He has forgotten me." Will slipped completely out of my arms and moved past me.

"It's okay, I promise," I said to his back. "Don't blame

yourself. It's crippling you."

Black clouds rolled through the sky, devouring the afternoon light until the landscape was so dark, it seemed as if we were suddenly trapped within a pitch-dark room. I gasped as our forms disappeared into shadow, but as soon as the light went out, a dim glow like moonlight came from an unseen source. All I could see was him and me.

"What's going on?" I asked. "Are you doing this?"

"I can't stop the nightmares," he replied absently. "All I can do is fight. It's all I ever do, but I know nothing else." His sword shimmered into being, the sudden silver brightness blinding me for a moment.

Then he was swinging. The shapes of lupine reapers materialized in the darkness, black fur glistening in light that seemed to come from nowhere, and I drew my swords on instinct. Trees grew from the ground, sprouting leaves lightning fast. The reapers came from the trees like a plague of rats, snarling and snapping their jaws, and on the other side of Will, I saw *me*.

In the midst of the swarm of reapers, I—or rather, Will's mental projection of me—swung the unmistakable Khopesh swords swallowed in white angelfire. My dream self fought effortlessly, sword strokes fluid and well-placed. I'd never seen myself fight before. It was as if the phantom me knew her enemies' next moves before they occurred, blades meeting flesh, ash and fire billowing toward the forest canopy as one by one the reapers met their deaths by her hand. The glimpses I caught of her face made my breath stop. She was every bit the avenging angel striking down her enemies, her face hardened with determination, and the shadows in her eyes made her seem older. Will matched her every move, but no matter how many enemies they cut down, there were just too many.

She let out a smothered cry of pain and her blood painted the ground.

"No!" Will roared and destroyed the reaper between them with a final swing of silver through flesh. He moved fast, taking hold of my dream self before her knees hit the grass. His sword was gone and she was in his arms, and then they took to the sky in retreat. The sensation of being shot from the ground like a rocket flattened my stomach and I almost lost my balance. Their forms blurred away and reappeared as Will knelt and gently set my dream self on the grass in a quiet grove of trees. She groaned and clutched her chest. Blood steadily leaked from deep, jagged claw marks that ripped through her clothing and skin.

Will frantically pushed her hair away from the wounds and tore off the sleeve from his shirt, revealing his tattooed right arm, and pressed the cloth to her chest. The fabric turned bright red instantly. He murmured fearful things under his breath and cupped her cheek.

"I'm so sorry," he whispered, and it was all that I could make out. "I'm so sorry."

She gargled something back, gruesomely choking on her

own blood. I felt strangely detached from the moment, watching myself die in agony. I couldn't move, couldn't speak, as I watched the horror unfold before me. Her body became limp in Will's arms, his anguish naked on his face, and her eyes lost their focus.

Will bent over her, clutching her tightly to his chest, before he laid her back onto the grass. "I can never save you. You always die like this, in my arms, and I can't bring you back."

I watched my dream self shudder into silence, the blood leaking from her like a river. "That's not me," I told him, finding my voice at last. "Well, it *was* me, but I'm right here. This is just a memory. A dream. This isn't real."

"It's always real." His fingers brushed my dream self's cheek as his jaw tightened and he closed his eyes. "It hurts so much. You're dying, and I can feel it like acid through my veins, through my bones. You're so sad and I know your sadness is for me, not for yourself. I feel everything that you feel."

"Then feel me," I pleaded. I knelt beside him, trying to focus on him and not my dream self dying on the ground. I took his face in my hands and made him look at me. Forgotten, the body faded away. "Feel that I'm right here. My heart's beating. I'm alive and I'm right next to you. I'm not hurt, can't you see?"

His lip trembled as his eyes roved over me. A tear slipped over his cheek and disappeared. "How? How are you there?"

"You're dreaming, Will," I said, smoothing a hand over his hair, trying to stop my own tears from coming. "Believe me. This isn't real, but *I* am. I'm right here."

"You're okay?"

His voice was so heartbroken that I was breathless for a few seconds. I nodded and drew in a quivering breath. "Yes," I whispered. "I'm okay." I took his hand and pressed it to my chest. "Feel my heartbeat? I'm okay, I promise."

He swallowed hard and his shoulders sagged with relief. He squeezed his eyes shut and buried his face into my shoulder, pulling me into him. "Ellie," he sighed. "I miss you where I am. It's dark here."

I hushed him, resting my cheek against his hair. "I'm with you. I'm right here."

The scene changed and we were on the cliffs of Scotland again, and the misty wind shoved against me, but I didn't feel its chill. The crashing waves and crying gulls were in the distance and it was just him and me.

He lifted his head, his green eyes bright and gazing up at me. He pulled me into his lap and my knees sank into the cool grass on either side of him. He cupped my face, brushing his cheek against my skin, moving against me, drawing my hair over my shoulders and pressing his lips to the locks as he inhaled. "Jasmine," he whispered, and smiled wistfully.

I nodded and a soft sob escaped me. I still wore the perfume I'd put on for prom. "Yes, Will."

"I miss you," he said again.

"I miss you, too."

"I keep looking for the light, but I can't find it. Come back to me."

My fingers brushed his lips and I pressed my forehead to his. "I will, I promise."

He tilted his head back and his mouth opened against mine, his lips soft, and I melted into him. He held me as close as he physically could, his hands gentle but tight, as if he were afraid I were a tiny bird that might fly away if it escaped. An overwhelming rush of sadness and longing passed through me, because I knew this wasn't real, that we weren't really together. His torment broke my heart and I felt like I was falling through the sky, like the ground wasn't really beneath me, like my body wasn't really against his. None of this was real. None of it.

It's not real.

No matter how hard I tried to believe the words circling in my mind, I could only focus on Will, who kissed me like he needed my lips to breathe, like we were sinking beneath the ocean beyond the cliffs and we'd drown if he pulled away. I could only think of how much time I'd wasted, all these centuries of denying how much I was in love with him, and now he was dying.

Something tugged at my core, pulling my stomach out my back. I broke our kiss and stared into his face, confusion wrapping around me. My body jerked involuntarily and he tightened his grip on me.

"Ellie?" he asked.

"I don't know what that is," I confessed, holding on to him.

"Please don't leave me," he begged. "Please stay here so I'm not alone."

A vice clamped down on my heart. "I can't control this."

"Ellie—"

Then something yanked me back at a lightning speed and Will's form blurred to nothingness at the end of a dark tunnel as he cried out my name. The sensation of flying through the air came to a halt when I woke up in a soft bed. I thrashed in the sheets with a desperate gasp of fright and I sat bolt upright. My pulse hammered beneath my skin, which was damp with cold sweat. Once again, I had no idea where I was, but this place was real. I was truly awake this time.

The room around me was dark and unfamiliar, and I pulled back the sheets to find myself still wearing my clothes from earlier. They were ripped and dirty from the fight at the nightclub. As I started to slide off the bed, a door on the far wall opened and Cadan appeared with a frightened look on his face.

"Are you okay?" he asked. "What's wrong?"

"Where am I?" I demanded, ignoring his concern.

"Relax. We're back at my apartment. You fell asleep on the drive so I brought you here. I tried to wake you, but you wouldn't respond. I figured you were exhausted so I let you sleep in my bed. Are you upset? I'm sorry if I—"

I realized that tears soaked my cheeks and I wiped them away. "No, it's okay. I had a bad dream, or something. I didn't know where I was for a second. Just freaked me out a bit."

He sat down on the bed beside me and smoothed my hair back. "Do you always sleep like that?"

"Like what?" I asked defensively. I touched the corner of my mouth to check for drool.

He studied me curiously, his opal eyes bright in the dim light pouring in from the doorway. "You were practically out cold. I was pretty worried about you."

I shook my head. "Just a deep sleeper sometimes, I guess." I wasn't about to confess to him what had really happened. How I had been sucked into Will's dream was a mystery, but part of me wanted to fall immediately back to sleep in case I could be with him again. I could still feel the ocean wind, his touch on my skin, my lips numb from his kisses. I closed my eyes at the memory and inhaled, but instead of Will's scent, I caught Cadan's.

"You should go back to sleep," Cadan offered. "Stay here a few more hours and we can figure out a plan once you've had some more rest."

"Sleep . . . here?" I asked, suddenly remembering I was in Cadan's bed.

"It's okay," he said. "I've got a couch." He gave me a kind smile that made me feel a little reassured.

"I don't mean to take your bed."

"Sleep. Just come on out when you're ready. The world

won't end if you sleep a bit more."

I wanted out of my dirty clothes, but I was too tired to think of an alternative. I crawled back into the bed and sank into the silk sheets. Cadan rose and walked toward the door. I rested my head against the pillow and watched him.

He paused with one hand on the doorknob. "Sleep sweet," he said softly and closed the bedroom door behind him.

I could only muse over the strange, almost archaic phrase for a few moments before I fell into a fitful sleep, one in which Will was noticeably absent.

4

WHEN I WOKE IN THE MORNING, I WAS FAR TOO
aware of the blood on my skin and clothes from the night
before. My hair was crusty and stuck together in clumps
with the stuff, and there was even blood under my nails. I
was so used to gore by now that instead of being as grossed
out by it as I used to be, I just found it annoying. I felt sorry
for sleeping in Cadan's bed while covered in filth. The afternoon sun poured across the carpet and walls through the
floor-to-ceiling windows. I bathed in the warmth for a few
precious seconds before the task ahead of me tore into my
thoughts.

I left the bedroom and found my way to the living room,
which was overlooked by the kitchen. Beyond the bar counter, I saw Will rummaging about several cabinets and my
breath caught in my throat. I blinked, and then it wasn't Will

I saw; it was Cadan. I stood frozen, unable to approach him until my pulse settled. A memory hit me hard, the memory of waking up late after that stupid college party to find Will cooking breakfast. When I looked at Cadan, now that I knew that Will was his younger half brother, I could see how strongly he resembled Will. It was the curve of his lips, the straightness of his nose, the heavy line of lashes over his eyes. But they weren't Will's emerald-green eyes. The fire opals that made up Cadan's irises flickered when he saw me, the prism flames spinning for a heartbeat.

"I hope you slept well," he said, and focused back on the food in front of him. "I can't cook, so I had lunch delivered. You've got to be starving."

As a matter of fact, I was. But when I glanced at the blood caked under my fingernails, I couldn't imagine eating before I showered. "That was generous of you," I replied, "but I've got to clean up. I'm so gross right now. There's still blood and . . . *stuff* . . . everywhere on me. Do you mind if I get a shower first?"

"No, of course not." He led me to the bathroom and offered me a clean towel. I took a scorching-hot shower and scrubbed myself until my skin was raw but clean. I gingerly stepped back into my dirty clothes, unhappy I had nothing else to wear.

Back in the kitchen, Cadan and I made small talk while I ate. It was obvious how hard he'd tried. "Thank you so much. I ought to get going."

He nodded. "What do you think should be the plan? Regarding Antares?"

"We find her," I said clearly and surely. "If she's in the Rocky Mountains, the same place you saw her last, then we go there. I'll pack and we can get going today."

"Tonight," he corrected. "Sunlight and I don't get along."

"Right." I surprised myself with how easily his demonic nature escaped me. "Okay. Why don't you arrange travel plans for us? I need you with me. You're the only one who knows where Antares is."

He stared at me, his gaze firm and drilling. "Are you sure you want me along?"

"Absolutely," I said, recalling how well we fought together last night. "We're a good team."

He watched me a moment longer before tearing his eyes away, and he put the food away in a bag and slid it across the counter toward me. "I hope you liked the stir-fry. It's from my favorite Thai restaurant. A little hole-in-the-wall downtown. You should go there sometime."

I smiled at him. "I appreciate this—everything you've done for me. Thank you."

The corner of his mouth pulled back for an instant before he shrugged. "All right. Get out of here so you can get back. I'll find us plane tickets into Denver."

On my way out, I glanced back at him. He leaned over the counter heavily on his hands and he wore an expression hard with determination and worry. I had to force myself to keep going.

"I'm beginning to dislike seeing you come home covered in blood," Nana said as I dragged myself through the front door. She didn't seem pleased in the slightest. "We have a visitor as well."

Marcus stepped into the foyer, his expression a mixture of relief and irritation. "Where in the—"

"Save it," I hissed.

"My car had better be in one piece," he growled back, and I shoved past his shoulder. Then he grabbed my arm. "Hey—"

I jerked away from him and gave him a scathing glare. "Don't you dare touch me, or I'll torch your stupid car."

He wasn't amused. "Where have you been? For the love of God, please tell me you weren't with that demonic vir."

"That is none of your business."

"It sure as hell is!"

I laughed bitterly. "How is it your business? You are not my Guardian and I am doing whatever is necessary to save the one who is. I'm not sitting around on my ass like you are while he wastes away!"

"You're going to get your ass *killed,* that's what you're doing!"

I crunched my teeth together so hard they squeaked.

"Get out of my face, reaper."

"You're an idiot," he said exhaustedly. "Running off with Cadan? What's the matter with you?"

"Don't you dare say a word against him," I warned Marcus. "All he has ever done is help me. He told me that Bastian found the sarcophagus, about the necklace they used to give Lilith corporeal form—not to mention he *killed* Ivar and Bastian to protect me. He's even the one who warned me that Bastian feared we'd find something called the hallowed glaive, a weapon that can destroy the Fallen. Once Will is better, we're going to find it."

"I can't believe that you'd trust a demonic reaper, that you'd risk everything by doing so."

"I'm not an idiot to risk everything for Will," I snapped back. "He's done the same for me for hundreds of years. I'm going to save him and I'll do whatever it takes."

"He would hate you risking your life for him—"

"Too bad!" I shrieked. "Cadan knows where Antares is and he's going to take me there."

His eyes bugged. "Antares? That's who you're after? You're mad for going after a Grigori, let alone a Cardinal Lord. She'll eat you alive."

I lifted my chin in defiance. "If she tries, then I'll at least make sure I get what I need from her first."

"*Listen* to me," he rasped hurriedly, leaning over me. "The Grigori are powerful and beyond dangerous. You don't know—"

"I *do*, actually," I shot back. "Cadan has already warned me. You all seem to forget who I am. I am the archangel Gabriel. I commanded the legion of Heaven that defeated and banished the Grigori to Earth eons before the first reapers were created. I know better than anyone what they're capable of. Antares may be too much for a reaper, but she knows who I am just as well as I know her."

He seemed to deflate. "Fine. Then go. You're making a huge mistake."

I bit back a snarl. "I wish everyone would stop telling me how stupid I am and at least offer to help me."

He was silent. After the longest moment, I shook my head and marched up to my room to change my clothes and pack a bag. I threw in jeans, warm- and cold-weather tops, toiletries, and then raced down the stairs to find Marcus and his car gone. Nana stood on the porch, her arms folded over her chest. I eased around her carefully, peering at the sad look on her face.

"Come back, okay?" she asked.

I fought a sob in my throat and dropped my duffle bag to the ground before hugging her tightly. "I promise, Nana. I love you."

"I love you too," she replied. "And I trust your judgment. No one's perfect, but I believe that you believe you're on the right track. Do what you need to do, and I'll be here waiting. Go save your Guardian."

It was so hard to pull away, but I had to hurry. I threw

my things into my car and peeled out of the driveway, forcing myself not to look in the rearview mirror.

Cadan and I caught a direct flight to Denver and I slept almost the entire way. He rented us an SUV that was blacked out all over to offer himself protection from the sun and we headed northwest toward the Rocky Mountains. After a few hours of driving, I had him take the wheel so I could rest. When I woke again, it was after dark and my ears were popping from the altitude. Somewhere in the mountains, we would meet another of Cadan's "friends," but he assured me that this one was friendly through and through. Antares's location was too remote for access by car, so we would travel the last few miles by horse and foot.

"You're going to need to sleep here pretty soon," he said, glancing over at me. "In a real bed where you can get some rest instead of in a plane or car."

I watched the headlights paint the winding road ahead a dull yellow. The higher we climbed into the mountains, the more upset my stomach got. "I'm fine. Just keep driving."

He huffed. "I'm getting a room at the next town. I'm not dealing with your attitude the entire time I'm risking my ass for you. You at least owe me a good mood and a continental breakfast."

I rolled my eyes and ignored his remark. "There better be a room with two beds. If we have to spoon in a double, I'll be even grumpier."

"I hog the blankets anyway."

"I kick crotches in my sleep."

A small smile curved his lips and he caught me watching him from the corner of my eye. I pinned my gaze back to the road. "So we sleep for a few hours, grab a bagel in the morning, and head out. Deal?"

"Deal."

He managed to find us a moderately not-seedy motel in a small town with a few stoplights. Once we checked in, I dragged my duffle bag into the room and tossed it on the bed closest to the heat register and put the vents on full blast. It was almost June, and yet Colorado hadn't caught on.

I hugged my arms to my chest and, exhausted, flopped onto my bed.

"You need the shower?" Cadan asked me.

"Not yet," I grumbled. "I want to just lie here for the rest of my life."

He huffed a short laugh. "All right. I'll be out in a few."

I must have drifted off because I opened my eyes what seemed like seconds later and he was already out. He was bare from the waist up and ruffling through his bag for a shirt. I tried not to stare too hard, deciding then and there that reapers just automatically came with Photoshopped chests, arms, and abs. Ridiculous.

"All yours," he said without looking at me.

I grabbed the baggie filled with my shampoo and stuff, and before I disappeared into the bathroom, I caught a glimpse of Cadan's muscled back out the corner of my eye. My breath caught. Burn scars were shredded down his back, a marbled and gleaming slash of them. They mirrored Marcus's scars almost exactly, and I knew only divine fire could cause such a permanent injury. Cadan wore scars from angelfire.

He glanced over his shoulder at me before tugging a shirt over his head. "Don't forget that I know what we're about to walk into," he said, understanding what I'd been staring at. "I never fear anything unless I have a good reason to."

I said nothing, or rather I could think of nothing to say, and I closed the bathroom door behind me. I paused for a minute, absorbing what I quickly began to understand. Only angels could wield angelfire, and the only angel Cadan knew besides me was Antares. She had done that to him, nearly killed him.

I undressed and ran the water as hot as I could stand it before hopping into the shower. The water practically scalded me, but I savored it. Hard as I tried, I couldn't think of anything else but what would happen tomorrow. Only when we found Antares would I know if I could save Will's life. What if Antares wasn't there? What if she refused to or couldn't help me? What if Marcus or Ava called to tell me Will had died in the night? As tears fought to break free, I stood under the water and let it hammer my face, the stinging heat and pressure keeping me from concentrating too hard on the horrible thoughts. If I cried, Cadan would surely hear me with his stupid super reaper hearing and then he'd bug me with questions. Why was it that people always asked you about why you're crying? If you're crying, then something shitty happened and you don't want to think about it. In this case especially, it was better for me to be left alone.

The hot water had turned my skin pink, but it didn't hide my puffy eyes and generally crappy appearance as I'd hoped. If I was lucky, Cadan would keep his questions to himself. I combed out the tangles in my hair and let the damp curtain fall over my shoulders. My pajamas never felt more comfortable. I felt so sore and tired everywhere, but my journey had barely even begun.

When I left the bathroom, I plopped onto on the edge of my bed and Cadan turned off the TV from his seat on his own bed. He moved to sit across from me and rested his elbows on his knees, peering into my face studiously.

"It'd be stupid to ask if you're okay," he said softly.

I gave him a pathetic smile. "Good thing you're not stupid." I waited for him to respond, but he was quiet. "Would it be stupid to ask if *you're* okay?"

"I'm fine, I promise. And everything else will be fine too. Antares will be where I left her. It's been a few years, but I'm sure she'll remember me."

"You left that big an impression, huh?" I joked.

"In a way." His tone was serious.

"What did she have that you tried to kill her for?" I was just as grim that time.

"I didn't want it," he replied. "Bastian did. He wanted the grimoire. She didn't have it, but I thought she was lying. Bastian ordered me to bring him the book and I'd been tracking her down for years, so there was no alternative, and I was desperate. Of course she beat me to a pulp, but she'd tossed me beyond the reach of her bindings and couldn't finish me off. I was even luckier to walk away alive from Bastian after he was through disciplining me."

"It couldn't have been easy growing up with him, and then working for him."

He wore a distant look, licking his lips as if tasting for the response he wanted. "I suppose. A birth to any reaper is rare, but things are different for the demonic. My mother worked for Bastian, following the Christian armies invading the Holy Land. She had a taste for the most pious of souls. It was easy for her. She was good at hunting humans and fighting the angelic. When I was born, she went right back to it and I was handed off to others to be raised, as most demonic children are. Bastian believed that his fatherly duties stopped at teaching me what he deemed important life lessons. He taught me how to fight, how to kill, and how to use what power he gave me through his blood. He was cruel, but if he hadn't been, then I'd have died in battle a long time ago. But then again, look at Will."

Cadan was right. Will's mother and Nathaniel had raised him with love, and he was a better fighter than anyone. I wondered what Will would have been like if Bastian had known Will was his son all along.

"I'm so sorry," I told Cadan.

He shrugged. "I don't know any different." He watched me carefully, curiously. "I'd like to, though."

"What's your mother's name?" I asked. "Is she still around?"

"Isolda," he replied. "I only saw her a few times. She wasn't interested in caring for me and I knew she'd died. In battle, of course. Bastian never mourned her. I remember she had hair like mine, but more silver. Eyes like chilled amethyst. I think I look a little more like my father, except for my hair. Will looks a bit like Bastian too. It's the sharpness of his eyes that gives his lineage away. Eyes that see straight to the pit of your soul. I never liked when Bastian looked at me in anger. Both he and Will give that look like they won't just kill you—they'll obliterate you."

I'd seen that look in Will's eyes infinite times, and every time he gave that look, he destroyed. He wasn't known for his mercy on those who tried to hurt me. "I wish that Bastian didn't have to die, but I guess it's rather naïve of me to hope that we could've worked things out. He was still your father. And Will's. Family is family. They're a piece of you no matter what."

"It isn't naïve to hope one can change," Cadan continued. "But for Bastian, it was all he ever knew. He knew he had a purpose on Earth, as do the rest of our kind, that we are at war with the angelic, and that we are on the eve of an even greater war, one that could destroy the races of both Earth and Heaven. He grew up learning that the humans, angels, and angelic reapers are his oppressors, and this war proved to him what he'd been taught. My life has taken the same path, but my heart is not as cold as Bastian's was. He couldn't see beyond the hate he was conditioned to feel. Perhaps we will never know if the demonic are born evil or the angelic born good. What really determines good and evil, anyway?"

"I've been trying to figure that one out for a long time," I said. "You're my argument against perfect evil and perfect good."

"It's never too late to start over," he mused. "After eight hundred years, this dog can still learn new tricks."

That made me smile a little, but it vanished as quickly as it had appeared. "I wish the same had been true for Bastian. There had to have been something good in him." I remembered what he had said to Will—that he'd loved Will's mother, Madeleine. If he could love, could feel true love, then there was hope that he could've changed. But now it was too late to save him, and considering what could have been only weighed on my heart even more.

Cadan considered my words thoughtfully. "I don't know if he was inherently evil. He was a reasonable and logical man, though his reasoning took a darker turn. He lived over a thousand years in the world of demonic reapers. They were his people, his kind—*our* kind—and he wanted to help us.

To him, to many of us, the demonic aren't 'evil.' The Fallen in Hell aren't monsters. They—we—are just another group with different views from the angels and their angelic reapers. I grew up believing the angelic were our oppressors, that there really was a place for us in a peaceful afterlife. That we could go to Heaven if the humans weren't standing in our way. Now, though, I realize what is truth. That all reapers are an accident, playthings of the divine that were never meant to be. Reapers are pawns in a proxy war. I've always doubted what the others believed, ever since I learned that Antares's blood runs through my veins. Not a whole lot dilutes her power mixing with my line, and that's what makes us so much stronger than other reapers. We are so close to the pure source, to pure divine power."

I became so restless with thought that I got to my feet and paced along the wall. I wondered if the small piece of angelic lineage was what drove Cadan to want to be good, but I realized Bastian had even more angelic blood, and he'd been less inclined to see the light. It didn't make sense, but it made me realize that I had to be right: that despite a reaper's heritage and tendencies, he could change, become the kind of person he wanted to be. Bastian had no heart, no goodness in him at all, but his first son, who had even less angelic blood in him, chose to leave the demonic behind.

Cadan stood and eased toward me, moving like a wave. I pressed my back into the wall as he stopped inches from me. "Whatever I am, I'm not evil."

"I know you aren't," I said, and swallowed, fully aware of every part of him and feeling the heat of his closeness. "You have a good heart."

He rested his head heavily against the wall and closed his eyes, taking a deep breath. He raised a hand to touch my arm, but stopped and put it back down. His eyes opened to mine. "I'm trying to change. I know all that I've done wrong, the things I've let others do because I was too much of a coward to stop them. I want—*need*—redemption. And I know you can give me that."

He touched me then, smoothing his hand up my arm, fingers catching on the strap of my tank top before wrapping around the back of my neck. He turned my face to his and his hand molded to the curve of my jaw and lifted my chin.

"I want to help you," I told him. "You've done so much for me."

His gaze fell to my lips for a heartbeat. "You're an archangel and I can feel your goodness in you so strongly. I felt it in you even before I knew what you were. The night we met, it was only you in that crowd for me. I walked into that party, knowing you were there somewhere, but I could sense you a mile away. I had to know you. I was sure that if I could save you, then you could save me. God knows I need it." He smiled only just, and something like wings beat through my chest. His thumb brushed my cheek and lips, and my heart pounded as I considered what else he wanted me to allow him to do.

"You've done so much to save yourself already," I said. "You're strong, Cadan. You just need to realize it."

"I have," he replied, his smile widening as he watched me. "You make me feel strong, like I can get out of this hell I was born into. I love the way you make me feel. I love *you*, Ellie. I really do."

"Cadan—"

"I know you don't think it's real," he said, cutting me off. "But it is. Nothing fake can feel this powerful, this *invincible*. I'm aware of the effect you have on all reapers, but I don't feel what the other demonic do. None of them feel the way I do about you. I know what this is because I've felt it only once before. And I won't let things happen the way they did last time."

"I'm not Emelia," I said, my lip quivering.

He squeezed his eyes shut for a heartbeat and his fingers spread into my hair. He opened his eyes again, and the bright orbs captured mine. "I know you aren't. No one ever will be her, but no one will ever be you, either. Nothing that has ever set foot on this Earth in countless millennia could be compared to you. And I know you'll never be mine." His voice broke on those last words and his jaw tightened.

I exhaled, speechless. Nothing I could say would make him feel better. I cared about him deeply, but the limits to what I felt for him would never be enough to satisfy him.

"I know you're his," Cadan breathed, "but please, one kiss. That's all I ask before I give you up forever."

I swallowed hard. "If I'm his, then I can't kiss you. I won't. Not even once."

He pushed his chest into mine, dipping his head so close I could taste his scent. He was all over me, filling my every sense.

"Please give me just one kiss. I only want to know—"

"Cadan, I am going to slap you."

When I felt his lips brush mine, I hit him. He nearly fell to the ground, but he let me go and hobbled to his feet. He pressed one hand to the wall beside me to catch his balance and he touched his blazing red jaw with his other. His opal eyes stared wide at the floor in surprise and after a few moments, he blinked at me.

"I'm so sorry," he gasped.

"That was wrong," I told him firmly. "If you know the difference between right and wrong then you have to feel like an asshole right now. I'm not going to kiss you when Will is lying on his deathbed a thousand miles away. Cadan, you are my friend. Don't ruin this."

He turned his back to the wall and slid down to the floor, his shoulders slumping and his head hanging heavily. "I am such an asshole."

"Yeah, you are." I dropped to sit beside him. "How's your jaw?"

"Hurts like hell," he replied, moving his jawbone back and forth with a hand. "If you'd actually put some force behind it, it'd be broken."

"Well, I wasn't going to punch your jaw right off your face," I said. "That would make a mess and the hotel would make me replace the carpet. I have more important things to worry about than carpet and dislodged body parts."

"I'm sorry, Ell. I lost it for a second. I felt fearless, thinking I could have you if I took you from him. That never would've happened."

"I love Will. I have for a long time. I'm not sorry for that."

"I'm not him," he said as the air rushed from his lungs in an awful, defeated sigh. "I'll never be good enough, will I?"

"That's not what it's about," I assured him. "I can't explain what it's like between Will and me. If things were different . . ."

"If I were angelic, you mean."

"No. It's not about what you are, either. That doesn't mean anything. It's *who* you are that I care about and what makes you my friend." I touched his jaw, which didn't look so red anymore. "And if you were anything but what you are, like if you were human, then I'd be making a run to the ice machine to get you something for this shiner I just gave you."

He gave me a little smile and I released his face. I walked to my bed, pulled back the blanket, and settled into the firm mattress.

Cadan was slower to reach his own bed. He sat on the edge and leaned forward. He ran a hand through his hair and exhaled. "I'm sorry, Ellie. I really am."

"It's all right," I said, peeking up at him from my pillow. "Get some rest. We both need some."

"You've got a better heart than me."

"You've got a heart and soul of gold," I told him. "You just haven't quite figured out how to tap into all of it yet. I have faith in you, Cadan. I believe in you. Once you can believe in yourself, that you really can do good, you'll see a huge difference in yourself."

"Thank you, Ell."

"Now, sleep," I said firmly. "Don't make me slap you again."

He shook his head and laughed gently. "Okay. Sleep sweet."

I smiled at him. "You sleep sweet too."

5

I DREAMED OF WILL AGAIN, BUT THIS TIME THE landscape was familiar. The marshes in southern France were wet and earthy, but they were incredibly beautiful. The sun was rising and we followed his dream projection of myself to a nearby village after pursuing a demonic reaper who'd showed up in town. The patch of dense forest we navigated made travel even more difficult, and up ahead of Will and me, my dream self had to hack the Khopesh swords through thick brush and vines. Her gown was tattered and the gold fabric was splattered with mud, and her hair was long, wild, and loose from its ribbons. In all honesty, she was in desperate need of a shower and a pair of sweats to relax in. I remembered wearing boys' breeches and boots during hunts back in the days when it wasn't proper for girls to wear anything but dresses, but this hunt had been unexpected.

Gowns were very inconvenient when off killing monsters in the dark.

"Will," I called to him, and he glanced back at me. "Why this memory? The fight has already happened and the sun's coming up. There won't be any more demonic out here."

"This was a significant moment in my life," he answered casually, almost a little detached. Of course my dream self was in her own little world, trudging through the marsh completely oblivious to my presence and my conversation with Will.

"How so?" I asked, but got no reply from him.

Through the trees, I could see a clearing, and the rising sun was nearly blinding. As we approached the tree line, I shielded my eyes with one arm and followed my dream self and Will into a lush meadow. As soon as my eyes adjusted, my breath stopped. In the center of the meadow, caught in the golden glow of dawn, was a band of white horses.

We halted just past the trees and the horses lifted their heads, jaws swinging back and forth as they chewed the rich grass. Their necks, thick with muscle, shook long, tangled white manes as locks fell down their faces and over their eyes. Some lifted their noses to catch our scents and they snorted.

"The horses?" I asked, taken by the sight. "They're what make this memory important to you?"

The corner of his lips turned up in a brief, small smile, and he shook his head. "No. Never the horses. They're just animals to me, but to you . . . you've always loved them."

My dream self moved toward them carefully, her tattered dress dragging through the thick, tall grass, and she clucked softly as she lifted her hand to coax them toward her.

As soon as Will took a step forward, the white horses spooked, squealed, and galloped off into thicker brush, splashing through mud and water.

"Will!" my dream self snapped in frustration, spinning around to glare at him. Her hair, deep, dark red in the burning sunrise, blew in the wind and strands caught on her lips and eyelashes. "You frightened them!"

He seemed unaffected as he crossed his arms over his chest. "Animals don't usually like reapers. You were so mad at me for scaring the horses, not that I really cared. You were such a brat sometimes—the bossiest person I'd ever met."

"Thanks, jerk," I grumbled.

My dream self began to follow the horses, but she turned back to glare once more at Will. "Don't come any closer, okay?" she asked, her voice softer now. "They can smell you and you've spooked them, so stay there. Please. I just want to see them."

She crept closer to the edge of the meadow where the horses had gone and she held her hand out once more. A large horse—the lead stallion—slowly stepped out from the trees on her left, his body flowing like foam on the sea, powerful muscle rippling beneath his white coat. He snorted and gave a throaty rumble, his gray nose questing toward my dream self's outstretched hand. The rising sun cast a soft glow over his coat, like the golden dawn on pristine, newly fallen snow.

"I don't believe I breathed the whole time you were out there," Will whispered. "The stallion could have spooked any second. Even now, I seem to want to hold my breath."

He wasn't the only one. I watched the white horse stretch his nose out to my dream self's fingertips. He sniffed, snorted, drawing back for a heartbeat, and disappointment hung over her face. And then he pressed his nose into her palm, pushed it, and closed his eyes, long lashes folding shut. His entire body seemed to sink and relax as if her touch—*my* touch—had done it.

Behind him, one by one, his band of white mares and small gray foals slipped through the trees and brush fluidly. They moved as a group toward my dream self, surrounding her, daring to stretch their own noses out to sniff her, touch her. She smiled brightly, her eyes gleaming in the dawn light, the color of her hair intensifying until it flickered like flames down her back and shoulders.

"I couldn't believe it," Will breathed, "how they all came out of the trees like that, like they were drawn to you—as drawn to you as I was. Like they could feel you as I could. To this day, nothing I've experienced has been sweeter than your touch or your voice—when you weren't fussing at me, that is. You feel and smell like sunlight, like God's grace."

I forced my gaze away from the horses to Will, whose

lips were parted in awe, his eyes neon green and flashing. I stepped up next to him, aching to touch him, but afraid to. He seemed trapped in a world I couldn't join him in.

"There were so many of them," he continued. "Until that morning, I'd never seen true beauty in its purest form. Nothing compared to this, seeing you there, surrounded by white horses, in a moment of such quiet serenity after a night of carnage and bloodshed. I'll never forget this for as long as I live, and longer still if I'm granted a life after this one. The image is burned into my mind, into the deepest, most untouchable regions. I'll never forget it."

Though I wasn't as close to the horses as my dream self, I remembered the smell of them, the scents of wet grass and soft earth on their white coats. The puffs of their breath against my hands, muzzles burying into my hair, the slickness of their coats beneath my fingertips. I closed my eyes and remembered myself encircled by the white horses, that strange mixture of contentment and joy. I remembered grinning ear to ear that day so long ago and looking up toward the trees at Will, who smiled that quiet smile of his, and I felt a riptide of longing and sadness drag my heart back out to sea.

Will spoke again, his voice even softer, his gaze pensive and distant. "You were such a pain sometimes, and made it so difficult at first for me to fall into my duty as your Guardian, to obey you when most of the time, I just wanted to snap back at you. But you never gave up and you fought with everything you had. I saw your kindness, your fathomless selflessness and immeasurable, divine beauty. It was moments like these, where even wild horses couldn't deny the strength of your presence and heart, that made me want to fight until I couldn't fight anymore—just to be by your side. I remember this very dawn, in this very meadow among the white horses, because in this very moment, I realized that I was in love with you."

I opened my eyes and I was back in my body, standing next to Will in this memory-dream, watching his projection of myself, and I looked back into his face.

"I want to return to this place," he said with a smile. "It's been a long time. I'd like to see it again. With you. Maybe the descendants of these horses are still there."

"Okay," I said, nodding. My eyes began to burn with salty tears.

"I know that I'm dying, and I don't want to die," he said, "because you will be sad."

"I'm going to save you," I promised. "It's my turn to protect *you* now."

He fell quiet, breathing softly as he watched the horses. "I can't die yet. When I wake up, I've got a few things to take care of. I want this war to end and if my mother is alive, I want to find her. Then I'm coming back here."

"We will," I said. "We'll do all of those things." I touched his cheek and turned his face to mine. "You have to keep fighting the way you've told me to keep fighting. Do you understand?"

"You'll come back for me?"

I smiled. "I always do."

He closed his eyes and touched his forehead to mine. I felt myself waking up, but I fought it. I didn't want to leave this place—leave *him*.

I tightened my jaw in disappointment and pressed my body into his. "But for now, I have to go. I have to go back to the real world."

"I don't want you to leave," he breathed, his hands cupping my face.

"I can't save you if I'm sleeping," I replied gently. I kissed him and forced myself to back away. "I love you, and I'll come back for you."

He said nothing as the vision blurred and faded. A moment later, he was gone, and so were the horses. I woke to a different dawn from my bed in the hotel room in Colorado. I glanced over at the other bed, but Cadan was gone. The shower was running. I turned over, pulling the blankets up to my chin, burying my face into the pillow as the fabric eagerly drank my tears.

"You're very quiet this morning."

I glanced over at Cadan as I drove, but that second was long enough for me to absorb the concerned look on his face. Eyes back on the road, I decided that I couldn't reveal to him my dreams with Will. Even I didn't fully understand how our minds could unite through sleep. It had to be the link the angelic magic forged between us in the tattoos on his arm. The closer I become to Gabriel, the stronger it should grow, and the closer I should grow to Will. Even now, a thousand miles away from him and despite his grievous condition, I sensed him. When I closed my eyes, I could catch his scent. But when I opened them, Cadan was sitting beside me, and Will's scent drifted away.

"I'm focused," I replied.

"You'll let me know if you need a break, right?" he asked in return, and the uncertainty was clear in his tone.

I exhaled, but the sound was more like a growl. "You keep saying that and—seriously. When I need a break, I'll take a break. And I don't need a break, I need to keep going. If I wanted to bring my grandma with me, I would've brought her, but I didn't, so shut up."

He opened his mouth to reply, but wisely clamped it shut. I pressed on the gas and the SUV surged faster. We didn't say much to each other for the next hour and a half, until the GPS had me pull onto a narrow dirt road full of potholes. Soon enough we passed a sign for Red Mountain Ranch, and not long after, the ranch itself came into view. I pulled the SUV into the drive, rolled under a rusty iron gate arch, and clunked over cattle guards beneath the wheels. There were a few free-range steers I had to dodge, including some chickens that, flailing their pitiful wings and hopping their fat bodies short distances over the ground, seemed more inclined to get out of the truck's path than the cattle.

"Pull right in front of the house," Cadan instructed.

I aimed for a long, rambling single-story house with a rickety porch that wrapped around the front and western side. It faced a pasture filled with black cattle and spotted cow ponies. Behind the house was a barn that had seen better days, but it was age, not neglect, that wearied it. A few ranch hands bustled about their chores, leading animals in and out of the barn, dragging hoses to water stalls and pasture troughs. I shut the car off and climbed out with Cadan just as the front door of the house swung open and a tall, lean, elderly man in a cowboy hat, plaid shirt, jeans, and cowboy boots stepped out, wiping his hands on a clean dishrag. He had a gray mustache and even a freaking twinkle in his eyes. I liked him already.

"Cadan," the man called cheerfully. "Wish I could say I was glad to see you, but the old lady's in the house and I know soon as she gets a look a' you, she'll leave me. Even after thirty-two years. Why is it I keep gettin' older and you're strappin' as ever?"

Cadan grinned—and I swore I caught sight of a little color in his cheeks—and he ran a hand through his hair. "Good genes, I guess. Great to see you, Judah."

The cowboy smiled at me next. "And this . . . this must be her." He descended the porch steps and reached for my hand, but before he took it, he asked, "May I?"

I watched him confusedly, unsure if he was really asking for permission to touch me. I blinked and nodded.

Judah took my hand at last, cupping it with both of his. "Welcome," he said. "I know who you are, so don' be shy. I know who that scoundrel over there is too."

I glanced at Cadan, who watched me almost sadly. It surprised me that Cadan would know this human and would even reveal himself to him. How much did Judah know? If he said he knew who I was, did that mean he knew my name was Ellie—or Gabriel?

Judah let go of my hand and put his own on his narrow hips, beaming down at me. "I've got the boys saddling up the horses for you. I'm sure you want to be on your way. Grace's fixin' up pulled pork sandwiches for your trip. You should eat one before you go."

My stomach growled at the thought, so loudly that Judah heard and laughed. "That sounds awesome," I said.

He turned to the house and waved us inside. The front door led into the kitchen, where a woman worked at the counter over stacks of shredded meat and bread and little baggies for each sandwich.

"Grab me a coupla' those, will ya, Grace?" Judah called with a pat on her shoulder. "Guests are here."

She smiled at Cadan and me with bright eyes and flushed cheeks. "Cadan." She greeted him warmly and pulled him into a one-armed hug with a kiss on his cheek.

"Hey, now," Judah said, the amusement in his voice passing through his frown. "Don't make me arm-wrestle the boy for my honor back."

Grace rolled her eyes and moved away from them both. "That would be unwise, dear. Who's your girl? You're a vision, darlin'. Are you like him?" She gestured to Cadan, but gave a smile with it.

"She's nothing like me," Cadan interjected gently, his gaze avoiding mine.

"Not a reaper," Grace surmised. "Just a lucky girl, then. What's your name, sweetheart?"

"Ellie," I told her.

"How'd you two meet?"

Cadan opened his mouth to speak again, but Judah was quicker. "Grace."

She seemed to understand the tone of his voice and took it no further. She grabbed a sandwich for each of us and poured two glasses of sweet iced tea and placed them on the round kitchen table. Again, as I inhaled the sandwich and tea, I was left wondering what exactly this couple knew about Cadan and me. I feared saying anything at all.

"All finished?" Grace asked with a smile.

Cadan sat back in his chair and exhaled. "That was delicious, as always. Thank you so much."

She took both our plates to the sink. "Why don't you come with me and we'll make sure your packs are all ready? I double-checked the tent and it has no holes, but we'll see how many blankets you'll need. Remind me to grab the grain bags for the horses."

She beckoned to Cadan and he followed her from the

kitchen. Then it was just Judah and me. One corner of the old cowboy's mouth curved into a knowing smile beneath his scruffy mustache.

"Grace makes the best pulled pork in Colorado," he said. "Pretty sure that's why he keeps comin' back here."

I studied his face carefully. "You know he's a reaper?"

"I do," Judah replied, taking in a long breath.

"And you know what it means for him to be what he is?"

"I know he looks pretty darn good for his age."

"Do you know the difference between a demonic reaper and an angelic reaper?"

"I know the difference between a good man and a bad one," he replied. "No one's perfect, and that boy wears his heart on his sleeve. I am also an imperfect man. Who am I to judge someone else based on where they come from? What counts is what that man does with his life and for others."

"I agree with you," I said. "Did Cadan tell you who I am?"

Judah leaned forward and rested one arm on the table. "He did, but Grace don' know. You seem surprised that I trust him, but I'm even more surprised that *you* trust him."

"'What counts is what a man does with his life and for others,'" I replied, repeating his own words. "And Cadan has earned my trust ten times over."

"He's not as lost as he used to be. I think he's finally found the right trail."

"Are you one of the psychics?" I asked. "Is that how you know him?"

Judah shook his head. "No. Cadan told me about them, though. No, I found him torn to pieces up the mountain one day, a *long* time ago. Thought a bear mauled him. Looked like he'd dragged himself a long way, but he was out cold when I came across him. I tossed him over my horse and rode back to the house. Grace helped me stop as much of the bleeding as we could, but even before we got him in the truck to drive him to the hospital, we noticed somethin' was strange about that boy. Skin don't just knit itself back together without a needle and thread. We didn't know what to make of it. By the time he came to, he was almost completely healed, save for the brand-new scars all over his back. I guessed he must have had a hell of a day, barely surviving a bear attack *and* a fire. Grace is sick of my Smokey jokes, though, so I'll spare you."

"But it was a Grigori Lord," I said.

"That's what he called it too," Judah continued. "We never learned about them in church. All that stuff's in Enoch's book and Pastor Jim don' like that one. Anyway, that boy we found had a lot of explainin' to do. After what we'd seen, it wasn't too difficult to accept what he told us. He stayed here for a few weeks and didn't seem to ever want to leave. He said the ones he would return to empty-handed would be very angry with him, and that no one like Grace and me would be there to make sure he heals safely."

"So he told you everything?" I asked, wholly surprised. "About the reapers, about my role, and the angels and the Fallen?"

"Yep. He said the book he was lookin' for up the mountain would be the thing that stops you in the end, you the killer of his kind. It's been interestin' over the years, watchin' him linger and never age as I get old and tired. He's changed a lot in other ways. He told me what the demonic reapers do to humans, but he's never once harmed us and I believe him when he says he has only fought other reapers. I used to ask him, 'Boy, why do you think that Prey-lee-what's-it kills you reapers? There's a reason why you don' hunt humans. You think it's wrong, and so does she. Don' that make sense?' So, I guess it did, 'cause now you're sittin' in my kitchen eatin' my wife's pulled pork sandwiches."

I felt my eyes burn, but before any emotion broke through, footsteps sounded through the house. Cadan and Grace returned.

"Everything looks good," Cadan said to me. "Are you about ready?"

I gave him a smile but I felt it tremble. "Yeah. Let's go get the horses."

We followed Judah out of the house and into the barn. The air smelled thickly of hay, and in the aisle were three tied-up horses. Two horses were being saddled with heavy Western gear while the third was already loaded with camping equipment and a couple extra bags.

"You'll be on Peewee," Judah said to me, and patted the fat belly of a cute bay mare with stockings. She turned her head to shove at his pockets for a treat. "Cadan, you take Savvy."

"You're letting me ride Savvy?" Cadan asked. "I'm honored, Judah. Thanks."

"How long will we be out there?" I asked, peeking into a couple bags on the pack horse named Star and finding food and water. I scratched the horse's furry face and moved on to give Cadan's gray gelding a pat on the neck.

"Two days' ride," Cadan replied. "And hopefully two days back. We'll camp comfortably, I promise."

Instinctively, I wanted to crack a joke back at him about our differences in the definition of comfort, but as I slid my hand down the horse's neck, the warm silk of its coat brought on another painful sting to my eyes. I remembered my dream with Will so vividly that when I closed my eyes for an instant, it was the coat of a white horse in France that I touched and not that of this big gray gelding named Savvy. Will had promised me months ago that he would take me riding someday. I was supposed to be with him right now and not with someone else.

"Are you okay?" Cadan was right beside me, his head dipped low and close to mine, the breath of his words against my hair.

I tried to look up at him, but a glance was all I could muster and I rested my cheek against the horse's shoulder. His leg stomped at a fly and he gave his head a good shake. My fingers twined around his mane as he turned his head to nuzzle at my pockets.

"Let's get going," I said, and put my back to Cadan. I

would not cry. I wouldn't allow myself to. All Cadan wanted was to comfort me. He was sweet, but the only thing that could comfort me right now was finding Antares and getting her to heal Will.

The constantly overcast sky during the day and thick forest canopy were a blessing for Cadan. I'd worried about him being in the sun, but he seemed to handle it fine as long as he didn't cross into direct sunlight. By the time twilight had fallen and the clouds went away to reveal a beautiful starry sky, my entire body felt like I'd fallen all the way down this mountain instead of having ridden a horse all the way up it. How could anything make someone so sore?

Suddenly all three of the horses' bodies grew stiff and jittery as they snorted, their breaths billowing in the cold air. They danced, fearful, and made slow rumbling noises and spun in the trail. Their hooves kicked up snow and they looked around themselves, wild-eyed and terror-stricken. I pulled hard on the reins to keep Peewee from taking off beneath me, but she, Savvy, and Star were ready to bolt any second.

"What's the matter with them?" I shouted to Cadan, who was having as much trouble as I was in controlling his horse.

"They smell demonic reaper," he replied, eerily calm.

"They just *now* noticed you?"

He shook his head, one hand holding the reins, the other stroking Savvy's neck. "No, not me. The horses know me. It's someone else. I can smell them too."

My gaze grew hard as I surveyed the surrounding trees. "They must be after us or Antares. There's no way we can take care of this on horseback. They're going nuts."

"Let's dismount and tie them up," Cadan suggested and hopped off Savvy.

I followed his lead and helped tie the horses to sturdy branches. They still seemed frightened as we trudged away, but the sooner we intercepted whatever reapers were out here with us, the sooner the horses would calm down and we could continue up the mountain.

I felt a power surge not far from us and when I glanced at Cadan, he signaled to me that he had felt it too. I called my swords and let my own energy buzz, knowing the demonic reapers would sense it the way a shark smells blood and come straight for me. I was right.

The first reaper zipped through the trees on my right. The second was a blur many yards away and Cadan took off after it. Something heavy slammed into me, knocking me into the trunk of a tree. Clawed hands grappled for me and I blindly swung a sword. A grunt from my attacker assured me that I'd struck flesh and he paused just long enough for me to refocus. I slashed again, this time with flawless precision. The reaper's flaming head hit the snow, rolled, and crumbled to ash with the rest of his body.

"Cadan?" I called, hoping he'd dispatched the other reaper just as easily.

Smothered whimpers told me otherwise. "Over here," came his reply.

I followed his voice to find him standing over a struggling body lying in a pool of blood in the snow, skewered by his long, thin sword. The female demonic reaper, whose arms had been chopped off at the elbow, looked like she'd been out in the woods for a while. Her skin was dirty and her hair was tangled and matted. Her clothes were torn and stank something foul.

"Look," Cadan said, beaming. "I found a new friend. She was just about to tell me what she's doing all the way up here."

Her eyes, bright red balls of fire, fixed on my face. "Preliator!"

"Excellent guess," Cadan said, and kicked her in the belly. I heard a crack and she writhed and howled.

"I didn't even think to keep one alive for questioning," I said, and crouched by the fallen reaper's side. "Smart move. So, new friend, what brings you round these parts?"

She snapped her jaws at me before shrinking away and cackling. "Looking for an angel, but we found the wrong one."

"That hurts," I said, frowning. "Really. My heart. It's broken."

"Are you after Antares?" Cadan demanded.

Her stumps for arms leaked blood gently, as if she were almost out of it. "Merodach sent us for the Cardinal Lord. We must've been close since we ran into you, Preliator."

"Sammael wants all of the Grigori dead, doesn't he?" My tone had grown serious, all the humor gone from me.

She wheezed in pain, closing her eyes. "How should I know? I'm only looking for the beast."

"Are there others looking for the rest of the Grigori?"

She snarled up at me. "We will purge this world of all divine things."

"I'm taking that as a yes," I said, and turned my gaze to Cadan. "Let's take care of her and get going. We've got to find Antares before someone else does."

I stood and turned my back to the skewered reaper. As I walked back to where we'd left the horses, I listened to the reaper hiss obscenities in four different languages at Cadan until he silenced her with a final swing of his sword.

6

I WANTED TO KEEP RIDING, BUT CADAN INSISTED
that both of us and the horses needed to rest. I reluctantly
accepted defeat and we found a place to camp. I was so distracted by thoughts of the demonic reapers beating us to
Antares that I didn't even notice that we'd only brought one
tent until Cadan had it halfway set up.

"Why just the one?" I asked nervously, slowly removing
the stakes from the sack on Star's back. I glanced over at
our horses, which were tied to a nearby tree. Savvy snoozed
while Peewee eyed me intently in between bites of grass.
Every time he let out a soft snore, she pinned her ears and
tossed her head at him.

Cadan took a stake from my hand. "We could only take
one packhorse for the two of us and the horse can only carry
one tent bag. It's all right. I only brought this for you."

"Where will you sleep?"

He gave a reassuring smile. "Out here. I've had worse, believe me. And besides, the stars out in the middle of nowhere are incredible. I'd rather be out here, really."

I helped him get the last couple stakes into the ground. I was still a bit wary of him and didn't want an awkward repeat of last night. Despite feeling better about sleeping arrangements, I was freezing. The temperature must have been cut in half almost as soon as the sun began to set and the clouds faded. I'd pulled on a hoodie over my long-sleeved shirt and wrapped a blanket around my entire body, but I still shivered. Cadan sparked a fire and I spread my sleeping bag on the ground close to it and soaked in the heat.

"We've got a couple sandwiches left over if you're hungry," Cadan offered, digging through the food bag.

My stomach grumbled and tightened. "Yes, please. I'm dying over here."

He dragged his own sleeping bag out onto the ground beside mine and dropped a bottled water and sandwich into my lap. As I ate, I listened to an owl hoot nearby and I finally gave the night sky a good look. My breath caught. It had been so long since I'd seen such bright stars. The sky seemed almost multifaceted as the stars twinkled. The enormous moon was so clear and close that it seemed unreal.

"You were right about the sky," I said to Cadan.

He shifted next to me as he finished his sandwich. "Not many places on Earth have a view like this."

"No, they don't," I agreed. The chill began to creep through my layers, so I burrowed myself into the sleeping bag like a burrito. Cadan, like all reapers, seemed unaffected by the icy air, and I glowered bitterly at him. "Did you ever find anything more on the hallowed glaive?"

He shook his head. "I've been trying to dig up information, but no one seems to know what it is. We'll need to find an expert on relics, or something. I don't even know where to start."

I frowned, thinking of Nathaniel. He'd been a genius and seemed to know everything there was to know about our world. He would have been handy right now—not just so he could help us figure out this mysterious weapon, but I could really appreciate one of his terrible jokes. But he was gone, and so was my mother. And Will would be too if we were unsuccessful. I studied Cadan, who always seemed so cool and collected. I never imagined that he'd lost someone he loved before. "Can I ask you about something?"

"Of course."

"Can I ask you about Emelia?"

He exhaled, long and tiredly. "Sure. What do you want to know?"

"What happened to her?" I asked. "If you're not comfortable talking about her, that's totally fine. I'm just curious and I'm learning so much about you. To be honest, you're a bit of a puzzle."

He looked down and he gave an uneven smile. "It's okay.

A long time has passed and I can talk about her. I met her in 1928 at a party in Los Angeles. She had been seeing Ronan for a while and knew what he was. Their relationship was so interesting to me—I'd never known a demonic reaper to show any sort of affection toward a human. It was obvious he was crazy about her and the more the three of us went to social things together, the more Emelia and I became friends. Ronan made mistakes, though. He had a temper and a sharp tongue, as you must have noticed when you met him. I'd seen Emelia cry more times than I could count. When they split for good, she and I remained friends, and I fell for her hard. I was stupid for a blink of an eye. I should've known better."

"What do you mean?" I asked.

"I was in deep, working for Bastian," he said somberly. "I had to keep her secret, which I did for almost a year. I knew that if Bastian found out I'd been seeing a human girl . . . he'd have me flayed alive just to heal his own pride. Then the other demonic would eat her. They'd have taken her soul without a doubt. I should've walked away, but I didn't. Ivar was the one who found me out. We'd had our fun together, but she was maniac. There are crazy girls, and there are *crazy* girls. I never got involved with her beyond anything physical, but she was just as jealous as she was insane. You saw her."

I did. When Cadan had met me at the library a few months ago and we'd talked for a while, Ivar had tried to rip me apart in the parking lot. Cadan had killed her while defending me and to protect the secret that he was helping me to stop Bastian.

"Anyway," Cadan continued, "Ivar followed Emelia after I left her one night and she killed her. I doubled back, but it was too late. I'd left her defenseless and Ivar hunted her down like a rabbit. Before Ivar could . . . take Emelia's soul . . . I fought her. I beat her to hell but I couldn't kill her. I couldn't do it and I should have. Every day since I have regretted that." He sucked in a heavy, trembling breath and his hands rolled into tight fists. "I just stared at her on the ground and then I took Emelia and left Ivar. I was stupid and a coward and just *left* her there. *Alive.*"

I watched him as he suffered internally. His pain and regret was so clear over every inch of him that I felt terribly sad for what happened. "I'm sorry," I said.

He shook his head. "No. I'm the one who's sorry. I hope I suffer for the rest of eternity for what I did to that girl. I knew—I *knew*—I never should've gotten involved with Emelia. I should've been more careful. But I'm selfish. Still am. As I am with you."

"It wasn't your fault," I assured him. "Ivar—"

"Yeah, Ivar took her life, but I handed it to her." He shook his head again, this time less angrily. "I'm so impulsive and completely aware of it. You remind me of Emelia a little. It's your eyes and your big smile. She loved to go to parties and dance and have fun. Both of you are so bright and full of life. You scared me too. Still do."

"Good," I said with a grin. "Then I'm doing my job right."

I was rewarded with a small smile. "I mean about the way you make me feel, how quickly what I felt reminded me of when I had Emelia. That night when Ivar attacked you, it was like a flashback from Hell. At least I finally found the courage to avenge Emelia. By killing Ivar, I'd broken myself from Bastian completely, my allegiance to him, and then I killed him too. How sad it is that by dealing death, I gained my freedom?"

He gazed back up at the stars, the breeze blowing his hair a little. I hadn't realized he hurt so much inside, that he felt so much guilt about serving Bastian and for Emelia's death. The fire crackled in front of us, all heat and light and comfort. I rested my cheek on Cadan's shoulder and rubbed his arm soothingly.

"It'll be okay," I whispered, and took his hand in both of mine. There was nothing I could do to convince him that what happened to that girl wasn't his fault, despite what he'd convinced himself. It was up to him to forgive himself.

"Whatever happens tomorrow with Antares, I've got your back," he said. "Hopefully Antares won't be up for round two with me, but a few decades is a blink of an eye to a creature like her and she'll know me when she sees me. Who knows, though—it may be different with you here."

"I swear, I won't leave without the cure," I said. "I can't."

He sighed, relaxing. "We'd both better get some sleep if we want to be functional in the morning."

"Yeah," I agreed and groggily finagled myself out of my sleeping bag burrito and got to my feet. "See you in the morning."

"Yep," he replied.

Behind me, I heard him rustle his own sleeping bag as I climbed into the tent to make my nest of blankets. It took a few minutes to get comfortably warm, and it took even longer for me to fall asleep.

I woke the next morning without having dreamed about Will and was so afraid for him that I had trouble finishing my breakfast. An ill spin in my gut matched the horrible thoughts in my mind. I didn't have cell reception way up here so there was no knowing if something had happened to him. Marcus or Ava had no way of contacting me. All I could do was keep going.

Only a few miles higher than the elevation we'd camped at, it was snowing. The ground was lightly dusted and snowflakes fell slowly, sticking to my eyelashes and to Peewee's mane. The air grew colder and harder to breathe the whole way we climbed. We stopped for lunch around midday and then were on our way again. At last, Cadan pulled his horse up and dismounted, his boots thudding gently in the snow.

"Is she close?" I asked and slid from the saddle to the ground. I led Peewee by the reins up to where Cadan had stopped.

"From here we go on foot," he said, and tied Savvy to a

tree. "Judah has a map of our route and if we don't return, he'll come this way up the mountain and at the very least, find the horses."

I gave Peewee a good-bye kiss on the nose and a scratch between her ears. I smiled a little to myself when I realized I worried the horses would be left all alone. For a second it felt good not to worry about the dire situation I was soon to walk into.

"You probably won't want to bring your heavy jacket," Cadan said almost dismissively.

I gaped at him. "Are you serious? Did you not notice the snow? Or the mountain?"

"All right. Your choice."

"I feel the cold, remember, Superman?" I grumbled.

"What I mean is that the Cardinal Lords make things change," he said.

"How so?"

A pause. "You'll see."

I decided to trust him and leave my coat and wool hat behind. I hopped up and down a couple times to get my heart rate up and blood pumping. "You'd better not make me regret this," I warned him.

Cadan led me through the narrow path parting the dense thicket, brambles catching on our sleeves and collars, tugging at my hair. I heard the horses nicker and rustle behind us and I prayed they wouldn't break free and strand us here. The farther we climbed up the mountain, the warmer the air seemed to be. Not summer warm, but like a late October afternoon's gentle sun on your skin, and I was glad I'd left my jacket behind. The snow was disappearing, melting away more and more up the path until fallen leaves appeared beneath our feet, crunching with each step. I looked up at the trees and the snow had gone from them, too, their bark dry and dark, limbs still full of red and gold leaves. It was as if time had gone backward; the late spring mountain snow had melted away and autumn emerged before our eyes.

The forest opened to a small golden meadow with an enormous tree in its very center. It looked thousands of years old, its trunk easily thirty feet around, and its boughs so massive and heavy that many of them hung twisted and gnarled to the ground. They curled and coiled in every direction, weaving in and around each other, some of them so wide that I could probably have fit my entire body inside them.

"What is going on?" I asked. "Cadan?"

I looked around for him and spotted him stepping up to the giant tree. He drew a knife from his belt and pressed it to his palm, slicing a fine, thin line of red. Then he touched his hand to the trunk and pushed his blood into the bark. He looked up twelve feet or so, where the branches began to unfurl, and he whispered something.

Immediately the great tree gave a shudder, its branches shaking loose golden leaves. The bark began to morph and I had to blink my eyes hard, certain I was losing my mind. Something began to grow right out of the base of the branches.

It shimmered in the sun, glossed in the shade, and looked nothing at all like bark. It looked like the top of a head. Human limbs rippled smoothly from the bark, extended along the branches at shoulder height as a torso emerged from the tree's trunk. The body pulled itself from the tree, arms tugging hard, but vines wrapped tightly around the wrists, refusing to release. Hair fell from the figure's head, gleaming red-gold locks, and pale gold robes wrapped around the body to form a dress that looked unlike any fashion from the last several thousand years. The face stared at the ground as the body pulled forward to free itself from the tree, the hair spilling over narrow shoulders and dainty arms. Bare feet touched the leaf-covered ground, more vines coiling around delicate ankles as if they were chains binding a prisoner to the tree.

Once the body stepped toward me, chains of vines and branches binding its limbs, I could see that it was clearly a she. Her face rose to gaze upon Cadan, eyes blazing like a wildfire beneath heavy lids, lips a natural rose-red, skin golden and shimmering with light as if autumn leaves burned just beneath the surface. She appeared my age, perhaps a couple years older, and she was beautiful in an unnatural way, a frightening, fiery way. She was ancient, never-changing, and I was terrified of her.

When she spoke, her voice seemed to seep through my ears, eyes, and mouth like warm milk and honey, making my brain fuzzy, my limbs heavy and tired. *"Audes provocare mei?"*

"Antares—"

"*Non loqueris nomen meum.*" She cut him off sharply with a wave of her hand. "You swine, *vermis*, you insect of earth and rot." Even when speaking English, her voice was edged with an accent, the crippled remnants of a language long since dead. Her bindings stretched and groaned, refusing to allow another inch of freedom. "I am the Grigori Lord of the West. You dishonor me by breathing in my forest. Be gone!"

Cadan flinched at her voice. "I have not come for myself. I beseech you on behalf of the archangel Gabriel."

The ageless Grigori laughed, her voice making my spine shiver and heartbeat slow. I could taste sugar in my mouth with every one of her words. "*Tu me delectas.* I know who Gabriel is and she would have nothing to do with you, demonic spawn. Leave me in peace."

"Gabriel is here now. With me. In human form."

Antares's head tilted to the side inquisitively. She looked past him and her fire eyes met mine. It felt like her gaze was digging straight into my soul. "And so she is. What a delicate thing you are now, Strength of God. Have you come to destroy your Fallen sister at long last?"

"No," I said, swallowing my fear. "I need your help."

Her lips curved slightly, barely a smile. "My help? How curious."

"My Guardian is dying. He was poisoned by a demonic reaper's venom."

Antares looked at me without emotion. "Your Guardian is a reaper?" she asked, her voice lilting.

I nodded. "Of your bloodline. He's angelic."

She said nothing at first. Then she raised a hand and beckoned to me. "Come forth then, mortal archangel."

I took a hesitant step forward with a glance at Cadan. His expression was gentle and comforting, and he gave me a small amount of courage. She grasped my wrist and yanked me forward. I cried out in surprise. Her fingers were hot and they moved up and down my arm as if she was trying to feel every vein and tendon beneath my skin. She touched my hand and opened my palm flat.

"Your Guardian," she said musically. *"Amas eum.* You love him. This reaper. He protects you at the risk of his own life. How very noble of him—and how very unwise of you to come to me."

The ice in her voice made tremors of fear stab through my inside. "Will you help me?"

"I know of demonic venom very well. Whoever poisoned your reaper Guardian wanted you both to suffer long. This is a cruel death."

I brightened. "Then you can save him!"

"I can," she said dismissively. She stepped back and her power pushed into my body, propelling me away from her. "But I will not. I do not see the benefit in it."

My veins ran cold as fear settled once again on me. "But you *can* save him! Why won't you help me? Just tell me how to cure him. You don't have to do anything. Just tell me the antidote. Please!"

She watched me silently, her brow furrowing with curiosity. "Who are you, Gabriel? How far you have fallen, my sister, to feel so much? I barely recognize you. Your human soul has diseased you."

"No!" I shouted back. "Don't you see the difference in us? I was like you before I became human. Now I have a heart, a soul, and all I want to do is protect the ones I love. Your selfishness is your own disease, Antares!"

She laughed, her voice musical as it rustled the autumn leaves. "Go now, Gabriel," Antares said tiredly. "Leave me in my purgatory."

"You're here to help the humans!" I cried. "You watch over them, guide—"

"Watch them, yes," Antares hissed. "Do you know what I watch of them? Every moment, I watch a murder. With every word I speak, countless children around the world are defiled. A man beats his wife until her face is unrecognizable. War. Genocide. I see it all behind my eyes so that I can never close them and have reprieve from the suffering I am forced to witness as punishment for bearing my own thought and desire. For daring to have a mind of my own, it was taken from me and replaced with thousands and thousands of years of horror. Do you, Gabriel, truly believe I was sent here to aid humanity? Now do you see that I am chained to the Earth and forced to watch humanity destroy itself?"

"You aren't supposed to be angry," I said. "The angels are not meant to feel emotion."

"But was it not inevitable? All I know now is hate and pain."

"I'm human," I told her. "It's not so bad."

"You are not human. You are the same as Raguel, the one who bound me here in the name of Justice. I owe you nothing."

She turned her back to us and I couldn't stop the sharp intake of breath as I glimpsed the two burnt and bloody stumps protruding from her shoulder blades. The skin was blackened and grotesque, her robes torn and singed. I knew then that the stumps were what was left of her wings. The wings she had used to fly before she fell to Earth.

"Antares," I begged her and collapsed heavily to my knees and dropped my head. "Please. *Please* help me."

Warm fingers lifted my chin and I looked up into the face of Antares, who watched me with interest. Up close, her eyes were like liquid gold. Rivulets of iridescent pearl flecked with chips of ruby swirled in their depths, hypnotizing me.

"You . . . kneel before me?" she asked, her voice slow.

"I'm desperate." A tear rolled over my cheek and slipped into the corner of my mouth. A shock of salt on my tongue.

The Grigori Lord stood, pulling her hand away from my face, and I let out a terrible sob. My body shook as I cried, letting out everything I'd held in for days, all of my sorrow and rage and exhaustion. I buried my face in my hands. It was so hard to stay strong every second of every day, but I had to. I allowed myself to be weak for one minute, but now it was time to suck it up and do what I needed to do. When I let my hands fall and looked back up at Antares, she still watched me.

"Gabriel," Antares whispered. "What has your humanity done to you?"

I pushed myself off the ground and stood shakily, staring right at her face. "Being human has taught me to love and that's why I'm here. I will do whatever it takes to save him."

"Why?" the Grigori asked. "Why would you want to save your Guardian if this is what he has made you become? This sorrowful, weakened thing fallen so far from the creature I once knew."

"I am not weak," I growled, rolling my hands into fists. "If I were weak I would not be standing here. It is not weak to admit your limitations and ask for help. It is not weak to feel sorrow. It's *human*. I have changed since you last saw me, because I have *become* human."

"And the rest of humanity? Why do you still fight for them? This world drowns in grief and pain."

"That's true," I told her. "I've lived a thousand lives. I know as well as any human how much suffering there is in the world, but there's also joy and love."

She shook her head. "The human race is still as it was before the Fall. They have not changed."

"There's also hope," I pleaded. "To hope for a better

world—*that* is why I fight. That's why I've been fighting for so long. The humans are young and imperfect, but they are strong. They would not still be here if they weren't. This is why I stand before you now. I need my Guardian's help. And I love him. I can't save humanity without him."

She seemed to weigh me with her gaze for a moment before looking at Cadan and then back at me. "You have moved me, Gabriel. Your passion is beautiful in a way that I have never seen up close. If your human soul has taught you to love, then there may yet still be hope."

"Will you help me, Sister?"

"For the antidote I require a payment," Antares said.

Cadan stepped forward before I could stop him. "If you want blood, take mine."

A stab of ice hit my heart. "What? Cadan, no!"

I reached for him, but he tore away. Antares's face filled with amusement.

"You would sacrifice yourself to save her beloved?" she asked, tilting her head at him curiously. "How you have changed, reaperling."

"I've done a lot of bad in my life," Cadan replied. "It's about time I did some good."

"*No*," I ordered and grabbed his arm. "You've done enough. This is for me to do."

"Fortunately for you," Antares interjected, "you are not the one who can pay me."

Cadan called his sword, silver flashing in the golden

autumn light, and he stepped in front of me. "You will not harm her!"

"Silence, fool," Antares said, and waved her hand. Cadan's body was thrown to the side and his back slammed into the trunk of a tree. "Have you not learned your lesson?"

I trembled, but held my chin high. "What do you want?"

Antares beckoned me forward. "For the antidote to heal your Guardian, I want you to free me."

"Free you?" I asked in confusion. "I don't understand."

"Send me home," she said. "To Heaven. Restore my wings, redeem me. I only want to leave this wretched place."

I wasn't sure if I had the power to do that, if I even knew how, but I nodded anyway. For the chance to save Will, I'd at least try. If I left her there chained to that tree, then Sammael would eventually find her and kill her. Antares might have never learned about mercy, but I knew it well. "Okay. I'll do it."

"Swear it!" Antares roared, her eyes flashing white gold. "Swear it on your life's blood!"

I swallowed hard. "I—I swear on my blood that I will set you free."

Antares paused for the longest moment of my life before lowering herself to the ground. She hovered her palm just over the ground, the tips of short blades of grass brushing her skin, and a light shone brightly. Something slid out of the dirt, something dark and coiled, and Antares broke off a piece. She stood and came toward me and I struggled to see what she had. She held her hand out and revealed something that looked like organic plant material, a root maybe. She nodded to me, motioning for me to take the root, and tentatively, I obeyed. The thing was soft and flexible, but its outermost layer was rough against my skin. It looked so ordinary, so plain and powerless.

"Only the root of a tree that binds a Cardinal Lord can heal reaper venom," Antares explained. "You need to make a poultice from it and cover the wound entirely. The healing process will take three days."

I stared at the root in my hand. "That's it? And he's healed?"

"Yes," Antares replied firmly.

"With everything in me," I said, "I thank you."

She gave me a nod of solidarity. "Now send me home."

I stuffed the root into my jeans pocket and lifted my empty hand to cup Antares's cheek. Her shimmery skin was warm and soft, but smooth like stone. I closed my eyes and reached deep within for my archangel glory, pulling it to the edges of my power and feeling its comforting burn through my body. A light grew in my hand, much like Antares's had moments ago when she retrieved the root. Her chest rose and fell heavily, her breath quickening and deepening. From somewhere far back in my mind, words whispered to me, words that Gabriel knew and Ellie was only beginning to understand.

"By what grace I have been given," I called out, and my

winged necklace grew blazing hot, so hot that I gasped, but I forced myself to keep speaking, "I release you, Antares, from your earthen bonds."

The more I invoked of my blinding-white archangel power, the closer I felt to Heaven. I could hear voices far, far away, voices I recognized that belonged to my brothers and sisters, lending me their own power to help me save this Fallen angel. I fought to keep my eyes open, gritting my teeth against the searing heat of my pendant, and Antares erupted in energy. Her charred and broken wings grew tall and wide and healthy, skin covering new bone, white feathers spreading long and gleaming as if they radiated a light of their own. Antares let her head fall back and her arms lifted above her waist, palms up toward the sky. The roots holding her to the ground withered and peeled away, disappearing into the earth. The enormous tree shuddered and shrank, boughs retreating into the trunk, leaves disappearing, until nothing was left of it. Antares stepped away from me, her dress flowing, hair flying in the tornado of power circling her, her wings spread their full sixteen feet, and every inch of her aglow.

"Thank you, Gabriel," Antares said, her voice giving off that strange echo, like Azrael's and Michael's did.

A tear rolled down my cheek as I took in the beauty of what unfolded before me. Antares's wings lifted and she jumped into the air. And then she was gone in a crack of white lightning.

When the brightness dimmed, snow began to fall.

7

THE JOURNEY HOME SEEMED FASTER, BUT I FELT
much more stressed now than before we found Antares. On
the plane, the deafening roar of the engines let me slip into
a white noise coma that let every single rational and irra-
tional fear cross my mind over and over. I worried that the
root wouldn't work, that Will would die as soon as I walked
in the door, that I would be intercepted by Merodach or
Lilith and Sammael before I could return, that something—
anything—would happen and I would fail. That I wouldn't
be able to save Will, my soul, or the human race.

The red-eye landed in the chilly early morning and the
sun hadn't yet risen. Immediately I called Marcus to let him
know I had the antidote and to expect me shortly. I drove
directly to Nathaniel's house—*Will's* house, I had to keep
reminding myself, now that Nathaniel was dead—with

Cadan in the passenger seat. I parked sideways in the drive-way and shoved the front door open.

"It's better if I stay out here," Cadan said as he climbed out and rested an elbow on the roof of my car.

I took his hand anyway. "Come in with me. You never abandoned me and I'm not leaving you behind now."

He wet his lips and exhaled. "All right."

"Ellie?"

I spun around.

Ava stared at our clasped hands from where she stood on the porch. There were many questions in her eyes but she only asked one. "What is he doing here?"

"Because he's the only one who would help me," I said, and led Cadan up the porch steps.

It was good to see Ava again, but the look of hate on her face as she stared Cadan down made me grit my teeth and walk right by her and into the house.

Marcus pulled me into a tight hug and I only let go of Cadan's hand to hug Marcus back. I held my breath and tried not to cry into his chest. "I'm so sorry," he confessed, "for what I said to you."

When his grip loosened a little, I looked up to see his gaze locked on Cadan's. I pushed a hand into his chest on instinct. "Please don't fight," I begged him. "Marcus, he's done so much. Please just leave him be. He deserves to be here."

When he took a step toward Cadan and lifted an arm, I pushed myself between them to keep them apart. But Marcus didn't hit Cadan. His hand was out, palm open. Cadan and I both stared at it until Cadan raised his own hand to shake Marcus's.

"Thank you," Marcus said tightly, but the soothing blue of his eyes assured me that he meant his words.

Cadan gave a single nod back. I relaxed, relieved to see that the demonic and angelic reapers weren't going to just tear each other up right then. It was a strange sight to see, these two enemies looking past their differences for a common cause, to save Will's life.

"Where is he?" I asked Marcus, and he motioned up the stairs with his head.

Understanding, I left the reapers and went to Will's room. Sabina kept sentry in the hall, just outside the door. I gave her a weak smile in greeting and she patted my shoulder comfortingly as I passed her. Lying in his bed against the far wall, Will slept. I eased toward him, covering my mouth with my hand to hold my composure. Seeing him there, the reality hit me full force again and I was unable to prevent my tears any longer. I touched his face, brushing my fingers along his jaw. He turned into my hand, but he didn't wake. His skin was hot, scorchingly so, and I found a cool, damp cloth on the nightstand. I dabbed his forehead and cheek softly.

"I have it, Will," I whispered. "I'm going to save you like you've saved me so many times. You'll be all right, I promise."

I felt a vice around my heart when my gaze found the

silver cross his mother gave him around his neck. I was happy to know that they hadn't taken it from him. He'd want it close to him. I touched my winged necklace at the hollow of my collarbone and remembered how lost I felt when I wasn't wearing it.

When Sabina entered, I welcomed her calm presence. "What do you need?" she asked, her voice low.

I pulled the plastic bag from my pocket and removed the root. "A poultice needs to be made from this. Do you know how to do that?"

"Yes," she replied. "I can do that for you."

I handed the root to Sabina and she promptly spun on her heel and left the room. I gave a last look at Will before following Sabina. In the dark hallway, images flashed in my mind from the night my mother died, when I'd torn myself from that same room and down the stairs, screaming for Will. This house held so many wonderful and terrible memories for us all. I steadied myself on my feet and took a deep breath. As I descended the staircase, Cadan looked up at me from the same spot I'd left him in, a quiet pain in his expression. There was no telling how difficult it was for him to see my joy at seeing Will again, but there was nothing I could do to help Cadan except to not lead him on. I went into the kitchen, where Sabina took a bowl from the cabinet and set it on the counter. As she mashed the root, the others joined us.

"Glad to have you home," Marcus said, stopping beside me.

I rested my head on his shoulder. "I'm glad too. And I'm

glad all of this will be over soon."

"What happened out there?" he asked.

"We found Antares."

Ava rounded Marcus, her arms folded. "And she just gave you that thing?"

"No," I replied and caught Cadan's eye. "She wasn't going to give it to me at all. And then she did."

"You convinced her?" Marcus asked.

"I guess so," I said. "I set her free. She gave me the root, I released her, and she went home. If I hadn't been able to release her, then Sammael would have killed her. He has been hunting the living Grigori in this country, killing anything that might be a threat to him. We ran into some of his demonic reapers searching for her. But Antares is safe now and Will has a chance to live."

"Hopefully this will work," Ava said. "He hasn't woken at all since you left."

I moved to the pantry to look for plastic wrap to hold the moisture in the poultice and bandages to wrap it with. "Antares said it will take three days. We'll need to make sure the root lasts that long. The tree disappeared with her, so this is all there is."

"You won't need much between bandage changes," Sabina said over the bowl. "This root is potent. I can smell the magic."

"Good," I said. "However weird it is that you can *smell* magic."

"The sun is rising," Cadan said from the other side of the kitchen. "I'd better take off."

I looked up at him, not failing to notice the sad and tired look on his face. "I'll come say good-bye."

I followed him through the house to the front door and out onto the porch. He turned to face me, smiling softly. There was a quiet gleam in his gaze, the fire in those gemlike eyes brightened by the reddening dawn.

"There aren't words enough for how grateful I am," I said.

He shrugged and grinned playfully. "It was nothing. Don't mention it."

I huffed. "Yeah, all right. Risking your life for me is nothing."

The grin faded to seriousness. "Call on me for anything. I mean it."

"Thank you," I whispered, and threw my arms around his shoulders to hug him tightly. "Thank you, thank you, *thank* you. For everything. I'm in your debt."

When he pulled away, he pushed my hair behind my ears tenderly. "I'll be back tomorrow night to check on you, okay?"

"Yeah," I said with a nod and a sniffle.

He backed away and turned to leave the porch. Out on the grass, his silver birch-colored wings slowly spread. "Hang in there, kid." With a final warm smile, he bent his knees and jumped into the air, his form vanishing into the Grim.

I hugged my arms close and hesitated another few

seconds before walking back into the house. Even though Will had rebuilt everything that'd been destroyed during Kelaeno's and Merodach's attack, in my mind I saw the front door blasted open, the walls torn down, the staircase shattered—everything looking as if a bomb had gone off. I passed the spot in the hallway where Nathaniel had punched through the wall to retrieve hidden weapons, the place where he had said his final good-bye to Lauren before meeting his doom upon Merodach's sword. Will hadn't had time to replace all of the flooring in the hall and kitchen, and I glanced at a dark stain in the wood that was once someone's blood. I didn't know who it had belonged to. So many had died here that night.

When I reached the kitchen, Sabina turned to me. "The medicine is ready."

"Okay," I replied. "Let's get to it."

I marched back up the stairs to Will's room and sat on the edge of his bed. I put the poultice and fresh wrappings on the nightstand and removed the dirty bandages from around his arm. The wound was even more vicious-looking than I remembered. I bit my lip as I peeled the cloth from his skin and he moaned in pain. The black spider-webbing of poison in his veins rippled through his arm and chest. With my fingers, I took just enough of the poultice to cover Will's wound completely. Then I pulled the plastic wrap and wound it all the way around his arm before adding fresh gauze wraps.

"What now?" Ava asked.

I watched Will's face, seemingly so peaceful until his brow furrowed in pain. "We wait."

I rushed to make it to school on time. I'd missed a couple of days, but Nana had called me in sick for Monday, Tuesday, and Wednesday. My abrupt absence from Kate's prom after party had my friends asking a lot of questions, but my mind was far away all day. Thursday's preparations for our final exams of high school were maddening, as I'd missed three days of review and hadn't slept. They were the last things I needed to worry about, but I'd made a promise to myself that I'd finish high school. It was a desperate, naïve attempt to cling to a normal life.

As soon as class let out, I drove to Will's house. Marcus sat in the living room watching TV and Lauren came out of the kitchen when she heard me arrive.

"Hey, Ell," she said with a supportive smile. "Good to see you."

I gave her a big hug. "You too. And I'm so glad to be out of class. I'm finding that the harder I try to stay normal, the less I enjoy it. God, school *sucks*."

Marcus laughed and got up. "Ready to drop out and just skip the last week?"

"No way," I said very firmly. "I've come this far. No going back now. How's Will today?"

"He's sleeping better," Lauren said. "Not a huge improvement, but it's noticeable."

I sighed with relief. "Awesome news. Are Ava and Sabina out hunting?"

"Yeah," Marcus replied. "Lauren and I are standing guard over Will's recovery, while the girls get to go play. I'm admittedly a little jealous. And bored."

Lauren smiled and put a hand on his shoulder. "Your shift is over tomorrow. You can hold out until then."

"I'm going to go up and see him," I said, and started up the stairs.

Will's room was dark, so I rolled up the blinds to let in the afternoon sunlight and opened the window. The fresh air was warm and sweet, and I returned to Will's bedside. The poison was less visible through his skin already and he looked better, just like Lauren had said. His skin even looked less sallow. I felt satisfied, but tired, so I pulled a book down from the shelf and curled into the bed beside Will, tucking my legs close to my body and resting my head on a pillow. I brushed his hair back once and then opened my book to read.

I must have dozed off, because a knock on the open doorframe startled me into groggy awareness and I noticed Cadan standing there for the first time. He said nothing as he came in and sat down on the chair across from the bed. I smiled at him and he smiled back; it was our only exchange.

Ava passed by the room and poked her head in, giving us both a questioning look, before continuing on her way down the stairs. I heard voices below, perhaps Marcus trading duties with Ava and Sabina. He would be pleased to get out of the house and hunt the demonic reapers—minus the one keeping vigil in the room with me.

After school the next afternoon, I stopped by Nana's house to see her, since we'd only spoken on the phone since my return. Our reunion was emotional and teary-eyed, and I told her everything that had happened with Antares and Cadan. We sat on the patio outside, soaking in the springtime sunlight as it faded into evening's twilight.

"You really trust him, don't you?" Nana asked. The question sounded more like a statement, and she didn't seem like she thought I was crazy.

"Yes," I replied. "No one else has seen how much he's done for me. I trust him with my life."

"Good," she said. "You need more people you can count on, and despite his colorful past, the demonic reaper has proven himself."

My tone became grim. "When Will wakes, I have to tell him about Cadan. He still doesn't know that Cadan is his half brother and he'll find out that Cadan was the one who took me to Antares. He won't be happy, but he's going to have to deal with it. I just have to time the conversation so that it's soon, but not on top of a lot of other bad news."

"True," Nana agreed. "It's sensitive information and better it come from you than anyone else. Will is smart, though.

He'll take the news in stride."

I nodded. "I've got to get going. It's almost dark and he needs all the protection he can get while he's healing. He'd be helpless against an attack and Merodach knows where we live. If he knows, then the worst of our enemies know."

"Should you maybe leave that house?"

"Where would we go where we wouldn't endanger innocent people?" I asked. "Sammael is gathering strength. We're relatively safe right now, because he used up too much energy when he was resurrected and battled not only us but Azrael too. He needs to recharge and this will take time. However, 'relatively' isn't positively, so we have to be careful. His lackeys could show up at any moment. Besides, that house is home."

"You know what you're doing," Nana said with assurance. "Will I see you tomorrow?"

"I think so," I replied. "I'll watch over Will with the others tonight, *attempt* to study, and then finals start Monday. I'll call you and let you know what's going on."

Nana got to her feet with me and we hugged good-bye. "Come by soon, sweetheart."

"I will," I promised. "I've got a lot to do before I can relax."

I drove to Will's to join the guard shift with Marcus and Lauren. Replacing Will's bandages let me get another look at his wound, which continued to heal well. One more day.

One more day.

* * *

Even with studying all night, I wasn't feeling confident about my exams, but at least I only had two today. I was exhausted physically and mentally. Sleep was inconsistent and fitful, and I hadn't had a chance to rest after the journey to find Antares. The only thing that kept me going every day was knowing Will would wake soon and we could finish this fight with Sammael at last. I took up my post in Will's room, napped a little beside him, studied, and waited. When I changed his bandages, the wound had closed and he seemed to be normal again. He just wouldn't wake up.

I'd been dozing when I felt movement beside me. My heart leaped into my throat and I looked down into Will's face, holding my breath. He moved his head left and right as he tried to speak.

"Will?" I asked softly, touching his cheek, barely able to contain my joy. "Can you hear me?"

His eyelids fluttered and he groaned. "Ell . . ."

"Yes," I said, and kissed his forehead. "It's me. It's Ellie."

His eyes opened and my breath caught. It felt like I hadn't seen that incredible green in years. He looked right up into my face, squinting blearily, but there was recognition there. "Ell . . . ?"

My smile was ear to ear as I brushed the back of my hand across his cheek and he leaned into it, closing his eyes again. "Hi," I whispered.

He lifted his hand to mine and gazed back up at me. "Dreaming . . . again. . . ."

I squeezed his hand tight. "You're not dreaming anymore."

His smile was weak, but the sweetest thing I'd ever seen. "Miss . . . you . . . Ell. . . ."

"How do you feel?" I asked. I put a palm to his forehead and then tested his pulse on his wrist. His fever had gone down and his heart rate seemed to have returned to normal.

"Came . . . back . . . to me. . . ."

I shushed him and kissed him again. "Of course I came back to you. I promised you I would. Do you remember? Do you remember the horses?"

"You . . . ," he whispered, taking a deep breath between pauses, "found me . . . in the dark. . . ."

"I did," I replied. "Don't try to speak, okay? Just rest."

He closed his eyes and his brow creased. "No more . . . rest. . . ."

"Just lie here with me," I told him. "You'll feel better soon."

I worried that the lamp on the nightstand shone a little too brightly, so I switched it off. When I looked up, I saw Ava and Sabina standing in the doorway, watching Will and me, and I wiped at a tear that fell down my cheek. They began to retreat into the darkness of the hallway and I gazed back down at Will as he breathed gently, holding on to me, and I curled myself up tighter against him.

8

I SPENT THE ENTIRE NIGHT SITTING NEXT TO WILL on his bed. He never went back to sleep, but occasionally I did, and I would wake curled in his arms, and for the first few seconds of wakefulness I feared that I still dreamed. But it was real and he was alive and awake and recovering.

"Do you remember the dreams?" I asked him once, my voice slipping through the dark.

His fingers touched my face, tracing the curve of my cheek down to the corner of my lips. "I do. I remember you came, that my mind hadn't just created you. You weren't a part of my dreams like everything else was."

"Somehow I entered your dreams," I explained. "I think it had something to do with the bond, the magic in your tattoos, or that I'm tapping into more of my archangel abilities. I just don't know."

"It's better to see you now," he said gently, "with my true eyes."

I smiled against his fingers. "I didn't think I'd ever see them again."

He was quiet for a few moments. "How did you do it? What happened?"

"Rikken's bite was venomous," I told him. "We didn't know how to heal you, but I knew where to start looking. We didn't have any of the texts about angelic medicine, so I went to the source."

"Source?" he asked, unsure. Then his eyes went wide. "No. Tell me you didn't . . ."

"I found Antares," I confessed. "In exchange for releasing her from the Earth, she gave me a root from the tree she was bound to and it healed your wound."

"You went to the Lord of the West?" he asked in that disapproving-Will way of his. "Ellie . . ."

"Do you love me?" I stared him straight in the face.

"Yes."

"Then trust me."

"That was so dangerous. . . ."

"Oh, shut up," I grumbled and slapped his shoulder gently. "I did what I had to do to save you and I'm not hearing any of your crap about it. Now I'm going to try to sleep a little. I'm in the middle of studying for final exams. You picked a very bad time to almost die."

He gave me a silly, lopsided smile. "Sorry. We'll talk

about Antares tomorrow."

"Any chance you'll forget to scold me about it again?" I asked with a hopeful lilt to my voice.

He kissed the top of my head. "Nope."

I held on to him tighter. "I'll remember to bring my armor then. And the swords."

"I love you," he said against my hair.

I closed my eyes, my cheek against his chest, rising and falling with his breaths. "I love you too."

I woke alone in the bed and on the verge of panicking, because I didn't know where Will was. The house was quiet, so I went through the kitchen and out onto the back porch. Will and Marcus were hanging out down by the lake, the afternoon sunshine gleaming off their hair and skin and the calm water's surface. I bounded off the porch and down the lawn toward them. They turned to look my way and I let out a squeal of happiness as I leaped into Will's arms. He caught me around my legs with a laugh and I threw my arms around the back of his neck and kissed him. It was wonderful to feel him again, to feel him hold me tight, to feel his lips against mine. He was warm from the sunlight, and he smelled like Will and felt like Will and he was back to his old self again. My Guardian, my Will.

"I'm still here, you guys," Marcus grumbled. "Really. I'm going to gouge my eyes and ears out."

Will set me down and I still clung to him, wringing my

fingers around the bottom of his shirt. "How are you feeling?" I asked him.

"Great," he said, and lifted his injured arm. "Like I'm
back to normal." The bandages were gone and the wound
had just about disappeared. There would be no scar, as if
nothing had ever happened.

"That's wonderful! We should take it easy one more night
before we get back to work. We shouldn't take any risks right
away."

He raised an eyebrow at me, flashing a smile between
Marcus and me. "How long was I out, again? I like this new
you."

"Let's just say this new me is a lot more like the old me,"
I corrected him.

"In a strange way that sort of makes sense," he said. Now
his smile was all for me.

Later that evening, Marcus left with Ava and Sabina to go
patrolling while I stayed with Will. He was restless and itching to get back into the field, but Lauren had come over to
help me convince him to relax. As we finished cleaning up
dinner, Will stopped, frozen, mid-drying a dish.

I stared at him. "What's wrong?"

And then I felt that soothingly familiar energy signature,
but for Will, the energy was enraging.

I put my hand to his chest. "Will, relax. I can explain
why Cadan is here. I'll go talk to him and tell him that now

isn't a good time. He's not here for a fight, trust me. He only wants to make sure everything is okay."

I could hear his teeth grinding together and I got nervous.

"She's right," Lauren assured him. "Everything's fine, Will."

"I'll be right back," I said. "You have to trust me. Do you trust me?"

He nodded reluctantly. "Fine. You get him out of here."

Relieved to know that no confrontation would occur, I left Will and Lauren in the house and found Cadan waiting on the porch. His expression was curious, but stone-hard, as he stared at the front door behind me. His light eyes and pale gold hair were bright in the moonlight.

"He's awake?"

I should have known that Cadan would be able to sense us as we had sensed him. "Yeah. He's good as new."

"I'm glad for you."

"Thank you," I told him. I pulled him into a tight hug. His arms were warm around me. "Thank you so much for everything. I couldn't have done this without you."

We parted and he grinned down at me. "You would have eventually. I don't doubt that. But I'm happy to have helped. I wanted to apologize also."

"You don't have to," I promised. "Whatever happened, it's in the past and I know you didn't mean anything."

"No," he said sadly. "I'll never be able to apologize enough for the way I behaved."

"Well, I forgive you. And that's all that matters."

"Ell," he sighed. "I tried to make you kiss me. You ought to hit me *again*—"

The front door blasted open and in the same instant, Cadan was sent tumbling down the porch steps to the ground. When I overcame my surprise I realized that Will had just coldcocked Cadan in the face.

"My turn for that," Will snarled as Cadan struggled to his feet, cupping his jaw.

"Will!" I cried in anger, turning on him hotly. "What the hell? If anyone's going to hit either of you, it'll be me!"

"I can explain," Cadan said as he held up one hand defensively and spit a glob of blood onto the grass. When his eyes met Will's, Will disappeared, moving like a flash in the darkness, and he reappeared on the ground in front of Cadan. He hit him again. Cadan's head snapped around. More blood flecked his shirt.

"Stop it!" I shrieked. "Both of you!"

"What's going on?" Lauren burst out the front door, shocked and afraid. She gasped when she saw Will and Cadan fighting.

Will's fist slammed into Cadan's face and he was thrown to the side. As soon as they parted, I jumped between them and grabbed Will's shirt as he moved to strike Cadan again, and the demonic reaper whirled out of reach. His wings sprang free, their leathery hide slick and gleaming beneath the moonlight.

"Ellie, this is between him and me," Will growled and yanked free.

"It sure as hell is *not*!" I snapped at him. "You have nothing to do with what happened between us. He got a little pushy, I slapped the crap out of him, and he apologized. It's over, done, *finito*! It's none of your business, you idiot!"

Cadan held out an arm and his thin, elegant, rapierlike sword appeared out of a flash of light. Will tilted his head with a derisive smirk.

"Is that all you got?" he asked darkly and held out his own hand. The archangel sword, six feet in length, shimmered into existence.

Cadan's sneer matched Will's maliciousness. "Some might say you're compensating for something."

Will huffed. "Believe me. I'm not."

"This is shockingly mature, you morons!" I yelled at them, but they ignored me.

Lauren held my arm tightly with both her hands, clinging to me in fear. I knew what she was thinking. The last fight that happened in this house had killed the man she loved. I was determined to end this before someone really got hurt.

With a roar of rage, Will swung his sword as hard as he could and cut Cadan's blade in half with a shriek of metal. The tip of Cadan's sword helicoptered through the air and he took a single step back in shock. Will relinquished his blade and lunged for Cadan. Will grabbed two fistfuls of Cadan's collar and picked him up off his feet before slamming his back into the ground with a thick thud. Will crouched over him and smashed his fist into Cadan's face again and again as I screamed uselessly. Cadan wasn't even fighting back. He was just letting Will beat the hell out of him. I threw myself on top of Will, pulling at his shirt. I grabbed his wrist and held his arm back, using every last ounce of my strength.

"Will, *stop*! You're going to kill him!" I shrieked, and pulled him off of Cadan.

We were finally standing and I was still dragging him away as Cadan rolled on the ground, groaning. He spit up a thick gob of blood, his face torn and his eyes already swollen and purple. The bones in his cheeks were working themselves back into their rightful places beneath his skin, fractures mending and sewing themselves. Will yanked away from me but I darted around him, fitting my body against his, blocking him from getting at Cadan again.

"He's your *brother*!" I screamed, and shoved his chest hard, knocking him back a step. I gasped for breath and he grew very still while I shook like an earthquake. "He's your brother, Will. He's Bastian's son too, and he saved your life. You'd be dead if it weren't for him!"

His mouth opened as he stared at me. His arms fell loosely. "What?" he asked in the smallest voice.

"He's the one who took me to Antares. I couldn't have saved you without him."

Will shook his head so slightly the movement was almost invisible. "*No*. No way."

"It's true," I said breathlessly. "You and I owe him a lot."

"We don't owe him *shit*!" Will cried, casting an angry finger at Cadan. "He is *not* my brother!"

Cadan struggled to stand, gasping from pain, and he wiped his sleeve across his face, smearing blood. "I wasn't too keen on the news, either, *Brother*."

When I looked back at Lauren, I saw her hands covering her mouth and all the blood had drained from her face. She fluttered back into the safety of the house and away from the angry reapers.

"Are you all right?" I asked Cadan.

He gave me a nod and a shrug. "I'll live."

When I turned back to Will, he was staring at me, his green eyes wide and hurt. "Why didn't you tell me? How long have you known?"

"I've known since Bastian told you that you were his," I confessed. "Cadan had already told me that Bastian was his father. I'm sorry."

"Why him?" Will gasped. "Why did you go to him? Marcus could have helped you—Ava or Sabina. . . ."

I stepped close to him and put my hands on his arms to try and comfort him, but he was frozen beneath my touch, unyielding. "Because there was no time and he was the only person I knew who had met a Grigori. Please don't be angry with either of us. As much as you hate him, Cadan risked his life for you. Please forgive him for what happened between him and you."

"He touched you," Will said, the words just an exhale. For an instant, he trembled, and his face filled with pain and vulnerability before locking back up again. It was barely a crack in his composure before he sealed it up with concrete. "He tried to force himself on you. I can't let that go."

"He didn't force himself on me," I said firmly. "He was a little pushy, yeah, but only for a second. He was a jerk, and I handled it. There's nothing you need to do now. Just chill out, okay?"

His jaw set tight and he glanced up at the sky before meeting my eyes again. "For centuries I've watched you with everyone but me," he said. "Not him, Ellie. Not after what he did to me, to *you*. I could have protected you the night Ragnuk killed you, but Cadan and Ivar stopped me. Instead of killing me, they kept me alive so that I would see you dead. That kind of malice can't be forgiven and every time I see his face, I see what was left of you when Ragnuk was finished."

My eyes started to burn, but I was determined not to cry. "He's trying to make up for the things he's done wrong. I don't expect you to forgive him right now, but please believe that you might be able to one day. You'd be in much less pain if you stopped trying to hate him so much. Be happy to know that you have family and he's right here. He's *family*, Will."

Will looked over his shoulder at Cadan, who stood stooped over as his face put itself back together. He'd need to eat a lot very soon to make up for the energy he spent in order to heal. It was possible for him to exhaust himself and run out of energy before he was fully healed, and I wondered if Will was thinking the same. He had a pathetic look on his face, a strange mix of remorse and satisfaction, as he watched his broken older brother heal from the assault. He must have been waiting a long time to beat the hell out of Cadan, but now that he had done it, he seemed ashamed of himself—as he ought to be. He looked down at his hands. Cadan's blood was splashed across his skin up to his elbows.

"If you trust him," Will said in a low voice, "then I accept that. But it doesn't mean that I have to trust him too."

Will moved away from me and went back into the house without uttering another word. When he was gone, I turned to Cadan and winced at his appearance. He was mostly healed now, but blood still caked his face and his black eyes remained puffy. I watched his skin stitch together a gash in his lip and he wiped the blood away with the back of his hand.

"I'm so sorry," I told him. "You look awful, like you got hit by a bus."

He coughed up a hunk of red stuff. "I had it coming. He got it out of his system finally, so maybe now we can move past this and focus on what's important, like stopping Sammael. It'll be a while before Will is ready to accept me. We shouldn't push him."

I nodded, knowing he was right. This situation only added more stress that none of us needed. "He sure likes to hold grudges, doesn't he?"

The corner of Cadan's lip pulled into a tiny smile. "Again, I deserved it. When you're immortal, time is different. Things that happened years ago still sting like they happened yesterday. Grudges are hard to let go. I understand how he's feeling and I think we both need to let him feel it. He'll let go when he's ready. If he doesn't, then it's not like I deserve any better."

As I let his words sink in, I couldn't help cringing at the mess Will had left him in. "I should get you a towel or something, help you clean yourself up."

"Nah. I need to get going. I'm exhausted and just got my ass kicked inside out. And I need to eat like crazy." His expression softened. "I'll catch you later, okay? And next time I'll give you a heads up if I need to drop by. In the meantime I'll try to gain back my pride by beating up things for information."

I put a hand on his shoulder. "Let me know if you hear anything interesting, okay? The next step is to find this hallowed glaive and the copy of Antares's grimoire."

He gave me a puzzled look. "Why do you still need it?"

"I need to summon Azrael and ask for his help in fighting Sammael," I said. "If that doesn't work, then I need to ascend, to become Gabriel again, if it's possible."

His eyes bugged. "Well, if you think it'll give us an edge, then let's do it."

"Thanks," I said. "If I can be at my full archangel power, then I have a chance to wipe out Sammael *and* Lilith."

"I'll find out what I can about any copies of the grimoire for you. Night, Ell." He winced before spreading his wings and disappearing into the Grim.

Will had mangled him pretty bad and I felt partly responsible. I should have told Will everything, that Cadan was his older brother, that without Cadan's help, I never could have found Antares in time. Will could have had time to digest the news before seeing Cadan's face. Perhaps their altercation would've been less bloody and traumatic.

Back in the house, I headed up the stairs. Behind the closed door of Nathaniel's and Lauren's room, I could hear the TV on and see light flickering around the doorframe. I felt awful every time Lauren was around a fight. As a psychic, she had her own incredible talents, but superhuman strength wasn't one of them. I couldn't even imagine how vulnerable she felt when reapers turned a brawl into a demolition derby. I found Will in the upstairs bathroom washing his hands. The white sink was stained red with blood that wasn't his.

"I'm sorry," I said weakly.

He didn't look up. "For?" His voice was dry, low, and empty of emotion.

"For a million things." I sighed and leaned against the wall. "For not telling you that I knew Cadan is your brother. I was afraid to tell you. I'm also sorry that I didn't tell you that Cadan took me to Antares. And I'm sorry he came over tonight."

He turned off the faucet and set his hands on the counter on either side of the sink. At last he looked up and his gaze caught mine in the vanity mirror. That green was so very dull. "I understand why you didn't want to tell me. I wouldn't have wanted to know."

"I would've told you when . . ." My voice trailed off. When would I have told him? Under what circumstances would I have had the balls? "I just wasn't sure when was the right time. I would have told you. I swear."

"I know you would've."

He turned around and scooped me into a hug. I clung to his iron grip, soaking in his heat like I'd been freezing to death. I buried my cheek into his chest, breathing in his scent and smoothing my hands over the hard contours of his back beneath the soft cotton of his shirt.

"I just wanted you to live," I whispered against him. My tears melted into his shirt. "You've saved me more times than . . . than there are stars in the sky. I had to do whatever it took to save you in return."

He squeezed me tighter and nestled his face into my hair and I felt his warm breath. Then we just held each other in that still and quiet place.

9

AFTER AN INTENSE LAST FEW DAYS OF HIGH SCHOOL, I passed my exams and guaranteed my admission into Michigan State in the fall. The night before commencement, Kate and I had a sleepover at Nana's house with angelic reapers prowling the area on full alert, as danger these days was extremely imminent. Kate and I did the lame girl things I once loved, like giving each other a mani/pedi, flipping through magazines, and scrolling through gossip blogs. But I hadn't realized until then how much I'd changed since last fall. While Kate showed off the new designer dress she bought to wear beneath her graduation gown, I realized that I didn't really care. I had just grabbed the first dress I found in my closet and a pair of heels that would match, feeling no excitement at all. I hadn't even wanted to go shopping. Dresses and shoes didn't matter. The only excitement I felt about graduation was getting to be with my friends and family, because I understood now how limited our time with them was. If only I'd known that before it was too late. Maybe then my mom would've been able to watch me receive my diploma.

I was, however, a little excited about Josie Newport's Blackout Graffiti Party after commencement. Kate had bought a giant bag of highlighters to doodle all over ourselves and our clothes. The white tank top I would wear would inevitably be covered in vulgar sayings and genitalia by the end of the night. I wasn't sure I'd ever understand boys' obsession with drawing penises all over everything, including other people.

In the morning I rode to school with Kate to prepare for commencement. The grounds were packed with my rowdy classmates and most of the faculty—who were either beaming with pride or grinning with relief to see us go. We filed into lines to head out onto the football field and take our seats. Cheers roared through the stadium and everyone looked up into the bleachers to spot their families. Kate's mom whistled at her from where she sat with Kate's dad, grandparents, and other family members. Sitting close to the Green family was my own. There was Nana, and beside her sat Will, Lauren, and Marcus. They were here partly as my bodyguards and backup while Ava and Sabina lurked within the Grim, watching the perimeter of the school. Kate grabbed my arm giddily as she blew a kiss to Marcus, who playfully stuck out his tongue in disgust, to which Kate flipped him off, much to my

Nana's shock. If she had pearls, she'd be clutching them.

Commencement was hellishly boring. I picked at my nail polish while we sat through a bunch of faculty and student speeches. Kate was busy dirty texting with Marcus, having somehow snuck her cell phone in by tucking it into her bra. I kept myself occupied by looking around at the equally bored faces of my classmates. After tonight, I'd probably never see 95 percent of them again. After tonight, things would stay about the same for me: hunt, kill, and fight for my life. If I was lucky enough to survive and defeat Sammael, then maybe I could move into a dorm with Kate in the fall.

When I was called to get my diploma, I shook the hands of my teachers, got my photo taken, flipped my little cap tassel, and went back to my seat. I looked up to grin at my family. Will, Lauren, and Marcus weren't just my friends. They were honest-to-God real family. Even Kate's mom, practically my second mom, was on her feet roaring with cheers for me. She would never know what I'd been through to get here, but she clapped and whistled like she did. It was a while before everyone finished receiving their diplomas, but when it was over, the principal congratulated our class on graduating and then hundreds of caps were tossed high and flying through the air. I might have used a little bit of my Preliator power to throw my own cap the highest.

That night at Josie's Blackout Graffiti Party, I'd managed to avoid having any highlighter boy parts scribbled onto my white tank top—*so far*. Landon and Chris had managed to draw genitalia on most of the partygoers, targeting the cuter girls the most. I felt like I'd need to bust out my Khopesh swords to deter them. To my dismay, my angelic reaper backup team were here to protect me against the demonic, not pesky human boys. When I caught them sneaking up on me for a third time, Kate grabbed me and dragged me into the bathroom. I should have ditched the stupid tank top like she had. She'd also made it clear to everyone that if anyone scribbled on her glittery purple leopard dress, she'd stab their eyes out with her stilettos.

"Let's do my hair!" she squeaked in rabid excitement. She was a little drunk already, which made me feel even more sober than I actually was.

"Are you serious?" I hesitantly accepted the handful of highlighters she stuffed into my palm.

"Let's make rainbows." She plucked the cap off a blue marker and began tracing streaks through her blond hair. She skewed her Egyptian-style highlighter-outlined eyes in the mirror. This was clearly a daunting task for her.

"I don't think this is what the magazines mean when they talk about 'highlights.'"

"You're funny, bitch." She handed the blue marker to me. "Do the back."

I sighed and did as she'd asked. I highlighted her hair in blue, purple, green, yellow, orange, and pink. Her rainbow hair clashed with her purple disco leopard dress and monster stilettos. She looked like a hooker Rainbow Brite about to be sent to rehab.

"We should wash it out," I suggested dismally, picking at the mutilated strands of rainbow hair.

Kate gasped and swatted my hand away. "Oh, *hell* no. Let's go marvel at my amazing hair!"

She dragged me out of the bathroom and back out into the cavernous room Josie's parties took place in. The black lights made the neon graffiti splashed over everyone glow in the dark as they twisted and jumped to the music. I had to admit, Kate's hair looked ridiculous and awesome at the same time. We took a break from dancing over by the hors d'oeuvres and were immediately descended on by Landon and Chris like marker-happy vultures.

Landon squeezed between Kate and me and threw his arms around our shoulders. "The two hottest chicks at the party!"

"You're like girl-next-door hot," Chris said to me. "Kate is like supermodel-hot. You're like the two hottest options in a porn buffet."

I narrowed my eyes. "Thanks a lot."

Landon wiggled away from us and began to compulsively scribble dirty images on Chris's cheek like he'd missed a spot. "You guys should think about a webcam. You'd make so much money. You could get a Ferrari or something."

Kate gave them a sugary sweet smile. "How did either of you graduate high school?"

Chris's expression exploded as a lightbulb seemed to click on in his head. "Landon, dude. Don't you think it would be hot if Ellie and Kate had a baby?"

"What the hell are you talking about?" Kate snapped.

I put a hand to my forehead and scanned the crowd, hoping to find a distraction. "I'm so disturbed right now."

Landon examined both of us a little too thoroughly with his gaze. "You mean if they banged? Yeah, man, two chicks is always hot."

"No, no, I mean like if they banged and had a baby together. It'd be the hottest, most perfect baby ever."

Landon looked like he was about to barf. "Babies aren't hot, dude. That's sick."

"Well, it's got to grow up first. But right? They would make the perfect baby together."

I stared at them both. "You two are the dumbest people I have ever met in my life."

"You don't mean that." Chris grinned.

"Yeah, I do actually. Good-bye."

I grabbed Kate and dragged her onto the dance floor. There were so many people packed together that I lost her in the crowd in minutes, but managed to locate Will keeping guard by one of the exits. When I saw his bored face and nothing written on his skin, my fingers suddenly itched to scribble with a highlighter.

"Hey." He greeted me with a warm smile.

I stood close to him, my shoulder touching his arm.

"I'm ready to go when you guys are. I think I've made enough of an appearance. I really just want to go kill stuff."

"Me too," he agreed.

I frowned at him. "You didn't let anyone write on you? How does that happen?"

He gave me a disapproving look. "Seriously, Ellie?"

"Ah," I said. "You must have glared at them just like that. I'm the only one who's not afraid of you. Maybe I could draw over your tattoos so they glow and write *BADASS* on your forehead. All I've got is pink, though. Hope you don't mind."

"Please, don't. I beg you."

I laughed and kissed him, standing on my toes to reach him. "You're looking a little green there, homeslice. You going to pull through?"

"Not if you draw on me in pink highlighter, I won't."

I laughed even harder. "Okay, okay. You're safe, I promise. Let's get out of here. I'll try to find Kate and everybody and say good-bye. Find Marcus, okay?"

He nodded and moved through the crowd. I pushed my own path through the dancing mob, hoping to spot Kate's rainbow hair over the sea of bouncing heads. I really needed to get a leash on that girl, or some kind of tracking device for long distance. I passed by Evan and Rachel, who seemed to be having a blast dancing. I hadn't seen much of either of them since they began dating, but it was good to have hung out with them tonight. To be honest, I wasn't sure how much more of my friends I'd be able to see. There were some serious missions about to go down.

A pang of hurt hit my heart. I ought to be relishing every moment with them, living those moments to the fullest, and not wishing I were somewhere else. Once this was all over, I promised myself, I'd try to spend as much time with my friends as I could.

A girl screamed. I looked around, hoping the screams were just from kids goofing around, but the crowd seemed to have gone still. A few people were still dancing to the music, but in seconds all heads turned in one direction. When I followed their gazes and spun to the right, I bumped into the giant body of a demonic reaper.

Merodach.

I wasn't breathing. I blinked a few times, hoping the mirage would go away, but it didn't. He was difficult to see beneath the black lights, but his dark form blocked out a large number of highlighter-covered people. His horns spiraled toward the ceiling, his wings folded tightly to his back, and his moonlight eyes gleamed, the dim light reflecting off his pupils like an animal's. It took me that long to realize he wasn't in the Grim, and everyone else could see him just as well as I could. They were all staring at him, but he was only staring at me.

"No," I whimpered, but the word was only an exhale. I doubted anyone could even hear me speak.

"Hello again," Merodach said, his heavy voice like scraping gravel. "Gabriel."

"If you have any honor at all, then you and I will take this outside."

He smiled, an unsettling gesture. The crescent scar I'd given him was bright, gnarled, and angry-looking. "And let all these souls go to waste?"

Before I could respond, more screams erupted. My head snapped around. There were more demonic reapers in the room. They shoved through the humans, grabbed at them, and then all hell broke loose. Everyone was screaming now, darting in every direction, most fighting their way toward the exits. I saw one of the demonic reapers grab a girl and bite into her neck, splashing blood over himself and the bodies of other kids. Beneath the black light, the blood was like a bucket of neon paint tossed through the air.

I took off like a shot to help the girl, leaving Merodach at my back. The demonic reaper took another chunk out of the girl before I got to her and he bared his bloody teeth at me. He dropped her; legs tripped over her, bodies slammed into him, and I called my swords. Angelfire lit up the dark room like a bonfire and more shrieks echoed off the walls. I heard two voices screaming my name in the distance.

The reaper slashed his claws, catching my tank top and shredding a long tear through the front. One of my swords took off the arm that clawed me and the limb disappeared in flames as the reaper screeched in pain and fury. His remaining hand lunged for my throat, but I jammed my blade into his chest and ripped it back out sideways, turning his heart to giblets, and the rest of him erupted in angelfire.

The panic only grew worse. People trampled each other, bodies hit the floor, and more reapers filled the room. I spun around, breathlessly surveying the chaos, and my shoe tapped the body of the girl I couldn't save. She stared wide-eyed up at me, dead, half her body eaten, her soul surely in Hell. An explosion of energy made me look to my left. Will had another demonic reaper cornered. I let my swords go and dug out my phone. I texted to Cadan "HELP!" I prayed he'd check his messages immediately and get over here.

"Ellie!" Kate seized my arm. "We have to get out of here!"

I looked over at Will, who was now battling a different vir, and I faced Kate again. "You go. I have to help Will."

"No way!" she shouted. "I'm not leaving you here! What are those things?"

I shook my head. "You have to go. Trust me, Kate, I can take care of myself. Just go!"

Marcus appeared, taking Kate securely by the arm. He dragged her toward the exit as she fought him, screaming my name, and her frightened gaze didn't leave mine until we were separated in the crowd. I silently prayed that she would make it out all right. I had to stop the demonic reapers from taking anymore souls.

I called my swords again and jumped back into the fray.

Shoulder to shoulder, I pushed my way through the scrambling crowd as they went in the opposite direction toward safety. I stepped over another body. I held my breath and didn't look. I didn't want to know who it was, if it was someone I knew. A firm hand took my shoulder and I raised my sword, but it was only Marcus.

"Kate's out," he assured me. He was out of breath and a gash was healing on his cheek. His sword was completely red. "I don't know about your other friends. I couldn't find them. There has to be at least seven or eight demonic vir left in here, Ellie. This doesn't look good."

"I know," I said. "They're here for me, but they're distracted by the humans. We have to kill as many of the vir as possible and even our odds more. Get to work."

Marcus left me and I caught the eye of one of the vir a ways down the wall. His lips, corpse-blue against his ashen skin, curled into an ugly grin. My heart pounded as I looked around. The crowd was thinning, allowing for a little more maneuverability. A little was all I needed.

The demonic reaper called a sword of his own and the blade shimmered into his hand out of thin air. He charged at me. I raised mine just as we were about to collide, and I jumped high. He slowed, his head tilted as his gaze followed me in confusion, but it was enough to throw him off. My shoe touched the wall and I kicked off. My blade swept down in an arc and cleanly through the reaper's neck. He and his flinging skull were gone in seconds. I landed hard, my knees folding on impact. A crescent of blood from my sword strike glowed neon in front of me beneath the black light, as did the splashes of gore across my white tank and skin.

I looked up into Landon's face and my heart stopped. Instead of having fled, he stood staring at me as I held my swords, covered in blood. Bodies streaked behind him, some darting in terror, some falling to the ground.

"Landon," I rasped and rose slowly.

His brow creased as he tried to piece together what he was seeing. "Ellie, did you just—?"

Then his face smashed into the wall with an ear-splitting crack. I choked on my tongue as I watched the demonic reaper lift Landon up by his shirt collar and bare her fangs to bite. I moved so fast that I don't think she saw me coming. I reeled my arm back and swung my sword. The fiery blade buried right into the side of her skull, splitting her head in two. The white flames drowned her and she was gone, letting Landon crumple to the floor. I collapsed with him, letting my swords disappear and helping him to roll onto his back. My entire body went numb and my stomach churned. Landon's face . . . He was dead. Landon was dead.

Someone grabbed a fistful of my hair. I screeched as I was dragged across the floor, away from Landon's body, kicking and tearing at hands that gripped me like steel. The pain made it hard for me to open my eyes, but when I did, I caught the silhouette of an enormous horned shape.

"Humans," Merodach spit. "I don't know why you even

bother. All they do is scream and scatter like birds. You can't protect them and you can't win this war."

He released my hair and the relief on my scalp was instantaneous. I pressed my hands into my head to soothe my skin as I gathered my limbs together and pushed myself to my feet. I picked my swords back up. "You reapers keep saying that, like you're trying to convince yourselves it's true. That's pretty pathetic."

"Xastur!" he barked, his pale eyes frozen on my face. Another demonic reaper appeared beside Merodach. "Wrap it up."

Xastur nodded and vanished in a flash. Merodach tilted his head at me with a curious look. He opened his mouth to speak, but a form materialized right where Xastur had just gone from. The figure was lightning-fast and I was able to make out a hand—a hand that took hold of Merodach's throat and sent him flying across the room and crashing through a window. He disappeared into the darkness outside as glass rained down. As the newcomer slowed and his blurred form took shape, I recognized Cadan.

"Are you okay?" he asked me, his eyes blazing.

"Yeah," I said, and the nausea began to spin in my gut again. "They killed my friend. Oh my God, Landon is dead." I wanted to grieve for him, but now wasn't the time. "I think Xastur is helping Merodach run the show. Find and stop him."

Cadan nodded and disappeared after Merodach. I looked

around, hoping to figure out how many reapers were left alive. Will was covered in blood and his sword was stained neon beneath the black lights. He finished off the last of them, and when his gaze caught Merodach climbing back through the window, Will's face twisted with hatred.

"Marcus!" he roared to rally the other angelic reaper.

Marcus appeared in the room, his own hands and clothes tattered and bloodied from battle. "They're dead," he said. "They're all dead, except for Xastur. He took off."

Merodach surveyed the other reapers and his gaze rested on me. He bared his teeth, flashing bright fangs in the black light. "The coward. You win this one, Preliator."

Will roared with rage and launched himself in the air toward Merodach, sword swinging. Merodach whirled to the side to avoid the blade, but Will followed him. They were neon blurs in the darkness, nearly invisible—until Will's body rammed into the wall and Merodach appeared above our heads, black wings spread wide. Feathers drifted to the floor. Merodach's hands rolled into fists and he loosed a bellow of fury and frustration. And then he vanished. When Merodach didn't reappear, I ran to Will's side and helped him to his feet. He punched the wall, his fist burying deep, and he swore at the top of his lungs.

"He'll be back," Marcus offered. "You'll have another shot at him. At least we didn't lose anyone."

"Ellie did," Cadan said in a low voice.

Reality came crashing down on me. I didn't want to look

at Landon's body, but my legs moved toward him anyway. He was crumpled on the floor against the opposite wall, his limbs tangled like a tossed doll's, and what was left of his face stared straight up at the ceiling.

One of my best friends was dead. I wasn't sure if that fact would ever begin to make sense. Merodach had taken someone else I loved from me. There was one deafening thought repeating itself in my head, so loud I couldn't think, like I'd forgotten the entire English lexicon but for five words.

I will kill them all.

10

"I WANT TO KNOW WHERE XASTUR WENT," I SAID, my tone sharp and commanding. "I want to play croquet with his head by dawn, do you understand?"

The three reapers nodded in unison.

"Someone has to know a demonic reaper named Xastur," I continued. "I want Ava and Sabina on this too. Marcus, call Ava and tell them to drop whatever they are doing."

Without questioning me, Marcus took his phone out and dialed. He began to relay what had happened as Ava listened on the other end. Will stepped close to me. The scent of blood on him was gut-wrenching.

"We may not track him down tonight," he warned. "But eventually we will. He will die for what he did to Landon and the other humans."

"I swear I will make him suffer," I said.

Will studied my face for a couple moments before exhaling. "Xastur may give us something on Merodach too."

"He's right," Cadan added. "There's a chain of command in their ranks. This guy obviously isn't a grunt, and there's a good chance he is privy to crucial information. He may even have artifacts that will help us."

"Like a relic?" I asked.

"Maybe," he replied. "Xastur might even have the copy of Antares's grimoire that you're after."

My mind raced with possibilities. "Better yet . . . if Bastian figured out how to summon Lilith, then they might know how to summon others."

"Other Fallen?" Will asked, surprised.

"No," I said. "Summon an angel like Azrael. If we don't find the grimoire copy with Xastur—which is likely—then we might still find out if Xastur knows how to summon Azrael. He's an angel, an *ex*-archangel, to be exact. He has to know if it's possible for me to ascend and become Gabriel."

Cadan's expression hardened. "Do you still want to do that?"

"I have to do whatever it takes to destroy Sammael and Lilith," I said. "We start with talking to Azrael. We have to find out how to summon him."

"Guys," Marcus interjected. "Sabina knows who Xastur is."

"Does she know where he is?" Will asked.

Marcus flashed a dark, satisfied grin as he slipped

his cell back into his pocket. "Yeah, she sure does. She's never infiltrated his hideout before because it's too heavily guarded. So, what do you say we crash someone else's party and pay him a visit?"

"Let's go." I didn't wait for a response before I began marching toward the front door.

In the distance, countless sirens from emergency vehicles wailed mournfully.

I plugged the address Sabina gave us into my GPS. Will rode shotgun beside me and the rest of the reapers flew through the Grim straight for our destination. My heart pounded so hard in my chest that it was painful, but there was no way for me to relax. I stared hard at the road ahead, desperate to drive the images of the bodies of my friends and classmates from my mind.

My phone buzzed. Kate was calling. I took a deep breath and caught Will's glance out of the corner of my eye. "Hey," I answered.

Kate's response was a string of unintelligible angry sobs and curses.

"Kate, slow down," I ordered. "Are you safe?"

"I'm home!" she cried shrilly into my ear. "Where are you? What happened? Oh my God, Ellie—"

"I'm with Will. Just calm down and stay where you are, all right?"

"They won't tell us what happened! People were *dead*, Ellie!"

Landon's mangled face flashed in my head. I just couldn't bring myself to tell her, to say out loud what I didn't want to be real. "I know. It was horrible. People just panicked and stampeded. It was a horrible accident—"

"Oh *please*," she snarled on the other end. "You saw those things. We all did. Don't even lie to me."

I couldn't deal with this right now. "I've got to go," I said. "I'll call you in the morning, okay?"

"Don't you *dare*—"

I hung up and turned my phone off. I had to. There was no way for me to explain to her what happened without thinking long and hard about a realistic story. The police would be all over the scene and questioning everyone who'd been there, including myself, I was certain.

But I couldn't think about that. Not yet. I had to stay focused on the danger I was about to walk right into. This reaper, Xastur, would be the last to get his blood on my blades tonight.

"I am so sorry about Landon," Will said in the smallest voice.

A tremor rippled through my chest. "I'm the one who should be sorry. It's all my fault."

"Please don't say that."

"Yeah, it is," I snapped back a little more sharply than

I'd intended. "I brought the reapers to that house. It's my fault they were there and killed all those kids. If you guys hadn't been there . . . I don't know how many more would have died."

"The demonic are the ones who did this," Will said, his voice firm. "We took them all out except for two. We'll find Xastur and then we'll find Merodach."

The muscles in my jaw clenched, my teeth squeaking against each other. "Yes," I said. "Yes, we will."

Xastur's hideout was a dilapidated old textile factory, and as my car rolled nearer and the building loomed overhead, an ache of dread shuddered through me. I let the car idle to a standstill and I stared up at the factory. Demonic energy oozed from its crumbling walls and broken windows, coiling around frightening memories I'd shoved deep into the pits of my mind.

"Ellie."

Will's voice shook me from my reverie and I realized that I'd been squeezing the steering wheel so hard my hands had turned white and I was shaking. Even so, I couldn't let go.

"What's the matter?" he asked. "We can turn around, take you home. I'll return with the others to get what we need."

Lights flickered in a couple of windows in the top floor. I jumped when a shadow passed over the glow. "I remember this place."

"You've been here before?"

"I died here." I unbuckled my seat belt and climbed from the car.

Will followed. "What? When?"

"Ragnuk," I replied distantly. "I followed him here and this is where he killed me."

He fell silent, and I realized he had never known where I had died last. I understood that the memory was painful for both of us and I didn't want us to let it become a distraction. I wanted revenge for Landon's death and Xastur was the last culprit remaining alive besides Merodach. I would return to this factory, but Xastur would be the one to die tonight. He and whatever other demonic things crawled through the hallways.

"Come on," Will said at last. "The others are waiting."

It didn't take long for us to rendezvous with the rest of our team. The angelic reapers, Marcus, Ava, and Sabina, stood with our own demonic reaper, Cadan. He and Will exchanged looks, but in their attempt to be civil, nothing was said between them.

Sabina stepped forward, clad in black, her blond hair pulled into a high, tight ponytail. She pulled out two guns and checked the clips in both. Two long daggers were strapped to the sides of her boots. "Xastur keeps his office on the top floor. There are vir protecting the upper levels and mostly ursids patrolling the lobby. I've seen two different vir outside of the building since we've been here. I don't have a definitive number, but so far I've counted seventeen ursid reapers. I don't know how many are deeper within the factory or how many vir reapers we will meet."

Marcus swore under his breath. "That's a bigger party than I thought."

"Let's go for it," Ava said eagerly and called her sword into her hand.

"There are six of us," I said, agreeing with Ava. "If we're careful, then we have nothing to worry about. I'm not sure if we'll have much of an element of surprise, but we should approach as if they don't know we're here. Xastur will need someplace to regroup, but if he's returned to his main hideout, then he's either completely stupid or completely oblivious. This place shouldn't be so heavily guarded if there isn't something important inside to guard."

Marcus shot a grin at Will and flicked his brow. "Well then, boss lady. Let's move in."

I was flanked by reapers as we marched toward the factory entrance. The overgrown lawn revealed nothing, so one by one, we slipped into the Grim and let the world of reapers fill our senses. There was no way to make it all the way to the top floor without alerting Xastur and his goons. We would have to fight, and that was hard to do without making a ruckus. I could only hope that we'd have enough of a jump on our enemies to keep them from all descending on us at once. A handful of reapers at a time was something we could handle, and not a couple dozen. That was too big of a risk. I wouldn't let anyone else I cared about die tonight.

As we neared the front door, flashes of darkness and my own blood on the dirty basement floor hit my mind's eye like distorted, grainy tintype photographs, but I stared hard at that door. No more would I walk in fear of what had happened to me. I wouldn't let death haunt me any longer. I would hunt death. I would be the reaper.

I kicked down the door, full force, and the sheet of metal crashed into the opposite wall. Outside light drenched the shadowed lobby. They now knew I was here, but they wouldn't know I'd brought an army.

Movement blazed to my left and a demonic vir tore from the darkness and into view, but Will was there in an instant and he slammed his fist into the reaper's face. A hideous crack echoed through the lobby and the vir's head twisted almost all the way around on his neck. His body was pale stone before it crashed to the tile floor.

Marcus stepped up to the vir's remains and slapped Will's shoulder. "You are one bad motherf—"

He was cut off by a cacophony of earth-shaking roars resounding from deep within the cavernous factory. The walls shook free of dust, and yellowed paper and debris blew toward us from a dark hallway. I called my swords and angelfire lit up the room. Eerie white light danced off the walls and ceiling, and we waited for the ursid reapers to descend.

I heard their hollow loping through the halls, claws

clicking cement, large bodies panting, snarling, growling orders to each other. Black fur rustled in the darkness and gnashing teeth appeared. I bolted toward the reapers as they appeared. Claws and fangs slit through the air past my skin and my knees hit the floor. I slid across the cement and was lost to them in the tangle of legs and paws, too small for them to keep me in sight. Bodies jumbled above me, snouts crunching, and I cut flesh. My blades spilled blood and bowels, and reapers went up in flame and ash. When I was past them, I jumped to my feet and whirled to face the remaining enemies. Sabina was caught in the jaws of an ursid and was thrown against the wall with a thud. Before it could make a killing bite, Marcus shoved one of Sabina's guns to the temple of the beast and fired until bullets pounded rock. Will split a reaper in two with his blade and spun around. Ava ducked and his blade swept over her head and buried itself into the rib cage of another ursid reaper. Cadan's sword jammed through the chest of a rearing reaper and as it fell, I hacked its head off.

When the blinding flames and cloud of ash settled, no more ursid reapers remained and we headed for the stairwell. It was quiet except for the echoes of our footsteps. I counted five stories in total as I looked up. Dying fluorescent lights flickered at each level.

Ava stepped ahead of me. "See you at the top." Her wings sprang free and she shot into the air. Marcus and Sabina followed.

Cadan exchanged looks with Will. "You got her?" he asked.

Will's gaze narrowed and darkened. "Yeah. I do."

Cadan's mouth formed a tight line as he accepted this without another word and followed the others, his wings lifting him with ease. Will wrapped his free arm around my waist and pulled me close to his body. I hugged his body tight in anticipation of liftoff.

"None of that tonight, please?" I begged him.

His green eyes met mine for an instant before he lifted his chin to the dark shaft above us. "None of what?"

I pinched his skin through his shirt with my fingers. "You know what I mean."

His wings spread wide; feathers brushed my skin and he looked back down at me. There was a whisper of a smile and then he kissed me hard. He pulled away only a few inches and said, "I've got you."

Then we rocketed through the shaft, five stories up. We landed and he set me down delicately. The others had already breached a cavernous room, and the popping sounds of gunfire and the *shing* of silver against silver assaulted my hearing. I caught Xastur making a dash for the exit and I chucked my sword. The angelfire went out as it whipped through the air end over end and pounded into the reaper's chest. He snapped back and shrieked as the blade buried in the wall, nailing Xastur with it. I stomped toward him with my remaining sword still lit.

"Going somewhere?" I asked him. "You're developing quite the reputation of loyalty to your buddies—or lack of, more like it."

Blood oozed down the reaper's front and squeezed between his teeth before dribbling down his chin. "Get this thing out of my chest," he sputtered.

"If I free you, then you're likely to do what you do best—*run*," I sneered. "We can't have that."

"Ellie!"

I spun at the sound of my name. Cadan jogged to a stop in front of me.

"Sabina," he said, and I didn't miss the desolation in his voice.

A shudder of fear went through me. "Watch this worm," I instructed and left Cadan with the pinned Xastur.

I passed piles of rubble littering the floor of the room as I hurried toward the group of angelic reapers huddled over something rumpled in a heap at their feet. It was Sabina. Her blond hair was tangled and matted with blood as her head lay cradled in Will's hands. Her clothes were drenched dark and a horrible wound gaped wide open in her chest. On the other side of her lay a large sword painted red. The stench of blood was nauseating and I covered my mouth with my hand. Will looked up at me from the ground and his head shook almost imperceptibly.

I knelt beside her and took her hand. Her skin was cold. Her black eyes were dulled to gray as she watched me, lips trembling, mangled chest rising and falling with struggling breath. "Gabriel," she murmured.

With my other hand, I smoothed her hair away from her face. "Thank you, Sabina," I said, emphasizing every word. "You have been an incredible soldier."

"I wish I could keep fighting for you," she replied. A trickle of blood slipped past her lips.

"You've fought enough."

"I wanted to see the end," Sabina continued. "I wanted to see us win."

"It'll just be more blood," I told her. "Are you sure you can't heal from this?"

When I looked at our hands clasped together, I realized why her skin felt so cold. Her fingers had already begun to harden and turn to stone. I bit hard on my lip. Sabina gave me a tiny smile before throwing her head back and groaning with pain. She seemed so small, shuddering on the floor in front of me, bleeding to death.

Ava crouched beside me. "Don't worry, my friend. We will have victory. Someday I'll see you on the other side."

Sabina huffed a tiny laugh and coughed before swallowing more blood. "There is no other side."

"You say that only because no one knows for sure," I said. "There is Heaven for human souls and angels, and there must be a place for the souls of reapers. A paradise all your own."

Sabina's eyes, even lighter than they were moments ago,

slowly rolled over to meet mine. Her face and lips had begun to turn gray. A crack split across her cheek. "Do you promise, archangel?"

"I believe it," I said firmly.

"Good-bye, Ellie." Sabina breathed in and out and closed her eyes. Her grip on my hand loosened. "Make it bright," she whispered. And with those peculiar words, she was gone.

Rage boiled deep within me, a torrent river of fury and bloodlust. We weren't supposed to lose anyone else. Sabina shouldn't have died. I rose to my feet and called my sword again. Angelfire blazed as I marched toward Xastur. Cadan stepped aside, the heat of the divine fire nearly scorching his skin. Xastur's eyes were wild and he struggled against my Khopesh sword impaling him to the wall through his chest.

"Do you see what you've done?" I snarled at him and pointed my fiery blade in the direction of Sabina's remains. The other angelic reapers had closed in behind me and watched in silence.

"That wasn't me!" Xastur howled. "I didn't kill her!"

"The one who did was acting on your orders," I shot back, and poised the blade at his face. "So did the ones who murdered my human friends only hours ago. Their blood is on your hands, along with countless other lives."

"It was Merodach's idea! He's the one—"

"He's next on my list," I said. "Don't you worry. I'm going to kill every single one of you."

"Him, too?" Xastur barked, motioning to Cadan. "What about him?"

I looked over my shoulder at the demonic reaper with the fire-opal gaze pinned on my face. "Bastian's son fights for me now. He's risked his life for me and for the ones I love."

Xastur swore and spit a red glob on the cement floor at Cadan's feet. "Traitor! The Lord of Souls will come for you."

Cadan said nothing.

I pressed the tip of my sword to the base of Xastur's throat and he hissed at the angelfire turning his skin red. "We will meet Sammael sooner or later. But first, we deal with you. There is a reason why I haven't yet split you from collarbone to crotch."

"What do you want?" The demonic reaper laughed. "Information? You think I'm going to tell you where our Lord is?"

"No," I said. "I need something else from you. I will let you go if you cooperate."

He laughed even louder. "How would you know I'm telling the truth?"

"That's the million-dollar question, isn't it?" I asked. "I suppose I'll just have to make you *want* to tell me the truth."

My Khopesh sword opened his skin and let the angelfire in. The reaper's screams echoed through the factory.

There was so much blood on the floor by the time Xastur started squawking that a wide river of red split the room in two. The bits I'd cut off of him had turned to stone at my feet and I'd kicked them away. Not much of his face was left recognizable, and I could never take enough flesh from him to make up for Sabina and Landon and the other kids murdered tonight.

"Please," Xastur sputtered through blood. His head hung low and one eye struggled to focus on my face. His other eye wasn't there anymore. "I'll tell you anything. *Anything*."

"Ellie," Will said in a careful voice. "I think he's had enough."

But had *I*? I felt so much hate in my blood that it seemed like I couldn't spill enough of it onto the ground. Xastur was nearly dead, almost where I wanted him, but a dark, coiling part of myself enjoyed torturing him. My mother would hate to see what I'd become.

But this wasn't me. The ice forming around my heart had crept from the deepest, darkest pits of my past, from the lost part of me that had never known any of the things that now made me human: love, compassion, regret. This part of me, the whispers of an archangel who'd had a taste of my human emotions and preferred the flavor of hate the most—even savored it. The archangel I had once been now desired to take control and I'd handed the reins right over to her.

I tilted my head as I studied Xastur's shredded face. I plucked my sword sticking out from his chest and he moaned in pain and slumped over. "Do you know how to summon an angel?" I asked him.

"Me?" the demonic reaper muttered, and tried to stand straight. "No. That stuff's in the book that Merodach has."

"The grimoire of Antares?"

"Yes. There are more spells like the one that summoned Lilith, but I don't know what the spell is, I swear. I only know that it's in there."

"Does Merodach have the only copy of the grimoire? He has the original, but are there others that you know of?"

"There's one copy," Xastur said, and wheezed. "Merodach is trying to find it before you do."

This had to be the copy that Nathaniel had written. "He doesn't know where it is?"

"No, but he knows who has it. A collector named Ethan Stone. Merodach has been combing the eastern seaboard looking for this guy. We suspect he's a psychic and has found a way to hide from the demonic."

"Thank you," I said, and turned to the others. "We need to find Ethan Stone."

They nodded, but all four of them paled when they saw my face. I assumed that was because of the blood.

Cadan stared at me with a look like he was trying to see the path in a maze. "What is wrong with . . . ?"

"Ellie, I think we should go," Will said carefully, his expression tight with worry. He even seemed a little afraid.

"I want his head first," I replied and lifted my blade.

Xastur's face lit up. "No! You said you'd let me go!"

"I didn't say that I'd let you go alive."

I stepped back, swung my sword over my shoulder, and ripped it screaming through the air. The blade bit through flesh and bone and crunched into the wall. The reaper's head toppled over and hit the floor before rolling past my feet. The body crumpled to the floor and shattered into gravel. I had to give the blade a strong tug in order to dislodge it from the wall. When I looked up, I caught my reflection on a shard of glass from a broken window and saw what had frightened Will. For an instant, I thought it was angelfire shimmering off my eyes, but my irises had all but disappeared on their own, replaced with the bright white light I saw in my nightmares and feared more than almost anything.

11

I WOKE EARLY THE NEXT MORNING FEELING STIFF and wretched. Although I'd managed to avoid anything involving news coverage or peer speculation about the events of last night, a difficult conversation with Kate still loomed ahead of me. I was still too shaken. By now she had to know about Landon. His mom had already called Nana so there was no doubt she'd called Mrs. Green, too. All I wanted to do was run away from everything as fast as I could. Will quietly agreed to go for a run with me and we traveled at a quick pace down the winding country road close to Will's house. I didn't believe I'd ever run twenty miles so fast in my life. Even when my lungs burned and my legs turned to jelly, I couldn't stop. If I slowed down, then it would all catch up with me.

Back at the house, I trudged up toward the front porch, but

Will caught my arm. I turned to him. The early-morning dew coated our skin, mixed with sweat and the scent of grass. The warm glow of sunrise brought out the color in his hair. My own tresses looked like they were on fire.

"Hey," he said softly. "You haven't said a word since we left. Are you okay?"

"Trying to be." In truth, I only wanted to be strong and to keep going. I couldn't allow myself to curl into a ball because I'd lost so much. I still had something left to fight for.

He pulled me close, his hands sliding up to cup my face. His lips brushed mine, warm and soft, a scent I could drink, and I kissed him back harder, desperate to cling to him. When I broke the kiss, I held his gaze and smoothed my hand across his rough cheek. My bottom lip trembled as an intense wave of despair crashed over my heart. It seemed as if the closer we came to victory, the more people I loved were lost. If I lost Will, then my soul would die. I'd had a taste of what life felt like without him and I couldn't endure that again. For an intense, fleeting moment, I thought of suggesting we go for another run, only this time we'd never come back.

"No matter how hard it gets," he whispered, "I'll be by your side. I'll never stop fighting."

"I won't either," I promised and kissed him again. "Come sit out back with me?"

I took his hand and led him into the backyard to the swing where I used to sit with Nathaniel and talk. I only wanted to swing and let the motion rock me into senselessness. Will sat next to me and I rested my head on his shoulder and rocked back and forth, staring out onto the lake. A loon drifted not too far from shore, crying its mournful call to no one in particular.

"Do you ever feel guilty?" I asked him.

"About fighting?"

"About things like last night. What I did was pretty messed up."

"It may have been," he agreed. "And though this doesn't excuse the wrongness, we got what we needed out of that vir. This information could change the course of the war."

"As sick as it is, I feel better after what we did to Xastur," I confessed. "His blood can't bring back the souls he's taken over hundreds of years, including the souls of my friends he murdered last night, but I'm glad for what we did to him. It was his turn to hurt and we came nowhere near giving him exactly what he deserved. I don't feel any guilt at all and I know how messed up that is. I feel like I lost a piece of myself last night."

"You lost two friends," he said gently. "And you wanted revenge."

"That didn't mean I was allowed to torture that reaper."

"I'm not going to judge you, Ellie. Don't be too hard on yourself."

I hesitated, feeling a heaviness in my chest. "What I did made me as bad as them."

"I think we're past worrying about fighting dirty."

"Were you afraid of me last night?" I asked him, my voice tiny. Just a squeak. "When you saw my eyes?"

This time, he hesitated. My heart only beat once or twice, but it seemed like a lifetime passed in those moments. "Yes."

The silence that fell between us then thankfully didn't last long. Marcus appeared out of the Grim midflight and he landed in the yard. Will and I slid off the bench swing and headed toward him.

"Hey," he greeted us, stretching out his wings and taking a deep breath. "Wanted to see how you're both doing and to let you know we might have something. I put in a call to Lauren and—"

"What the hell?"

All three of us jumped and spun. Kate stood at the top of the hill beside the house, staring down at us—right at Marcus's wings. She was frozen solid and her hands covered her mouth, the shock and confusion splattered across her face like an Impressionist painting. I, on the other hand, was staring at her extremely *blue* hair.

"What the *hell*?" she repeated.

My jaw dropped. "Oh my God, Kate. What the hell happened to your *hair*?"

She looked aghast. "Why the hell does he have *wings*?"

Marcus withdrew his wings in a flash and started toward her. "Babe," he said gently, like coaxing a frightened animal. "Babe," he said again.

"I am not on drugs," Kate murmured, her voice blank. "I

am not on drugs and I just saw you had wings."

"No, Babe. What are you talking about?"

He reached for her and she slapped his hands back. "Don't even lie to me! You had freaking *wings*! I saw them! Just like those things from last night! What the hell? *What the hell?* You're one of them!"

Then she lost it. She loosed a blood-curdling scream and wheeled away from him, but he grabbed her and pulled her to his chest and held her tight. She thrashed and shrieked as he crooned gently to her, but she wouldn't relax.

I bolted toward them and held Kate's face in my hands. "Kate, calm down. It's okay." I shushed her, but she was crying hysterically.

"I'm crazy," she rasped over and over again. "I'm crazy. I'm totally crazy."

"You're not crazy," I said.

She sagged heavily in Marcus's arms. "Just let me go. Let me *go*, damn it."

I could see on his face that this was the last thing he wanted to happen. If he'd ever wanted to reveal himself to Kate, it was clear that this wasn't the way he'd planned to do it. He slowly loosened his grip on her and she stumbled away, wiping her tear-streaked face with her arm.

"Please tell me I'm crazy," she begged. "Please tell that what I saw last night wasn't real and I didn't just see your wings and that you aren't one of those monsters. Marcus, don't freaking lie to me."

"I would never lie to you," he said, the ache in his tone brimming with honesty and shame. "You aren't crazy. What you've seen was real."

"Stop screwing with me!" she shrieked in anger.

"I'm not!" he shot back.

"He's telling the truth," Will said, the look on his face deadly serious.

Kate stared at him and then looked pleadingly at me. "Ellie, you're my best friend. Please don't screw with me. Landon is freaking *dead*, for Christ's sake. He's dead! I haven't slept. I'm still terrified. Please, *please* tell me—honestly—what the hell is going on."

"I don't—don't know what to say," I stammered. "But you aren't crazy. Marcus, show her. It's too late to hide it anymore."

He closed his eyes and his jaw clenched and he did something he'd likely never done before. He showed his wings to a human. The sparrow-brown feathers gleamed gold in the morning light, that unusual reaper quality giving them a sort of shimmer. Kate's eyes grew wide as apples and she collapsed to her knees in front of Marcus as he spread his wings.

"What are you?" she breathed. "Are you an angel?"

He shook his head. "I'm a reaper. Like Will."

Will looked at me, questioning me with his eyes. I nodded and he knew what to do. He slipped his shirt over his head and dropped it onto the grass. Kate gaped up at him, a tear sliding down her cheek. Will's white wings sprang free and Kate jumped in surprise. Her hands covered her mouth and she whispered something I couldn't make out. I knelt next to her and pulled her into my arms. She shook and shuddered like she was freezing.

"What is happening?" she murmured under her breath. "What is happening? It's not real. It's not real. . . ."

"Kate, sweetie," I said to her and put my forehead to her temple. Her skin was cold and clammy. "It's okay. Don't be afraid. I'll explain everything to you if you want me to."

"How can you explain this?" she asked. "None of this makes any sense. Those things killed my friends, people I've known since kindergarten. They're *reapers*? And Marcus is one of them. And Will. And . . . *you*?" She pulled away to stare at me, her eyes wide and pupils tiny pinpricks of black drowning in blue.

"No," I swore. "I'm not like them and they aren't the things that attacked the party. Those were demonic reapers. Will and Marcus are angelic reapers. They help us, help *me* fight the demonic ones."

"Help you *fight*?"

"Will and Marcus aren't angels," I explained. "But I am."

A little bit of Kate's old self came back. "Just because you're sheltered and kind of a prude doesn't make you an angel."

I couldn't help but smile a little. "No, literally. I'm the

archangel Gabriel. I was sent here to protect human souls from the demonic reapers, the same creatures who killed my parents. The angelic reapers are on my—our—side. Will is my Guardian, the strongest angelic reaper the archangels could find. He's like my bodyguard and that's why we're together all of the time."

Her lips parted and I could tell she was calculating in her mind. "I always knew he wasn't your tutor. No tutor is that hot."

I laughed out loud, a nervous but happy laugh. I hugged her tight, feeling an enormous amount of relief and fear. I was so happy to finally get to spill my guts to my best friend, but I was also terrified of bringing her into the world I was so desperate to share with her. "Let's go inside, huh?" I suggested. "Get some coffee."

Kate's hands no longer trembled as she held the steaming mug of coffee. Straight black. She said that she needed the kick in the face to think clearly. We sat next to each other on the couch in the living room while Marcus sat in the chair on Kate's other side and Will leaned against the wall some ways away, his arms folded over his chest.

"I can't believe what really happened to your mom and dad," she said weakly. "I'm so sorry you had to keep all of that inside—keep *everything* a secret."

"It hasn't been easy," I agreed.

"Does this mean that Landon is in Hell?"

"No," I said. "I killed the reaper before it could even try. I don't know how much a demonic reaper needs to ingest in order to take a soul, to be honest. But it takes at least one bite and that's not a bite I'm willing to risk."

Her eyes moved from Marcus to Will and back. "And you two. You don't eat people. You fight the ones that do."

Marcus leaned forward, putting a hand on her knee. "Right. We're soldiers, basically. Some of us fight in battle, others protect holy relics from those who would use them for evil. We live for hundreds, thousands of years."

She swallowed hard. "How old are you?"

"Two hundred twelve . . . ish. I lost count."

"Wow," she breathed. "That explains so much, though. You've had a lot of time to gain experience. I wondered how you were so damn good at—"

Will cleared his throat and she gave him a curious look. Marcus beamed far too satisfyingly.

"And you?" she asked Will.

"Six hundred twenty."

She huffed. "Let's hope the pattern sticks, for Ell's sake."

My cheeks lit up in flames and I gaped at her. I wasn't sure if I'd ever been more embarrassed than in that moment. "Wow, *really*, Kate?"

"Yeah, really. I have to look out for my girl, right?"

I grinned at her and sighed. "There are more important things to think about right now, you know."

She shrugged. "If you insist," she grumbled.

"Like your blue hair!"

Kate sighed. "I can't get the blue highlighter out. I must have taken six showers and it's still blue. I'm sure I'll have to get the color stripped and redone."

I tried to offer her a sympathetic smile. "It's not so bad, really."

"Liar."

"Do you want to talk?" Marcus asked.

She gave him a sad look disguised with a little smile. "Yeah. We should."

Kate and Marcus stepped out onto the porch, leaving Will and me alone. He watched the floor, hands clasped together, lost in thought.

"I feel so conflicted," I told him. "I'm so happy that Kate knows, but I can't get what happened to Landon out of my head. I tried to protect them by keeping them away from this world, but Landon is still dead. My parents, Nathaniel, Sabina, Landon . . . I can't lose anyone else. My heart can't take it."

"Some things are out of our control," he said. "We have to learn to accept and adapt."

"I never wanted Kate to have to adapt," I confessed. "Not to this."

"Now it comes down to what she wants. She may be happier. Her relationship with Marcus could improve. You haven't been the only one hiding a double life from her."

I knew what he meant, but I wasn't sure if I could stand

the danger Kate would be in and the vulnerability of being an ordinary human girl in a relationship with an immortal reaper who had many, many enemies. I thought of Emelia, the girl Cadan had loved a long time ago. I didn't want Kate to end up like her, but it wasn't my place to decide what was right for Kate. Her life was her own, and if she wanted Marcus in it, that was something I'd have to learn to accept.

I rose from my seat and went into the kitchen. The windows were open and I could hear Kate and Marcus's conversation out on the porch. Even if I had no say in what Kate would do, it didn't hurt for me to try and find some consolation.

"Were you ever going to tell me?" Kate asked him.

"That's a funny question," he said, "because last night I decided that I would. I hadn't been sure if I wanted anything to change between us, because I loved things the way they were. If you knew what I was, what Ellie was, what's really out there . . . I didn't want to scare you and I didn't want to endanger you. But last night, when the reapers attacked, you were so brave and determined to get your friends out. I practically had to drag you out of that house. I watched you drive away and I couldn't help thinking what a hell of a reaper you'd have made. Better yet, you're a hell of a girl."

He smiled at her and she grinned back. "If I was as strong as you, I could definitely kick your ass."

"I don't doubt it," he said. "But you don't need my kind

of strength. A simple look from you alone cripples me. I am at your mercy."

She lifted her hand and drew a finger down the length of the scar on his face and neck. "Will you tell me how you really got this?"

"Demonfire," he said. "I didn't lie when I said I got this in a fight. I just didn't say with whom. The Fallen Belial, a demon. He almost killed me."

Her expression grew serious and grave, all humor lost in her eyes. "So what happens now?"

"You have to decide," he said, "if I'm worth it. You can walk away from me today, and to be honest, you probably should, but you have to hear me out first. For what it's worth, I don't want you to go. I love you, Kate, and I need you in my life."

She bit hard on her lower lip and wiped at a tear cresting in the corner of her eye. I wasn't sure when was the last time I saw her cry. "Why? Why do you love me? You're over two hundred years old and you're a freaking monster hunter. Why do I even matter to you?"

"Because I can't remember the last time I had as much fun as I do when I'm with you," he said, and a smile began to grow. "You're my match. You're hilarious and strong-minded and beautiful. You're human and supposed to be so fragile, but you're not. You're made of stone and when I'm with you, you help me feel stronger. I can forget what I am, this instrument of destruction and warfare, existing only to kill and die, and I can be a person. God, I don't want to let go of that. I can't let go of you."

Her tears were free-falling now. "You don't have to. I'm not afraid of you and I love you, too. I'm glad that I get to know this side of you. I want to know everything about you."

He cupped her face in his hands, his fingers twining through her blond hair. "I'll tell you. I'll tell you everything and I'll show you everything. I want you to know me."

He kissed her fiercely, their bodies melding together, and I felt the relief that I'd longed for since last night. It was dangerous for her to be with him, but he could protect her from those who'd use her to get to him. He would keep her from them and keep her close to his heart. His being an angelic reaper wasn't his secret. *She* was his secret.

12

IT WAS A LITTLE WHILE BEFORE KATE AND MARCUS returned to the living room and they sat beside each other on the couch. "I got a bit sidetracked, but I was going to tell you what I got from Lauren this morning," he said.

I looked questioningly at Kate. "Are you okay with hearing this?"

She nodded, her lips tight. "Yeah. I'm in."

"Okay," I said. "What do you have, Marcus?"

"It's not a huge lead, but it's something," he continued. "I called Lauren because Xastur said that this Ethan Stone may be a psychic. She said she knew the name and that Nathaniel had been in contact with him. She's going through old phone records, emails, everything to find a possible location for this guy."

"That's good news," Will said with a sigh. "It's a break

we really need. Is she at her place?"

"Yeah," Marcus said. "You and Ellie should head over there and see where she's at so far. I can hang here and go through Nathaniel's office. If I find anything that her clairsentient abilities could help with, I'll give you a ring."

"Great," I agreed. "There's got to be records of communication. Nathaniel kept everything when it came to dealing with psychics and Lauren's abilities can really speed this up."

"Clair-what?" Kate asked. "What does that mean?"

"It means she can read an object's psychic signature just by touching it," I explained. "She feels things and sees information in her head: what something is, where it's been, who it belongs to. She's probably going through Nathaniel's stuff to feel out a connection to Ethan Stone. If he's as powerful a psychic as we were told, then Lauren won't miss him."

"That's pretty cool," she replied, but seemed very sad. "She was dating Nathaniel, right? Will's friend who died?"

Marcus took her hand and squeezed it. "Yeah."

Her gaze fell and she seemed to piece things together, getting a better understanding of what her relationship with Marcus could mean.

"Let's get going," I said to Will. The tension in the room had just become too thick to breathe and it was time to get to work. He and I stepped outside and headed for my car, leaving Kate and Marcus to work out whatever they still needed to.

On the third knock, a woman I didn't know answered Lauren's door. She had a pleasant expression until she appeared to recognize me. She looked from me to Will and then slammed the door in our faces. I jumped and stared at the closed door in shock. I knocked again. Two people argued in hushed voices on the other side before the door opened up a second time and Lauren appeared.

"Ellie, Will." Lauren greeted us with an apologetic smile. "Great to see—"

The door opened wider and the woman returned with a disgusted look on her face. "You have to go. Both of you. Now."

"Mom, please," Lauren begged her. "They're okay. They're my friends."

Lauren's mother shook an angry finger at us. "You will leave my daughter alone. Do you understand? You are not welcome here."

"It's okay," I said, and began to back away. "We'll go. Come on, Will."

We started toward the car, and Lauren's mom disappeared behind the door.

"I'm so sorry," Lauren said as she caught up with us. "My mother doesn't like reapers. Hates them, actually."

"I thought your grandmother was the other psychic in your family," I said. "How did she know what Will is?"

"She knows who you are," Lauren explained. "And she

knows, from growing up with my grandmother and from raising me, that you have a reaper Guardian. Two and two, I guess. Please forgive her rudeness. Knowing about reapers her whole life and knowing what they do and being unable to see them hidden in Grim has given her a great fear of them. She doesn't want anything to do with even angelic reapers and she's always resented how I help you. She's afraid of what she doesn't understand."

"It's all right," I said honestly. "We can come later if your mom is over. I don't want her to be upset."

"No, no," she replied. "This is way too important. I'll grab my things and head to the house. Let me say good-bye to my mom really quick."

"Sure," I said, and watched her disappear back inside.

Will crossed his arms. "I'm sorry you had to see that. I didn't know her mother would be here."

"It's no big deal. She has her reasons for her feelings."

"I'm glad you're not upset," Will said.

Lauren returned with an armful of books and files stuffed with papers, which Will promptly took from her and carried to my car. We drove back to Will's house, where Marcus and Kate were going through boxes in the basement. Some were labeled DON'T THROW OUT and others CORRESPONDENCES. Papers were strewn across the floor as they leafed through each and cast all of them aside. They seemed too glad to see us trudge down the steps.

"Please don't tell me you do this kind of stuff every day,"

Kate said, sighing. "I had a very different impression of your Supergirl adventures."

I laughed. "My adventures are usually a lot more dangerous than the threat of paper cuts. Have you guys found anything?"

"Not yet," Marcus said, appearing entirely exhausted. He gestured to the armloads we'd brought from Lauren's house. "Is that more of Nathaniel's junk?"

"Yeah," Lauren replied. "I haven't gone through this stuff yet, so I brought it over."

"Let's get started then," Will said. He grabbed a box and slid it across the floor to me. "Look for anything that might say 'Ethan Stone' or reference to a location on the East Coast."

It took a few hours before there was any break at all in our search—and it was a pretty vague break. I came across a torn-open padded envelope addressed to Nathaniel from a P.O. box numbered 184 in Saugerties, New York.

"Here's something East Coast-y," I said, and tossed the envelope to Lauren.

It landed in her hands and she gave out a shriek before dropping it immediately. Everyone stopped what they were doing to stare at her and I jumped to my feet to cross the room to her.

"Are you okay?" I asked, putting a hand on her shoulder. I picked up the envelope and peeked inside. "Spider? Will is good at squishing them. Will!"

Her wide eyes were fixed on the tan paper wrapping. She reached for it gingerly and when her fingers touched it, she swallowed hard and trembled. Her eyes rolled up into white orbs and her head snapped back, mouth wide open to release a skin-ripping scream. The envelope went flying out of her hands and the lightbulb above our heads shattered in a blinding flash and shower of glass. In the darkness, the basement was suddenly silent.

From somewhere unseen, Kate's disembodied voice said, "Guess we have a winner."

The envelope, address side up, sat on the coffee table with five pairs of eyes fixed on it. Lauren and I had sat at the kitchen table until she stopped shaking and then we joined everyone else in the living room. She'd assured me that she was ready to talk about what happened in the basement, but I kept a close eye on her.

"This package came from and was directly handled by Ethan Stone," Lauren said. "I'm positive. There's no telling what Stone sent to Nathaniel, but his psychic signature is all over it. So is Ellie's, for some reason, only hers is very faint. I can't explain that, but there is something very, very powerful laced into this man's energy, something terrifying. I believe there may be much more to him than you were told. He can't possibly be just another psychic human."

"What did you see when you touched it?" Will asked.

"A huge house surrounded by trees," she described.

"Inside, there are sculptures, paintings, pieces of bones that belonged to dead saints, jars of cursed coins, trinkets dripping blood magic. . . . These images came in flashes, but I repeatedly caught glimpses of a leather-bound book with no title or author name on the cover. This book may not be Nathaniel's copy of the grimoire, but I believe if you go to the town this envelope came from, then you can find Ethan Stone."

"Let's go for it," Will said. "It's our best lead."

I nodded. "Marcus, you in?"

"Oh yeah," he said. "I'll give Ava a call."

"I'll ask Cadan to join us," I added. "I know that doesn't make you happy, Will, but our little team is one less with Sabina gone. We need all the help we can get and he's strong. We're lucky to have him as our ally."

His mouth was a tight line for a few moments before he spoke. "No. You're right. Call him and tell him we leave tomorrow."

"Thank you," I said. "I'll get plane tickets for the two of us. Marcus, would you and Ava travel or fly using . . . other means . . . ?"

He laughed. "Do you mean fly by wing instead of machine? It wouldn't take as long if we traveled by plane and would be much less exhausting. She and I can get our own tickets. We've got the identification we'll need to travel. Not the first time we've taken a plane."

"Then we roll with what we have," I said. I was nervous

about undertaking this mission, but I'd have my friends I could count on at my back.

"So you'll be gone for a few days?" Kate asked.

"Yeah," I explained. "We're going into this one a bit blind, so it may take longer. I'm counting on figuring out Stone's location once we get to Saugerties."

"Will you let me know how you're doing?" she asked.

"Of course," I promised with a smile.

It was no trouble to purchase two plane tickets into the Albany International Airport and book a couple of rooms at a gorgeous bed-and-breakfast in Saugerties. The trouble was figuring out what to do once we got to Saugerties after two in the afternoon. While I took a shower to get rid of my jet-lagged-ness, Will looked up the location of the post office on my phone. Marcus and Ava wouldn't arrive for another two hours, and Cadan was flying in after dark, of course, so it was just Will and me for now. I dressed in the bathroom and took my blow-dryer out into the room to finish getting ready.

"Any news?" I asked Will. I plugged in the dryer and sat down on the edge of the bed.

He plopped down beside me and eyed my blow-dryer. "You tell me. You're the one with the satellite dish."

"What?" It took me a moment to realize he was talking about the diffuser attached to the end of the dryer. "It keeps my hair from getting frizzy."

"It doesn't receive messages from space?" he asked, his

voice ringing with sarcasm, and he took the blow-dryer from my hands to examine it.

"Give me that," I grumbled and grappled the dryer back from him. "You're ridiculous. So, did you get an address for the post office, or what?"

"Of course."

He winked at me. I turned on the blow-dryer and blasted him in the face. He pinched my side and I couldn't stop the squeal that escaped me. The entire time I dried my hair, he was right next to me, watching me curiously, touching the warm, dry, wavy locks of my hair, playing with my sleeve. . . . Finally, I turned the dryer off, set it down on the bed, and stared at him.

"Do you want something?" I asked him with an impatient huff.

He gave me an innocent look. "Never."

"Then quit pestering me."

"Never," he replied with a grin and inched a little closer.

I rolled my eyes. "I'm going to kick you out of the room and ignore you."

"Never."

He was so close now that I could taste his breath and when he kissed me, it sent a rush of electricity to my toes. It only took seconds for the heat between us to flame, his body scorching against mine, pushing me into the bed. I wiggled toward the pillows and away from the edge of the mattress, and he followed me, molding his body to my shape. Kissing him now, feeling his lips against mine and his tongue against mine, reminded me of how long it had been since we were alone together and truly happy. The kisses we'd shared in his dreams felt tangible at the time, but now I knew that nothing could substitute for the feel of Will's body in the real world. I'd missed him so much, missed the smell of his skin and the warmth and roughness of it brushing my own. I wondered what he felt when he kissed me back, if there was anything better than this to him. The brief moments I was able to forget why we were in that hotel room together were relieving, but there wasn't time for this yet.

"Will," I said, prying my lips from his to gasp for air.

He grinned at me before he buried his face into my neck, nuzzling and mumbling in response.

I laughed and untangled myself from him. "Will. Hey."

His eyebrows raised questioningly and he gave another gruff, unintelligible answer. I pressed a hand into his chest, guiding his back into the bed, and his hands ran up my thighs as I positioned myself over his hips. Now that I was in control, I raised a finger at him to let him know that I was serious.

"As much as I'd love to stay here all day—maybe even forever—we have things to do," I said firmly.

"I don't disagree."

"You are terrible," I said, laughing. "We need to get going!"

His hands settled on my hips and suddenly he flipped me

around until I was beneath him again, the mattress bouncing. He kissed me hotly and I gave in, throwing my arms over his neck, hands digging into his strong shoulders. His fingers brushed the skin of my waist beneath my shirt. We kissed for what felt like hours, until my lips were swollen and tender, and his shoulders had turned red beneath my grip. Yet again, we came to that familiar stalemate, where we waited for one of us to make the first move to back off for good. This time, it was him. The cloudiness in my senses began to fade and reality came crashing back down. For some time, I lay against the bed beneath Will, his fingers twining through my hair and my own curling around his shirt, folding my body against his like I was trying to climb into his skin to get that much closer to him. But the peaceful dream had to end sometime and we had a mission to complete.

Once we were all ready to go, we navigated the sprawling bed-and-breakfast out to the parking lot where the rental car was parked. The hotel dated back to the Colonial period and had that classic East Coast charm to it. I really wanted to explore its many wings and the property it sat on, but we had stuff to do first. We found the post office easily, but as we walked inside and the local elderlies glared at Will's tattoos spiraling out from under his T-shirt, I had severe doubts that we would find much information here.

I scanned the wall of gray metal mailbox doors and found box 184. At least we knew that this particular box existed.

Question was, did it belong to the mysterious Ethan Stone?

There was an older woman working the single register behind the counter, wearing a pink cardigan with kittens over a pink shirt. She glared at me from beneath her halo of frizzy gray hair. "Can I help you?"

"Yeah," I began, unsure of how to work this. "Could you tell me who rents box 184?"

"No," she replied rather tersely. "That would be against federal law."

I bit my lip and thought hard. "Well, does it get used often? As in, recently and still in use?"

"Yes, mail comes in and out," she grumbled. "It's a P.O. box. That's what happens."

The kittens on her pink-on-pink ensemble weren't very intimidating, despite the woman's harshness. "Thanks for your help," I told her smugly.

Outside the building, we stood on the sidewalk. Will didn't seem too disappointed. "At least we know that the box is still active."

"Yeah," I said. "But we'll never find out who's using it. So . . . if I were a bored, small-town local kid and there was possibly a gazillionaire living in a gigantic house around here, possibly a psychic or something else supernatural, meaning he possibly doesn't chill with regular people, meaning he's possibly a recluse . . ."

"How can you say all of that in one breath?"

"Shut up. I'm thinking," I said. "This guy is probably

the only cool thing to talk about around here, except for the horse shows advertised everywhere. People really like horses in Saugerties, I guess. Anyway, Ethan Stone would probably be like this town's Boo Radley, you know?"

"The who?"

"Meaning, he'd be an urban legend, only he really *is* something supernatural," I said. "Meaning, while the adults in town might glare at us, the local kids would love to spook tourists with the story."

"But why?" Will looked at me a bit cross-eyed. "I don't understand why they would care."

"That's because you're a replicant. Now let's go."

I took his hand and dragged him down the street. This part of Saugerties was like a postcard, seriously. It was creepily quaint. We walked down the picturesque street until I spotted a local ice cream shop, its benches out front packed with teenagers. *Jackpot.*

I hauled Will up to the window to order. I figured we ought to blend in with everyone—and I'd get an ice cream out of this as well. After I got my regular cookie dough, I made Will order something. He got a small root beer float, of course, and then we sat at a bench with another couple. The girl smiled politely at us and the boy gave Will a nod of manly solidarity.

"Nice tats," the boy said. "Get them done in the city?"

"New York City?" Will replied. "No, in Rome."

"Interesting style and the symbols are really cool. I hear

the Italian tattooists are the best."

"She isn't Italian, but she's amazing."

I beamed and took a bite of my ice cream. I happened to have been the not-Italian, "amazing" artist of his tattoos five hundred years ago, when he became my Guardian.

"Are you guys from around here?" the girl, a cute, curvy blond, asked.

"No," I replied. "I'm from Michigan and he was born in Scotland."

"Wow," she said. "Both of you came a long way. Are you on vacation?"

"Pretty much. You guys live here?"

"Yeah," the boy said. "Born and raised, both of us. I'm Scott. This is Leah."

"Ellie and Will," I said, and gestured to him beside me. "So, you guys probably know all the cool stuff to check out. You know, the stuff that isn't advertised every five feet."

Scott shrugged. "Not really. It's pretty boring here. There's a few places people say are haunted, and there's this compound up off of County Road Thirty-Three—"

"Compound?" He got Will's attention.

"People say it's a government facility or something," Leah said almost dismissively. "Like they're building robots up there. It's stupid."

"You only think that because you've never seen it," Scott sneered at her.

She rolled her eyes. "It's not real! You guys are so dumb."

Scott turned his head to us. "I've seen it. Trust me. It's got a huge wall all around the property and always has guys out at the gate packing guns. There's a house on a hill that the driveway leads to and it's huge. We're pretty sure they do mutant experiments or something."

"I heard the house was owned by some crazy billionaire," I offered, hoping I'd get more information out of him.

He shrugged. "Yeah, some people say that he's some master thief who steals valuable stuff from all over the world. I've never seen him, though. Just seen the guards out front and lights on in the house."

"Cool," I said, and looked right at Will. "We should check this place out."

"Sounds like a plan," he agreed.

I turned back to Scott and Leah and leaned over the table. "Where did you say this house was again?"

13

MARCUS AND AVA ARRIVED AT THE BED-AND-breakfast at last and after they checked into their room, we regrouped in mine. They sat in the couple of chairs at the small table by the big window overlooking the garden outside, and Will and I sat on the edge of the bed, briefing them on what we found out in town earlier. Meanwhile, the angelic reapers had ordered a ton of delivery, which overran the room. I had some fried rice and a couple pieces of pizza, but that was only a fraction of what had been ordered—and quickly devoured. Will took the guards Scott had mentioned very seriously. When Cadan arrived, I filled him in and we suited up. We didn't have a whole lot to expect from this mysterious Ethan Stone. I mentally prepared myself to be ready for anything.

Getting past the front gate of the mansion was extremely

easy. There were two guards visible, but we flew over them, hidden in the Grim, and landed safely deep in the wooded area that stretched across the property. The house was well lit even so late at night, and we could spot no reapers in the Grim aside from our own forces. Cadan split from us to find a way inside that wasn't the front door.

"The demonic could be protecting the interior," Ava suggested.

"We don't know for sure that this is Stone's house," Will said. "We have to proceed with extreme caution. I don't sense any demonic power, but they must be suppressing their energy."

I nodded in agreement. "If Stone or the grimoire copy aren't in there, then we need to get out quick and clean. I'm not losing anyone else."

I was suddenly deafened by the wail of a siren coming from the house. My hands clamped over my ears and I peered through the trees in confusion.

"They know we're here!" Marcus shouted.

"Cadan!" I cried out in horror. He was probably what had set the alarms off and he was out there by himself in whatever mess he'd walked into. I couldn't let him fight alone. I raced through the trees and burst into the open lawn, which was now lit up with roaming floodlights. I did my best to dodge the lights and to stay hidden. I could hear the footsteps of the angelic reapers keeping pace behind me and the crackling of gunfire everywhere.

There was no more time to find a way inside that could provide cover. I soared over a balustrade and nearly slipped on the terrace leading up to the mansion. I bounded up the stone steps and ducked between towering columns to burst through the front doors.

"Cadan!" I screamed, skidding across the glossy marble foyer floor in near complete darkness. The searchlights roving the grounds cast stark beams that lit up the interior of the house for only a moment before disappearing again. *"Cadan!"*

The response was gunfire. I ducked and rolled across the floor to dive into a parlor leading from the foyer as bullets pounded into the walls and glass all around me. Will, Marcus, and Ava went to work, colliding with our attackers. Black shadowy bursts of reaper power and the short, disorienting flashes of light from firing guns made it hard to see anything at all. Bullets tore off chunks of marble columns, ripped through wood and plaster, and above the roar of destruction I heard men shouting orders.

But where was Cadan? A frightful knot tightened in my gut.

I darted from my hiding spot to another room as bullets made the archway frame explode into splinters. I caught sight of one of the reapers who had his back to me and was stepping farther away from the others. I crept behind him quickly and shot my hand forward and knocked the gun from his grip. I grabbed his throat, digging my hand hard under his jaw, and I yanked him toward me and slammed his back against the wall. His petrified appearance didn't faze me.

"Where is Cadan?" I shrieked, knowing—and not caring—that I probably looked as wild-eyed as he did.

He shook his head and mumbled at me. I jerked him forward and smashed him into the wall again, crushing plaster, and he screamed in pain.

"Where is he?"

"Ellie!"

I looked over my shoulder and saw Ava racing toward me. A reaper between us swung the butt of his rifle up and into the side of her face with a crack. She growled at him, grabbed him by the neck, and threw him across the room. His body crashed into a chandelier in a shower of glass and crystal, and then a fireplace, destroying the mantle and everything on it before hitting the ground and not rising.

As my gaze returned to the terror-stricken eyes of the reaper I had pinned, I became aware that something was very wrong. He grappled at my hand, pulled at my fingers clamped around his throat, and I barely felt anything. Reapers were stronger than that—even the weaker ones. I drew in a sharp breath and released him, stepping back and letting him crumple to the floor.

"They're human," I called, waving my arms to the angelic reapers. "They're human! Stop! Don't kill them! *They're human!"*

A bullet struck my shoulder. It was a pain unlike anything I'd ever felt before, like a major-leaguer swinging a baseball bat into my body at full strength. The force swung me off my feet and my back hit the floor, knocking the air from my lungs. The bullet lodged in my shoulder hurt so bad I couldn't breathe, and I could feel the heat from my blood seeping from my wound. Will crouched over me, shouting, but I couldn't hear his voice at first over the heavy thudding of my pulse in my ears as the blood ran out of me. The tissue and muscles trying to heal and right themselves inside me was probably even more agonizing than the initial hit itself. I could feel my body pushing the bullet toward the surface, but what should have been relief was only the blinding sensation of a power drill grinding through my shoulder.

Cadan's face appeared in my blurry vision and a wave of relief crashed over me at seeing him alive. "Oh, God," he murmured fearfully. "Did she get shot? Can she heal from this?"

"I don't know," Will admitted, the terror in his bright green eyes obvious. "I have no idea. Ellie, please stay with me. Please, don't go. Please."

I did my best to give him a nod and tried not to move anymore until I felt the bullet surface through my skin and *plink* to the floor. Once the wound had closed and the pain began to dull, I weakly sat up with Will's and Cadan's help, grimacing in pain. "Wow, that hurt," I grumbled, clutching my shoulder.

"Are you okay?" Cadan asked as he stared at me in disbelief.

"Yeah," I grunted. "Give me a sec." It was still hard to breathe. The deeper tissue trauma the bullet must have caused seemed to take longer to heal. Until then, it would hurt like hell. "You didn't kill the one who shot me, did you?"

"No," Will said, sounding disappointed with himself. "I was more worried about you than with taking off his head."

I sighed with reprieve. "Good. The guards are humans, not reapers. Tell the others to stop fighting."

"Stand down!" A voice echoed from across the room.

Will and Cadan shot to their feet and I turned my head to see a man emerging through the crowd of armored humans. He was tall, dressed in a suit, and looked to be a little older than my dad had been, with sharp features, and his sandy-blond hair was trimmed neatly. His eyes, a dusty hazel beneath a light brow, surveyed the scene and then glued firmly to mine. His lips, soft but thin, carried a curve of amusement, and the wrinkles in both corners of his mouth told me he was fighting what could have been a smile.

"We wouldn't have had all this trouble if you hadn't sent in a demonic reaper first," the man said in an English accent. "When did you start working with Hellspawn, Preliator?"

Will vanished and reappeared with his fist tightening around the man's collar and lifting him off the floor. The guards' rifles raised and clicked into position. "Who are you?" Will snarled, lifting the man higher.

"Don't fire," the man shouted to his guards. "Set me down, Guardian, and we can work this out like civilized creatures."

"Tell me who you are first!"

"Stone," the man said finally. "Ethan Stone. Now, if you'll kindly—"

Will dropped him and the man crumpled to the floor with a grunt. "Okay, Ethan Stone, how do you know who we are?"

Stone picked himself up and brushed the dust from his suit, giving Will a cocky grin. "I didn't need to summon any telepathic talents to tell the obvious once I got a look at you. Again, all of this could have been avoided if you'd simply knocked on the door instead of sending in a demonic reaper. That was asking for a mess of trouble."

I took a painful step toward Stone and put my hand protectively on Cadan's arm. "He's my friend and brother to my Guardian."

Stone's hazel eyes brimmed with surprise. "That certainly wasn't the response I'd anticipated. Not only friend, but *brother*?"

"Long story," Cadan replied. "Very scandalous."

"We aren't here to chat," Will said as Ava and Marcus stepped close to either side of him. "We've come to take back what you've stolen."

"Yes, yes," Stone said tiredly, waving a dismissive hand. "I know this already. You want the angelic reaper's copy of the Lord of the West's grimoire. I knew you were coming."

"If you knew we were coming, then why open fire on us?" I asked, confused.

"Like I said," Ethan Stone replied, "I wasn't expecting the demonic reaper. My men were only defending—and unfortunately *destroying*—my property from what they were trained to fight against."

"You're a psychic, aren't you?"

He shrugged. "In a manner of speaking."

"Then you understand why we need that book," I said. "I don't want to take it by force. If you know who I am then you know that I only want to stop the Fallen."

"I know what you're trying to do," Stone replied. "And I want to help you. I want you to have the book."

"Thank you," I said earnestly. "Where is it?"

He started to turn, beckoning for me to follow him. "Come. The Guardian may join us, if you wish, as long as he doesn't try playing the strangle tango with me again."

I nodded to Will, happy to have him accompany me. There was something strange about Ethan Stone. His response to my asking if he was psychic was unnerving and dodgy. There really wasn't an easy way to prove what he was, but I had to assume that I could handle myself around him, as dangerous as that assumption was.

Stone led us through his mansion and it never seemed to end. The architecture was unlike anything I'd ever seen before. The corridors had short flights of staircases in the strangest of places and each hall had a different color and shape to its design; some were arched and lined with columns, others had sharp angles and corners with vaulted ceilings. Intermittent alcoves with elegant lighting and tapestries decorated the walls, and some windows stretched two stories high and were covered with enormous drapes.

"Did you design this place?" I asked. I was acutely aware of Will's steady closeness and preparedness for whatever might occur around each corner.

"I did," Stone replied. "I construct additional wings every so often when I begin a new collection. They all have their own themes. I'm a bit obsessive-compulsive that way."

I gazed up at the forty-foot ceiling painted with biblical scenes. "I see."

"I apologize for this rather long trek," Stone said, glancing over his shoulder at us. "The book in question resides in my rarer-books library."

"Rarer?"

"I have too many rare books to fit into one library," he explained. "So I have a second library for the even rarer books. This one is smaller than the normal library. For example, it doesn't have its own wing."

I decided that this guy was a maniac, but when I saw the library in question, my eyes about bugged right out of my skull. His "smaller" library was about the size of the public library in my town. There was a main room lined floor to ceiling with books, smaller rooms off to the side filled with more books, and spiraling staircases that climbed to lofts covered with even more books. If Nathaniel had been there to see it, he would have had a heart attack. In the middle of it all was a sitting area with giant fluffy chairs and ottomans surrounding a coffee table that was more like a polished slab of wood taken from the biggest tree trunk in the world. When I stepped close to the table, there were so many rings in the wood that I guessed there to be a thousand. Above the sitting area was a chandelier made of dozens of very unusual-looking antlers and horns.

Ethan Stone must have noticed my curiosity and confusion, because he was suddenly next to me explaining. "These were all taken from reapers. Horns and antlers aren't especially common, even on the demonic, so this piece was *extremely* expensive to procure."

I had no desire to know what was "*extremely* expensive" by his standards, or how he managed to "procure" the chandelier of reaper antlers.

"You don't want to know," he said casually and walked right on by me.

I stared after him as he climbed one of the staircases. Will and I exchanged looks and followed the odd psychic. Stone navigated the second level and followed a curved wall of books into a narrow hallway that led to a beautiful stained-glass window featuring an image of an avenging angel striking down what appeared to be a demon with an enormous sword. In front of the window was a wooden pedestal with a glass case on top. A worn, ancient-looking leather book sat beneath the glass. Stone pressed a button on the underside of the pedestal and the glass lifted, freeing the book within.

Stone stepped aside, motioning for me to come forward. "It's been in here for many years, beneath UV-filtering glass, so it's in perfect condition."

I lifted the book, finding it heavier than I thought it would be, and the leather cover was supple and creased after centuries of use. A beam of hope stewed in my heart as I stared at Nathaniel's copy of the grimoire in my hands at last, but that hope blinked out like a candle flame when I saw Will's sword shimmer into existence.

"Good-bye, Stone," Will said, and raised his blade.

"Wait!" I cried out, aghast. "Stop!"

Will turned to me, his gaze hard. "He's too dangerous to leave alive. He's knows too much that can jeopardize our chances at winning this war. This entire compound is a goldmine for demonic and angelic artifacts. If Merodach found—"

"He's human," I said, and put a hand on Will's arm, lowering his blade. "Please don't do this. Don't kill him."

"It's a mistake to let him live."

"No," I said in anger. "Are you no different from the demonic? Killing innocent humans? Will, you're better than that, I know it."

"He isn't innocent," he contended.

"But he's human." I tightened my hold on Will's arm. "Please, *please*, Will. You promised me that you wouldn't kill any humans. This includes Ethan Stone."

His body stiffened and his jaws ground together hard. He watched Stone's face with an angry, conflicted expression, but that meant he was at least considering my request. After a few heart-pounding moments, he withdrew his sword and Stone let out a huge breath of relief. "The lady has spoken. You're lucky she has far more compassion than I."

I let go of Will's arm and touched his face. "Thank you," I said, and kissed his cheek. "Thank you for this."

"Thank *you*, Preliator," Ethan Stone said.

I turned to him and made sure the tone of my voice ensured that Stone would heed my warning. "Don't make me regret my mercy, or I'll come back here and kill you myself."

"You won't," he replied. "I am in your debt."

"For now," I began, "I'll take this." I clutched the grimoire close to my chest.

He regarded me shrewdly. "What do you plan on doing with it?"

"I have an angel to evoke."

"Ah," Stone said. "Dangerous creatures, angels. I would have thought you were interested in getting in touch with your *inner* angel."

"That's not something I'm willing to talk about with you," I said coldly. "We're leaving now. Thanks for the book."

Will let his sword disappear and he followed me down

the stairs and toward the exit.

"You'll want to take a closer look at the *Ars Goetia*, Gabriel," Ethan called from behind us.

I faced him, looking up at him leaning over the loft balcony. I longed to stay and ask him about everything he could possibly know and about all of the secrets in his cavernous libraries, but there was no time. I now had what I came for and I wouldn't stop here.

A smile split Ethan Stone's sharp face. "Happy reading, archangel."

14

I SPENT THE NEXT SEVERAL HOURS SCOURING THAT book, turning crisp, delicate pages, my eyes straining to read Nathaniel's elegant medieval script. If there was a way to evoke the angel of death, it was not in the grimoire. It may have been in the original scroll written by Antares, but Nathaniel didn't include it here. It wasn't until we had landed in Detroit and were driving through Southfield that a light-bulb switched on.

"Oh my God," I murmured as the cryptic last words of Ethan Stone unraveled in my head. "The *Ars Goetia*. Stone, you smartass."

"What is it?" Will asked and glanced over his shoulder at the open pages in my lap. "*The Lesser Key of Solomon*. Why does that sound so familiar?"

I was practically bouncing in my seat. "The *Ars Goetia*

is the first book in the *Lemegeton*, also known as *The Lesser Key of Solomon*. The version Nathaniel wrote here is the original Middle Latin text naming and describing seventy-two demons that can be evoked, but he also included the English version published in 1904 by Aleister Crowley for reference."

"Crowley? The occultist Crowley?"

"That's the one," I said. "And I know what Stone was getting at when he recommended I pay close attention to this section. Crowley believed that the Ring of Solomon, also called the Pentalpha, was real. This ring is said to be able to summon and control the Fallen bound in Hell."

"I've heard of the Pentalpha," Will said. "But no one's ever found it. Just because some lunatic strung out on opiates believed something mythical exists doesn't mean it really does."

I couldn't help but smile. I felt like I was the only one in the world who knew that this war was about to turn in our favor, thanks to Ethan Stone.

"The Pentalpha does exist," I said, "because I'm the one who made it and gave it to King Solomon. He was a psychic who engineered one of the earliest reaper-hunting groups."

Will grew quiet and seemed to digest what I'd told him. "Okay, say this Ring of Solomon is real. How will it help us? We don't exactly have any Fallen we want to evoke."

"Because I created it, I have complete control over it," I explained. "Instead of summoning a demon, I can make it summon an angel. I will evoke Azrael."

"Do you think you can really do that?"

"Without a doubt."

"Okay then," he said. "Let's find it. A relic that powerful is bound to have a guardian—a very strong guardian. We should look into the known guardians and narrow down possible leads. Ava can help with that, but with a relic that can summon demons, it's likely to be very well hidden and—"

He stopped midsentence and stared ahead onto the busy road. The car slowed, but the countless headlights and neon flashes of traffic signals were too disorienting and I couldn't quite see what he saw.

"What's the matter?" I asked him.

"There's something in the road."

A moment later, I could make out what his reaper eyes saw: the silhouette of a figure shaped like a man stood in the middle of the busy road. "Oh no," I breathed as a pair of wings stretched from the figure's shoulders, wings that were in plain view of human beings.

Will smashed the gas pedal to the floor. The engine roared as the turbochargers kicked in and we raced past cars in the other lanes.

"What are you doing?" I asked, my voice trembling. My hands tightened on both the dashboard and console. "Will, please slow down. Slow down!"

His foot jammed harder on the pedal and the figure zoomed into closer view. I caught an electrifying blaze of moonlight eyes before the reaper launched himself off the ground and out of the path of the Audi's grill. Will swore and slammed on the brakes. The tires squealed as the car fishtailed. He avoided the other cars in the lanes by swinging into the parking lot of a strip center and the tires screeched to a halt. The reaper landed in the middle of the street with a bend of his knees and his back to us. Headlights from passing vehicles fell on gleaming black membranous wings that spread high and wide, and his inky black power rolled across the ground toward us, the pressure like extremely low frequency in my ears.

"Who is it?" I asked.

"Merodach."

My stomach dropped. As the demonic reaper faced us and marched closer, Will's grip on the steering wheel tightened until the leather whined. He hadn't gotten out of the car yet, and I realized that I wasn't sure if either of us was ready to face Merodach yet—and I was positive we weren't ready to fight him on an insanely busy seven-lane street. There were just the two of us against him this time, and if the demonic reaper favored his odds, then he wasn't likely to retreat again.

Will kicked the door open and stepped out onto the pavement. "Merodach! I'm going to—"

The demonic reaper vanished in a blur and Will's back slammed into the hood of the Audi, crunching steel and pushing on the car so hard that the nose ground into the pavement and the rear tires lifted into the air with me in it.

Merodach's hand had clamped around Will's throat as his form refocused in a burst of shadowy power that drenched his body and shoved Will harder into the hood.

"To what?" Merodach crooned. "You're going to what, Guardian?"

It was hard to hear the reapers' voices over the noise of evening traffic and the panicked cries of pedestrians. I fumbled with my seat belt, rattling metal and plastic, until it sprang free. I pushed open the door and Merodach looked up at me as I jumped to the ground, breaking his concentration just long enough for Will to overpower him. He grabbed Merodach's wrist and squeezed until the demonic reaper hissed in pain and released Will's throat. Will's sword shimmered into existence in his hand and plunged into Merodach's gut, spilling red. Will shoved the demonic reaper away and kicked him hard in the chest, forcing his body to peel off the sword and to stagger back. With a roar, Will lifted the enormous blade and swung it through the air, marking a shallow slice through Merodach's clothes and skin in a flying sheet of blood.

Will poised his sword toward the demonic reaper. "Not going to run with your tail tucked between your legs again?"

"When I walk away tonight," Merodach said, "my footsteps will paint the ground with your blood."

Will launched himself at the vir, but Merodach's own blade slashed across Will's abdomen. Will doubled over, clutching his wound, and Merodach turned on me. My sword caught his, stopping it, but he spun the double blade and evaded my second sword. Merodach swept the sword toward my chest and I made a sharp intake of air, unable to raise my weapons quickly enough to stop him. I whirled out of his way, but he followed me and sliced again. Will threw an arm over my chest and knocked me out of the path of Merodach's blade, and the silver cut deep into Will's arm instead of mine. He hissed in pain, but he didn't remove himself from between the demonic reaper and me.

Merodach backed off, whirling his double blade, daring us to come for him. Will charged and leaped into the air, sword striking high, but Merodach grabbed Will's foot and swung him hard into the busy road. I screamed as Will slammed into the door of an SUV, crunching metal, and both of them spun into more traffic with a deafening crash as vehicles collided. Cars in all seven lanes fishtailed to screeching stops, some drivers exiting their vehicles to run toward the overturned cars, others staring at Merodach and me. Others screamed.

"Will!" I darted toward the carnage, but he was already climbing out of it.

Before I could see how badly injured he was, I sensed a darkness that made my stomach turn and my throat close up. I halted in my tracks and turned back to Merodach. The air behind the ancient demonic reaper took on an elastic form, disrupting paths of light from their sources as shapes took form—no, slipped through the Grim. Demonic reapers, at least two dozen of them, emerged into our world, the seam between planes pulling at their limbs like tendrils of shadows and ink. There were so many, and they kept coming. It was no wonder why Merodach seemed so cocky tonight. What a coward he was to fear fighting Will and me unless he outnumbered us several to one.

Will returned to my side and I called my swords. My angelfire flickered and flared in the darkness and I watched Merodach's wounds close up. "Will," I breathed. "What are we going to do?"

"Kill all of them," he said.

I wanted to ignore the frightened people in the street with us and the cars slowing down to gawk or to help the injured escaping the wreckage. But there was no chance. People already had their phones out to call for ambulances and police, and I was suddenly more terrified of that than I was of the reapers. We'd gotten lucky in the fight against Orek in Detroit when neither of us could be identified in the grainy footage caught by onlookers. Playing dodge-cars with reapers in the middle of Southfield Road and 10 Mile wasn't likely to put fortune on our side tonight. The authorities would arrive in minutes. We had very little time to either eliminate these reapers or relocate to a more secluded area.

The demonic vir grew closer, weaving between vehicles or hopping over them, but I wouldn't wait. We met in a flurry of swinging swords and gnashing teeth. I cut open the throat of a reaper and kicked his body away, but another appeared at my side and I barely saw the flash of her eyes before I cracked my elbow into her jaw. She stumbled into her comrades and I slashed a sword across her chest, splitting her wide open, and she was dead before she hit the ground.

I buried my blade into the heart of another reaper and looked around wildly for Will to make sure he was okay. He had one of the vir skewered in the street, but an eighteen-wheeler roared right toward him, its airbrakes screaming. He ripped his blade free of the reaper's body and sprang into the air. His wings burst through his shirt and beat, taking him out of the path of the truck's grill. Its tires screeched as the trailer swung out of control and smeared several of the demonic reapers across the pavement. Will landed heavily, wings spread, and a horn blared behind him. He turned just in time to slam a hand into the car's fender and shove his power as hard as he could, caving in steel and sending the car spinning away. Before he could recover, more reapers descended on him, blocking him from my view. A wall of vir came toward me, drawing me away from Will—separating us. As soon as I realized this, I felt Merodach's hot breath in my ear.

"I've come to claim you in the name of the Lord of Souls."

I slashed a sword and Merodach grasped that wrist and then my other, holding my arms still with unmatched physical strength. The blaze of my angelfire was close enough that it seared his skin, but he acted as if he couldn't feel it.

"Come quietly with me and I may let your Guardian live."

"But I won't let *you* live," I snarled and buried my knee between his legs, and he loosed a roar of pain and rage. My instinct was to run to Will and make sure he was all right, but he could take care of himself.

"You stupid, stupid girl," Merodach snarled as he recovered. I held both my swords as I circled him, waiting for him to strike. "You and your Guardian have been overwhelmed tonight. Have you had enough?"

"Have *you*?" I shot back. "Or do you need another kick to the nuts? I'd be happy to oblige."

A vicious smile curled Merodach's lips and he laughed, a sound so deep and earthy that it made my bones shiver. The streetlights gave his scar a sickly glow. "This fight is nothing compared to the ten thousand demonic reapers we have gathered. I will take the grimoire and feed your soul to Sammael. How many more of your friends will I enjoy killing? After I'm done with you, your Guardian is next. And then I will hunt down the last of your pathetic little flock of angelic reapers before I feast on your little blond human friend and your seer grandmother. Yes, Preliator. Don't think that I haven't been keeping my eye on you."

Terror stabbed like metal spikes into my muscles as my body went stone rigid. I believed him when he said that he would murder my friends and family. He had already stolen from me so many people I loved and so much of who I once was. It felt like he was taking me apart piece by piece, ripping out chunks of my soul until there was nothing left.

But Merodach was wrong. I would never allow him to take all that I knew away from me. I had to survive. I had to kill him and protect everyone and everything I loved. All of the beasts of Hell knew they couldn't stop me. I was the archangel Gabriel, the Preliator, and they knew that no matter how many times they killed me, I always came back to kill them. No matter how much they frightened me, I remembered what Cadan had told me about the stories of me he had grown up hearing. Even demons feared something. The demonic reapers had nightmares of their own, stories they told one another to terrify, a legend that haunted them in their sleep. That was me. I was Hell's nightmare.

I charged at him, slashing my Khopesh blades and splitting his skin with silver and angelfire. He drew his double-bladed sword to counter my attacks, but I was fast and determined. Merodach backed toward the wreckage in the road as I drove him, shoving my power into each sword strike. With a rage-filled cry, I leaped into the air, kicking off the hood of a car to send me higher, and I smashed my boot into the reaper's face. He hit the ground hard before I even landed, but was back on his feet in a flash. The instant he lifted his blade, I slammed him with another blast of my energy, a lightning strike of white light, and he soared, roaring, through the air.

Merodach landed heavily on the pavement and skidded to a stop while cars raced past him. The driver of a sedan blared the horn before swerving to avoid him at the last minute and almost sideswiping one of the immobile wrecked cars. Merodach got to his feet and I threw my power at him, knocking him back off his feet. He rolled on the ground and howled in rage as he rose again. I could feel his power building almost exponentially, gathering strength like a tidal wave. Even from the sidewalk where I stood, I could see the pure, undiluted fury in his blinding eyes.

Merodach crossed the lanes as he stomped toward me and another car came rushing down the street, but he didn't give it a chance to swerve. His power detonated in a burst of shadows and smoke and he lashed out behind himself in anger, smashing the bottom of his fist into the grill of the car. The force behind his blow sent the car careening through the air above his head and it slammed upside down into the road with a shriek of metal against pavement. I gasped in horror, praying for signs of life. When no one emerged from the debris, Merodach stepped up to the car and kicked the frame, sending it sliding and screeching over the curb and out of the street. The humans who had tried to help ran in the opposite direction or tumbled to the ground in fear.

"Freeze!"

The command came from a few yards down the side-walk, accompanied by the shuffling of footsteps and *click-clack*ing of a firearm. I spun to find a police officer with her gun drawn and pointed at the demonic reaper. Her cruiser, lights flashing, was parked across multiple lanes to stop anymore traffic. My heart pounded. If one cop was here, then more would arrive very soon.

"Drop the weapons, hands behind your head," she ordered.

It took me a moment to realize that meant *me*. I was the one standing there with flaming swords in both of my hands. Merodach was the only bad thing here, but the officer didn't know that. With my entire body trembling, I let the angelfire die and I placed my swords on the ground before raising my hands. I really didn't want to get shot again.

"You." She gestured with her head for Merodach to get out of the road. "On the grass. Hands on the ground."

He just stared at her with a blank look and didn't move.

"Hands on the ground!" she repeated, her voice breaking with fear.

"Merodach," I called to him, hoping he would ignore the officer, but after what he'd done at Josie's house, I didn't think he would. No innocent humans needed to get mixed up in this mess. The demonic reaper ignored me and I felt my pulse quicken. I had to try and talk him into taking this fight someplace else. I considered running. If he wanted the grimoire and to take me to Sammael, then he had to follow me, but I couldn't risk bolting and leaving the bystanders defenseless. Will was taking on the last of Merodach's reapers and I was on my own here.

"Merodach," I repeated more firmly. I stepped back on my heel, bracing myself to dive for my swords if he attacked. "Forget about the humans. If you want me, then come for me."

The demonic reaper's eyes flashed with his power and his sleek, double-bladed sword rippled into existence.

"Drop the weapon!" the cop shrieked.

Merodach ignored her and started toward me, swinging his sword, and I dived to sweep my own off the ground.

"I *will* fire!"

"Don't shoot him!" I cried at the officer, trying to warn her. "You'll only anger him!"

Her gun moved back and forth between the reaper and me, and she cursed under her breath about her missing backup. Merodach raised his sword at me and the cop fired. The bullet slammed into his chest and he didn't even miss a beat. The cop swore again, this time loud with fear, and she shot a second bullet right between Merodach's eyes. His head snapped back and he stopped in place, but he didn't fall. He straightened slowly, anger twisting his features, and he turned his gaze to the police officer as a line of blood rolled down his nose.

"What the hell are you?" she whimpered, eyes wide. There was no doubt she now realized that the wings and horns weren't part of a costume.

Merodach moved so fast that I lost him for an instant. Suddenly he was right behind the cop, grabbing a fistful of her hair and yanking her head back. She shrieked and shot a wild bullet, but he was unfazed.

"No!" I stepped toward him, but stopped myself. If I made a move to save her, he'd kill her for certain. I was the one he wanted, not this frightened young woman. I began to walk backward very slowly. Sirens belonging to police, ambulances, and fire trucks wailed in the distance, growing closer every second.

"If you run," Merodach crooned, "I'll rip her head off."

"Why are you even wasting your time with her?" I asked him. "Your fight's with me."

He gave me a thoughtful look and said, "You're right."

His jaws spread so wide they cracked and seemed to dislocate like a snake's, and then he chomped down hard on the woman's neck. Blood showered from her wound, soaking everything close to her with red, and she gargled and choked through her own screams. I nearly threw up when Merodach ripped his jaws away, taking with him the fleshy majority of the woman's neck, and he gulped it down. Her head drooped over her shoulder, hanging on by a few strips of skin and ligaments, her mouth gaping as she died midscream. The reaper tossed the limp, still leaking body to the ground. The gun clattered across the pavement.

I couldn't move—couldn't breathe—from the horror of what I'd just seen. The remaining people watching the fight all shrieked and ran in every direction, finally finding the sense to get out of there. I wasn't sure if the reaper had consumed enough to take the woman's soul, but I prayed that she had been spared Hell at least.

"Why?" I asked Merodach.

He licked his lips and sighed as if the gore on his face

was delicious. "Because you didn't want me to."

I let out an exhausted cry of fury and swore as loud as I could. "I'm going to rip you apart!"

I launched myself off the ground, swinging my swords. He knocked my arms away, gliding past my swords, and he backhanded me in the face. I hit the ground with a pained grunt and he grasped me by the neck before I could do anything. He lifted me until my feet were dangling in the air and he squeezed my throat, but I kept struggling. I wouldn't let him strangle me. I couldn't let him take me to Sammael.

I summoned my power, pulling everything I had from those dark depths that I was so afraid of, tapping into the infinite well of strength given to me in Heaven. I stared into Merodach's ever-brightening eyes as the torrent of energy circled us both, lifting my hair and lighting the red streaks like wild flames. I slammed my power into him and he gritted his teeth against the force, but he didn't release my throat. I threw energy into him a second time, but still he held on, even when I kept pushing and pushing at him until he was practically hanging on to me or else he'd be blown away. When I summoned my archangel glory, I became aware that I was screaming—a raspy, desperate wail—as everything was drowned in white, hot light. The glory boiled Merodach's skin, his hands burning red where he gripped my neck, and soon he was roaring with pain and effort. My glory flared, setting his hands ablaze. His face, twisted with wrath and agony, started to sizzle and his skin split into strips of charred gashes that cut through the scar I had given him the night Sammael was released.

"I cannot let you go," Merodach wheezed as his lips were cut and burned.

"I will make you," I rasped and cried out as my power exploded.

Everything I had in me slammed into the demonic reaper, drowning his entire form in energy and glory until he released my throat and disappeared with a scream. He blew away from me and was sent tumbling into the road. His claws left jagged white streaks in the asphalt as he ground to a halt. Merodach picked himself up, his body covered with open wounds and raw burns.

"I won't let you destroy anything else that I care about," I swore, and pulled my energy back into myself and marched toward him. "Your life of killing and reaping is over."

Appearing out of nowhere and drenched in blood, Will pounded his fist into Merodach's jaw so hard he knocked the demonic reaper off his feet, cracking his back into the road. Will called his sword and slammed it into Merodach's chest, staking him to the pavement. Merodach roared, spitting blood as red pooled on the ground beneath him. What skin of his that had been shredded and charred by my glory was unable to heal from the angelic power. He hissed at Will and gnashed his teeth, tugging uselessly at the giant blade, but he only cut deep slices into his hands. Wounds that should have healed in seconds struggled to knit the skin back together. By the calm look on Merodach's face, he seemed to understand that he was about to die.

I waited to see if Will wished to fulfill his oath to take Merodach's life. Both of us had a claim to revenge now, but the image of Merodach's sword buried in Nathaniel's heart had haunted us since the night it happened.

Will and I exchanged looks and I gave him a slow nod, acknowledging that I wanted him to have this kill. Will shoved his boot into Merodach's rib cage and tugged his sword from the reaper's chest. Merodach shuddered and moaned, gagging on his own blood.

Will, splashed with blood that mostly belonged to others, pressed the sword's tip to the demonic reaper's neck. Wounds that streaked across his face, arms, and chest healed quickly. "You came here with a force of over two dozen and still you were outnumbered."

Merodach laughed, a horrible wheezing sound. "You can't stop Sammael. You think you know what you have to do to beat us, but it will take your lives."

"The words of a dead man mean nothing to me," Will snarled. He buried the blade through muscle and bone, severing Merodach's head. His skin hardened to stone and within seconds, the demonic reaper's remains resembled very little of the beast he'd once been.

For a few moments, neither of us moved or spoke. We were paralyzed by surprise and relief to have this great enemy dead at our feet. We stared at Merodach's remains as if we expected his pieces to glue themselves back together and rise to continue the fight. When they didn't, I let my swords disappear and I touched Will's shoulder. He was frozen solid. I put my other hand to his chest and looked up into his face. The wailing sirens let us know that the police had to be just blocks away now.

"Will," I murmured to him softly. I moved my hand up to touch his cheek and gently turned his face to mine. His crystalline green eyes blazed back at me. "Are you okay?"

He nodded. "Yeah. I'm okay now."

With that, the tension washed away from him like the receding tide and he pulled me into his arms, hugging me close. I buried my face into his chest, soaking in his warmth and comfort. He held me for so achingly long that I almost forgot everything that had happened. I pulled myself out of his arms and turned to gaze toward the carnage Merodach had caused, at all the bodies littering the ground.

"It's not your fault," he whispered into my ear. "Merodach did this."

"But it's not fair. There shouldn't have been collateral."

"The only thing we can do is stop the demonic from hurting anyone else," Will said.

He was right. While Merodach's death gave us a sense of relief, having avenged the deaths of our friends, things almost didn't feel that much different. His death was a stepping stone. There was still so much more to be done.

"We should get out of here," he said. "We can't get caught up with the police."

He took my hand and guided me back to my car. The hood was caved in, but the engine started up with no trouble. We drove away, but I stared into the mirror long after the battle site faded into the night.

15

WILL AND I WERE QUIET FOR THE REST OF THE drive home. I brought Nathaniel's copy of the grimoire inside and hid it among the rest of the books in his study, hoping it would blend in, just in case someone tried to steal it again. Will grabbed some quick food so he could heal his injuries before showering and I went ahead to take a shower in the bathroom connected to Nathaniel's old room. I tried not to close my eyes, because every time I did, I saw Merodach's last moment flash in my mind, heard his last words, and then saw Will's sword separating his head from his neck. I wished I could scrub the memories away like I could scrub the blood from my skin. It was over, he was done with, and all I wanted was to forget his frightening face and move forward with my life and my mission.

After quite a while, reluctant to leave the soothing hot

water, I finished in the shower and dressed in a tank and shorts for bed. Will had already finished his shower and sat in the chair in the corner of his room, leaning forward on his elbows. His body was stiff and motionless, his hair still wet from his shower and his shirt was patched dark with dampness from his chest and back.

"Are you okay?" I asked as I leaned against the door-frame and crossed my arms.

He took a long, deep breath, letting his shoulders relax. He nodded.

I stopped in front of him and ran a hand through his hair. He closed his eyes at my touch. After some time, he leaned back in the chair and looked up at me. "How's your arm?" I asked.

He rolled up his sleeve to expose the ugly red slash, all that was left of the deep gash Merodach's sword had cut into him. I traced the line gently before pulling his sleeve back down. That slash had been meant for me, not for him, a blow that could have killed me. I looked up to find his gaze locked on my face.

"And the other place you were hurt?" I asked, my voice trembling.

He stood and lifted the bottom of his shirt to show me the mostly healed wound across his abdomen. My heart pounded as I lifted my hand to his skin, my shaking fingertips brushing over hard muscle, and he rested his forehead against mine. When I pulled my hand away, he straightened and looked down at me calmly and collectedly.

"I should go." I turned and took a step toward the door, but he grabbed my hand and spun me around, yanking me into him hard as I let out a gasp of surprise.

"Don't," he said. His eyes were green orphic fire, piercing me for a heartbeat that felt like an eternity, and then his mouth opened hungrily against mine. His kiss was scorching, exploring, his chest pushing into mine. My arms wound around his neck as his mouth moved over mine and his hands smoothed around my waist. My back. My cheeks. Threading through my still-damp hair. My fingers dug into his shoulders and glided up the back of his neck as his lips found my throat, his breath hot against tender skin. His nose and lips brushed against my neck and he kissed a trail from the delicate spot behind my ear down my throat. He let the strap of my tank fall and his lips pressed to my bare shoulder. He was smiling and then so was I, laughing quietly into his hair, filled with so much happiness and *rightness*. I was ready for this. I wanted this. My hands touched his neck and jaw, playing with his ear and shirt collar. He laughed too, but there was something in his laugh that made my stomach flip and flutter, something rich and raging. My fingers traveled south and dipped into his waistband and fumbled with his belt.

He stopped abruptly, just as he had when he'd driven me home from that stupid college party and I'd tried to seduce him. Only this time, he didn't move away from me. His next kiss was light and brief, unsure, and I sobered up instantly.

He stared at me, searching every inch of my face and body. His hand went through my hair and cupped my cheek, thumbing my bottom lip.

"I love you," I said against his thumb, kissing it once.

He was suddenly breathless. "I've loved you forever."

His lips found the place under my jaw, that ultra-soft skin there, and I tilted my head back as fire raged through me. His free hand rested on my hip, his thumb making little circles on the point there. We stood there shakily, stuck again at that place that always caught us, my body trembling nervously against his. There wasn't any going back now. He couldn't walk away from me this time. He couldn't tell me no and tear his eyes away from mine. Not again. So I made a move.

My hands slid across his skin and I pulled the hem of his shirt up. He stood frozen for too long until he finally, slowly, raised his arms and I pulled his shirt over his head and touched him, the muscle sculpted over centuries of war. He was beautiful. For a moment I forgot to breathe. *Breathe*, I told myself.

Oxygen brought my mind back to where my body was—against his. He dipped his head and kissed my lips, sweetly this time, with careful concentration. I squeezed my eyes shut as so much emotion poured through me in that instant. Desire had numbed my thoughts, but with that kiss, I suddenly remembered that I'd loved him for centuries, the way he'd loved me. I cursed myself for forgetting how deeply I cared for him and for forgetting his face and his name when I returned to this world as Ellie Monroe.

"We don't have to do this," he whispered. "We can stop."

"No," I said quickly. I took a breath to steady my voice. "I don't want to stop."

He nodded gently and his mouth returned to mine. Expert hands traced along my spine, sending shivers to my toes, erasing my doubt. I raised my own arms over my head, inviting him in, and he slid my tank top off. I fought my nerves, trembling all over, as I allowed him to see me. He only paused for a few moments, gazing down at me, before he pressed himself to my body and kissed me fiercely. When his bare skin brushed against mine, I took in a sharp breath and trembled. I could feel how strong his heart beat in his chest, echoing my own pounding pulse. It was alien to feel someone's bare skin against my own, even if it was his—a body I knew as well as my own, or at least I'd thought so. He pulled back just a little and looked into my eyes. His lips were parted and my own were swollen with his kisses.

"Are you sure?" he whispered, his eyes moving over every inch of my face. His gaze was heavy, as if he felt too much all at once for him to contain it.

I answered by taking his hand and leading him to his bed. He lay down with me, his body hovering over mine. He'd never touched me more gently than he touched me now. He moved slowly and his gaze was glued to mine as he shimmied my shorts over my hips and down my legs. The hesitation in his touch had vanished completely, but he was no less tender. One of his hands slid down my side and around the back of my thigh, tugging me closer to him. He kissed my mouth and his lips moved southward, kissing and touching me in places I never knew could experience such things. Time moved in waves of consciousness . . . moments where I was completely aware of where I was and then other moments where I slipped away and knew nothing at all but a beautiful sense of physical touch. The pain, when that moment finally came, was so brief, so fleeting, that as soon as it had passed, what rushed through me in its stead consumed my senses. Every part of him moved as gracefully as he did in battle, just as fluid and just as precise. Each time our eyes met, the connection was so fierce that it took my breath away. After everything we'd been through together, after hundreds of years, I had never imagined we could find an intimacy stronger than we'd felt before.

Then, even as he kissed me and his body moved with mine, an unwanted spark of worry made me wonder if things would change between us after tonight. Had they already changed between us when he'd kissed me for the first time back in the wreckage of the warehouse? But nothing about this was wrong. It was beautiful. I felt more loved and alive than ever before. After spending so long feeling more and more inhuman as my divine power claimed me, he brought me back. The battles I fought and the blood I shed threatened to unravel my humanity, which I clung to so desperately, but he held me together with ease. With every kiss and touch, he saved me, brought me closer to Earth, to him. I'd never felt more human. I'd never made a more right decision. It seemed like we'd been falling through the sky for centuries and we'd found the ground at last. His soul had been so beaten and torn and aching to return home. For him, I was home. And for me, he was the tide carrying me there.

Hours later, I woke with a gentle intake of air and my eyes fluttered open. The room was still dark and I was still lying in Will's bed, naked, with only the sheets covering us both, and we were tangled in each other's arms. He lay on his side facing me with his eyes closed. I touched his bottom lip and the back of my finger traced his jaw up to his ear. The silver cross and chain around his neck were splayed across the pillow. He made no sound other than his long, gentle breaths as he slept. He huffed and rolled onto his back and let out a soft snore.

I wrapped my hand around his cheek and kissed his neck. His lips curved into that secret smile of his and he groggily stirred out of sleep. Before he was fully awake, I kissed his throat again, barely able to keep the silly laughter from my lips, and then I kissed his chest, his shoulder, his cheek, his temple, and his lips at last. He wrapped a hand around the back of my head and tugged me closer to deepen the kiss. I drew away, leaning over him, and my hair fell over his face. His eyes were bright, gazing up into my mine, with a wonder and satisfaction that I'd only ever dreamed of seeing in them.

The backs of his fingers grazed my cheek. "I want to wake up like this every day," he said.

My body warmed all the way down to my toes and I smiled at him. He pulled me down to him and kissed me gently, his hands working their magic. I broke away and brushed my nose across his cheek. He looked at me and thumbed my chin.

"How are you?" he asked, his voice soft and serious. "How do you feel?"

I brushed his hair up off his forehead so that it stuck out messily, but adorably. "Wonderful. Amazing. Beautiful."

"Are you happy?"

I smiled, leaned over him, and kissed him again, slow this time. "I have never been happier."

He smiled back. "I love you, Ellie. I don't want to let go of this moment. I want to be lost in you forever."

I settled back into the bed and curled up against him, resting my cheek on his chest. "I wish we could stay here and let the world go on without us. I wish we could be normal."

He wrapped his arms around me and tugged me closer. "Without us, the world won't go on at all. When all of this is over, we'll be able to breathe. I promise. And you know I don't break my promises."

"I know," I said. I traced his lips with my fingertips and he kissed them.

We drifted in and out of sleep until the sun rose and bathed the room in golden light. As much as I'd have loved to lie in bed all day, my growling stomach was very demanding and very vocal about its needs. I dragged myself out from under the sheets to dress myself, feeling the butterflies again and totally aware he could see all of me. I tugged on my shorts and pulled my tank over my head, glancing back at Will, who watched me. I bit my lip, unable to stop myself from thinking about how incredible he looked lying there.

"I want breakfast, but you are too tempting," I told him.

He grinned. "We have all day, you know."

A warm rush fluttered in my stomach and I had to force myself to leave his room. I prodded around the kitchen and decided that today was a pancakes day. It wasn't long before Will joined me in the kitchen, pretending to be curious about the griddle I'd started to heat up. As I mixed the pancake batter at the counter, he stepped up close behind me, pressing his body against my back and dipping his head over my shoulder. His lips brushed my neck and his hands squeezed my hips.

"Will . . ."

"I like kitchens, don't you?"

I laughed and wiggled away from him, bowl in hand. "I'm trying to make you food here. I'm not domestic in the slightest, so you should cherish this."

He expression became somewhat serious. "Always."

Understanding the other meaning in his response,

I closed the distance between us and kissed him before returning to the counter to finish. I sprinkled cinnamon into the batter and dropped globs of the pancake goo onto the griddle. As I cooked breakfast and joked around with Will, it was such a relief not to worry about anything for a few minutes. It felt like we hadn't had a break in so long.

I finished my breakfast, took my plate to the sink, and returned to the table. I stopped next to Will's seat and he looked up at me with a curious look. I climbed onto his lap, a leg on either side of him, and I draped my arms over his shoulders. My sly grin matched his.

"Hello," I said.

His grin widened and his hands fell on my waist. "Hello. Can I help you?"

I cupped his face and kissed him, not failing to notice there was something different in my kiss. He seemed to notice it too. There was a casual ease in my kiss, a lack of any lingering shyness or doubt between us. I could now kiss him in the way I'd dreamed of kissing him, letting him know exactly how much I wanted him without feeling like it was wrong to do so. There was this intense sense of freedom in our touch, no reason to hold back anymore. And it was incredible.

He took hold of my thighs and stood, kissing me as he carried me upstairs.

16

A GROUP MEMORIAL SERVICE WOULD BE HELD AT the high school for all of the teens killed at Josie's house. I made it a goal to scout leads on possible locations of the Pentalpha before the service, and we would act the day after. I knew I had a special connection with the relic since I was the one who made it and I'd likely be able to sense its energy. That would be very helpful once the search began.

I didn't get the chance to hang out with Kate before the memorial service and/or tell her about what had happened between Will and me. Every time I thought about it, I found myself biting my lip and feeling those unbidden butterflies. I knew that conversation would warrant a sleepover and long girl talk. Kate and I had so much to say to each other before I left.

The candlelight memorial brought a somber mood to

the recently graduated teens and their families. My smiles from the past couple of days couldn't have shielded my heart from the sadness that overwhelmed me when I returned to my high school for the first time since commencement. I sat with Kate, Chris, Rachel, and Evan among the rest of my former classmates in the football field beneath the endless night sky, and Landon's absence was heartbreakingly noticeable. In my hands, I held one of the roses he had given me for my seventeenth birthday that my mom had dried for me. She had always loved drying flowers. In a way, this rose was for both of them. There were several faces I looked for but did not see, and the missingness that was felt in all of us was a low, heavy, suffocating cloud. There was no way to explain how strange it was for everyone to be so sad when the last time we were here and all together, we had felt nothing but pure joy and excitement.

Our principal closed the service by giving a speech that brought us all to tears. Kate squeezed my hand as we got up from our seats and filed out of the rows of chairs to line up and pay our respects. An altar covered in framed photographs of the dead, flowers, and candles stood on the platform the speakers had presented from, and everyone in line passed by in a gloomy, teary procession. People left small gifts that had meaning between them and those that had been lost: friendship bracelets, a football, a ribbon that said "Daddy's Little Girl," and more photographs of the deceased and their friends and family. I decided then that I wanted to write letters to each of the families, to express my condolences for their losses. I left Landon's rose in front of his picture and Kate took my hand and laid her cheek on my shoulder as we stopped to gaze at his picture. The three of us had been so close for nearly our entire lives, and it truly felt as if there was a hole in me now. I knew Kate had to feel the same. Losing Landon gave me so much sorrow, but I also felt an intense anger at the demonic who had done this to us. To all of us.

Kate and I went to meet up with Will, Marcus, and Ava afterward, who had accompanied us and kept a lookout. We rounded the bleachers where the students' families sat, and a hand grabbed my wrist and pulled me into the beams supporting the stands. I gaped in surprise when I recognized the red and puffy faces of Harper Knight, Josie Newport, and a couple of their friends. Harper released my arm roughly, glaring at me something vicious.

"What?" I asked, but I was more concerned with Josie's appearance. She looked absolutely anguished, with fresh tears smeared across her cheeks and her usually perfect makeup and hair a total mess. "Are you okay?"

"We saw you," Harper snarled, her face twisted in anger. "You know what really happened, don't you?"

I stared, speechless. "I—"

Kate stepped between us, turning on her pit bull charm. "Hey. Back off. We have no idea what you're talking about."

"No, I think you do!" Harper shoved Kate and Kate

would have swung her fist if I hadn't caught it.

"Stop it!" Josie cried, and grabbed Harper's shoulder. "Let's just go."

Harper ignored her. "Don't lie to me, Ellie. We saw you with those monsters. We saw you with freaking *swords*. I'm not blind and I'm not the only one who saw! What did you do, you psycho? Did you kill those kids?"

I almost choked on the air in my lungs. "Oh my God! I lost one of my best friends too!"

"How dare you?" Kate demanded and shoved Harper in the chest, knocking her back. "What the hell is the matter with you?"

I started to walk away, feeling the tears stinging my eyes and nausea creeping up my throat. I already felt guilty enough for Landon's death and the deaths of all the other people, but the last thing I could handle was being directly accused of killing them.

"We saw you, Ellie!" Harper yelled at my back. "You can't deny it!"

I spun around and stomped right into her face. "You want to know what I was doing? I was trying to *save* you, bitch. You'd all be *dead* if I hadn't been there! All of you!"

Kate took my arm. "Ell, don't."

I knew she was afraid of my blowing my cover, but I'd already lost my temper. "I don't care anymore! Harper, you're right. I do know what happened. Those monsters were real and I'm the only one who can kill them. That's what those swords are for. I did everything I could that night. I fought. All I *ever* do is fight. And fighting *you* is not worth my time, so get out of my face."

She gaped back at me, Josie whimpering beside her, their other friends silent. I spun and walked away as quickly as I could, Kate on my heels. Will appeared out of nowhere, pulling me into his arms to comfort me. Marcus stood behind him, watching the girls we'd just left with disgust, and Ava joined him, her own expression hard and angry.

Will lifted my chin to meet his gaze. "What's the matter? Are you okay?"

I shrugged, exhausted and heartsick. "Yeah. Just someone giving me crap."

He looked up suddenly and I was surprised to see Josie walking toward me, wiping her tears away with the thin sleeve of her shirt. Harper and the others were nowhere in sight.

"Ellie, I'm so sorry," Josie sniffled. "I know I shouldn't make excuses for her, but she's angry and hurt. One of the kids who was killed was her new boyfriend. That doesn't make it okay for her to lash out at you, though."

I gave her a tiny, grateful smile. "I understand what it's like to want someone to blame."

Her eyes flickered to the ground and past my head, and she seemed hesitant. "Is what you said true? About those things that were in my house, killing people? I saw you with the swords too." She looked at Will. "And you were there too.

Do you really fight them?"

"You told her?" Will asked me, surprised.

"Yes," I confessed. "They're what killed my parents, Mr. Meyer, and those people at your party. I'm sorry I couldn't save everyone. It's impossible for me to, but I still try so hard."

"Do you need any help?" she asked with genuine sweetness.

"I've got help," I said. "Thank you. I'm about to leave, Josie. Tomorrow, actually. I have to find something very important that can help me stop something even worse than the monsters who killed our friends. If I don't come back . . . if I never see you again . . . well, thank you for being kind, Josie. You're a good person and you've always been nice to me."

She frowned. "You sound so sad."

I smiled at her and fought back a tear. "I've got to go. Bye, Josie."

To my shock, she yanked me into a hug. "Bye, Ellie. Be safe."

I let my shoulders relax after a moment. "You too."

When we parted, I was sad to leave Josie. She really was a nice girl and I'd miss her. If I survived this war, I would visit her. I would do a lot of things. I would go antiquing with Nana again like we used to. Kate and I would waste a million hours wandering around the mall. Maybe I'd even join a rock band. If I survived this war, then I would really live.

I'd savor every moment in the sunshine, catch as many snowflakes on my tongue as I could, and I'd love as fiercely as my heart would allow. I wouldn't let the demonic take anything else from me. I wouldn't let anyone take from me what made me . . . me.

Will and I sat in the living room at the house, hard at work with Ava, Cadan, and Marcus, going through known relic guardians and choosing which were the most promising to check out. We could pick a few locations out of a hundred, but in the end, the Pentalpha might not be in any of them. Our odds of success didn't seem so great.

"What about this one?" I asked, pulling the photo of a girl—no, an angelic reaper—out from the pile.

Ava shook her head. "She protects a demonic relic, a blade Lilith used to murder babies in their cribs."

I exhaled in frustration. "You know all of these relic guardians and what they're guarding, but none of them can help us."

"Most of them I know," she agreed. "Not these three."

She pushed three file sheets toward Will and me, and we peered over the table to take a look. The first document had a small photograph of a male reaper paper-clipped to a sheet of his known physical traits, apparently for identification purposes, and the name of a town was circled in red ink in the top right corner: Apache Junction, Arizona. The second file listed the guardian's name as "Unknown" and featured a map of a region in Brazil with a small village near Manaos highlighted. The last file had only a question mark scribbled in red above a map of Belgium.

"What do you have?" Cadan asked.

"This is all the information there is on these guardians and their relics," Ava explained. "I have the most comprehensive collection of information on relic guardians and these three are a mystery to me. It must be that secrecy is their top priority. They want to remain unknown because whatever they are protecting is of the greatest power. These are the three relics we need to track down."

"Excellent," Will said. "Ellie and I will track down the Arizona guardian. Marcus and Ava will go to Brazil."

"I can check out Belgium," Cadan offered.

I shook my head. "You aren't going alone."

"I'll be fine," he said.

"You're working with us now," I said. "We work in teams. You're not going alone."

He shrugged, seeming disappointed but accepting of my terms. "What's my job, then?"

"Guard Nathaniel's copy of the grimoire," I said. "I trust you to keep it safe. Merodach wanted to keep its power from us and Sammael may send more thugs to stop us. We still need this book to summon Azrael and hopefully perform my ascension, but I need the Pentalpha first."

"Let's get ready to ship out, then," Marcus said excitedly. No one got more pumped about a mission than him.

"I'll get us on a flight into Phoenix tonight," Will said to me.

"Sounds good," I replied.

He got up and headed to the study to use the computer. Ava stood and bade us good-bye and good luck. Marcus gave me a hug as I walked him out the front door.

"I'd better let Kate know what's going on before I go," he said. "She'll be furious if I leave without a good-bye."

I laughed. "Yeah, she would beat you to a pulp for sure."

"See you soon," Marcus said, and gave me a kiss on the cheek. "Go kick some ass, okay?"

"You too."

I closed the door behind him and turned back to find that only Cadan remained in the room. He stood and settled his hands on my shoulders.

"You'll be okay without me?" he asked, his gaze warm and searching my own.

"Of course. Will *you* be okay without *me*?"

He grinned. "I might not."

"I'll be fine," I assured him. "I don't expect a fight. We're just going to check out this relic and if it's the Pentalpha, then we'll bring it home. Don't worry about me."

"I will anyway."

"Just don't give me a reason to worry about *you*, okay?"

"You won't need to."

I pulled away from him and started toward the hallway to the study. "Let me grab Nathaniel's book for you before we forget it," I called back to him.

Will wasn't in the study when I got there, but the computer still hummed and our flight information was printed out beside it. I pulled the grimoire from the shelf where I'd hidden it and made my way back to the living room. I slowed when I heard Will's and Cadan's voices.

"I wanted to thank you," Will said, seeming to force the words out, "for saving my life. And for keeping her safe."

"It was nothing, really," Cadan replied. "Don't mention it."

"I mean it. That wasn't nothing. I've been . . . less than kind to you. I'm sorry for hitting you."

"You had every right to."

"Regardless, I shouldn't have hit you," Will said. "I apologize. Honestly."

"I'll try not to give you another reason to beat me up."

Will paused and I peeked around the corner at them. "You've done so much for both of us," he said. "You've proven your loyalty. It has been hard to let go of the past, but you've earned my respect. And my trust."

This time, Cadan was the one who didn't respond right away, but when he did, his words were heavy with sincerity. "Thank you, Will."

"Brothers?" Will asked him.

"Friends?" Cadan held out his hand.

A hesitation. "Yeah." Will shook Cadan's hand. "Friends."

I couldn't help my own smile. This was the moment I'd

been waiting for. I turned the corner and bounced up to the reapers, giving them both an enormous, knowing grin. *"Hello-o-o-o-o,"* I sang and shoved the grimoire into Cadan's hands. "Good to see you guys are getting along."

Cadan flashed a little, embarrassed smile. "I'll see you two around."

"Bye!" When he was gone, I turned to Will and gathered the hem of his shirt between my fingers, beaming up at him.

"Enough of that," he grumbled at me, but the corner of his lips tried to pull into a laugh. "You're such a . . ."

"A what?"

"A spy!"

"I wasn't spying!"

"You were eavesdropping." He narrowed his eyes and tried not to grin.

"Maybe I was. So what?"

He kissed me, hard at first, but he sighed against my lips and relaxed into a slow, gentle kiss. When we parted, he looked a little sad.

"What's wrong?" I asked him, searching his eyes for answers.

"I wish we didn't have to leave again," he confessed. "I wish we could just stay here and be happy."

"Well, we wouldn't get much done if we did that," I said. "Think of the mission as a vacation. I'll bet Arizona is hot this time of year."

"Heat and cold don't really feel like much to reapers."

"And you're a Debbie Downer," I told him bitterly. "We'll be back home in no time. The sooner we get all of this done, the sooner we can relax."

He nodded, but it seemed halfhearted. "We should get packing."

"Can't forget my satellite dish. The aliens might have valuable info."

He laughed. "Maybe they can tell us where the Pentalpha is."

My smile faded a little bit. "Before we go, I wanted to write letters to the families who lost their kids that night."

He gave me a gentle look. "Is that something humans do for each other in times of loss?"

"It can be," I replied. "I just want to express how sad I am in a way that doesn't involve shedding more blood. After losing my parents, Nathaniel, Landon, and Sabina, I'm feeling so much right now and I may be one of the few people who understands what these families are experiencing."

"If you're mailing them, I can put them into envelopes and stamp them," he offered.

"That would be great."

We went into the study and I pulled out a loose-leaf notebook, envelopes, stamps, and a pencil. Will sat in the chair opposite my seat at the desk and looked curiously at my notebook and pencil.

"Don't you need cards?" he asked.

"Cards feel so generic and insincere," I said. "I don't want to say the same thing to each family."

I spent a little while writing the letters. I shared my memories of my classmates to their parents, wrote how sorry I was, and how I wished that night had ended up differently. I paused in horror when I saw Will cramming the letters clumsily into their envelopes.

"What are you doing?" I snatched the paper out of his hands.

"I'm putting them into the envelopes, just like you asked," he said.

"Fold them hot dog style so they fit."

"Fold them—*what*?"

"What's the matter with you? You're folding them hamburger style, the short way, and they don't fit like that."

"What are you talking about?"

I took a piece of paper and folded it lengthwise. "Hot dog style, see? Looks like a hot dog." I folded it crosswise. "And hamburger style. Looks like a hamburger."

"It looks like a piece of paper."

"And you look like an idiot. Just fold it this way and don't cram the paper into the envelope."

He shook his head and grinned as he carefully folded the letters the way I wanted him to. "You are so ridiculous."

"I'm aware," I replied. "I just want the letters to look neat, you know?"

"I do. Sorry I messed a couple up."

"That's okay," I said. "What do you say we get to packing and drop these off in the mailbox on our way to the airport?"

"Sounds good."

I finished the last letter and gathered all of the envelopes. "Well, that's it," I said, and took a deep breath. "Adventure time."

PART TWO

Requiem for a War

17

"I REALLY HOPE THIS RELIC IS SOMEWHERE THAT'S air-conditioned," I mumbled as I threw my duffle into the backseat of the pickup truck we'd rented.

Will rolled his eyes, smiling. "We'll stop at a gas station on the way and get you a battery-powered fan."

I made a pleased little noise of approval and hopped into the passenger seat. "You have to drive, though. I'm not taking on the responsibility of dodging armadillos on the highway."

He rounded the front of the truck and got into the driver's side. "I'm pretty certain there aren't any armadillos in Arizona."

"Why would you know that?" I asked him, looking at him like he had a third eye. "Armadillos should be in Arizona. And Michigan. They're so cute."

"You are so weird."

"Just drive. No complaints."

"Yes, ma'am."

We headed east from the airport on the 202 loop and took the exit toward Apache Junction. We drove around downtown and the surrounding neighborhoods to try picking up any trace of the relic's or its guardian's energy. The town seemed entirely normal and we could sense no reapers, angelic or demonic, and certainly no relics. By the time the sun began to set, I'd already lost my patience.

"How certain was Ava that there was a relic here?" I asked Will, looking over at him.

"She might have only marked the largest nearby town."

I groaned. "This is like looking for a needle in a haystack. Or rather, a needle in a desert. Let's head to the more rural areas."

He glanced at the GPS on the dashboard. "How about we take 88 out of town and go north through the mountains toward Tortilla Flat?"

"Why not?" I rolled down my window and let in the fresh air. "The heat's not too bad at night and the stars are incredible. It's nice out here, huh?"

"Yeah," he replied. "Lots of sun during the day. Good place to hide a powerful relic. The sunlight makes this place more unpleasant for the demonic."

I sighed. "Always the practical one. Do you ever enjoy something just to enjoy it? Besides root beer floats and playing music, I mean."

"Not really."

"If there is one thing I'll teach you, it's to enjoy the little things."

He flashed me a beautiful smile. "We've still got a ways to go. Teach me now."

"Okay," I said. "I'll take that challenge. Roll down your window."

He eyed me suspiciously, but lowered the window anyway. "And?"

"Stick your elbow out. Like this." I propped my elbow on the door and hung my head out my open window. "Feel the warm wind in your hair? The dusty smell of the desert? There's some good tunes on the radio. There's no traffic or anything way out here. It's a nice night, you know?"

He took a deep breath and let the wind catch his dark hair. He gazed up at the stars for a few moments and then he looked back at me. "Yeah," he said. "It's a nice night."

I smiled and closed my eyes, soaking in everything my senses could hold—and that was when my senses picked up something I didn't expect. There was a hum of electricity on every inch of my exposed skin, much like the static on a television set.

"Will," I said, watching all the tiny hairs on my arms rise straight into the air. "Will, turn off at the next road."

Without question, he took the next right onto a narrow and rocky road. I gripped the door handle as the truck nearly bounced me out of my seat. The presence grew stronger the longer we stayed on this road, as if whatever emitted the energy called to me. I was certain whatever I'd detected was a relic. There was too much power here for it not to be. I prayed that we'd found the Pentalpha.

It took a couple miles of rolling through the empty desert before the headlights shone on a trailer home that looked like it had been sitting in the dust for way too long. The roof sagged a bit and the handrail of its tiny porch was broken and hanging off. The worn and beaten front door hid behind a battered screen that swung on its hinges, and the windows were covered with a thick layer of dirt. Honestly, the place looked abandoned.

"It's there," I said to Will.

There was no visible driveway, so he pulled off the road in front of the trailer, driving over rocks and scrubby plants. His game face was on as he shut off the truck.

"Should we knock on the door?" I asked, unsure of how we would proceed.

"That doesn't matter," he replied. "The guardian already knows we're here. Be prepared to fight just in case."

I nodded but hoped we wouldn't have to. As we climbed out of the truck, an angelic reaper appeared through the door of the trailer and stepped down the creaky stairs. Will moved ahead of me, approaching carefully. The reaper wore clothes much cleaner than the state of his house, and his hair was shorn close to his scalp. His eyes, a soft plum color that glowed a little bit in the darkness, studied us curiously. He seemed to have concluded that Will was also angelic, but the way he rubbed the whiskers on his chin made me doubt he knew who I was.

"State your business," he said, his voice carrying a light, unusual accent. "I don't like people showing up at my door. And get rid of the girl. I don't allow humans."

"This is the Preliator," Will announced, and the reaper's eyes shot wide. "I am her Guardian. We've come to investigate the relic in your possession."

He walked toward us, gaze locked on me, his steps slow and even. "Is it true? You are the Preliator? You're very little."

I chose to ignore that last addition. He seemed nervous, so I made an effort to appear friendly. I held out a hand for him to shake. "Hi. I'm Ellie."

The reaper watched my open hand for a few moments, long enough to make things pretty awkward, and he gave Will an unsure look. When Will didn't immediately break his arm, he took my hand and held it firmly. "It is an honor. I am your servant and my name is Icarus."

I gave him a warm smile. "Great to meet you, Icarus. Can you show us to your relic, please?"

"Yes, yes," he said. "Come on in."

Will and I followed Icarus into the trailer. The interior was dark, with only a few sparse pieces of tattered furniture. The cabinets in the kitchen were broken and the carpet smelled thickly of mold. I didn't want to seem rude by covering my mouth and nose from the smell, but it was very difficult not to. Will, politely, gave no sign of discomfort, though his sense of smell had to be a hundred times stronger than mine. Icarus held a hand out, motioning for us to stand still, and he crossed the narrow living room to one of the windows. He pulled on the blinds cord and the floor between us slid apart with a mechanical hum, revealing a grated steel spiral staircase descending into a brightly lit shaft.

"That's not what I expected," I murmured to Will. He seemed unfazed by the secret passage, as if they appeared all the time in real life.

"What relic are you looking for?" Icarus asked as he returned to where we stood.

"It's called the Pentalpha," Will explained. "It's extremely powerful and crafted by Gabriel herself. It has the ability to summon the Fallen."

"Ah," Icarus said. "One of your own creations, Preliator? I'm sorry I don't recognize this word, but I'm happy to show you what I have. Perhaps you will know it when you see it." He started down the stairs. "Follow me. All relic guardians have their own way of surviving and protecting their charges. The house above this facility is camouflage, more or less. People don't usually come knocking, and if the demonic track me down, then they won't find much. It also acts as a fallout shelter. You know, just in case. After World War Two, the fifties had me a little nervous about these humans and their affinity for explosives. So I upgraded when bomb shelters were all the rage during the Cold War. Not that I'm paranoid. I'm careful. Just in case."

I shot Will an uncomfortable look. "No, of course not. So you've been down here for sixty years?"

"Is that how long it's been?" he asked. "I've had modifications done a few times. Be careful where you step and where you touch the walls. There are defensive devices triggered by touch."

"This place is booby-trapped?" I asked, suddenly panicked.

"A bit," he replied. "Yeah."

I stopped dead in my tracks, making Will bump into me. "Why didn't you say something? How do we get past them?"

"No worries," Icarus said casually. "I deactivated them when I opened the doors. I have an ability to control metal and electrical devices. But you never know. I could have missed one, so be careful."

I gulped. "Just in case?"

"Yeah."

I bit my lip and decided to proceed at my own risk. Icarus seemed content navigating the booby-trapped staircase, so I wanted to give him the benefit of the doubt. We reached the bottom of the shaft and found a hallway made entirely of steel, which led to an enormous heavy door with an elaborate adornment of high-security locks. An angelic spell repelling the demonic was painted in red across the door and on the metal floor in front of it. I didn't need to get close to smell that the paint was actually blood—*fresh* blood.

"Have you ever had a breach by the demonic?" I asked Icarus.

"They've never gotten this far," he replied. The locks clicked and buzzed and retracted, allowing the door to swing open. Beyond the door was another hallway, but this one looked like it belonged in an ordinary house. A runner stretched over the carpet and the hall opened up into a living area with leather couches and an insane number of books scattered around and stacked in leaning towers. Despite Icarus's talents with metal, there weren't many appliances to be seen.

"Do you live down here?" I asked.

"Yep," he said. "I don't get out much except to get food and anything else I need."

"Couldn't tell."

"Such is the life of a guardian," he mused. "Yours ought to know."

I peeked over my shoulder at my hard-faced Guardian. "Will definitely doesn't get out much unless I make him."

Icarus led us into a bedroom. "When one has something precious, one tends to be unwilling to let it out of sight," he said.

"I understand all too well," Will replied.

Icarus gazed up at the ceiling, and a panel hissed free and slid to the side, allowing a metal safe to be drawn out of a dark space on a high-tech dumbwaiter of sorts. I marveled at all the strange devices Icarus had in here and wondered how he managed before electricity was invented. I imagined he was pretty bored back then.

"You probably haven't opened this up in a while," I said. "I hope you remember the combination."

"There is no combination," the relic guardian replied and stared at the safe door. After a moment, mechanical things inside clicked and whirled and the door popped open, just as the locks on the passageway door sprang free. Icarus reached in and removed an object larger than I'd expected. It was a statue—not the Pentalpha ring.

I let out a tired breath of disappointment. "That's not what we're looking for."

"No?" Icarus asked. "This is the idol of Pazuzu, capable of summoning the demon of that name. I've been protecting it for two hundred years."

While the relic was incredibly powerful, strong enough to make me feel a little light-headed, it was definitely not the one we needed. "The relic we're after can summon any demons, not just Pazuzu. It's a ring, kind of."

Icarus frowned. "I'm sorry. I don't have anything like that. I wish I could help you."

An awful, nauseating dread began to creep through my belly and the worst worries whispered in my head. We'd come so far to find this thing, but it was a dead end. I'd have to call Ava first thing in the morning to see if she had found anything. We had to find the Pentalpha before anyone else did. Everything depended on it.

A hand touched my shoulder. "Hey," Will said gently. "Just because it isn't here doesn't mean we won't find it. We still have to check in with Ava and Marcus, and there's still Belgium. If we can't find the Pentalpha, then we'll find another way to evoke Azrael."

"Belgium, you say?" Icarus asked. "It's a very well-kept secret among the guardians that there is a supremely powerful relic hidden in Belgium, protected by the same guardian for nearly six hundred years. No one knows the guardian's name. That's how well-hidden he is."

"That sounds promising," I said, hoping to seem positive, even as doubt crept through my thoughts.

"We'll head out in the morning," Will said.

"Do you two have a place to stay?" Icarus asked. "You're welcome in my house. I insist. This facility is a whole lot safer from the demonic than a motel."

After all of the traveling and fighting I'd done in the last seventy-two hours, I was more than willing to crash on the first soft surface I found. "That would be great, Icarus. Thank you."

He seemed pleased with that and returned the Pazuzu idol to its safe and hidden place in the ceiling. "I'll show you to a room. There are a few bedrooms, but I rarely have guests, as you might imagine. I promise you'll find the accommodations very comfortable. Are you hungry at all?"

"We should both eat," I said.

Icarus's plum eyes grew to a vibrant hue with excitement.

"I love to cook. I must have a hundred books on it. Since I don't get to cook very often for others, let me make you this incredible dish I've been dying to try out. . . ."

He chattered away as he made us several delicious dishes. As eccentric as he was, I liked him. He was a very interesting guy. I imagined that we could even be friends. But I knew too well what life was like for a guardian. Friendship didn't often mix.

When we finished eating, I was so stuffed that it killed me to move around and help the boys clean up. When everything was put away, Icarus led us to the small bedroom we'd stay in for the night.

"I'll show you another room, Ellie," Icarus offered and began to leave.

I stopped him. "One is fine."

He gave me a curious look. "Oh." He paused, thoughtful. "Okay, then."

"I'll get our bags," Will offered and disappeared from the room to navigate the strange underground house.

The room was cozy, with walls painted a forest green and a big fluffy bed against one wall. I collapsed on the mattress and considered falling asleep before Will returned with my stuff. When I plucked at my dust-caked hair, however, I realized I couldn't sleep without a shower first. Perhaps the desert wasn't for me after all.

I also realized that Icarus hadn't left yet. Sheepishly, I sat up and smoothed my hair out of my face. His head was slightly cocked to the side, sort of like a bird checking out a worm. Thankfully, he was angelic and I was in no danger of sharing a worm's fate. Maybe.

"You are very strange," Icarus observed.

"Thanks," I replied, a little unsure. "So are you."

"I accept that."

"Fantastic."

He hesitated, his expression blank. "You're also very different than I imagined you to be. You're an archangel, but you're so . . ."

"Human?" I finished for him.

"Yeah," he said. "You're very human. Why?"

I blinked, again uncertain. Then I shrugged. "Well, if it quacks like a duck . . ."

"I don't understand."

"I've been on Earth for a very long time," I continued. "I've been human for a very long time. I don't really remember what it's like to be an archangel."

"You and your Guardian seem close."

"We're together," I explained.

"Interesting."

"Is there something wrong with that?"

"No," he said. "I don't think so. But I wouldn't have expected it."

"Our relationship isn't without its challenges," I said. "I believe it makes us a stronger team, though. Love makes you fight harder on instinct."

"Also interesting," Icarus noted. "I wish I could understand that kind of fortitude."

"One day you might."

"I won't," he replied. "But that's okay. I'm happy that you
have found it. Keep it close to your heart."

"I will," I promised.

"I'm glad to know you, Ellie," Icarus said. "Good night."

I smiled at him. "I'm glad to know you too. Thank you."

He gave me a slow, shallow bow before he walked from
the room. A few moments later, Will returned and tossed my
duffle bag on the bed.

"Got your stuff," he said.

"Thanks. I'm going to catch a shower. Are you crashing?"

He nodded. "Yeah. I have a feeling we won't get a lot of
rest after tonight so I'm going to get in as much as I can."

"Good call," I said with a tired smile. "I'll be back in a
few."

I hoisted my bag over my shoulder and searched down
the hall for the bathroom. I took a quick shower to get the
dirt out of my hair and when I returned to the bedroom, the
lights were off. I climbed into bed beside Will as quietly as
I could so I wouldn't wake him. I nestled against his body
and rested my cheek on his chest, his heartbeat a metronome
lullaby.

I drifted in and out of sleep for a little while, each spell so
short that I wasn't asleep long enough to dream. Something
kept pulling me back out and awake, but I couldn't quite tell

what exactly. Before I realized what I was doing, I was sliding out of bed and into my shoes and tiptoeing out the door. I felt an energy pulling me out of the underground house and outside into the night. The doors all unlocked before me, swinging wide to let me through, and I climbed the winding staircase to the surface in a sort of trance. My shoes made soft footsteps on the creaky wood floor of the rickety trailer, and when I pulled open the front door and pushed the torn screen aside, I became too aware that I'd just let myself get lured out into the open.

And something else was out here, too.

18

I WAS NO STRANGER TO THE HEAT AND LIGHT OF an archangel's glory. Michael stood before me in all his brightness, that cold, hard stare fixed on me. I felt so primitive and fragile in that moment when I looked at him and saw what I had once been. But in all his beauty, there was no life in him, no happiness. There was something different about him tonight, something flickering in his emotionless face that he was fighting with all his might to hide—something I could have sworn was anger.

Even though I was wary of his presence, I hoped he was here to deliver a message, something that might give us an edge against the Fallen. "Michael? Are you here to help us?"

"I'm here for the Guardian," he answered in his icy, hollow voice.

In the next instant, Will was at my side. His power

hummed around him and I knew he could sense through our bond that I felt threatened. Michael wasn't here out of peace. Neither of us was fool enough to drop our guards.

"I know why you've come," Will said, his voice dark and challenging.

Michael's robes fluttered beneath his golden armor in an unseen breeze, his wings spread high and wide. His feet were firmly on the ground, but he towered over us. "I warned you, Guardian."

I suddenly realized the exact reason for Michael's arrival. "Are you *serious*?" I spit at him. "You turn your back on this war, refuse to step in while Sammael is running rampant, while demonic reapers massacre humans in public and threaten not only Earth, but Heaven as well, and *now* you show your face? Is my sex life really your priority? No wonder our side is in such deep shit."

"Accepting the life of Guardianship is to accept the life of servitude," Michael boomed, his voice ringing out above mine. "The Guardian is not to pursue his own longings and desires, and he is especially not permitted to pursue an archangel."

"Is this about him breaking rules I've never heard of, or is it the fact that he's a reaper?" I demanded. "Whatever rule you insist on enforcing has no grounds here. In Heaven, I'm an archangel, but this is Earth and down here, it doesn't matter that I have an archangel's power. On Earth, I'm human and I answer to no one."

"The Guardian's punishment doesn't involve you, Gabriel," Michael said.

"Like hell it doesn't!"

"Ellie," Will said in a careful, quiet tone, warning me. I understood his concern, but now wasn't the time to be careful not to anger an archangel.

"You knew I would come if you disobeyed me," Michael said to Will. "You have overstepped your limits. Have you no respect for your charge, reaper?"

"How dare you ask him that?" I shouted. "This *reaper* has shed more blood for me than you or any of our brothers and sisters have ever shed. None of you have any clue what it's like down here. The angelic reapers are the only reason there's any life left on Earth at all and you have no reverence for them because of what they are. They are losing their lives for your cause!"

"They are tools," Michael said, his gaze piercing me. "As are we."

I shook my head in disgust. "If that's what you think, then you have nothing to fight for. And if you have nothing to fight for, then there's no way you can win this war. That's the difference between you and me. I *do* have something to fight for. The reapers and I aren't mindless drones. We're fighting for our lives, for *everyone's* lives! No thanks to you, *we* will win this war."

"The Guardian's mission is to keep you alive until he is dead," Michael said. "He accepted this duty when I offered it to him and he has disobeyed my orders."

"He isn't yours to command!" I cried. "Will is my Guardian and he's free to live his life."

Michael's lip curled. "He is not free. He is bound to the will of angels."

"Honor binds me to *her*!" Will roared suddenly. "I will follow her to the edge of night and back. You've said yourself that I am hers."

Michael drew his sword from its sheath and Will called his own in a flash of light and silver. "You *will* obey an archangel."

Will poised his sword at Michael and his power surged around him, a violent clash of shadows and darkness. "I don't obey you. I obey Gabriel, and I love her. That makes me stronger than everyone else, because I will never give up. There is nothing in existence that I hold more dear. She is everything to me. She is mine as I am hers, in every way. I will not yield to you, Michael, for you are not my master. I answer to Gabriel alone. Strike me down if you wish to, but I'm not giving her up without a fight, and I've been fighting for a very long time. I've still got plenty left in me."

"Then you have chosen death," Michael said icily.

I drew in a sharp breath of horror and threw myself between them. "No!" I cried to Michael. "If you kill him then it's practically a death sentence for us all. Will has been my Guardian for five hundred years. No other Guardian has ever come close to protecting me that long. Why would you even consider killing the best soldier you've ever had when we're so close to the end? How could you be angry about him and me?"

He gave me a blank look. "I am not angry. I feel nothing."

"And that's your weakness, Michael! You can't feel anything! That means you don't understand. But I do, Brother. I understand. I feel. I love. I love my Guardian. You gave him to me! God made me human! How many thousands of years have you watched humanity? What have they all done? They've all loved. How could God have made me human and you have given me my Guardian and have expected me not to love him?"

"Love is the illness that overtook Lucifer," Michael replied. "It was what began the war."

"No," I said firmly. "His hatred and jealousy of humankind were stronger than his love for God and for our brothers and sisters. If the only emotion he felt was love, then he could've accepted that our Father was also devoted to His human creations. But Lucifer didn't just love and you know that as well as I. Love had nothing to do with the evil Lucifer has done since his rebellion."

"That may be true," Michael said. "But love is just as dangerous as hate. I have stayed strong and true to God, because emotion does not cloud my mind. I must focus on my mission and so must the Guardian."

"Michael, *please*," I begged. "You have given me incredible wisdom before. Please hear my own wisdom for you. Will isn't dangerous. He gives me something to fight for and he makes me happy. You can't execute him."

"He disobeyed. Disobedience warrants death."

"I love him," I said in a small voice, my lips trembling. "No love can ever warrant death. Why would you take that away from me?"

Michael grew silent, his gaze softening as he looked from me to Will, and a dim light of hope flickered in my heart. "You would mourn for him."

"Yes," I said. "I would mourn him forever with a broken heart. This human soul has given me so many blessings and curses. I'm the only one of our kind who has ever felt the most perfect happiness and the truest sorrow—*because* of this soul. My love for my Guardian is one of those blessings. It's not a curse."

"I want to trust your judgment, Sister."

"You *can*," I promised. "Please trust me. I need all the help I can get, and that includes yours. If you kill my Guardian, then I will never forgive you. I can't be at war with you too. Please, *please*, Michael, my brother. Don't kill him."

I was sobbing now and the archangel stared at me with abject amazement. He glided toward me and bent down, peering into my face like I was some sideshow freak. I buried my face in my hands as I cried, wiping the tears from my cheeks and making an awful shuddering noise high in my throat. I hated the way Michael regarded me then, as astonishment leaked through his emotionless exterior. He lifted a finger to my cheek and caught a tear on his lucent skin that was made of golden light. He studied the drop and looked into my face.

"These are human tears," he said, his disbelief clear.

I sniffed hard. "Yes. I *am* human. Why can't you understand that?"

"I have never seen you cry before."

The ridiculousness made me almost laugh. "I'm begging you not to kill the person I love. Of course I'm going to get a little emotional."

"I do not want you to cry," he said. "It makes me afraid for you. You are not supposed to cry and I am not supposed to feel fear."

"Do you hate me?" I asked him.

"Of course not," he said gently.

A tear caught on the edge of my lips. "Do you love me as your sister?"

His mouth opened to reply, but nothing came out.

"It's okay," I whispered. "You're worried about me, because you love me. Don't be afraid of feeling anything. Our Father made us this way. He wouldn't make a mistake."

"I . . . ," Michael said, and emotion spilled over his face. His brow furrowed with exhaustion and he seemed overwhelmed by what he felt. He closed his eyes and took a deep breath before opening them again. "You are my sister, Gabriel."

"Then don't do this," I begged him.

He was quiet again for several agonizing moments, returning to his emotionless state. "Keep him. I have faith in you, Sister."

Will and I breathed sighs of relief, but it was a few seconds before Michael withdrew his sword. His expression remained unchanging as he lifted Will's death warrant.

"Thank you," I said to him. "Thank you so much. I need you, Michael. Help me defeat Sammael and Lilith."

"If I could, I would," he replied. "But my orders are to remain in Heaven and to protect our world. It is your duty to protect Earth. I'm sorry, Gabriel."

"I can't do it on my own. I need more angels down here."

"We cannot disobey our orders," Michael said. "That includes me."

"Have you ever heard of something called the hallowed glaive?" I asked. "I was told that the enemy fears this weapon could destroy Sammael."

"Yes," he answered. "The glaive belongs to Azrael."

I looked at Will. "That's awesome news."

Will nodded. "Azrael must have used this weapon to defeat Sammael before and he's got to still have it. At least we know right where it is and won't have to go looking for it."

"Is it possible for me to become an archangel again?" I asked Michael. "If I had my full power, then I would be a match for Sammael."

"It is possible," Michael said, "but it will destroy you."

My belly felt like I was just socked by a fist, the shock of his words a mind-numbing disappointment. "What? Destroy me?"

"No human body can withstand that much energy," Michael explained. "A mere glimpse of an angel's glory will burn the eyes from a normal human's sockets. You have enough divine power in you to handle angelic glory for short periods of time, but trapping all of your true strength inside this mortal body will kill it. Death may not happen instantly, but it would be inevitable. You are unstable enough as it is already, with your human emotions in direct conflict with your angelic power. You must have felt this happening before when you summon your full strength."

"Are you saying that I would become a time bomb?"

He gave me a single nod. "In a manner of speaking."

Will closed the distance between us and put a comforting hand on my arm. "We should abandon the plan, then. It's too much of a risk."

"How long could my body survive with my full power?" I asked Michael.

"Ellie—" Will's hand tightened on me.

"You would live until you used that power," the archangel said. "And you would need it all to kill the Fallen."

"So I could survive until I killed Sammael and Lilith."

"That is possible."

"Ellie!" Will took hold of my chin and turned my face

toward his, drilling his eyes into mine. "We will find another way to win."

"If this is the only way, then I'm happy to do it," I told him. "I know it's awful, but if it kills me, then I can come back."

"That cannot be guaranteed," Michael boomed, drawing our attention back to him. "If you die as an archangel on Earth, instead of the human you are now, you will not likely be reincarnated."

I let his words sink in, considering what they truly meant would happen to me. I felt myself fading into my thoughts, but the pressure of Will's hand on my skin kept me grounded. I drew a trembling breath and looked into his face. Fear resonated in his green eyes and he gave an almost imperceptible shake of his head.

"There's always another way, Ell," he whispered.

I bit my lip and swallowed hard. "What if there isn't?"

"I will *make* another way," he swore and cupped my face in his hands. "I'm not losing you for good."

"If this is my fate, then I embrace it," I said.

His thumbs brushed my cheeks gently and his gaze was firm and absolute. "No. You have the power to change your fate. You can fight it. We'll fight it together."

"If I had more information, I would tell you what I know," Michael said. "But what you ask of has never been done before."

I pulled away from Will and approached the archangel.

"Then you're saying that you don't know everything, that there could be a chance you're wrong."

"That is possible."

I nodded, weighing my options in my head. There was always hope. I had to cling to everything I had, no matter how dim that bit of hope seemed. "Thank you."

Michael gave a low, sweeping bow. "I must leave now. I can feel my hold on this world slipping. Good-bye, Sister. Godspeed."

The archangel vanished in a flash of light, and my eyes took some time to adjust in the sudden darkness. I turned to Will, forcing myself to face him and the conversation we were about to have.

"Will . . ."

"Let's not make a decision until we've spoken to Azrael," he suggested. "He may still be able to fight."

"And if he can't?" I asked. "Or won't?"

"Then we'll figure out something else."

"I'm going to do whatever I have to do."

"You're not going to die for this."

"If I have to die in order to save everyone, then I will in a heartbeat. The world is more important than me."

He shook his head and inhaled a rage-filled breath. "I will never let you do it."

I threw up my hands, exasperated. "It's not your decision!"

"I'll stop you."

"Will," I said, my tone firm. "I order you to let me do what I need to do to stop the Fallen."

His bottom lip trembled and he sucked it in as he accepted defeat. His gaze fell and he didn't breathe for an agonizing few moments. "If you do it, then you'll kill me too."

I fought back a sob and touched his cheek, softly turning his face to mine. "No. You aren't giving up. You have to keep fighting."

"What about you?" he whispered, his voice breaking. "You can't give up either."

A tear rolled down into the corner of my smile. "I always come back to you."

The pain on his face was heartbreakingly clear. Suddenly he looped an arm around my waist, tugged me against him, and he kissed me. I broke the kiss, unable to breathe as I fought to keep myself from crying. He held me close and I buried my face in his warm chest and closed my eyes tight. I didn't want to die. I didn't want to end, but I would if I had to in order to stop this war.

19

IN THE MORNING, WE SAID OUR FAREWELLS TO Icarus. Will and I didn't talk much on our trip back to Michigan. I could tell that he wasn't angry, but he was definitely thinking. I decided to let him be, to let him work out whatever he needed to in his head. I had already made up my mind about my own plan of action, but a part of me hoped that Will would find a way to prevent me from doing what I had to do. Strangely, ending my life wasn't what I was so afraid of. Although I couldn't remember anything from Heaven or what it had been like to be an archangel, I'd seen enough of Michael, Azrael, and Sammael to be certain that I didn't want to be like them. I didn't want to change and to become someone who really wasn't me anymore. I wanted to stay who I was: Ellie.

Marcus and Ava had also come to a dead end, as we had,

and Cadan's guardianship of the grimoire for a few days was uneventful. No one had bothered to unpack anything and everyone's luggage sat around Will's living room as we discussed our next move.

"Ellie and I are headed to Belgium," Will said. "Icarus seemed positive that something big is hidden there, so it might be wise for all of us to go."

"I can get plane tickets for tomorrow," Marcus offered. "Finding lodgings shouldn't be difficult either. Once we arrive, we should split up to cover more ground."

"I agree," Ava said. "In case there's a situation that one team can't handle alone, we should remain close enough that we can meet up quickly."

I felt pleased with our plan so far, and despite my exhaustion, I was excited and optimistic for the next leg of our search. "Safety is a priority," I added to Ava's suggestion. "I think Cadan should join you and Marcus. Will and I can carry the grimoire with us to keep it safe."

"Done," Cadan said. "I know some demonic hangouts we can crash while we're at it."

"Don't get too distracted," I warned with a teasing grin. "We're out to kick specific ass."

"Right, boss," he said with a salute.

"One more thing," I said. "When we evoke Azrael, I want all of us to be there. If he won't fight for us, then we'll have to discuss our Plan B."

Will got up abruptly and left the room without a word. I

shifted in my seat and Cadan caught my gaze with a questioning look. I shook my head at him, hoping my nonverbal response was a strong enough hint to him not to open his mouth.

Marcus stood up, breaking the awkward silence. "On that note, I'm going to go see Kate and say good-bye."

On Cadan's way out, he dropped his head by my ear. "You'll let me know if something's wrong, okay?"

"I will," I said honestly. "We're under a lot of stress and he's just worried."

"I understand," he said with a smile. "See you across the pond."

"You got it."

He followed Marcus out the door and I turned to go find Will, but Ava caught up with me and took my arm.

"Ellie, hey," she said in a low voice. "Are you all right?"

I chewed on my lip, unable to hide my nervousness. "Things got intense out in Arizona."

"Did something happen?"

I wasn't sure how much I wanted to reveal to her about Michael's visit, because somehow, what happened out there felt like something that was between Will and me. "Michael showed up."

Her eyes widened and "*Oh*" was all she said.

Her oddly knowing response made me wonder how much she knew about the extent of my relationship with Will. I hadn't said anything to anyone yet about us sleeping together—and that wasn't something I especially wanted to discuss with Ava, given her short-lived history with him.

When I didn't say anything more, she continued in a careful tone. "Will told me he was worried Michael would pay a visit if certain things happened."

With that, I was pretty sure Ava had just let me know that she'd figured it out. "Our conversation ended on a good note, I think."

"So things are tense with you and Will because of Michael, not because of . . ."

This is so awkward. This is so awkward. "Yes, definitely because of Michael almost executing Will."

Ava studied my face. "That isn't everything, though. Is it?"

She was obnoxiously intuitive. "I asked Michael if there was a way for me to become Gabriel and to have my full power. He said that if I became an archangel, that tapping into my full strength would annihilate my mortal body. He was also unsure that I would come back if I died as Gabriel. Meaning, that would be it for me."

"Ah," she murmured, the sympathy in her indigo eyes warm. "And now Will is determined to keep you from ascending."

I forced a smile. "Right on the money."

"Well, the answer is to do what you believe you have to do," she said, "but that's pretty hard to accomplish around someone as strong-minded and determined as Will. He doesn't want you to die, that's all it is. And for what it's worth, I don't want you to die either."

"Thanks," I said with a little laugh. "You and me both. I hope there's a way to beat Sammael and Lilith without killing me too, but if there isn't, then I know what I have to do."

"I believe you can do anything," Ava said.

I fell silent, marveling at how far we'd come, she and I. "Thank you."

With a nod of her head, she motioned to the hallway Will had disappeared down. "Go talk to him."

It wasn't hard to find Will. When he needed to think and cool off, he usually went outside. He seemed to prefer the outdoors anyway. He sat on the swing bench out by the lake shore and watched me as I slid into the seat next to him.

"I'm sorry I brought it up," I said to him.

He shook his head. "Don't be. I shouldn't have let it upset me. The others needed to know everything we're considering. I'm just unwilling to consider this plan."

I didn't want to start the argument all over again and I got the feeling that he didn't want to either. I pulled my legs onto the bench and curled up against him, resting my head on his shoulder as he wrapped an arm around me. "We're going to be okay," I promised him. "We'll hop on yet another plane, find the Pentalpha, get Azrael to be our terminator, get him a leather jacket and sunglasses, and we'll be fine."

He said nothing and only held me tighter.

* * *

I said my good-byes to Nana later that day before heading over to Kate's to watch movies and relax. She opened the door and gave me a big hug. It felt so good to see her after the emotional roller-coaster that was the Arizona trip.

"When did Marcus leave?" I asked as we headed up to her room.

"I actually got back from his place about an hour ago," she replied. "Figured I might as well help him pack . . . and stuff."

"Tactful," I said, rolling my eyes.

She closed the door behind us and plopped down on her bed. "I made him promise to bring you home."

"We'll both work very hard at that," I said. I dragged her movie binder out from the cabinets under her television. "What do you feel like watching first?"

"Something awesome and fun."

I flipped through the pages, scanning the titles. "How about *Clueless*?"

"Perfect."

"Then *Mean Girls*?"

Kate let out a long, happy sigh. "How are you reading my mind right now?"

"Natural skills, obviously," I said, and popped the disc in the player.

Spending a few hours with my best friend, watching movies and joking around, helped me grasp that feeling of normalcy I hadn't sensed in so long. I had worried that this final night of peace would make it harder for me to let go of my life, but sitting there with Kate, tears in my eyes from laughing, and our senior yearbook wide open between us, I decided that I wouldn't give up without a hell of a fight—that I'd be unbreakable. I wasn't just fighting for my own life, I was fighting for Kate's too. For everyone's lives. I couldn't let them down.

She must have noticed my distant look, because she rested her head on my shoulder. "You okay, Ell?"

I gave a halfhearted shrug. "I just want this to be over."

"Marcus told me he was worried about you."

I made a mental note to kick him in the kneecap for getting me into this conversation with Kate. "I'll be okay. I promise."

She made an unintelligible noise of disbelief. "He also said that you and Will were acting weird, and that I shouldn't say anything. Which of course means I will. And I just did. So, explain, please."

A secret smile escaped my control. This was a conversation I wasn't afraid of having. "Something happened. Things changed."

"Something good by that stupid grin on your face." She laughed and then her eyes got huge. "Oh my God! You slept with him!"

I chewed on my lip. "Yeah."

"Why didn't you tell me right away?" she asked, sounding hurt.

"Things have been pretty crazy."

"I understand," she said. "So, spill. How was it?" She winked at me.

"He was very sweet," I replied. "He was good to me."

She smiled. "I'm happy for you. I'm glad that things have worked themselves out for you two. Your relationship has been so up and down for a long time."

"It's been hard," I agreed. "I'm sad that we waited so long to be together. It's probably too late now."

She watched me and the look on her face told me that she understood what I meant. "This trip won't be like the last one, will it?" she asked, her voice weighted with sadness.

I was quiet for a moment. I wanted to be honest with her, but I didn't want to worry her. If I died, I didn't want Kate's last memory of me to be a sad one. "No," I replied.

"You know you can tell me anything."

"I might not come back this time," I confessed and bit the tip of my tongue to keep my composure. "The best-case scenario is that we find this ring, the Pentalpha, and summon the angel who's defeated Sammael before. If this angel can't or won't fight, then we will need another angel. Me."

"You'll become an archangel again?"

I nodded. "There's a weapon that can kill the Fallen, but only another angel can wield it. But if I do, then all of that power will toast my human body."

Her lips parted and she shook her head in disbelief. "But

if you're killed, you'll just come back. You'll be reincarnated again."

"We have no way of knowing for sure, if I die an archangel," I said. "When an angel dies, that's it. It's the same for reapers. They just *end*. Heaven is for human souls."

A glimmer of hope shone in her eyes. "But you have a human soul."

"Exactly," I said. "So we don't know what would happen to me."

"At least there's a possibility that you would come back," Kate said. "Or maybe you would go to Heaven. I don't want you to die, though. I'd miss you too much. And I'd have no one left to tease."

"You've got Marcus to harass," I offered.

She made a little face. "Yeah, but I need my best friend more."

I smiled at her. "It'll be okay. Everything always works out somehow."

"I guess so," she said. "Will you be *you* after becoming an angel again?"

"I'll still be me," I promised, but I wasn't sure if that was true or not.

"Wings would be cool."

"Yeah."

"Hard to fit through doors, though. And you'd go through shirts like popcorn, like Will does."

I laughed. "Yeah."

We fell silent for a few moments. Our movie was still going, but neither of us was really watching it. We were both lost in our thoughts.

Kate drew a quivering breath as if she were trying not to cry. "I don't want this to be the last time I see you."

"If it isn't, then the first thing we do when I get back is go shopping," I said. "And then we'll go on a trip. I feel like saving the world should get us a week in the Caribbean at least."

"At least," she agreed. "We'll take the boys, lie out on an island beach somewhere, make them fan us with palm leaves—no, their *wings*. I'll bet my right boob no princess or A-list celebrity has ever been fanned by wings before. We're so legit."

"The *most* legit."

Kate's mischievous grin brightened her face. "You know, with that warrior-servant-thing you and Will have got going on, you could do some pretty kinky—"

"*Kate!*"

She started laughing so hard that she was gasping for air. "I'm kidding! Well, kind of. But you know I only say this stuff to make your face turn into a tomato, right? It's a hobby."

I glowered at her. "I had a strong suspicion."

She pinched my cheek. "You're so vanilla. I adore you."

"I'm going to miss you, girl," I told her.

She sighed and gave me a soft smile. "I'll miss you too."

20

THE JOURNEY TO BELGIUM WAS A LONG AND TIRING one, but as soon as our plane pulled into the terminal in Brussels, I felt a new life and new determination in me. I'd gotten a few hours of sleep during the flight, so I was rested enough to meet the rest of our team right away. Ava and Marcus traveled together and Cadan had to wait until nightfall to fly. We rented a small car and headed to the café where we'd planned to rendezvous before making our first move to locate the Pentalpha. The café was busy and had enough ambient sound that we wouldn't be overheard by anyone without superfreak reaper hearing abilities. Not to mention, my coffee was incredible.

Ava splayed a map over the table between us. She took a pen and circled a district in Brussels and the town of Liege, about an hour's drive away. "I know of two relic guardians in Belgium," Ava said. "Neither of them protects the Pentalpha, but they may be able to give us leads about the identity or location of the guardian who does. Maeghan is local, Berengar is in Liege."

"Shotgun Liege," I said quickly.

The reapers all stared at me like I'd grown a third eye.

"What?" I asked, not the least bit embarrassed. "Their waffles are world famous. I'm going to Liege if only for their powerful relics and awesome waffles."

"I like waffles," Cadan said.

I beamed at him. "All right. You'll be on Team Waffles with Will and me."

Will just shrugged. He accepted me for who I was and he didn't seem to mind being on Team Waffles.

Marcus gave Ava a pathetic look. "Why can't our team have a cool name?"

She glared at him before clearing her throat. "Moving on, I can't give you an exact location on Berengar. You'll have to search him out yourselves, and it won't be easy. The relic guardians like to stay hidden."

"Got it," I said. "If I get close enough to the relic itself, I'll be able to sense it."

"It shouldn't take long to locate Berengar," Will said with confidence. "I believe we will have the Pentalpha by nightfall."

Marcus stood from his chair. "Ava and I will head out,

then. The sooner we find this thing, the sooner this will all be over."

"Let's rock and roll, boys," I said to Will and Cadan.

We gathered our belongings and headed out, but I caught Ava's arm and she turned back to me.

"Something wrong?" she asked.

"You know so much about the guardians," I said to her. "How come you've never become one?"

"I don't like hiding," she replied. "I've spent too much time by myself in the dark. Being out in the field on the front lines is more like it."

I smiled at her. "Yeah, it is."

"Be careful out there."

"You too," I said. "We'll be in contact as soon as we find Berengar. One giant, delicious waffle says we find the Pentalpha first."

She returned my smile. "You have a deal."

"I spy with my reaper eye . . . ," Cadan grumbled, "something spotted."

I glanced over my shoulder at him from the front seat. "You're cheating. And it's probably a cow that's too far away for my human eyes to see. Pick something close to the road."

"Fine. I spy something green."

"Grass, trees, clouds, and sky don't count. You are terrible at this game."

He huffed. "It's a stupid game."

"Pick something or I'm making Will play."

Will gave him a reproachful look in the rearview mirror. "Please pick something."

Cadan sighed and scanned the landscape. "I spy something brown."

I stared out the window, unable to see much more than green hills and blue sky. "The fence?" I asked, pointing at it.

"You win," he announced dismally. "I concede defeat. You are far too powerful for one so feeble as I."

"Don't give up so easily. I'm bored."

"Count the fence posts."

"How about I count your face?" I grumbled.

"Ooh, burn."

I turned to glare at him over my shoulder, but as soon as I saw him, I burst out laughing. He shook his head and laughed with me—or at me. Could've been either.

Will pulled off A602 and headed toward the center of Liege proper. We didn't really have a plan once we got into the city, and this felt just as unorganized as our trip to Arizona. I suggested we park the car and grab something to eat while we wandered, waiting to sense something. Navigating the seemingly randomly plotted streets of Liege was difficult, but the incredible architecture and magnificent art made for a fun adventure. Night began to fall and we found a small restaurant that I made sure served waffles. I scarfed down two of them piled with chocolate syrup and whipped cream and was feeling pretty sick to my stomach by the time we left. I didn't really care that I ate more than the reapers, though I had the feeling that Will regretted not ordering a second.

We left the restaurant and traveled the stony streets well into the night, listening to the vibrant mix of French and Flemish conversations and music. When I picked up the sense of unsuppressed reaper energy nearby, I moved into the Grim with Will and Cadan on my heels. We hadn't spotted the reaper yet, but Will took my shoulder to slow me down.

"Be careful," he warned. "If we can sense him, then he can probably sense us. We aren't hiding our power and he might be alarmed by Cadan's demonic energy."

It was easy for me to forget that Cadan wasn't angelic. We had to be cautious when approaching other reapers—especially reapers who knew Cadan by sight. Though Will's paternal side might have been unknown to anyone but us, many reapers were aware that Cadan was Bastian's son.

"Let me go alone," Will offered. "The reaper won't feel so threatened."

"No," I said. "It's my responsibility. Stay with Cadan."

"Ell," Cadan said in a low voice.

I turned to him and froze when I saw a reaper standing not a dozen feet from us, the very one we'd followed. The reaper was tall, drenched in black that made him melt into the shadows. I wondered if he'd been within sight the entire time we'd sensed him, but was still able to elude us.

He stepped forward, his boots clicking on the cobblestone, and I could see that beneath shaggy black hair was a hard face with strong features and a thick beard. His brown eyes enflamed to red as his power churned around him, flashing shadows and smoke.

"We're not here to fight," I called to him.

His head tilted in a curious gesture and he kept walking toward us. Will held out his arm to call his sword, but I put a hand to his chest. The reaper gave Cadan a vicious glare, baring his teeth and hissing like an animal. Instead of drawing a weapon and attacking right away, he circled our group, studying us.

"Do you speak English?" I asked carefully, certain not to show any fear.

"Yes," he replied in a thick, gruff accent that I didn't recognize but could guess it was very, very old.

"Are you the relic guardian called Berengar?"

After a few seconds, he gave me a single nod.

"I'm the Preliator," I told him. "I'm looking for a relic known as the Pentalpha, the Ring of Solomon."

His eyes lingered on Will's tattoos. "I know who you are. And I know who he is. Your last Guardian was not so tall."

I was taken back with surprise. "We've met?"

"A long time ago. I've sensed your presence since your arrival in this city. I never expected to see you again, and especially not in the company of Hellspawn."

"He's my friend," I said firmly. "His presence will not

be challenged. Berengar, I ask that you surrender your relic to me."

He made a brusque sound in reply. "I won't be able to help you."

"Do you have the Pentalpha?" Will asked.

Berengar shook his head. "No. I possess Raziel's book. It contains all of the secrets of God."

I closed my eyes and exhaled as the disappointment of yet another dead end pulled me beneath a crushing wave. I knew we still had a chance to find the relic, but our goal seemed to drift further and further away each day.

"Don't worry," Will said softly. "It's out there somewhere."

"Do you know of the Pentalpha?" Cadan asked Berengar.

The relic guardian turned his gaze to Cadan. "I do not speak to the demonic."

Anger rushed through me. "Then speak to me," I growled.

"Yes," Berengar said. "I hear few rumors about it and its guardian. The Pentalpha never stays in one location very long, a few years at most. I spoke to an angelic reaper some time ago who told me that she knew the Pentalpha guardian and believed that it had been moved to Belgium. Whether it is still here, I do not know."

"Did the reaper happen to mention *where* in Belgium?"

"No," Berengar replied. "But you can ask her. Evolet lives across the river in Bressoux. If it please you, I will ask her to come to Liege."

"Thank you," I said, though it would take more than this

to make me like him. The way he scowled at Cadan even when he spoke to me made me mad, but I had to remind myself that Berengar didn't know Cadan.

Berengar arranged for us to meet this Evolet at a small café a couple blocks away. We found a table on the patio outside and it wasn't long before two reapers approached us and sat down. The girl I assumed was Evolet had blond hair pulled into a braid over her shoulder and blue eyes like burning stars. Her companion was a male reaper with curly dark hair and his expression wasn't very friendly. The girl studied my face intently and Will stiffened beside me. I put a hand on his arm to let him know he could relax, but whatever made him feel defensive affected me too.

"Are you really the Preliator?" the girl asked in a light French accent.

"Yeah," I said. "You're Evolet, right?"

She nodded. "I'm sorry for my imposing backup. Calix doesn't like to be out around so many humans. Neither do I, for that matter, but what Berengar had to say interested me. I don't trust him often, hence Calix's presence."

"That's shocking," I mumbled, dripping with sarcasm. "Berengar was so pleasant."

When her gaze rested on Cadan, a curious smile spread across her rosy pink lips. "How interesting. Cadan, son of Bastian. You're really rolling in the trash these days, aren't you, Preliator?"

"Hey!" I snapped.

"You'd better watch your words," Will said in a cold, dark tone. "He's not the only son of Bastian."

Evolet looked at Will now. "Even more interesting."

"Now that we've established your bigotry," Cadan grumbled, "can you help us?"

"I don't think anyone can help you," she replied.

Will shot up from the table, one hand tight in a fist, the other ready to draw his sword. Cadan stared at him with an expression of uncertainty.

"Relax," Evolet said with ease, sinking deeper into her chair. "It wasn't a threat."

"I don't understand," I said in disbelief. "You can't tell me that you've already given up."

Her blue fire eyes fixed on mine. "We're preparing for war against an enemy beyond any of us. Sammael will turn this world to ashes."

I stared harder into her eyes. "I will not let that happen."

She huffed, amused. "The Pentalpha is real."

"I know it is," I said, my patience waning. "I made it."

She was quiet for several moments and then she lifted one hand. Energy sparked from her fingertips and the black wisps of power danced in her palm. "There are two people on this Earth who know where the Ring of Solomon is hidden. I am one of them."

"I am the archangel Gabriel and you will tell me what you know," I ordered.

Cadan stood to join Will, and Calix crossed his arms over his chest, puffing himself out. The intimidation game wasn't going to get us anywhere. I needed Evolet to cooperate.

Suddenly Evolet smiled and relinquished her power. "I like you," she said. "You've got spunk."

"My life is complete. Really."

"You'll want to go to Aalst," Evolet said at last. "West of Brussels. The relic guardian is there."

I breathed a sigh of relief and mentally crossed my fingers in the hope that we wouldn't hit yet another dead end with this lead. "It looks like we're backtracking," I said to the boys.

"You're welcome to collect and attempt to use the Pentalpha," Evolet continued. "I wish you the best of luck. If you were wise, you'd find a quiet place to lie low like the rest of us."

I stared at her in disgust. "Are you serious? You coward. I will not hide in a hole and let the world fall to pieces because I'm too afraid to fight. How can you live with yourself?"

She smirked and her eyes flashed. "I *live*."

"You are the sorriest excuse for an angelic reaper I have ever seen," I snarled at her. "You have a duty to protect Earth and Heaven."

Anger twisted her face and she leaned across the table. "The things I know make me a top target for the demonic. Do you have any idea what they'd do to me if I were caught?"

I scoffed. "And you think *I'm* not a target? That your

worst nightmare has never happened to me more times than anyone can count? I've been caught. I've been torn apart. I'm *still* a target. And I'm still fighting, unlike you."

Evolet fell quiet, watching me coolly. "I do like you. And I hope whatever you're trying to do works out. For all our sakes."

I stood from my chair, sliding it back and letting it screech across the floor. "I wish I could say it was nice meeting you. We've got a mission to carry out. Thanks for the tip."

Will and Cadan followed me out of the café and into the streets. As we headed back toward where we'd parked the car, I slowed my pace to match Cadan's. His gaze was fixed on the ground as we walked and I hooked an arm around his.

"Are you okay?" I asked him.

He looked at me finally, his opal eyes quiet and distant. "Of course. I've been treated a lot worse, believe me."

"I do," I said. "But you're not trash. No matter what anyone says. No one can help where they come from, and where you come from doesn't make you who you are."

"Not entirely true," he replied, flashing me a sideways grin. "You're from Heaven, after all. Need I say more?"

I rolled my eyes and shoved his shoulder. "I'm serious! I know it must be hard for you, being around so many angelic reapers who only see what you are instead of *who* you are."

His smile faded and he lifted his head, gazing onward. "Not everyone will give me the chance you have, and even then with you it took time. It isn't fair for me to hold anything against those who haven't had the time to understand me. Besides, I'm not out to redeem myself to them. I want to redeem myself to *me*. And to you. That's all that matters."

I took a firmer grip on his arm and stopped us both in the street. He looked down at me, his jewel eyes brightening, glowing in the darkness.

"You have," I told him, feeling a little heartsick at his words. "To me, at least. You have to let me know if there's anything I can do to help."

His grin came right back and he wrapped an arm around my shoulders, pulled me close, and kissed the top of my head, very big-brother-like. "You just worry about saving the world, okay? I don't need saving nearly half as bad."

We started walking again to catch up with Will, who had stopped a little ways ahead. He watched us, his expression difficult to read. There was no anger or jealousy on his face, only a visible effort to understand. Just as Cadan had said, it would take time for others to accept that he had turned his back on the demonic. It was especially hard for Will, given their past, and though it would take more time for him to be as comfortable with Cadan as I was, I believed with all my heart that he would arrive there one day.

21

"WE'RE HEADED TO AALST," I TOLD AVA OVER THE phone once we were back on the road.

"Any specific location?" Ava asked. "Address, intersection, landmark?"

"None that we know of," I replied, with a glance over at Will in the driver's seat.

Silence, and then, "What's the plan?"

"You and Marcus go on ahead of us," I instructed. "We're an hour behind you."

"See you soon." She hung up.

When we arrived in Aalst, I found the town to be sublimely quaint in its sleepy quietness. Will parked on the side of a steep, sloping street and we walked down a street of brick too narrow for even a car lane, with picturesque buildings painted various shades of cream and pastels lining the passage on either side of us, until we found an open pub. Since we knew nothing about the relic guardian supposedly located somewhere near the village, I hoped that perhaps he had made an appearance at some point to one of the locals.

A few burly men with their mugs of beer were scattered at booths and tables inside the pub. It seemed like the tourist crowd had cleared by this late hour and the only patrons left were those seeking relaxation and a pint after work. I longed for an end to the day myself, but we'd already decided to find a hotel to stay the night only after we had finished investigating the village. The men in the pub gave us disgruntled but curious looks as we sat on empty stools at the bar.

The balding man tending to the bar asked us in Flemish if we wanted anything. I flashed my sweetest, apologetic smile at him. "Americans," I said, and gestured to myself, Will, and Cadan.

The bartender nodded, understanding. "American," he echoed in a thick accent. "Need a drink?"

"Yes, please," I said. "Do you have tea?"

He laughed and shook his head. "No. No tea. Are you three students?"

"Journalism," I replied, thinking quickly. "We're writing a story on local legends. Stories of flying creatures and things like that."

His hands fumbled around a glass and it slipped from his grip to clatter on the floor. I exchanged looks with Will and Cadan before watching the bartender curiously.

"No story here," he grumbled, his face reddening. "You should leave. There is nothing here to find for you children."

"I'm sorry," I told him. "I didn't mean to upset you. We're only interested in—"

"No," he said, his tone firm and harsh, and he leaned over the counter and got right in my face. "You will find nothing here."

Will launched himself to his feet and he slammed his hand on the counter, warning the man to back off. "That's close enough," he growled.

"Thanks, anyway," I said to the bartender and dropped off my chair. "Let's go."

As we hurried out the door and down the street, Will leaned close to my ear, and said, "We're being followed."

I turned to see that one of the men from inside the pub now stood in the narrow street, head bowed and hands stuffed into his pockets. I felt no threat from this man, but he was clearly nervous and that made the reapers nervous in return.

"American girl," he called in a hushed voice also thick with a Flemish accent. "You look for legends?"

"Yes," I said. "Do you know of any creatures like the one we're looking for?"

"I do." His eyes were huge in the dark. "But you will think I'm crazy. They all think I'm crazy."

I smiled. "Try me."

"You know Kasteel van Mesen?" he asked, low and guarded. He glanced over his shoulder once.

It took him mentioning the abandoned castle for me to remember it. "Yes, I've heard of it."

"The devil of Kasteel van Mesen," the man continued. "Black wings and glowing eyes. . . . The others think I'm crazy, but I'm not. They think the story is bad for business."

Will had a knowing gleam in his gaze. What this man described sounded like it could be a reaper. "And you've seen this creature with your own eyes?"

He nodded. "I worked as a security guard for years, but I am the only one to see the devil."

No wonder the poor guy's friends thought he was nuts. Fortunately for him, I believed in winged beasts. "That's a pretty good story," I told him. "Thank you. We will have to pay a visit and see if we can find this devil."

The man started back down the street, but just before he disappeared into the pub once more, he paused. "Be careful, fire girl. The devil will steal your soul."

I stared at him until he was gone and tried to shake off his final words. A terrible worry, that the reaper hidden in the crumbling castle might be demonic, crossed my mind.

We continued our trek back to the car and I pulled out my cell to call Ava. "How's the search going?" I asked when she answered.

"I'll let you know," she replied. "Evolet called. You made quite an impression."

"As did she," I grumbled. "Did she say anything *useful*?"

Ava laughed softly on the other line. "Just a lead where

we might find the guardian. She was surprised we were in Belgium. Have you found anything yet?"

"We're checking out Kasteel van Mesen right now," I said.

"Good idea. In fact, we're on our way to an abandoned factory."

"We'll regroup afterward. I can call you again after we've investigated the castle."

"One step at a time," she replied. "Luck to you."

"Right back at you." I put the phone away, resolved against meeting the others empty-handed. Evolet seemed certain that the guardian of the Pentalpha hid within Aalst, and a villager claimed to have seen a winged devil at the same location. I felt that we were close at last, and I wouldn't rest until I had the relic in my hand.

Will opened the car door, but Cadan put a hand on my shoulder and stopped me before I could climb in.

"I think I'll sit this one out," he said.

I stared at him in confusion. "What?"

"The relic guardians really don't like me and I don't want to cause any more trouble," he said. "I want you to go on. I'll sit tight until you find the guardian."

I knew he was right, but I didn't want to leave him behind, even for a few hours.

He appeared to notice my hesitation and he smiled. "You'll be fine. I'll be fine. Go with Will and get this ring. In the meantime, I'll keep my eyes and ears alert in case anyone follows us. I've got your back."

I nodded and swallowed hard. There was a chance that Sammael had ordered someone to tail us, or that Sammael and Lilith themselves could be hunting us at this very moment. Before he died, Merodach had made it clear that Sammael had regained his strength and was ready to take my soul and take this war to the next level.

Will cleared his throat. "I agree with you. The relic guardians have been defensive and potentially hostile. Hopefully this will be the last we'll deal with. We'll rejoin you when we're ready to summon Azrael."

"Then I will see you both very soon," Cadan said. He spread his wings, silver feathers flashing gold in the lamp-light, and he leaped into the night.

Kasteel van Mesen was dark, crippled, and yet still imposing. It had been built for a royal family in the early seventeenth century, but a couple hundred years later, it became a factory and was then renovated into a boarding school for the daughters of elite Victorian families. A magnificent neo-gothic chapel had been built adjacent to it, but the fortress was eventually abandoned and left to decay. Though it had been overtaken by the elements and by wild vegetation, I'd seen few things that were more beautiful. The roof had collapsed over many wings, but the columns, arches, and inlay of brick and stone still held their shape. The fallen castle had a very forgotten-fairy-tale feel to it.

We explored the perimeter until we found an entrance clear enough to get through, as most of the doors and windows on the ground level were blocked by debris and thick vines. We crossed through a tall double door with one side barely clinging to its hinge and entered a once-grand hall. The ceiling had collapsed long ago, and now patches of green and small, young trees grew from the floor, peeking out between chunks of the roof and heavy wooden beams.

"It's too dangerous to cross through here," Will said. "Let's find another corridor."

I followed him back through the door and down another dark hall. This one was lined with large windows, their frames intricate and lovely, but the glass was mostly broken and sprinkled across the floor. Chunks of plaster in the walls had been torn away to reveal ancient brick beneath.

"You should not be here." A young English woman's voice echoed from somewhere down the black hallway and my heart lurched into my throat. The sound frightened unseen birds and they scattered in the debris and vegetation.

"Hello?" I called, searching the darkness for signs of movement. "Are you the relic guardian? We are here for the Pentalpha."

Silence. I squinted, but still I could see nothing. I looked at Will, whose right hand was open, ready to call his sword. And then a shadow moved within the shadows and neither of us could draw our swords before a cloaked figure lunged at us from the blackness, dark wings spreading as wide as they could, filling up the corridor. A hand appeared from beneath the cloak's sleeve and a palm slammed into Will's chest, smashing him into the wall. Dust and chips of paint exploded in the thick air as he hit with a thud and a grunt. Most of the reaper's face was hidden beneath the hood, but full lips and a feminine build under her cloak gave away that she was female. The reaper threw a fist at me, but I blocked her. She threw a flurry of additional strikes that I managed to deflect off the hard bones of my forearms. She was fast—and *strong*. Every time I tried to draw breath and tell her who I was, I had to concentrate on blocking another attack.

I was forced to back away from her assault, all the way until my heel found the edge of the staircase we'd just ascended. I gasped as my momentum dragged me off my feet. The reaper leaped into the air above me to strike me down hard, but I kicked a foot into her chest as I fell down the flight of stairs, launching her over my head. My hands grappled for the wrought iron railing and my body swung to a stop, crumpling against the hard steps. The reaper's wings beat once in the high ceiling of the stairwell, taking control of her flight as she faced me from above, and her feet touched the far wall. Her knees bent and her power erupted; the folds of her cloak billowed in the smoky flares of energy and clouds of dust and debris. Then she launched herself at me. I twisted, hoping to dodge her fists again and afraid that if I called my swords, the guardian would feel even more threatened.

Before I could meet the reaper's attack, Will appeared above me. He grabbed the guardian's throat and threw her over the railing with a roar. I jumped up only to watch her land on her feet and bound out of sight. Will hopped the rail to dart after her and I followed him. As we rounded the corner of the stairwell to dash into the dark corridor, the reaper's black cloak swung into the space between us from a room on our right.

"Will!" I called to his back.

He whirled just in time to meet her blow, blocking her fist before it connected with his head. Clearly this reaper preferred to ambush. I grabbed her shoulder and yanked her around to get her away from him, but she deflected my fist and managed to block everything Will and I threw at her together. She was precise, moving as if she anticipated our moves, and I could sense some uncanny familiarity in her style. I jumped out of reach and she focused her attention on Will.

The relic guardian stopped suddenly, and as Will swung a fist, she stepped aside. Her face was full of recognition, but she also appeared puzzled and disbelieving. Was she surprised that the Preliator and her Guardian would try to take what she protected? However, it didn't seem like both of us surprised her—only *Will*. He was all she could stare at, and instead of striking her again, Will slowed to a pause and gaped back at the other reaper.

She pulled the hood from over her head and at last I

could see how astonishingly beautiful she was. Long, wavy hair the color of dark walnut framed a lovely face with large, almond-shaped eyes as extraordinarily green as Will's.

"William?" the relic guardian asked. "Is that you?"

He stared at her, disbelieving, as though he thought she was a phantom. At last he spoke.

"Mother?"

22

I GAPED AT BOTH OF THEM, BACK AND FORTH between their faces, their identical eyes—even the way they carried themselves was the same. I replayed their movements in my head, how graceful and calculated they both were, and I had no doubt that this reaper was Will's mother, Madeleine.

She rushed into Will, cupping his face in her hands, touching his cheeks. He stared down at her and his body was stiff in her arms, still in a state of shock. I couldn't imagine what he felt as his mother, whom he believed had been dead for most of his life, embraced him.

Will was breathless, frozen by astonishment. "You're alive."

"Yes," she answered, and tears rolled over her cheeks. "Yes, my son. I'm alive."

"How is this possible?" he asked, his voice breaking.

"Where have you been? I thought you were dead."

Madeleine smiled, a gesture so like Will's that it threw me off for an instant. "I became a guardian of a most powerful relic."

He swallowed and gasped for air. "*You* have the Pentalpha?"

"For many years." She released him and peered around him at me. "Who are you? You're not a reaper—that much I can sense—but your strength is incredible. I don't know what you are."

"She is the Preliator," Will said.

Madeleine exhaled sharply and stared at me. "You . . ." She trailed off and turned her gaze back to Will. "That means you're . . ."

He gave a single nod, his expression hard. "For five hundred years, I have been her Guardian."

"You are *the* Guardian," she said, blinking in shock for a few moments before smiling at him. "I'm so very proud of you." Her green eyes returned to mine. "It is a boundless honor to stand in your presence, Preliator."

"I'm just Ellie," I said with a warm smile. "It's an honor to meet you too. Will has told me about you."

Madeleine reached into the collar of her shirt and pulled out a gold ring strung on a leather cord around her neck. Even in the low light, caught between her fingers, the ring seemed to glow. "You must want this."

There were no words for the relief and excitement that

made my blood sing when I saw the Pentalpha at last. I recognized it immediately, but couldn't remember forging it since I could recall nothing of my time in Heaven. But this ring . . . This was what we came here for. "Please," I said. "We need to summon an angel."

She lifted the ring, pulling the cord over her head and free of her hair, and held it for a moment, gazing at it. "I've had this for a long time. It will feel strange not to be its protector anymore."

"That should be an enormous weight off your shoulders," I said.

She eased toward me and placed the ring in my palm. I felt its power on contact, the jolt of electricity and heat searing right up my arm and into my chest so fast I gasped. I knew I would be able to summon an angel with this ring that had, until now, controlled demons alone. I knew that I was the only one who could wield absolute power over it, that it was a part of me and of my own angelic magic.

"I have heard," Madeleine said, "from the tongue of the one who is my eyes and ears to the outside world, that the Preliator is truly the archangel Gabriel in human form."

"It's true," Will confirmed. "We intend to summon Azrael so he can fight on our side against Sammael and Lilith."

"So the beast is unbound." Madeleine wore a thoughtful, intense look. "Please, come to my rooms. I'm sure you have questions for me, as I do for you."

Madeleine led us back up the stairwell we'd destroyed,

down a hallway bright with moonlight, and into a room that had a few candles lit. There was a small round table in the center of the room with a lit candle and a single chair pushed in against it. On the far wall, there was a narrow bed with a worn quilt folded neatly across it. A generator hummed gently beside a dresser topped with another candle and a radio that was turned off. A stove and sink sat on another wall, and I wondered if this room may have been a tiny private apartment during the period the fortress was used as a school. From the cabinet above the stove, Madeleine collected a teakettle and filled it with water. The stove crackled until a small flame lit and she placed the kettle over it.

"Why did you leave without saying good-bye?" Will asked suddenly, blurting it out like he'd been trying to hold the question in for a while.

Madeleine gestured for us to sit on the bed while she took the chair at the little table. The mattress springs groaned beneath us. "I couldn't let anyone know that I'd become the guardian of this relic," she said, her voice sad. "Even you. I loved you so much and it broke my heart to leave, but I couldn't refuse Michael. When the relic's previous guardian died, he chose me for a reason. He placed something important into the most capable hands he could find. You, of all people, would understand."

"You could've said something," Will said. "Anything. You didn't have to tell me why you had to leave, but at least told me you were leaving. I thought you were *dead*."

"I'm so sorry, sweetheart," she murmured. "I never meant to cause you pain. I only wanted to protect you in case our enemies learned that I was the Pentalpha guardian. I feared that, if you knew anything, they would harm you to get to me."

He shook his head. "They would try. It would get them nowhere."

She smiled. "You've always been strong, William, and here you are, the Guardian of the Preliator."

"You never knew?" he asked.

Madeleine seemed sad. "No. I've been in seclusion for a long time in order to protect this relic. I've trusted Evolet to keep me informed of what was happening in the world every few months. I assume she's the one who led you to me. Where is Nathaniel?"

"He's dead," Will replied. "It's been a few months now."

Madeleine closed her eyes for several long moments. "I would have liked to see him again. I owe him everything. This war has given and taken so much from us all."

"How much do you know?" I asked. "About the war."

"Very little," she confessed. "I did not know until tonight that Sammael and Lilith are in our world. I've heard whisperings that Bastian had been searching for Sammael's sarcophagus."

Will's jaw hardened at the mention of Bastian's name. I studied him, knowing he had a million questions for his mother, and I wouldn't speak until he had said what he needed to.

"Did you always know Bastian was my father?" Will asked at last.

Her gaze faltered, but I wasn't sure that his question surprised her. "Yes, but I didn't tell him."

"Did you love him?"

"Yes," she said faintly. "I did."

"Why?" he asked, barely able to keep the disbelief from his voice. "How?"

She held her chin up defensively, as if she felt no shame. "Some things that are supposed to be wrong don't feel that way. He showed me more than once that he wasn't heartless. I'd hoped he would turn his back on Hell for me, but the pull was too strong." There was a crack in her defenses, just a hairline fracture, but sorrow showed there.

Will did not miss Madeleine's weakness and his own expression hardened. "Would it grieve you to know that he is dead?"

She drew a deep breath, pausing before she spoke. "Would it anger you if I said yes?"

"No," Will said. "If you once loved him, then I expect you would."

"How did he die?" she asked, her voice quiet. "By your hand?"

"By another's."

She was silent for a few moments before rising to tend to the kettle. She brought us each a cup of tea and I let mine sit in my hands to cool off before taking a sip. I tried not to feel awkward sitting here, meeting Will's mother for the first time, but I couldn't help it. Perhaps if things weren't so tense between them, then this would have been easier to endure.

"How did you even . . . ?" Will seemed to struggle with an end to that question.

"Get involved with him?" She wore a small, sad smile. "I knew who he was long before I met him, though I was still young. He was notorious, hunted by many of the most powerful angelic reapers. The first time I saw him with my own eyes, I had pursued some bottom-feeder right into an ambush led by Bastian. I killed six, until the only one remaining was Bastian himself. I was exhausted and wounded and certain he would kill me, but he didn't. He let me live. After that I seemed to keep running into him. It took me a while to realize it was on purpose, and it took me longer to fall in love with him."

Will shook his head. "But he was a monster." His hand tightened into a fist and I covered it with my own to offer him comfort.

Madeleine's gaze didn't miss the gesture. "He wasn't always. He told me his grandmother was Antares. The angelic blood in his veins made him different, created a light in his soul. But after a while, he just stopped feeling and welcomed only his dominant demonic side. He once told me that forever is a long time to keep fighting. I hadn't realized until it was too late that he meant fighting himself. I wish I knew how to explain to you what that goodness inside him was like and how he revealed it to me."

Will sat in silence beside me, his expression hard and contemplating. He was trying to understand what Madeleine explained about his father, but I didn't need any help. This was how I felt about Cadan, who fought with tooth and nail against what his father became and what he was also destined to become. From the first moment I met Cadan, I felt the light in him that Madeleine felt in Bastian, but that light had saved him from the darkness his father had been consumed by.

"It was hard for him," Madeleine said gently, "as I know it has been for you, William. But you're stronger than he was. Your heart is too pure for the demonic blood in you to take hold."

His green eyes met her identical gaze. "How do you know it won't? There's darkness in me and I feel it every day."

I squeezed his hand tighter. "You're not your father. You've proven that to me every day for five centuries."

Madeleine studied our faces and our clasped hands, but she wore the same ironclad, unreadable expression that Will wore when he was thinking.

Will exhaled and his gaze grew distant. "I have eternity to live, but not enough time to learn who I really am. Not until this fight is over. We have the Pentalpha and that's all that matters right now." He'd shut us out again, as I feared he would. He'd face Hell itself before taking on his own emotions, because the truth was a far more terrifying enemy and one that he couldn't control. He stood, his jaw set hard and shoulders tied into tense knots.

I stood with him. "Madeleine, will you help us?"

"Of course," she said. "I am no longer a relic guardian. My sword and life are at your disposal."

I was certain Will would be happy to have his mother by his side and that she would be an invaluable ally. I also wanted to know her. It was like meeting a legend, someone you'd heard about and wondered what it would be like to come face to face with. And her eyes . . . they were Will's eyes.

"We'll return tomorrow," I told Madeleine. "I need to figure out how I will use the Pentalpha to summon Azrael. We have a demonic reaper with us, so we have to take the sun into consideration. We'll likely arrive in the afternoon when the sun isn't so high."

Her brow made an almost imperceptible movement. "Demonic?"

Will spoke before I had a chance. "Another son of Bastian."

"Ah. I understand." She didn't seem surprised by the news that Bastian had sired another. At least Madeleine wouldn't be as hostile toward Cadan as the other angelic reapers we'd encountered, given her history with Bastian.

We said good-bye to Madeleine and headed to the car. As we navigated the abandoned castle, the cell phone in my pocket buzzed and I realized I'd completely forgotten to call Ava. I pulled it out and answered. "Sorry," I said guiltily.

"Where have you been?" she asked. She didn't seem angry, which made me feel a little better about not calling.

"We got sidetracked," I confessed. "But we have awesome news. I'm holding the Ring of Solomon right now."

I heard Ava exhale with relief and relay the news to Marcus. "That's fantastic," she said to me.

"How about we find someplace to get some rest?" I suggested.

"Perfect," she replied. "I'm not sure about you three, but Marcus and I are exhausted."

"Cadan split from us a few hours ago, so I'll touch base with him in a sec. While we head back into town, do you want to find a hotel to crash at?"

"Collect Cadan and I'll call you again when we've got rooms somewhere."

After Ava booked us a few rooms at the Best Western in Aalst, she texted me the address, which I plugged into the GPS. Cadan was closer to the destination than we were, so he met us there. Will and I had our own room, which I was glad for. He was troubled after the reunion with his mother and I worried that he was angry with her. I thought seeing Madeleine again would have thrilled him, despite the shock. Will had accepted her loss and mourned her long ago, and after losing my own mother so recently, I could imagine what old wounds of his had reopened upon seeing her face.

Will took a shower to remove the dust and grime caking his skin from climbing through the crumbling castle, but when he hadn't left the bathroom after some time, I started worrying about him. The door was cracked, so I knocked once and tapped it the rest of the way open. He stood over the sink, leaning heavily on his hands on the edge of the counter. His face was soaked as if he'd splashed it with water over and over. I touched his arm and kissed his shoulder, looking up into his face.

"Want to talk?" I asked him as I rubbed his back soothingly.

He took a deep, quivering breath. His pain was so naked on his face, etching scars into his skin that weren't traced by the edge of a blade. "For my entire life, I thought the reason she never came home that night was because she was dead. But she just *left*. And she didn't say good-bye."

"How old were you when she left?" I asked, and leaned on the bathroom counter beside him. I played with the Pentalpha with my thumb and forefinger. I'd looped the leather cord around my neck to keep it safe, as Madeleine had, and it hung just a little lower than my winged necklace.

He didn't answer right away, his gaze unfocused. "Fifteen."

I felt my heart break for him, a painful crack right down the middle. I had always been sure that he'd been young, even for a reaper, when his mother vanished, but I never anticipated how young he'd been even for a human.

"I wanted revenge for my mother's death and I'd only received basic training from her," he continued. "I went look-ing for trouble and would've gotten myself killed if Nathaniel hadn't found me. He and my mother had been friends, and then Nathaniel was all I had for a long time. Until you came into my life, anyway."

He looked back at me and I offered him a small smile. "And now you have your mother again."

"I can't tell you how happy I am that she's alive," he said, "but I feel so betrayed."

"I know," I said softly. "She isn't perfect. That's a hard truth to accept when it comes to parents. We idolize them and that isn't fair to them, or us."

He became quiet, but I understood how he was feeling. His entire life was spent believing his mother was this unfailing warrior, and now the image he'd woven of her in his mind had begun to unravel. He didn't want to accept that she was as flawed as the rest of us.

"When you're able to forgive her," I offered, "then you two can reconnect. She seems like an amazing person."

He leaned over me and rested his forehead against mine. "When did you start being so reasonable?"

I grinned. "One of us has to be. Usually it's you, but I appreciate you letting me have a go at it. Maybe I'm just tired and less argumentative."

It was his turn to grin, but there was a devilishness to his. "Well, then. I'll just have to keep you worn out so you don't bicker with me so much."

"Oh *jeez*—" was all I could say before he kissed me.

23

MY MOM PLOPPED DOWN ON THE COUCH BESIDE ME and grabbed a handful of popcorn before passing the bowl to me. I shook it up and frowned. She watched me and rolled her eyes.

"I'm glad you remembered a little popcorn with your salt," I grumbled and picked through the bowl, glad I didn't have a paper cut. It'd be like dunking my hand into acid.

"I like salt!" she said with a laugh. "Sue me."

"Why aren't you on a heart attack prevention regimen?" I asked. "Dad, help me out here."

He sat in his favorite chair on the other side of the end table and peeked his eyes over the top of the newspaper he was reading. Besides the TV, the only light in the room was the lamp switched on between us. "She has a point, Diane. How can you even eat that? Salt crunching between your teeth. . . . It's disgusting."

Mom threw her hands up in defeat. "All right! Fine. Make your own bowl. This one's mine. Keep your grubby hands out of it."

I looked back to my dad. "You're both terrible at watching scary movies. Dad, seriously. Put the paper down and turn off the lamp. You can't get scared with the lights on."

"Who says we want to get scared?" he asked, giving me a serious look.

"Why else would you want to watch a scary movie? Not for the gore, I hope." I grimaced. "Then I'd really worry about you."

He laughed. "No need to worry. You know how weak my stomach is."

Out of the corner of my eye, I caught a shadow passing by the window outside. I squinted curiously and stood, watching to see if the shadow appeared in the next window. In a few seconds, it did.

"I'll be right back," I said distantly and moved toward the front door. I turned the knob and pushed open the heavy door, peering into darkness. Crickets chirped and I heard tires on the road a few houses down. Across the large, wooded lawn, my closest neighbor's house was lit up.

Other than the usual, there was nothing outside.

Certain I'd just imagined what I'd seen, I went back inside and closed the door behind me. My breath caught in my throat when I saw the winged man standing in the living room between my parents.

I cried out, but my parents didn't seem to notice him or me. I ran to them, darting around a column that broke my line of sight. When I passed the column, I saw that the man had vanished. I slid to a stop and whirled around, searching for him. That's when he reappeared, standing only a few feet from me in the kitchen. I gasped and jumped back into the counter bar, nearly knocking over a stool. I caught my balance with a hand on the counter and stared at the man. He said nothing, but only watched me in return, and after a moment, I remembered his face.

He looked different—handsome, youthful, with bright, gleaming golden eyes beneath soft, silver hair. There were no horns or armor or bones that looked like children's bones. His wings weren't quite white, but more like the color of sunlight on snow, so unlike the charred and broken stalks I'd seen sprouting from his back last time we met. He appeared as he had when he was still an angel of the Lord.

"Sammael?" I asked, breathless.

He smiled, showing no teeth, only a widening split in his face that held no sincerity or emotion behind the expression. Soulless. "You remember me."

"But you fell." I shook my head, confused. "Am I dreaming?"

"Yes," he replied. "And yes."

Things began to add up. I glanced into the living room, where my parents had just been sitting, but they were gone.

Of course they'd be gone now that I knew I was dreaming. My parents were dead. This night was not real. It wasn't even a memory. Strangely though, I could still smell the popcorn.

"You've come into my dream," I said, and looked back at Sammael. "Why do you look like this?"

He stepped forward, his gait unnaturally smooth and effortless. The cloak he wore flowed at the ankles of his lightweight boots. Beneath the cloak was a high-collared soldier's jacket lined with gold fastenings and small jewels awarded to him for merit in battle. "My form in the physical world frightens you," he replied. "I thought it would be wise to appear to you as you knew me before Azrael cast me out, because I do not wish to frighten you tonight. I wish to talk."

"Why? You're only going to try to destroy me and send your thugs to kill more of the people I love. I have nothing to say to you except that I will destroy you first."

His face did not change, but his liquid gold eyes flickered. "Why bother to fight the inevitable? I know what you're doing. Collecting your trinkets and magic spells. You have the Pentalpha ring, this my spies have warned me of, but do not make the mistake of believing that since you possess it, I cannot take it. I will find you, Gabriel."

"You'll be too late."

"You're wrong in believing that you can defeat me once you ascend," he said. "But at least you admit that your human body is a weakness."

"It's not a weakness," I shot back, gritting my teeth. I

wanted to lunge for him, but it would be pointless to attack him in a dream. "This body just needs more power. I can't beat you as just a human girl or just an archangel, but combined? I will make deli slices out of you. You're afraid of the power my human soul will add to my unbound archangel strength. You know that's true, otherwise you wouldn't be here trying to scare me into giving up. I *won't* give up. That's something you should know too. Whatever you're here to do, tempt me to the dark side, or whatever—it won't work."

He grew closer to me, leaning over me, and his nose brushed my neck, inhaling slowly. "I'm not here to seduce you with flesh," he said, his breath hot against my skin. "I can offer you what you want, the very thing your existence depends on: *power*."

"Everything I have in me and everything I will gain I will use to destroy you."

He drew the backs of his fingers along the line of my jaw, but the feather-soft touch only felt like the brushing of flies' wings against my skin. I shivered in disgust. "You won't want to," he crooned into my ear. "Not after you've had a taste of what I can offer you."

"You're right," I chirped. "I'll probably barf. I'm getting indigestion just thinking about it."

Sammael's face hardened and his golden eyes blazed with fire. "Do you think this is a game, Gabriel?"

I glared at him, grinding my teeth together. "I absolutely do not."

He seemed to soften then, but it was false and momentary, like dirt turned to mud in the rain. "I can smell your soul. I can smell it like infection in a wound. When I take it, you will be purified."

"That's not how it works," I said, unwilling to move and to show my fear of him. "My soul has given me a sense of self, made me unique from everyone else. Don't pretend that isn't what you've always wanted."

He circled me, laughing. "A *soul*, Gabriel?"

"An identity," I corrected. "That's why you turned your back on Heaven. That's why all of the Fallen did. You were tired of being a mindless drone, a soldier who performed his duties and was never allowed to dream. You want your existence to mean something even now. Being human has given me a chance to really live instead of just survive. It's not enough just to exist."

He became quiet, his gaze studying me from head to toe. "Are you admitting your sympathies for the Fallen?"

"Yes," I said. "In a way. But you turned your longing into hatred, and instead of freedom, you only found bloodshed and misery and imprisonment in Hell. That's all you'll ever have. I feel sorry for you."

He lifted a hand and his long, slender fingers cupped my chin, lifting my face to his. "Do you honestly believe that you've found freedom on Earth, that being trapped in this limited mortal body makes you human?"

"Not just freedom," I said. "I have a chance to live here.

Freedom isn't just about getting to make your own choices. It's about getting to enjoy the life you're given, to live life to the fullest. That's the beauty of mortality, of what makes someone human. Time is treasured. The eternal . . . all they have is time."

"What's beautiful about mortality?" he asked. "You, Gabriel, a mighty archangel, stripped of your true power. A lesser thing. You live, you die, you live, you die. An endless cycle of violence and pain and suffering. There is nothing ultimate about your death, which is mortality at its intrinsic sense. Human souls go to Heaven or to Hell, but your soul—this shriveled thing you cling to so desperately—is shoved right back into your body and you're forced to do it all over again. You think that you're free? You're a slave to this mortal shell."

I swallowed hard and gritted my teeth. "At least I'm not hollow like you are."

Sammael stood straight, staring down at me calmly as though he were unaffected. As I considered the shadow of truth in his words, I broke. Just a small crack, but it was enough to let a tear roll down my cheek and pool into the corner of my mouth.

"Why do you hate them so much?" I asked in a tiny voice, my lips trembling.

"They disgust me," he replied, revulsion rolling on his tongue. "Earthly, living creatures with their feeding, bleeding, lusting. Pure beings like you—your angelic form, that is—and I, we require nothing like the breath and blood these impuissant life-forms depend on. I don't know how you can tolerate that decaying cage of a body. From the moment you are born, you are already dying. Can't you smell the rot?"

I shook my head, confused. "You hate them because they are alive?"

"Life-forms are impure," he said. "We angels are older than life itself, the first beings made from nothingness and given absolute power. We have no limits. But here you are consorting with these hybrid mongrel *reapers*. I can smell *him* on you. I can't articulate how disappointed I am in you. Come back to us, Sister. You can still reclaim your grace and I won't kill you. Heaven will fall and Lucifer will rise. Michael, Rafael, all of our brothers and sisters will die, but it is necessary for the purification. They are too loyal to God and his human creations to be swayed. Gabriel, my sister, help me cleanse the universe of the poisoning life and restore the dominion of angels."

I shook my head again. "No. I can't be swayed either. I have grown to love these humans and all life on Earth. If you would put your hatred aside for just a moment, spend any time at all among them, you'll see how incredible life is. There aren't enough words in any language—human or angelic—to describe how amazing the feel of sunlight is on your skin, or how soft is the velvet of flower petals, or what it's like to jump into a river. You hate too much to ever know what it's really like on Earth, what it's like to love and to feel love and to be happy. That's why I feel sorry for you."

"None of that should ever have been—"

"But it *is*!" I cried. "Sammael, you've been asleep for eons. Life has *thrived* and become something truly great. I love being human. Why can't you try to understand that?"

Flames raged in those golden eyes. "You can't be saved."

"No, Sammael," I said, shaking my head. "It's you who can't be saved."

He huffed—not quite a laugh—and grimaced. "Azrael can't fight for you. In the end, it'll be you and me."

"I'm counting on it."

He smiled, a hideous thing, like pulling apart a spider's web, and the world started to fade. I was glad to see him go and to return to the waking world.

The hotel room was dark, but the window boasted a halo of daylight threatening to shine through the dark shade. We'd gone to bed at dawn and now it was nearly noon. Will still slumbered next to me, breathing softly. I reached over to the nightstand and touched my winged necklace. It felt warm to the touch as always. I relaxed as I felt grounded to the real world instead of the nightmare-hijacking I'd gotten from the Lord of Souls.

As soon as I thought about him, the memory of something Sammael had said jolted me fully awake: *"You can still reclaim your grace. . . ."*

My grace.

I looked at the winged pendant and pulled it into my palm. "Oh my God," I murmured, turning the pendant over in my hand, examining it.

Will stirred, rustling the sheets. "Are you up?" he asked groggily. He hadn't even opened his eyes yet.

"My grace!"

He peeked one confused eye open at me. "What?"

"It was never gone," I said as the excitement of the revelation welled up in me. "The night Sammael was awakened, he said that he couldn't sense my grace. Kelaeno had broken my necklace and it fell—that's why he couldn't sense my grace. I've always had this pendant and it has always felt warm only to me. I feel lost, and like a piece of me is missing, when I'm not wearing this. That's because a piece of me *is* missing when I'm not wearing it. The necklace—Will, my angelic grace is inside it."

24

WITH THE PENTALPHA IN MY POSSESSION AND THE
iron certainty that my grace had never left me, I felt fueled to
get up and move. If I was able to somehow tap into the power
contained within my necklace, I might even be able perhaps
to uncover a new strength, or one that had been long lost to
me.

I dived into the shower before Will so I could tame my
hair and get ready, since he always seemed to take only five
minutes before he was suited up to walk out the door. Boys
were freaks, really.

Speaking of freaks . . . I grabbed my phone to text Cadan
and see if he was up.

R u ration yet?

It was at least a minute before he texted back. **What language is that?**

R U AWAKE

Much to my extreme dismay. The sun is no friend to my fragile complexion.

I rolled my eyes, entirely unsympathetic. **Poor baby. Come to my room asap.**

It's too early to proposition me, Ellie.

GET OVER HERE.

So frisky. Give me a minute to get some clothes on. Or should I not . . . ?

I let out a grumble and didn't reply to that. Boys were *freaks*. Next I gave Ava a call since she had never caught on to the texting thing. She wasn't quite as gung-ho about the twenty-first century as Cadan was. At least she had a phone at all. She and Marcus were already up and about, so they headed to our room right away. They arrived just as Will emerged from the bathroom, showered and dressed in fresh clothes.

"Have you figured out how to work the ring?" Marcus asked. He examined the relic between his fingers before letting it fall back against my skin.

"I don't think I need to do anything," I replied. "It's my own relic and it should obey me. I can make it do whatever I want."

"Well, it's great that you're feeling confident," Marcus said. "Let's hope that you're right."

Will stepped forward and crossed his arms. His game face was already on. "We should summon Azrael at the castle. We don't need an angel showing up where humans may see him. Our world has been exposed enough already. So, let's get a good meal first, get some energy, and head out."

Madeleine was waiting for us just beyond the threshold of Kasteel van Mesen. The reapers and I entered, but her gaze was glued only to Cadan's face. He, in return, was just as shocked.

"*You*," she exhaled. "They told me that they had a demonic reaper with them, but . . . you?"

"Whoa, wait," I interrupted. "You two know each other?"

Cadan opened his mouth to speak, but nothing would come out. At last he was able to tear his eyes away from Madeleine to then gape at Will. When Cadan looked back at Madeleine, he struggled to get the words past his lips. "You were pregnant?"

There was a lightning crack of anger in her toxic green eyes. "It was you, wasn't it?" she asked him between clenched teeth. "You killed him. Part of me always knew you would."

Cadan's silence said more than words could. Cadan had done what he had to do, and if he hadn't killed Bastian, then Will or I would've done it. I tried to read the expression on Will's face, but he was a wall of ice beside me.

"Yes, Ellie," he said finally, but didn't look at me. "Madeleine and I know each other. I should have known that she was Will's mother. Bastian didn't exactly make a habit of courting angelic reapers. Mostly he just killed them."

"What about you?" she countered. "Keeping the angelic for company instead of wading through their body parts? How you've changed."

He glared at her. "Yes, I *have* changed—something my father could never do. We've all done some pretty messed-up things. Not even you can deny that."

Without another word, she spun on her heel and stomped through the grass toward the dark hallway. I drew in a breath and took a step to follow her, but Will caught my arm. I looked up at him and he shook his head once. Ava and Marcus stood in silence behind Will, their faces grave.

"Why didn't you tell him that you were with child?" Cadan called to her back. "He never knew. Not until recently."

Madeleine stopped and, after a moment, she turned around. "Because I saw the way he treated you," she confessed. "And I didn't want that for my son. There was some goodness in your father, but he spared none of it for you."

Cadan flinched, as if the words stung like an open cut. "He stopped feeling anything at all after you left. If there had been any goodness in him, it had gone with you."

Madeleine looked over at Will before returning her gaze to Cadan's. "I never meant to hurt anyone, but I did what I had to do. You must understand why I left him."

He gave a miserable smile. "Better than anyone."

"I warned him that I would go," she said. "He did things that were unforgivable. When I realized that I would bear a son by a demonic sire, I had to get out and away from Bastian and the others. I loved Bastian, but he was dangerous. If he knew I was with child, then he would have tried to take William from me. You knew he wanted me to join his cause, and you know he would have raised my son to follow in his footsteps the way he raised you. Yes, Cadan, I've done things I'm not proud of, but hiding William from Bastian isn't among them."

Cadan exhaled, deflating a little. "I wouldn't wish what I lived through on anyone."

"Look," Madeleine said. "This is neither the time nor the place to settle old conflicts—*very* old conflicts. Ellie needs to summon Azrael. She's come a long way and we're running out of time."

"Yes," he said. "Right now, we've got more important things to take care of."

I touched his arm and offered him a supportive smile. "Thank you. Madeleine, we appreciate this."

"Let's go," she said to all of us now. "I can take you to a part of the castle that's big enough for the angel to come through. A lot of energy will be required to bring him to our world."

Madeleine led us to the great hall whose ceiling had caved in long ago. The stars in the night sky glittered so clearly, and the moon was heavy, low, and gigantic.

I drew the leather cord from over my head and closed my fist around the Pentalpha, feeling the power of the relic flow through my veins as if it were an extension of me. "I am the Messenger, Gabriel, she who is set over all the powers," I called out to the empty space above. "I evoke thee, Azrael, the Destroyer, lord of the shepherds of the dead."

It took a single instant for the ring to light on fire around my finger. The white flames licked over my fist but they didn't burn me. My heart slammed against my rib cage and the power erupted from the relic clenched around my lungs as it coursed through me, making me gasp for oxygen. The space seemed to shimmer and wave like air boiling over hot pavement, and something invisible tore a hole through the air, allowing for a single beam of light to blaze through. The light grew, forcing itself through the opening in the sky, and became so blindingly bright that I couldn't look right at it. I squeezed my eyes shut against it, turning my face away. When the light dimmed and I could see once more, a figure had come through the seam in space and his wings spread wide and shining as his boots settled to the ground. His dark skin and silver armor gleamed in the moonlight, corporeal and wholly in our world. He held out his hand and examined his open palm.

"It has . . . ," he said softly to no one in particular, "been a long time. The air feels cool on my skin. I can smell the trees."

I wondered if the last time he'd been corporeal on Earth was the day he cast Sammael out of Heaven. "Azrael," I called to him. "We need your help."

His gaze traveled across the faces of the reapers at my

flanks. "I am at your service, Sister."

"We need an angel to fight with us," I explained. "What we are isn't enough. You've beaten Sammael twice before. We need you."

"When Sammael joined Lucifer and the other Fallen, he kept his archangel strength," Azrael replied without missing a beat. "He is now more powerful than any angel below that rank. I would last only moments if I stood against him."

I stared at him in shock. "You won't fight?"

"I cannot."

"You won't even try?"

"Ellie," Will said next to me in his soothing voice. "Just because he can't fight doesn't mean he won't help."

"I may be outcast and weakened," Azrael said, wearing a gentle smile at Will, "but I never stopped serving. Michael chose well, Guardian. Faithful found among the faithless, faithful only he."

Will watched the angel as his words sunk in. "How can you help us?"

Azrael held out a hand and a staff shimmered into being out of a flash of light and energy, much like the way our own weapons appeared when we called them. The staff was longer than Azrael was tall, and at the head of the staff was a triple-bladed weapon reminding me somewhat of a trident, but the two outer blades were crescent-shaped and double-edged like a partisan. The weapon was vicious, but elegant in its design.

"The hallowed glaive," I murmured, recognizing it immediately. This was the weapon Cadan said Bastian had feared. This was the weapon I would use to kill Sammael and Lilith.

"Correct," Azrael said. "I will give you the weapon that banished Sammael from Heaven. However, you will not be able to wield the hallowed glaive in your human body. You must ascend to your archangel form in order to even touch the glaive."

I tried not to look at Will, whose eyes were glued to me and keenly felt. I wasn't ready to face the possibly of becoming the being again who was now a stranger to me, and to face what being an archangel meant. "But my angelfire doesn't work with any weapon other than my Khopesh swords."

"When you are an archangel, you will have no limits to your power. Any blade you conjure to vanquish the demonic will accept your angelfire. But you must wait to use the hallowed glaive until the moment you need it to conserve your archangel power. You must ascend, summon me at Armageddon, and I will give you the hallowed glaive. The armies of the Beast will await you there, and you will sing a requiem for a war."

"*At* Armageddon?" I asked, confused at first, but then I remembered. Armageddon isn't an event like people seem to think these days, it's a *location*. "You mean, the site of the End of Days is Armageddon, which is the same place as Har Megiddo near Jerusalem."

When I looked over at Will, I could tell he was thinking the same thing. "It's the hill of Megiddo in Hebrew," he said, his face lighting up. "Armageddon is the Greek name for this hill, not an event synonymous with the End of Days. It's the site *of* the End of Days."

"Correct," Azrael said. "It has been long foretold that the final battle will begin on the hill of Armageddon. Sammael and his legion will meet you there, Gabriel."

"Is there no other way for Ellie to use this weapon?" Will asked.

Azrael's gaze was sympathetic. "She must be an archangel to use the hallowed glaive and it is the only weapon strong enough to destroy the Fallen."

I tried not to let my sadness show as I understood what I must do, despite my fear of what would happen to me. "Then how do I ascend?"

"There is a spell that you and I wrote together when you were ordered to come to Earth in human form. I see you still have your necklace. You will need your grace. Along with the spell, you will need the fail-safe, which has been kept hidden in the event that one day you would need to shed your mortal bonds and become an archangel to fight on Earth."

"I have no memory of Heaven. Do you know the spell? What is this fail-safe?"

He stepped toward me, his movements fluid and inhuman, and he pressed his hand to my forehead. I gasped; the ancient words rushed into my mind in a thousand different languages. Images flashed of great humanoid beasts, the Nephilim, carving a path of destruction through civilizations long turned to dust, and of winged warriors painting the soil with the blood of those giants. I witnessed Azrael's memories through his eyes. I saw myself standing on a hill wearing armor made of a strange metal I didn't recognize. It looked as if it was made of mother-of-pearl, much like my winged necklace, and was splashed with blood, as were my Khopesh swords. My hair blazed like fire. At the bottom of the hill were the bodies of Nephilim, massacred. Azrael's memories whispered into my head, *"We were sent to eradicate the abominations."* The Nephilim were the offspring of the Grigori and human beings, but they couldn't be controlled or used like the reapers, who were bred from among the Grigori—the Fallen and Watcher alike. The flood that the world believed God had sent to destroy the Nephilim was not made of water; it was a flood of countless legions of angels, steel, and blood. Led by me. And then I was sent alone to destroy the demonic reapers. I was nothing more than an exterminator.

The angel of death drew his hand back and I stared up at him, feeling a tear run down my cheek. "We killed them all."

"No," he corrected. "You kept one of them."

I shook my head in confusion. "Kept . . . ?"

"For his heart."

Nausea wormed through my gut. "The fail-safe. The last

Naphil is alive, saved like a lamb for slaughter." I was so disgusted with myself, at what kind of monster I had once been—and the monster I would become again.

Azrael put a hand on my shoulder. "We do what we must to protect this world."

"Like murder?" I spit, anger boiling beneath my skin.

"Sacrifice," he said. "The Nephilim tore Earth apart and nearly wiped out the human race. We did what we were ordered to do, and we weren't supposed to feel shame. But you and I did."

When I closed my eyes, I sank into Azrael's memory again. I stood on the hill, my armor and white wings splashed with blood. My face flashed closer, soundless images clicking in sequence like an old silent movie, and I saw that my cheeks were stained with tears. My archangel self surveyed the battlefield littered with bodies of angel and Naphil alike, and I wept.

"God never again sent us in force," Azrael continued. "The damage was too great. Ever since, it has been your task alone to destroy the demonic reapers. Though I feel the war with the Nephilim may need to repeat itself against the beasts of Hell."

I reopened my eyes with a new determination. "Where is the last Naphil?"

"I'm sorry, Sister," he replied regretfully. "But I do not know. Only you do."

That determination threatened to flicker out like a candle

flame. "Yet another impossible thing to find. Thankfully, I've done several impossible things in the last few weeks."

"I must warn you, Gabriel," Azrael said, "that if you ascend, your unbound strength will be too unstable in this world. If you summon the power required to use the hallowed glaive, it will destroy your earthly form."

"You're certain?" Will demanded.

Azrael nodded. "There is no way her body could survive channeling all the power needed to destroy the Fallen. She will use the hallowed glaive and she will die."

Everything that Michael had said about my archangel power destroying my body once I ascended came crashing down on me. I'd held on to the hope that maybe I wouldn't have to ascend and if I did, that the angels would be wrong. That I could make it out of this and still destroy my enemies without destroying myself to do it. But now I understood that I had to die one last time to end this war.

"Then we won't do it," Will said with a hard finality in his tone. "We'll defeat Sammael without Ellie ascending and using the glaive."

"Will," I said, feeling a strange but settled peacefulness in me. I felt cloudy and lightheaded, detached. "It's okay. I've prepared myself to be ready for anything. I'm okay with this."

"But I'm not," he told me. "Remember what Michael said: if you die an angel, then you might not come back."

"So many lives will be saved if I do this," I said. "It's the only way I can destroy Sammael and Lilith and—"

"No," he said firmly, and his sword hand clenched. When he spoke again, his voice was tender. "No."

For a moment, it felt like there was only him and me in the room. Everyone else had melted away. Will's eyes fluttered shut, tightening with regret before he forced himself to meet my gaze again. He reached for me, his skin warm as his hands brushed my cheeks, and he sucked in his lip and shook his head very slightly.

"No," he said again.

"We'll be all right," I told him.

"There's always another way."

"This time there isn't," I said.

His eyes zipped back and forth between mine, his mouth open in shock. "How are you so calm?"

"I believe I always knew it would come to this."

"You aren't meant to die," he said. "You always come back. You can't be gone forever."

My heart was breaking, not for me, but for him. "I'm sorry that I have to do this."

"Ellie." He whispered my name, making me lose any determination I had to stand against him. "This is why I wasn't supposed to love you. Because I won't let you do what you have to. It's easy to do my duty when I have nothing to lose, but now I have everything to lose. I'll lose you."

I had a million things to say to him, but the words wouldn't string themselves together in my head enough to form anything coherent. All I knew and understood was that I had to stay strong. Sometimes, after people had accepted that they would die, they became self-destructive, as if it didn't matter if they wasted what time they had left. That wouldn't be me. If I would die, then I would make it count.

After an agonizing eternity, Will touched my hair in that familiar way of his, holding the lock in his fingers. "I don't have it in me to let you go."

I bit my lip to keep it from trembling as I watched the agony slowly dull the inimitable green of his eyes. "We must do whatever it takes to protect Earth and Heaven. It's okay."

He said nothing, only shook his head again.

"Gabriel," Azrael called. "What will it be?"

I looked up at the angel and swallowed my fear. "I'll do it."

25

AFTER AZRAEL'S DEPARTURE, EVERYONE GATH-
ered to discuss our next move and where the last Naphil
might be hidden. Everyone except for Will and me. Will was
thinking, calculating. Already he was resolute in figuring
out how to beat the Fallen in a way that didn't involve me ripping out hearts and growing wings. Azrael's news was hard
for both of us and I couldn't stand Will's silence.

I slipped away without telling anyone and retreated to
Madeleine's quarters, but it wasn't long before Cadan found
me. I welcomed his presence when he sat beside me, put an
arm around my shoulders, and let me lean into him.

"We don't have to talk about it," he said, his voice low
and soft. "I just thought you needed some company."

I took a long, deep breath and let it out slowly, but the

tension wouldn't leave me. "I'm not really sure what I need right now."

"Everything will be okay," he promised. "Things happen the way they're supposed to happen. If you become an archangel again, then you were always meant to. For what it's worth, I think you'll be a pretty badass angel."

"You don't know what they're—what *we're*—like," I said. "Azrael, Michael, me—Gabriel, that is—we're made of ice. We can't feel anything. I don't want to be like that."

He paused for a thoughtful moment. "I know you and you won't stop feeling. You have a soul. Probably the best one I've ever known."

I couldn't help but smile at him. "You're always so positive."

"I know you're scared," Cadan said. "And I know you're sad. It's okay to be both."

He and Will were half brothers, but they were so different. Cadan had somehow become this pillar of strength and support for me, the way Will was, but he always knew the right thing to say. The way Will expressed his feelings and dealt with things that troubled him was so much more physical. He was more quiet, but when he did open up to me, it was beautiful. Cadan had this uncanny intuition that made him an incredible friend.

"He's going to close himself up now," I said, remembering how Will had mourned Nathaniel in his own way. I didn't want him to mourn me already.

Cadan seemed to understand who I meant. "If he does,

it's not because he doesn't care."

"I know." I sighed.

"He won't give up searching for a way around your ascension," he continued thoughtfully. "He reminds me a little of Bastian in that way. They both have this relentless determination and are very thorough in everything they do."

He was right, I realized, but I'd never say that to Will. It would only make things a thousand times worse. Will would likely never fully accept that Bastian was his father, and he would certainly never take well to being compared to Bastian. Will was good and sweet and kind, but I'd seen his temper. His relentless determination also included kicking ass. And when Will kicked ass, he was very thorough. He kicked every last inch of it.

"I didn't mean that in a bad way," Cadan said, interrupting my thoughts. "I'm sorry if I upset you."

"No, I'm not upset," I told him. "I was just thinking what a terrible idea it would be to tell Will what you just told me."

"I have no plans to repeat that to him. Ever. And if you tell him what I said, before he kills me I'll tell everyone how you snore."

"I don't snore!" I laughed. "Will would know if I snored."

The air immediately grew thick with tension. I knew how Cadan felt about me, and what I just said was like rubbing Will and me right in his face. Why did I never stop to think before I opened my huge mouth? Cadan had sacrificed so much to help me and it had to be unbearably challenging for him to be around us all the time.

"He's too polite to say anything," Cadan said to break the awkwardness between us, but his voice was small and fragile.

I went along with it, trying to sound as if nothing had just happened. "My friend Kate isn't, though, and after the million slumber parties we've had, she definitely would've told me—*and* kicked me awake to shut me up."

"I'd have done the same," he said with a grin.

I narrowed my gaze playfully at him. "So you're admitting that you just lied. Slander's illegal, you know."

He scoffed and messed up my hair with his hand. "I'm a reaper. I live above the law. Human law, anyway."

The door opened and Madeleine appeared, her green eyes fixed with interest on Cadan and me. Cadan took his arm back from around my shoulder slowly, almost cautiously. "I don't mean to interrupt," she said in a low, slow tone.

"I hope you don't mind that I came up here." As awkward as I felt, she still scared the hell out of me. This was Will's *mother*. I wasn't sure if I'd ever get used to it.

"Of course not, Ellie," Madeleine said. "Everyone needs to retreat sometimes."

Cadan stood and the space next to me felt cold suddenly. "I'd better get back and make myself useful." He gave me a reassuring look, but mine in return was pleading and desperate for him to stay. His mouth tightened apologetically. It was clear he was just as scared of Madeleine as I was, but for different reasons.

As he left the room, Madeleine sat down next to me. Being alone with Will's mother before I really knew anything about her was really quite terrifying. I'd always considered myself a sociable, chatty person, but that all flew out the window with Madeleine, who was obviously one of the biggest badasses on the planet. For five hundred years, she'd been the guardian of the relic I'd made to be so powerful it could summon any demon. I'd seen only a glimpse of her prowess in battle, but it was enough to know I'd want to have her on my side in any fight.

This was *Will's mother*. Those two words kept spinning over and over in my head. She was impossibly beautiful. Her green-fire eyes and sweeping dark hair were the same as Will's, and she was also nearly as tall as he was. Though her body was lithe, she had strength and a groundedness in her curves that showed how unbreakable she was.

"I have a glaive-like weapon," she said, her lilting English accent breaking the harsh silence between us, "if you would like to train with one before you accept Azrael's blade."

"That would be excellent," I replied with a small smile. "Thank you."

"I could help you learn to use it."

I nodded. "I'm so used to using two small swords that this will be a big change. I can manage if I have help."

"Of course," Madeleine said. "And I apologize if I chased Cadan away. He left in quite a hurry."

I offered her a sympathetic look. "If you're worried that he's avoiding you, I think that he's still in a bit of a shock."

"We both are," she agreed. "He and I will be able to work things out on our own time. I wondered if I'd run in to him or Bastian again eventually, but to be honest, I'm much more shocked to have seen him with you and Will. That was a curious sight."

"Oh," I said. "You want to know how we became friends?"

"If you don't mind."

I sat there, looking back, and the image of seeing Cadan's face for the first time at that Halloween party flashed in my mind—after Will had punched the Phantom of the Opera mask off, that is. "There isn't much to it, I guess. He offered to help me. It took a while for me to trust him, but I'm glad I did. He's saved my life many times now. He's earned my trust."

"And Will trusts him as well?"

"It took a lot longer for Will to come around," I said honestly. I told her about Cadan risking his life to keep me informed of Bastian's plans and saving me from Ivar. I talked about his kindness and comforting me when I was at my lowest. I told her the story of what happened the night Sammael was awakened, about Cadan protecting us from Bastian and then killing him. I even told Madeleine about Cadan taking me to the Rocky Mountains to retrieve the root that cured Will from Antares. She listened in silence, and I caught the ghost of a smile on her face when I had finished my story.

"I don't know what he was like when you knew him, but the Cadan I know now is a wonderful, good person and he means a lot to me."

"I'm proud of him," Madeleine said. "Cadan was much younger when I knew him, and he was desperate for his father's approval. Beneath it all, he was good . . . and he was even my friend. He was there for me when Bastian was at his worst. I know Cadan only did the things he did to please his father, and his sins still seem to haunt him."

I knew that it had been Cadan, along with Ivar, who abducted Will to let Bastian torture him in the days leading up to my death by Ragnuk's teeth. That Cadan, I believed, was behind him—all of us—now. "What sorts of things?" I asked.

"He killed." Her answer was simple, straight to the point. "But no more than you or I, and it's unfair to hold that against him. The demonic and angelic are at war. At least he left the humans alone. I never knew him to hunt mortals. He'd tell Bastian of the souls he'd reaped, and Bastian was arrogant enough to believe that his subordinates feared him too greatly to lie to him. I, on the other hand, know a liar when I see one."

Madeleine was reasonable in her assessment of Cadan's actions. For as long as I'd known Will, he'd always been so firm in his belief that the ways of the world were black and white, that good and evil were clearly defined. I supposed that the hard centuries of being my Guardian had made him that way. Madeleine seemed to recognize the shades of gray that I sought and believed existed. This realization made me a less afraid of her.

"I'm glad that Will grew up away from Bastian," I told her, grateful. "I think you did the right thing."

"I wasn't even sure Bastian would let the baby live," she confessed. "Word of our relationship had already begun to spread, as had the rumor that he was half angelic himself. He was building his army then, making a name for himself among the most elite of the demonic. He couldn't afford to have anything mark his reputation—especially siring an angelic child. Those last few weeks made it easy to leave him. He had his moments and I still believe he loved me, but he was cruel at the core."

I studied her, surprised at what I saw in her expression. "You seem like a part of you regrets leaving him, even today."

She smiled at me, a terrible, sorrowful smile. "When you love someone so fiercely, they leave a mark on your soul that never goes away, no matter how much you dig and rip at it. He left a mark on my soul. At least the ones he left on my skin faded with time."

I had no response. I imagined that her relationship with Bastian hadn't been the healthiest, but knowing he'd physically harmed her made me grind my teeth together. No relationship was perfect all the time, and even Will and I could be rude to each other when stress levels were high, but violence was unforgiveable.

Madeleine squeezed my hand. "I didn't mean to startle you. There are countless things left unsaid about my time with Bastian. I've kept so much bottled up."

"I wouldn't *un*bottle any of that around Will," I warned her. "He might find a way to bring Bastian back to life just so he can kill him again. He might do this a few times, actually."

"That part of William hasn't changed then, I see," she said. "May I ask about you and my son?"

"I—no—of course you may. What . . . about?"

Her gaze became soft and gentle. "He's in love with you. And you love him just as much. I wondered at first, but tonight confirmed it."

I chewed my lip. "It's a little obvious, isn't it?"

She gave me a brilliant, wide smile. "A little."

"He's amazing," I told her. "Really."

Her smile became a little sad. "You've known him longer than I have."

"I'm happy that you and Will can have a chance to get to know each other again. It'll be good for both of you."

"He's changed a lot," she admitted.

"We all have," I said. "We've grown up."

"Strife will do that to you." She watched me carefully, but her smile remained. "We'll find a way for you to survive this. I'll need your help getting to know him again."

I huffed a little laugh at that. "I haven't given up hope. I'm going to do what I have to do—ascend and fight as an archangel—but I'll never give up hope. I don't want to die, but honestly, I'm so much more afraid of becoming some unthinking monster again."

"Again?" she asked. "I thought you couldn't remember Heaven?"

Azrael's memories of me as Gabriel flashed in my head once more. There had been tears in my eyes. I must have felt something after massacring the Nephilim. If I couldn't feel anything, then I would've shed tears for no one, especially not monsters. Remembering that I, as Gabriel, had spared one Naphil gave me hope for my archangel self, but then I remembered that I'd spared him only to harvest his heart, and that didn't sound like mercy. I hated to think about where he'd been held all these thousands of years. I didn't want to kill this creature. I had accepted that I might have to sacrifice myself to win this war, but sacrificing others was wrong. Still, there was no other way for me to ascend without the Naphil heart. Perhaps we had done a good thing in destroying them all. Yet . . . if they were just horrible monsters, then why had I wept for them?

"The other angels I've met have been like that," I explained. "And I know that angels aren't permitted to feel or to make their own choices. I don't want to stop loving my friends and family or to kill without discretion as I used to. When I ascend, I'll lose everything that makes me human."

"You'll still have your soul."

"Will I?" I asked. "If I do, I still won't know what exactly I'll turn into as an angel with a soul. And then after I lose everything that I am, I'm supposed to lose my life as well. No one seems to be able to tell me anything that's certain. I'm afraid of the unknown."

She smiled at me. "You're too much of a force to lose yourself to anything. If you forget who you are, then we'll help you remember. You've got incredible friends with you who believe in you and love you too much to let you lose who you are."

Madeleine was right. I had friends and family at home, and I'd brought friends—and family—with me on this journey. None of them would ever give up on me, no matter how many reasons I gave them to walk away. I had to do what I had to do, and they would follow me anywhere.

"What do you say we head back to the others?" she asked, rising to her feet and holding out a hand to help me up. "Then I will give you a tour of the armory and we can play with swords."

I grinned and took her hand. "Sounds like a plan to me."

26

MADELEINE HAD TRANSFORMED AN OLD CLASS-
room in the castle into her own incredible armory. The walls
of the room were lined with swords of all sizes and origins,
polearm weapons topped with vicious-looking blades, and an
assortment of battle-axes. There was even a tomahawk decorated with feathers, and an elegant parashu whose sweeping,
curved blade was etched with images of Hindu deities. I
strolled along the walls, examining and admiring the collection as if I was in a museum, but Will was like a kid in a
candy store. I bit my lip to keep from laughing, watching him
struggle to decide which weapon to pull off its display mount
first. He retrieved a fine example of a Celt-Iberian falcata
inlaid with gold, only to return it to its rack and bring down
the saya scabbard containing an unusual Yari spear.

"I take it that he inherited his weapon aficionado

tendency from you?" I asked Madeleine as I cracked up watching Will's giddiness over all the new toys.

She smiled in return. "Most reapers tend to bring beloved artifacts with them through the ages. I have few belongings I've held on to that aren't weapons."

I thought of the things Will had kept all this time: the cross his mother gave him, the books on his shelves, his guitars, and even a few of my own things he'd kept over my many reincarnations, like my winged necklace and the phoenix hair comb he bought for me from the peddler in Shanghai. I wondered about Cadan, if there was anything besides sad memories that he'd held on to over the centuries.

Speaking of Cadan . . . he sat on a raggedy, mildewed sofa beside Ava. Marcus leaned his back against the wall. The three casually observed Will and me as Madeleine gave us a tour of the weapons collection.

"Which one is the glaive you suggested I practice with?" I asked Madeleine.

She moved to the polearms section of her collection and retrieved a partisan that resembled Azrael's hallowed glaive, but in a far more primitive design. Every inch of the angelic-made weapons were not only unnaturally beautiful, but had an unearthly presence to them that gave them a faint feel of sentience. Will's sword had been given to him by Michael, and I assumed my own Khopesh had been crafted for me in Heaven. Our weapons had been forged with the purpose of being used on Earth. I could only imagine what sort of power the hallowed glaive could wield in our realm, a realm it was never meant to enter. Then again, I already knew the answer to that question. The power this divine weapon could wield, the amount of power I would need to summon just to use it, would kill me.

Ava put a hand on my shoulder and rescued me from my thoughts. "Marcus and I will do some research to find some possible locations of the Naphil."

"Good call," I said. "There has to be someone else who knows where he is. The Naphil may have angelic protection. Check with every reliable source you have. Every rumor should be treated as a lead."

She gave a curt nod and left the room with Marcus in tow. Cadan remained on the sofa with his arms crossed and his head tilted back. He looked as if he were dozing off. I turned back to Madeleine, who returned to me with the partisan staff in both hands. She handed it over, and I gauged the weight and balance of the weapon. It was hundreds of years old and yet balanced perfectly. The blades were double-edged and still sharp, with no signs of rust. Madeleine had taken care of this antique.

"Do you know what Sammael fights with?" she asked. "We should have you spar against something similar."

I shuddered as I remembered the weapon Sammael used to brutally glean a young girl's soul and devour it. "He had a scythe, but I don't know if that's his primary weapon. I saw him use it to take a girl's soul."

Her mouth turned down as she considered this. "I don't like polearm against polearm. These weapons are meant to be used from a distance, not in close combat where there is not enough room between you and your enemy to strike. Have you seen Lilith use a weapon?"

I shook my head. I wished I remembered something from my time in Heaven's army. I knew nothing about my enemies in battle, nothing that would give me an edge. However, once I became Gabriel, that might all change.

"Will," Madeleine called to her son. "Spar with Ellie using your own sword. The weapon is large enough to minimize the partisan's defenses and make using the partisan challenging."

Like I needed a spar with Will to be any more challenging. He called his sword as instructed and moved to stand about fifteen feet away from me, well out of reach of my blade.

Madeleine positioned herself next to me and laid her hands over mine to guide my stance. "Your right hand is dominant so it must be your rear hand. This is where your power comes from. Your forehand guides the direction of the blade." She lowered my rear hand, pivoting the staff so that the blade lifted to chest height. "This is your ward. Right heel stepped back, hands a great distance apart to keep the balance even. There you go."

She moved away from me and motioned for Will to prepare. "Let's work on defense first. Do not use the pole to stop a blade because the blade will sever the pole in two.

The partisan is designed to parry an attack by catching and entangling your opponent's blade with the outer blades of your own weapon."

Will rushed toward me, raising his sword over his head and sweeping it down in an arc. I pivoted the pole with my right hand as instructed and I lifted the spearhead. Will's sword caught in the hooklike outer blade of the partisan. Before he could wrench it free, I swung the pole toward the ground—Will's sword entangled in my own was unimaginably heavy—and he was unable to withdraw on his own. I slipped the partisan free and it became much lighter in my hands. I returned to my ward lightning-quick and thrust the blade toward Will's throat and stopped. There was no way I'd have defeated him so easily if he weren't going easy on me. This was only so I could get used to the techniques of using the polearm.

"Excellent instinct," Madeleine said cheerfully. "You've even moved on to offense without my instruction. Well done. Cadan."

He bolted awake and upright in the sofa so suddenly that one of the legs snapped and the sofa bottomed out. He swore as his butt hit the tile floor.

Madeleine strolled toward him and tapped the side of his head as he scrambled to his feet. "You. Let's go."

"What? Where?"

"Ellie can practice using the polearm while you and I say our piece," she elaborated. "We don't have much time."

On their way out the door, Madeleine paused to give me a knowing look and a little half smile. I realized then that her conversation with Cadan was partly an excuse to allow me a conversation with Will. They left and I faced my Guardian once more.

"Are you ready to have a go at this?" he asked, his tone careful and hesitant. "Maybe we ought to take it easy for the rest of the night."

"No," I said. "We don't have time to take it easy. Let's just do this."

He shrugged. "As you wish." He moved faster than my eyes could follow, reappearing right in front of me, swinging his sword. I swept to the side, avoiding his blow, but he'd anticipated that move and was already prepared to follow me. His sword swung again and I lifted the partisan to catch his strike. The human-made metal was devastatingly inferior to the angelic silver of Will's blade and I could feel it give and whine with each blow, threatening to break. As Will and I clashed, I became aware that he wasn't using all of his strength. There was no way this weapon could have survived even this long against his. I grew angry, pushing at him harder. I whirled and struck his ribs with the pole of the partisan. He grunted and stumbled, but he didn't counter my attack right away. He adjusted his grip on the helve of his sword and ducked out of the way of my next blow.

"Quit holding back!" I shouted at him. Didn't he take this seriously? I had to learn how to use a weapon like this or

I would fail. Did he decide there was no point now because I would die? I wasn't some dead girl walking. I wasn't precious or finite, and he was pissing me off treating me like so. "Just fight me!"

He shot me a hard look and stepped aside, letting his sword vanish in a shimmering flash. "No. Not like this. Not when you're angry."

"*You're* making me angry," I shot back. "We have to use what little time we've got left to prepare, and we might as well use the rest of the night to train. Do you think this is a waste of time?"

"No," he murmured low and harshly, but said nothing more.

"No?" I repeated. "That's it? That's all you have to say about everything?"

His green eyes pierced mine. "No."

I gritted my teeth with impatience. "I know what this is about."

"Do you?" he demanded. "Do you even care?"

I stared at him, bewildered. "What's that supposed to mean?"

He exhaled heavily as he shook his head and dropped his gaze. "Never mind."

"No you don't," I snapped at him. "Don't give me a non-committal response when you have something to say. What don't I care about?"

He whirled back to me, eyes blazing. "*Me!* You've just

agreed to throw your life away, just given up the fight, without asking for my help or how *I* feel. I told you that I won't—I *can't*—let you go and you don't care if you're taken from me."

My anger and shock had fled, replaced with only an immeasurable sadness. "I do care. God, I care so much. I know how much it hurt you when you thought I was gone after Ragnuk killed me—"

"I don't think you do," he said quietly. "You are all I know. If you fall, then I fall."

"Don't say that," I said. "I won't let you talk like that."

"I have done one thing for five hundred years," he said. "And that's protect you—fighting alongside you, *being* with you. You've shown me how to live, how to be human. When you were gone for decades, I didn't know what to do with myself. I don't know anything else. I have nothing without a purpose, without you."

I felt defeated. "I don't want to die either. I'm terrified of what will happen to me if I die an archangel. But this is so much bigger than you and me. We both came into this knowing and understanding the cost: enduring every adversity that comes with war. Only we've had to experience this for hundreds of years and the end is so close. We can finish this once and for all for *everyone*. Countless lives depend on us—on you and me."

He sucked in his lip in that familiar way, but it only broke my heart more this time. He shook his head. "I wish I could be brave and selfless for this, but I've given up every-thing for this war. *Everything.* I won't give up you. You're the only thing I refuse to lose. *Never*, Ellie." He drew a trembling breath. "Never."

"We don't have a choice," I told him.

"I *will* save you."

"You can't. Not this time."

"Then I will fall with you."

I shook my head and backed away from him, lifting the partisan glaive once more. "No. You can't talk like that. Whatever happens to me when I ascend and use the hal-lowed glaive will happen, but not until after I've stopped Sammael and his army. We have to focus. Now come on. Fight me. Train me like you want me to live."

He gave me a pitiful, beaten look, and called his sword. I gestured to him and he nodded in return as he took a deep breath. His raised his blade and I leaped into a jog, lift-ing the staff to drive it toward him, but he surprised me. He didn't wait for my move; instead, he struck first. His sword caught in the curve of the outer blades and I halted his attack. I shoved down in order to disarm him, but his extreme strength combined with the massive size of his blade kept me from yanking it right out of his hands. My con-centration broke—I imagined myself in this position against Sammael and a tremor slithered through me, allowing Will to overpower me. He forced me to take several steps back before shoving his foot into my chest. The partisan slipped free of Will's blade and I lost my balance. My back hit the wall with a hard thump, nearly knocking the wind from my chest. I just didn't have it in me to keep going tonight. I was too emotionally exhausted.

I slid to the floor, chucking the glaive aside and letting it clatter across the stone. When I didn't rise, Will withdrew his sword and came over to me. Then slowly, he sat down beside me, drew his arms around me, and slid me close. We remained there in silence with my legs tangled over his lap and my fingers curling around the hem of his shirt as one of his hands tucked my hair behind my ear. I wanted to stay like that, wrapped in his arms, until the world ended. I wanted to stay human. I didn't want to be an archangel again. I didn't want to change and become a heartless war machine. I didn't want to break Will's heart. I didn't want to use a weapon that would kill me. End me. I didn't want to end.

With my soul ripping in two, I pulled away from Will and forced myself to my feet.

He watched me, hurt twisting his features. "What's wrong?"

"Can I ask you something?"

"Of course."

"You told me once that you loved me because I was human," I said, my voice tiny. "Will you still love me when I'm an angel? Even if I won't be human anymore?"

"Always," he said, green eyes bright. "Even if you stop loving me."

I felt myself begin to crumble and I left the armory and him sitting on the floor.

The castle was eerily quiet as I wandered through the corridors and watched the dawn light peeking in through each window. I wondered where the others were. Ava was sure to still be hard at work uncovering the Naphil's location and driving Marcus on like a workhorse. I imagined Cadan either took a room in the castle or returned to the hotel to rest during the daylight hours. Madeleine . . . I wasn't sure. I didn't know her well enough. I wondered how her conversation with Cadan had gone and if they'd made peace.

Footsteps interrupted my thoughts. My first thought should have been that the footsteps belonged to one of my friends, but instinct sent my nerves running on hot coals. I let my senses stretch out to feel for the identity of the wanderer. I held out a hand and a single Khopesh shimmered into my palm. I turned the corner and met a face I hadn't expected to see in a million years.

It was Ethan Stone.

27

"YOU!" I SQUEAKED. "WHAT ARE YOU DOING HERE?"

Ethan wore a grin made of pure, sticky-sweet satisfaction. "I'm here to have a chat with an old friend."

"How did you find me?"

He scoffed. "My spies are far better than Sammael's. In fact, mine dispatched one of his in Liege. They're hot on your tail, little fireball."

I gaped in shock. "Your human soldiers can take on demonic reapers?"

"Mercenaries," he corrected. "Technically. They're ex-military, served in some of the most violent regions of the world. A few were on a special force that fought warlords in the Congo. They fared well against your own assault on my house, didn't they? The reapers tend to discredit human power because we are, well, mortal. To creatures who have the ability to live forever, mortality is a weakness. We may not have wings and claws, but we have explosives."

"Are you going to tell me why you're following me?"

"I've always kept tabs on you," he replied in a disconcertingly casual tone. "It's been in my best interest to. When you told me that you were looking to evoke an angel, I knew your next task would be to find Solomon's Ring. I also deduced that Azrael would be the angel you would evoke to fight Sammael since he's beaten the Fallen before, but I put my money on his answer being a big fat 'no.' Azrael was demoted—there's no way he could take on Sammael—and since he's the only angel with a tendency to bend the rules, you've got just one angel left that you can count on: yourself. Am I right?"

"Yes," I grumbled. "You get a stalker's gold star."

"Brilliant." His gaze shuffled toward both exits of the room. "I love gold stars and being right. Now, before your Guardian rushes in to remove my head before bothering to at least give me a good bollocking, we must move on. You spared my life and I would like to help you. Yes, you might have taken the next most valuable thing I possess, which was that magnificent book, but I have it in me to forgive."

"I'm pretty desperate, so I'll take what I can get," I told him. "How can you help me?"

"Being the collector I am, I also collect information," he explained. "I like stories, especially stories that happen to have truth to them. I learned a long time ago that you need the heart of a Naphil in order to ascend and so I deduced, since the Nephilim had been exterminated, that one or more were spared. I wanted one for my collection."

My jaw dropped. "You—*what*? You have one at your house?"

He laughed. "No, of course not. I found him and realized he wouldn't fit in my house so I left him where he was."

My brain grew numb with shock. "You know where the Naphil is?"

"That's what I'm trying to say, yes." All the humor washed from his expression and tone. "But I don't just want you to find the Naphil. Give the beast some mercy. I have seen barbarism, Preliator, but nothing like this."

My jaw set hard. "That doesn't surprise me."

"Another thing," Stone continued. "Did Azrael tell you what to do with the heart once you had it?"

"He didn't." I paused in horror. "I don't have to eat it, do I?"

"You can avoid that," he replied. "But you'll need a ritual out of the compilation of spells from the Antares grimoire your friend Nathaniel copied. I imagine he didn't quite understand what he had when it came to passages about you. We corresponded more often once he learned you were Gabriel."

I felt sad at the thought of Nathaniel. "We found you through a package you sent to him. Did you know him well?"

"We're both collectors," Ethan explained. "We understood each other. I'd been in contact with him for a number of years. Most of my life, actually. I was sorry to hear of his passing."

"He didn't '*pass*.' He was killed."

"Yes," Stone said, voice gentle. "I imagine you're very familiar with loss."

I didn't want to talk about everything and everyone I'd lost so far. "So, you and Nathaniel were friends? I know he kept in touch with psychics and you told me that you're a psychic."

"I told you 'in a manner of speaking.'"

I glared at him. "It's extremely annoying that you have to give me the most confusing response possible every time."

"I'm old and bored and running out of hobbies. This is a new one."

"Who are you, Ethan Stone?" I asked in a very serious tone. "Or should I say, *what* are you?"

He smiled. "That is the question, isn't it?"

And then it hit me. "The bloodline in America that Nathaniel told me about . . . you're one of the scions, aren't you?"

His smile widened. "I'm happy to know that I'm not descended from a moron."

My brain reeled as I circled him, gaping at him, studying him, picking out resemblances in his features that I saw in my own. I saw everything now. This was why Lauren had detected my presence in his psychic signature on the envelope, and why the energy was so intense and violent. She'd had a similar reaction when she used her abilities to sense a connection between myself and the sarcophagus Sammael had been entombed in. Only an angel had that kind of power. It made perfect sense for Nathaniel to keep in contact with Ethan Stone, and why he knew so much about our world even though he was psychic. But he was more than a psychic mortal. My power—angelic power—was in his blood.

"How long have you known?" I asked him, still breathless.

"Even as a young boy growing up in Surrey, England, I've always known I have abilities that normal people don't," he said. "But it wasn't until my mother introduced me to Nathaniel that I knew what I was. Your angelic blood has flowed through my mother's side for over three hundred years. Nathaniel had kept track of my entire family tree, since you married a mortal man and bore a child before that incarnation of yours was killed in battle."

Despite the incredible discovery of one of my descendants, this information stung ripe and raw. I hated thinking about the men I'd loved who weren't Will. If I'd known how he felt about me, I never would have even considered anyone else. I remembered what Will had told me when he found out Cadan had feelings for me: *"For centuries I've watched you with everyone but me."* Thinking about his words now made me so angry with myself, but he never told me he loved me until the night after we'd thrown the sarcophagus into the sea. If I'd *known* . . .

"Ellie?" Ethan Stone's voice shook me from my thoughts.

If I'd known and given my heart only to Will, then Ethan Stone wouldn't be here. His ancestors—my descendants—never would have lived. I couldn't regret what I'd done that gave life to others. I was the archangel of new life. Nothing was more precious to me. I was more than willing to give up my own to save all life on Earth.

Ethan Stone laid a hand on my shoulder. "That's a lot to absorb. I understand."

He didn't understand everything, but it was a nice gesture.

"Actually, I do," he said. "You and your Guardian fool no one, not even an old fool like me."

"Is being a creepy mind invader your only talent?"

"Of course not," he replied. "I'm also a talented smartass."

"That one has been apparent enough," I grumbled. "Nathaniel told me that my scions can't control angelfire, so what else can you do?"

"Enable my inherent laziness," he said with ease. He lifted his right hand and small objects zipped around my head toward him, very nearly nicking my skin. The objects—small rocks collected from the debris littering the ground—settled into his open hand. "I could have merely picked them all off the ground, but I don't need to. Brilliant, I know."

"In all seriousness, it is," I said, marveling at the rocks in his hand. I touched one and it prickled my skin with energy, like static electricity. "How strong is this ability? Can you pick up things that are heavier than little rocks?"

"Like a person?"

"Yeah," I said. "Could you pick up me?"

"I can do more than lift you," he replied. "When I was younger, I had less control over it. I had to learn quickly."

I cringed. "Did people get hurt?"

"They had it coming," he said with a dismissive wave. "Most of them, anyhow."

"Could you defend yourself from a reaper?" I asked. "Like if you were attacked?"

He shrugged and then he backed away several paces. "Rush at me."

I gaped at him. "What?"

"Attack me."

"Again, what?"

"Just *run* at me!"

I lunged toward him, but I only took three steps before his hand flicked up and my body was hurled in the opposite direction. My feet hit the ground the same instant his were lifted. Will had wound his entire hand around Ethan Stone's throat and he now held the man high over his head.

"It was just a friendly demonstration, I assure you!" Stone gargled, barely able to breathe.

"You attacked her," Will snarled, adding just a hair more pressure to make the man's eyes bulge.

"Will!" I shouted at him as I caught my balance. "Let

him go. He wasn't hurting me—just showing me his powers. He's one of my scions."

That didn't seem to make Will want to pummel Stone any less. In fact, Will glared even harder, but I understood. This human was descended from me and a man other than Will. Will had no reason to like him. Even so, he set Ethan back on the ground on my order and folded his arms.

"Thank you," Ethan said, and smoothed out his suit and his hair. Will didn't give him any room. I rolled my eyes. The stupid macho crap would never end.

"What do you want?" Will demanded.

"To help you!"

"He knows where the Naphil is," I explained. I turned to Stone. "Which is . . . where, exactly?"

"The Temple of Solomon," Ethan Stone said. "You really liked Solomon, I must say."

"But no one knows exactly where that is," I told him. "It's the same temple that protected the Ark of the Covenant for a long time. No one has ever been allowed to excavate the Temple Mount. If there's a Naphil buried alive in there, then there's no way to get to it."

He seemed unconcerned. "No, no. The temple in Jerusalem was sacked by King Nebuchadnezzar—completely plundered and destroyed. But there were two temples built. The one in Jerusalem protected the Ark of the Covenant, and a second in Aleppo, Syria, housed the last Naphil."

"Ain Dara," Will said in a low voice.

I stared at Stone, confused. "But that temple was built by the Hittites, not the Israelites."

"Parts of it, yes," he replied. "The twin temples are nearly identical if you look at the excavated ruins of Ain Dara and the descriptions of Solomon's Temple on Zion in the Hebrew Bible. The Hittites in the area Ain Dara was built believed the Naphil was one of their more destructive gods, a storm god called Addu. They worshipped him, built gigantic basalt lions and sphinxes around the cherubim reliefs, and carved enormous footprints into the earth leading toward the Sanctum, which is the inner holy room of the temple."

"Solomon built twin temples," I repeated, astonished. "Can you take us there? Can you help us find the Naphil?"

"I can do that," Stone agreed. "I have contacts in Israel and Syria."

"Will," I said, and caught my Guardian's attention. "Once we're finished at Ain Dara, we can head to Har Megiddo."

Ethan loosed a long whistle. "That's really where it will all end, is it?"

"It is indeed," I said dimly. "I'm tired of playing tag with the enemy. I'm doing everything I need to do in order to give our side the best chance to win this war and then I'm heading to Armageddon to face Sammael and end this once and for all. I'm just afraid that we won't have enough soldiers to help us fight Sammael's army. He will have thousands of demonic reapers to fight us there."

"All of the demonic spawn to meet the angelic," he

mused. "We need more angelic soldiers. I'm certain my mercenaries would be delighted to fight with you. I don't believe they've ever battled an army of reapers before. It'll be like Christmas morning for them, the bloodthirsty beasts."

"Ava and Marcus can rally the angelic," Will suggested. "My mother has her contacts, as well. While we find the Naphil, they can gather our friends and allies and *their* friends and allies. We can build an army within a week—days. We've all been waiting for this."

With a beam of hope, I realized that maybe we could do this after all. "Do you know where everyone is?" I asked. "Let's get the group together and figure this out. While the idea's fresh in our minds, we can organize how we'll assemble as many angelic reapers as possible."

"We can fly to Syria later this evening," Ethan offered. "We'll take my private jet into a military base I used the last time I traveled to Ain Dara. A lot of money can persuade many men to be very uninterested in our business. I warn you, this won't be any milk run."

"For now, let's get some rest," I said. "A lot is about to happen for all of us."

For the first time in a while, Will smiled at me.

I gave him a skeptical stink eye. "What?"

"Nothing," he replied. "Just proud of you, that's all."

Then I smiled back at him.

28

DESPITE HOW EXHAUSTED EVERYONE SEEMED, they were very alert while listening to my explanation of our next plan. While Ava, Marcus, and Madeleine rallied their allies, Cadan would call upon his own friends. I'd be surprised if Cadan had any other angelic friends, but he appeared confident nonetheless. Ethan Stone was already on the phone with his men and the pilot of his jet. Things were falling right into place.

I fell asleep on the ride back to the hotel, but I woke long enough to follow Will into the elevator and to our room. I lay sprawled on the bed wishing I could return to blissful uncon-sciousness, but Will wouldn't let me until we'd ordered room service and gotten some food in our stomachs. One meal a day wasn't cutting it for either of us. If I survived this war, I'd go back to Michigan and inhale some real food cooked by my nana. Even though the hotel only served breakfast at this hour, I ordered an omelet. After having had real Belgian waffles, I wouldn't waste my time ordering some cruddy hotel version. Unless I came back to Belgium, I'd never be able to eat waffles again, to be honest, now that I'd been spoiled. That was quite heartbreaking.

I couldn't remember when I fell back to sleep—or if I'd fallen asleep with my face in my breakfast—but I woke hours later to Will nudging my shoulder. I'd slept until after midnight, but now it was time for us to meet Ethan Stone and fly to Syria. I took a quick, cool shower to wake myself up and finish packing before we took our luggage down to the lobby. Ethan Stone was already waiting for us, leaning on a sleek black limousine. His driver grabbed our bags and set them securely in the trunk. He rushed around the limo to open the rear doors for us to climb in.

"We ought to arrive just after dawn," Stone explained. "This will allow us to travel safely through the desert. The sun is too direct for any demonic reaper to even consider attacking us during daylight."

"You are officially invited on all of our adventures," I told him as I slid across the seat and stopped next to the window. Will took his place beside me.

Ethan eased onto the seat opposite ours, sank deep against the cushions, crossed one leg over the other, and waved his hand over the panel under the windows. The panel slid away—a result either of a display of his power or the device being motion-activated—and a tray lifted into its place with a lazy hum, displaying crystal glasses, a pitcher of ice, and a bottle of brandy. Stone tipped the bottle over a glass.

"And we're off," he said, and grinned at us.

Ethan Stone's private jet was small compared to most commercial aircrafts, but it flew smoothly and in just a few hours we landed at a tiny airfield in the middle of the desert. The runway ended in a barrier of ten-foot-tall chain-link fence topped with barbed wire. On the opposite side of the airfield was a rickety, dusty building shadowed by a manned guard tower. I had a strong feeling there was more to this military base than we were told.

Stone exited the aircraft first and greeted a man brandishing a very large assault rifle. They spoke as if they were old friends, chatting in fast, happy-sounding Arabic to each other. Suddenly the man with the gun guffawed loudly and slapped Stone on the back so hard he lost his balance and frowned in pain. Ethan waved up at us and we climbed down the ramp, Will out in front like a bodyguard. The sun was insanely bright and hot, and I felt like my skin was frying right off my arms, even though I wore a thin shirt over a tank top and linen cargo shorts. Cadan, though he had braved daylight for me before, would never be able to handle this. Stone had been right that we'd be safe from demonic forces until nightfall.

We passed by groups of rough-looking men with so many weapons dangling from their uniforms they looked like twisted Christmas trees decorated by the Godfather. What kind of maniac were we traveling with who kept this sort of mafia-esque company all the time?

I tried to ignore the curious, leering gazes of the men, but I imagined they didn't have seventeen-year-old girls passing through too often. Stone's men took our luggage, but knowing that we'd be investigating ancient temples, I kept a backpack stuffed full of bottled water, food, a flashlight with batteries, and an extra change of clothes, just in case. We followed Ethan and the man he'd been chatting with toward the dusty building. Just past it, a Jeep was parked in front of a closed gate surrounded with more armed guards. This had to be our ride and I was more than giddy to get out of this sketchy "airport."

Stone exchanged a few more words with the man, handed him a fat envelope of what was likely cash, and returned his attention to Will and me. "Climb in," he instructed. "Yusri will escort us to our destinations today."

"Another driver?" I asked, peeking over the seat at the man in the Hawaiian-print shirt behind the wheel. He turned around and gave us a pleasant smile. He seemed like a nice enough guy, but I caught a glimpse of a gun sticking out the waistband of his khaki shorts.

"Of course," Stone replied. "Don't be silly. I never drive myself anywhere."

I studied the GPS on the dashboard as Yusri configured

the map. "Aleppo? Why are we going there first? I thought we're headed to Ain Dara. You'd better not try to bamboozle me, Stone."

"No *bamboozling*, I assure you," he replied. "The surface of Ain Dara has been reduced to rubble. There's no way to access the underground channels there. We'll be going in through a different door."

Will made an impatient noise. "Can you be a little more specific?"

"Ain Dara's underground system connects with the temple of the storm god Addu in the Citadel in the center of Aleppo. This temple is five thousand years old, older than the Ottoman palaces, the fortifications constructed by Ghazi after the Crusades, the Byzantine churches, the colonnades built during Alexander the Great's conquests. . . . It's older than everything built atop it. The passageways beneath run for miles and miles."

I nodded, understanding the plan. "So we will access Ain Dara from underground."

"I hope you brought walking shoes."

I frowned down at my sandals. "Meh," I mumbled in response. At least I had my backpack full of supplies.

"We'll need plenty of propane lanterns," he said. "It's dark as Hell down there."

Aleppo could only be described as a city built of gold—of golden limestone and sand brick, that is. The streets were a vibrant mix of languages, of people wearing Western and Middle Eastern clothing, and the scents of oils and spices. We navigated toward the ancient Citadel in the center of the city, past tourists and locals, automobiles, and carts pulled by donkeys. The Citadel, sitting atop a gigantic hill, was never out of sight so we'd never get lost, even though Stone seemed entirely sure of his path through the winding streets. We entered the same way the tourists did, across a grand stone bridge over what was once a moat and toward the towering entrance gate.

Ethan Stone pulled out a cell phone and dialed a number. "We're here. See you shortly." And he hung up. He led us past groups of tourists and their guides, and past open areas of excavations by archaeologists. The Citadel was an array of different levels of excavations, some sections cleared and others barricaded from visitors, and we had to hop up and off short ledges when there weren't any stone steps. The walls of some buildings still stood with little damage to their structure, while others had been reduced to rubble, though leaving clearly defined floor plans. We passed through archways of stone of alternating colors and through magnificent colonnades lined with gorgeous Hellenistic columns. The entire city, with its rich variance in ancient styles, was incredible. I wanted to veer off our path and go explore so badly, but we had a mission to see through. I wondered, for a fleeting, sad moment, if when I became an archangel again I'd even care about the beauty of the Citadel.

"Hello!" an attractive woman in her midthirties called out to us and waved. Dressed in khaki shorts and a wide-brimmed sun hat, she looked like she'd meandered off the set of an Indiana Jones movie not five minutes ago.

"Rebekah," Ethan Stone greeted her, and kissed both her cheeks. "Ellie, Will, meet Dr. Rebekah Massi. She is an old friend and accomplice on many adventures. She's treated me to archaeological finds not available to regular visitors, including some passageways still being excavated."

She flipped her long braid of dark hair over her shoulder and smiled at us. "It's wonderful to meet you," she said, accent thick. "Ethan has told me you're interested in climbing down into the tunnel system beneath the Addu Temple. It's really a very exciting maze of a system. The tunnels are still mostly intact. We haven't run into many that have collapsed."

My eyes bulged and my stomach turned. As claustrophobic as I *wasn't*, I had no desire to be buried alive in Syria. Or anywhere.

Ethan held an arm out. "Shall we?"

Dr. Massi steered us toward the storm god temple, which was an unearthed pit lined with limestone walls. To me, it didn't appear very different from the surrounding ruins, but Rebekah explained to us the intricate floor plan and what each room was used for. We headed to a section of the floor made of stone blocks that were free of dust, unlike the surrounding ground, and looked as if they'd been examined closely. She waved Ethan over and they both lifted the stones from where they fit, revealing a hatch made of wood that seemed to have been preserved in the scorching desert heat. I watched in utter fascination as the two carefully pulled the hatch open by an iron handle. Beneath was a shaft, barely large enough for a full-grown man to slip through, that descended into darkness.

"Cool," I murmured, and exchanged looks with Will. He seemed just as excited as I was.

"Are you ready?" Rebekah asked, a wide smile on her face. "It's a bit of a drop, but I've cleared the dangerous bank of sand that might have broken our necks and I've tossed down sacks to cushion our landing. I'll go first."

She reached into her bag and retrieved a propane lantern. She flipped a switch and a small flame flickered to life. It didn't seem like much, but as she positioned herself through the shaft, that little flame illuminated the darkness more brightly than I'd have guessed. Then she was gone, and a moment later her footsteps hit hard-packed earth with a dry thud and rustling of the sacks. I peered over the edge, deep into the shaft. Rebekah smiled up at me, holding the lantern over her head so that the glow turned her caramel skin to gold.

"I'll go next," Stone offered. He dropped his pack through the hole and followed it.

"Go," Will told me. "I'll close the hatch behind us and watch the rear."

"Or stare at it," I teased.

He licked his lips and they pulled into a little sideways grin. Smiling up at him, I eased my body through the hole until my legs dangled in clear air and all I needed to do was to let go. He gave me a reassuring look and I let my body fall. My senses quickened as I dropped and landed on my feet with grace and effortlessness. I stepped out of the way for Will to follow me and strained to see where Ethan and Rebekah had gone. They were talking just ahead of Will and me, lit by the glow of their lanterns. To my amazement, the tunnel had been carved out of solid rock. The air down here was cooler and less dry, and frankly it was more pleasant than aboveground. I picked up my pack and turned on my lantern. I started to get the second out for Will, but he put a hand on my arm.

"Save it," he said. "I don't need one to see. Three are enough."

"Show off," I grumbled.

"The passages open up into hidden locations all over the Citadel," Rebekah called to us from ahead. We walked a little faster to catch up. "I've found four that lead out into the city, but this one travels the farthest so far. On one of my explorations, I made the discovery of a lifetime: an ancient underground city between Ain Dara and Aleppo, much like the city of Derinkuyu, north of here in Cappadocia—now modern Turkey—which was once the homeland for the Hittite civilization. The Hittites seemed to have taken a preexisting city built by an unknown civilization and made it their home. I believe they have done the same with the city I'm taking you to today. I am itching to reveal the city, but not until I know what's beyond the door in the Sanctum. That's why I rang in Ethan."

"Door?" I asked.

"An enormous one, twenty feet high, and made of solid basalt," she replied. "There are engravings in a language I'd never seen before and reliefs of creatures I believed at first were cherubim, but upon closer inspection, were creatures I haven't seen in any Mesopotamian structure, or anywhere else in the world. The written language cut into the stone is far more complex than any language within thousands of years of its dating. It is almost alien."

"The language is Enochian," Stone explained, glancing back at us, the firelight dancing on his face and making him look a little younger. "The angelic language. It was no astonishment that Rebekah didn't recognize it."

"You can read it?" I asked, surprised.

"Again," he said, "I like knowing things."

My gaze fell to the tunnel floor. "I don't quite remember it. I didn't think anyone knew it anymore."

"You may again very soon."

This time Rebekah was the one who glanced back. "Remember it? You're a little young to be a linguist."

Ethan Stone gave an uncomfortable cough. I hadn't realized until now how poorly informed this archaeologist was about what was happening out there. I'd need to be careful about what I said from now on.

"Who are you again?" she asked, growing a little suspicious. "You also seem a little young to be a university student. Will, I can see it, though he doesn't look the type. A little brawny, he is. You're both quite curious."

"We're what he says." I wasn't sure how to explain myself, so I kept my mouth shut. The only reason Rebekah had even joined us was to help navigate this maze of tunnels since she knew it best. We continued for miles, for so long I began to sing songs in my head to pass the time. The passages branched off randomly and we took a couple of turns here and there. The floor rose and fell, and sometimes the tunnel grew wider or more narrow. We passed a few places where the ceiling had partially collapsed, forcing us to climb over fallen rock and debris. Every once in a while, we passed statues of sphinxes and even one of a winged man who had to be an angel. We must have been getting close.

A heavy rumble shook the tunnel walls and floor, and dust sprang free in thick clouds. Rebekah gasped and Ethan swore. Will remained silent and closed the distance between him and me.

"A cave-in?" I asked fearfully as I pushed my hands into the wall to catch my balance.

Stone frowned, studied the ceiling. "That didn't feel like a cave-in."

"Nor did it sound like one," Dr. Massi added.

I spun around to Will, who looked right at me. "Reaper."

A small noise of confusion escaped from me as I stared past him and into the blackness. I laid a hand on his arm, instinctively drawing my body closer to his. "Will?"

"It's not behind us," he said in a low voice. "It's up ahead."

I whirled the other way and looked past the two humans with us. There wasn't much room down here to fight and to protect our companions, but neither was there an escape route for the four of us. "Ethan, Rebekah," I said. "Get behind us."

"What?" she asked, gaping at us all. "Why? What's going on?"

Ethan took her by the arm and steered her past us despite her protests. "We should listen to them."

A second rumble reverberated, but this time the sound was very clearly a bestial roar.

"You both should start running," Will said. "Just keep going until—"

"*Will!*" I shrieked, cutting him off.

A figure appeared out of the blackness behind Will—a female vir—and grabbed two fistfuls of the back of Will's shirt and yanked him farther down the tunnel, her wings beating thickly in the narrow shaft as they disappeared. Rebekah screamed high and piercing as she flailed back-wards, dragging Ethan Stone with her, and her lantern clattered to the ground. It took me the longest moment of my life to decide whether to protect them or run after Will, but

I trusted Ethan to get Rebekah out of here. My Guardian needed me.

All around us in the tunnel, debris began to fall, small bits of rock and dust hit the floor. The sound of battle and thudding of bodies against stone made the tunnel rumble. Seconds later, chunks of rock tumbled from the ceiling. I stared in fear at the direction the humans had run.

"Ethan!" I screamed. "Cave-in! Get back this way!"

I could hear Rebekah's piercing cries as Ethan struggled to steer her around. The tunnel roared and shook as the ceiling caved in from somewhere in their direction. I spun and headed for where Will had gone with the vir. At the very edge of my lantern light's reach, Will shoved the demonic reaper into the wall of stone, his sword sparking against hers as she struggled beneath his strength.

"Move!" I yelled at him.

He tore away from the reaper, who was left in confusion, and darted farther down the tunnel and out of the way. I chucked the lantern at her head and she hissed and swung her sword to deflect the object. The blade punctured the small propane tank and it exploded. Fire engulfed her torso and she screeched and ripped at the flames burning away the flesh on her face. I called my swords, lit up the angelfire, and charged at her. She clawed through the last of the flames, her face scorched and raw and twisted with undulated rage. I lifted a sword and slashed it across her chest, splitting her skin and clothes wide open.

Will's sword crunched through her rib cage and jutted out the front of her body. She gasped and moaned in agony, staring down at the blade. She looked up at me, blood dribbling down her burned chin. She snarled as his sword withdrew.

"Sammael knows what you're doing," she hissed. "He knows of your planned ascension."

"Does he, now?" I asked. "He's invited to the party, if he's down."

She made a hideous, brutish sound. "You will never see the ends of his armies. They blanket the Earth as a storm blankets the sky, but the sun will never rise again."

I rolled my eyes. "Yeah, yeah. You demonic all think you're Shakespeare. Really nice. Good-bye." Then I took off her head and the rest of her burned up.

29

IT HAD TAKEN DR. MASSI SOME TIME TO CALM DOWN and speak in a reasonable tone of voice. She sat on the ground with her back to the wall while she devoured her sixth granola bar and we explained to her what she had seen. Ethan Stone returned after a short trek to check on the tunnel condition.

"The passage is completely blocked," he explained and exhaustedly took a seat beside Rebekah. "We can only keep going. I'm sorry about the reaper. I'd hoped I'd be right about the daylight."

I shrugged. "There's no daylight down here."

"She must have been waiting for us," Will said. "Sammael knows Ellie is trying to ascend and if he knew where the Naphil has been kept, then it's likely he'd have stationed demonic vir to intercept us. We'll need to be more careful and prepared for anything."

Rebekah began murmuring something and I had to face her in order to understand what she said. "Angels, demons, they're real. I believe in God, but never monsters."

Will stepped over to her and held out a hand for her to take and helped her to her feet. "This is the Holy Land," he said. "We all believe different things when it comes to God."

"We have to keep going," I told them. "We have four hours to sunset and a lot more tunnel to navigate. And now we need to find a way out of here that isn't the way we came."

"This is the only channel into the city," Rebekah argued. "The Sanctum has only one exit and that's our entrance."

I gave her a hard look. "There's always a way out. These passages can't all lead to nowhere."

"What are you even looking for beyond that door?" she asked, turning to Ethan Stone. "What is in the Sanctum?"

He took a deep breath, knowing his answer would sound like insanity to her. "The Sanctum of Air Dara is where the last of the Nephilim is imprisoned. I've seen him."

Dr. Massi didn't say or do anything at first. Then she laughed. "*Nephilim?* The half-angel beasts God flooded the world to kill?"

"Not with water," I added. "With angels like me. I am the human form of the archangel Gabriel. My brothers, sisters, and I wiped them out on God's orders to cleanse the Earth. I kept one of them alive in the event that I'd ever need to ascend to my full angel form."

"How are you an angel?" she asked, disbelieving. "You're a teenage girl."

"I became human to fight monsters on Earth," I told her. "Take it or leave it."

She shook her head in confusion. "How would this thing help you become an angel again?"

"I have to use his heart somehow," I answered grimly. "Right now, I just have to get it. One step at a time, right?"

"This is all absurd," she said.

Will hoisted Ethan's and Rebekah's belongings and presented them to their rightful owners. "Deny all you'd like, but you saw what happened here minutes ago. Now, we have to move. You can stay here, but I'd advise you to stick with us since there may be more reapers."

She gaped at him, clearly fearful of him since witnessing the battle, but she had to know he was right. There was no way out the way we came, and in case another monster showed up, she wouldn't want to be alone. After a few moments, she took her backpack and lantern from him and began walking alongside him.

"You're one of them, aren't you?" she asked. "Ellie is an angel, but you're not."

"No," Will said. "I'm a reaper, but I fight for her. I fight for Heaven."

Behind them, I moved nearer to Ethan. "You shouldn't have brought someone with us who doesn't know about our world," I told him in a low voice. "We put her in danger, and now she's slowing us down."

"Rebekah knows the underground system far better than I do," he said. "We will never find the city without her. She's an invaluable asset. I never imagined I'd ever be required to tell her about the reapers. Most people don't want to know that monsters exist."

That wasn't something I could argue with. I'd fought to keep this world a secret from Kate, but because I'd also fought to keep her in my life, that made it nearly impossible. Now she might have neon nightmares of that black light party at Josie's for the rest of her life.

"The entrance to the city is just ahead," Rebekah called to us over her shoulder.

Now that we were down to two lanterns, the underground passage seemed so much darker, and when the ceiling and floor began to widen, our lighted way became more and more dim. At last we came to a set of stairs that led into a large chamber with rows of support columns and archways that branched off into many rooms and hallways.

"We've excavated hundreds of underground cities throughout Turkey," Rebekah explained. "Many are connected through miles of tunnel systems like the one we came through from Aleppo. They're something like beautiful patchwork quilts, containing pieces from many different civilizations and expanded through the ages. I've found examples of Phrygian, Hittite, and even Byzantine period artifacts here. This room was likely an area for trade. The rooms off to the side were once stables and a granary. The underground temperature preserved food and kept living conditions comfortable. I don't believe these caverns were used much for housing, but mostly for storage and religious purposes. The Sanctum door is clearly marked."

She guided us further through the city, which was dark, cold, and quiet. I could hear the echoes of trickling water in the distance. We passed reliefs of Mesopotamian gods and demons, and when the door came into view it was even more gigantic than I had imagined. Jewels had been inlaid into the stone, and since they hadn't been stolen, I believed that no one had found this door before Dr. Massi and Ethan Stone. It was carved from floor to ceiling with images of the war against Nephilim: bodies of giants littered the bottom of the relief below a layer of images depicting a violent battle of Nephilim carrying stocky, archaic weapons against winged, armored angels wielding swords. At the very top, a winged figure surveyed the carnage from the crest of a hill, hair flowing, and both hands carried flaming swords. At the figure's feet was the name, the only Enochian word I remembered because it was tattooed onto Will's arm. My name: Gabriel. I swallowed hard, recalling Azrael's memory of me at the end of this battle, a frightening reflection of the carving I now saw with my own eyes.

"As soon as I saw this door," Ethan said, his voice breathy with excitement, "I knew what lay in the Sanctum beyond, that the legends were true."

"Not all legends are made from honorable heroes," I said quietly. "What does all of this say? I can't read the rest of this script."

"The Enochian along the edge of the door described the angels' victory over the Nephilim and says 'This barrier shall yield only to the flesh and blood of the Left Hand.'"

"Me," I said, gazing at the beautiful language describing such horrible acts of violence.

"For the most part," he replied. "It means that your human form, the vessel of flesh and blood, is meant to open this door. I believe I was able to open it because your mortal blood flows through my veins. We share genetic material."

"How does it open?"

"A pass phrase must be spoken," he explained. "And then you must offer your blood."

"Then go ahead," I instructed. "You're the one who speaks the angelic language."

"Enochian didn't work," he said. "In any case, we are here for your purpose, not mine. You were always meant to open this door."

"Which language worked?"

"I tried a handful of languages, but Old Hittite was successful. Your pass phrase will be different from mine, because your connection to the Naphil, the creature believed to be a god by the people who built this temple, is different from mine. They thought the angels were gods and you should regard yourself as such."

I stared at the door thoughtfully. "I should demand that the door open for one of their gods, for the Left Hand."

"I would guess that you need only tell the door who you are," Stone suggested. "And prove it with blood."

That sounded completely absurd. As if the door were a guard instead of just a door. What did one say to a door? I decided to take Ethan Stone's advice and tell the door that a battle among gods happened and I, leading my armies, won. Here went nothing.

I opened the skin of my palm with a sharp stone and pressed my blood against the door. I cleared my throat and made a silent prayer that I wouldn't trip over my words. Then I said: *"Huullaanzais siúnaan tarsikemi kisaat. Lim dinger-lim halziihhuun nu lukuran huullanuun."*

I held my breath, waiting for something to happen. A few seconds later, the door gave a stone-scraping-on-stone lurch, dust billowed, and the giant slabs of basalt heaved inward, revealing a staircase leading into a pitch-dark passageway. A second later, torches erupted with great flames that lit up a fifteen-foot-wide limestone staircase. We climbed. The steps were smooth and unworn through the ages, and the walls had been carved with more depictions of angels smiting enemies and the victorious winged ones standing over piles of the dead. As soon as we reached the top of the stairs, Rebekah let out a high-pitched whimper, visibly shaking with fear.

The body of a giant—sixteen feet in height—sagged against the far wall of the Sanctum. His torso rose and fell weakly as he breathed, but heavy iron chains draped across his wrists and ankles and around his neck. The carvings of angels at war continued on all four sides of the chamber, but where the images were within reach of the Naphil, they had been angrily clawed away until they were unidentifiable. Inside some of the jagged streaks were dried blood and broken fingernails. His head moved and his warm brown eyes—the only part of him that seemed human anymore—pierced mine from beneath long hair that had become twisted and matted into thick locks. He bared what was left of his broken, yellow teeth, blackened at the gums. His pale, dirt-caked skin had gouges cut deep and turned to black with rot that never healed, gouges that were elegant in the way they'd been cruelly carved. The marks were angelic script, a spell to keep his strength bound. If they healed, the spell would be undone, so another had been carved into his skin to keep the wounds from healing.

Tears ran down my cheeks and I covered my mouth with my hands to keep myself from breaking down sobbing. Ethan Stone had warned me of barbarity, but nothing could have prepared me for this.

"Do not weep for me, Gabriel," the Naphil said in a raspy, deep voice thick with the accent of a long-extinct human language, making the walls shake. "I am but a casualty of war."

I sniffed back my tears and forced out a response. "You know me?"

"You look different," he replied. His chains rattled as

his body shifted. "Very different. But I would recognize your face anywhere, even when it is not streaked with blood. Have you finally come to finish me off? I have been waiting to die for thousands of years."

"I am so sorry," I said. "I can't begin to tell you how much I regret what I've done to you."

"There is no need to lie. Angels do not feel regret."

"I do," I told him. "I have a human soul."

He dragged himself toward me like a spider, his chains and boney joints scraping across the stone floor. His body was deathly thin, all sharp angles and ghost-pale skin tight over bone, but somehow he had survived all this time. I could only imagine that it was his angelic side that kept him alive in agony. "You are a paradox, small Gabriel. You are not what you are, and you wish to lose what you have that makes you what you are not."

It took me a few moments of blinking to say, "What?"

"You are human, you are angel, you are neither now," the Naphil said. "Your humanity glows. Why would you wish to relinquish it?"

"I don't!" I said. "I don't want to be who I once was. I want to stay human, but I can't. The world is in danger."

He made an ugly noise. "*Again?* Who is your enemy this time?"

His words stung. "The demonic reapers, led by the Fallen Sammael and Lilith. They intend to take every human soul to Hell and destroy Heaven and Earth."

"You say that you regret what you have done, but you stand before me now prepared to repeat your actions. One must kill to save a life. That is the foundation for war, is it not?"

"That is a terrible truth," I admitted. "But seven billion human souls don't deserve an eternity in Hell. Even you can't deny that."

He studied my face, his eyes wandering and curious. "Who is to say who is right and who is wrong on either side of a battle?"

"My only wish is to protect the lives and immortal souls of the people in this world," I said. "The human race can't defend themselves against the reapers. This planet will burn and there will be nothing left!"

"I cannot deny the crimes of my kind," the Naphil said. "My own hands are permanently stained by innocent blood. But we never wanted to destroy everything. We only wanted more."

"We all want more," I said. "That's the part of you that makes up your human side. I feel that too. I want more. I want to live, but my life isn't as important as billions of lives."

A distant look grew in his gaze. "I would not know what it means to live anymore."

"Saying how sorry I am will never make up for what has been done to you," I said. "This is barbaric."

"I have deserved no less a fate," the Naphil said. "I have

done murder, Gabriel, and you imprisoned a criminal. That is the difference between our sins."

"Then you understand why I must kill you now?" I asked him.

"I have always known that you would come for me one day and why," he said. "I've had thousands of years to accept that I have done evil and that this is my punishment. I welcome death. Tell me about these beasts, the demonic reapers."

"They have gathered against us and are killing as many humans as they can and sending their souls to Hell. We can't let them do this anymore. We have to stop them once and for all. Sammael and Lilith, the Fallen leading the demonic, want to annihilate all life, everything."

The Naphil tried to stand, but his muscles had clearly atrophied. He slumped back over and his head lolled about on his shoulders. He stared sadly at the ground. "I am tired," the Naphil said. "I am tired of this hole in the earth."

"I wish I could offer you a better fate," I told him. I wanted nothing more than to free him and let him see the sky again, feel the sun on his skin, to let him live. But I couldn't. He couldn't live, and neither could I. I once asked myself if I could sacrifice others to win this war, and now that I knew I could answer that question with a 'yes,' I hated myself.

The Naphil's pitiful gaze found mine. "Kill to save many lives, Gabriel. Begin with me. Give me an honorable death."

"I'm sorry for what I have to do," I said.

"Do not be sorry for this," he said. "This is mercy. I do

not want to live like this anymore. Whatever fate greets my soul after death must be better than the weight of old iron chains."

Will stepped forward. "I'll do it, Ellie. Don't—"

"No," I said firmly. "I did this to him. I have to finish it."

The Naphil watched me as I moved toward him and called a single sword into my hand.

I would never forget the feel of the Naphil's skin breaking under the metal of my sword. I forced myself to watch him die as his life's blood poured from his haggard body. His eyes only left mine when he was gone. I wrapped his heart, which was about the size of a basketball, with linen that Rebekah gave me, and tucked it into my backpack.

The moment we left the Sanctum, the torches went out and the chamber turned to blackness, swallowing the corpse of the Naphil. We started back the way we had come and explored several tunnels that each ended in a wall of stone or another cave-in. Rebekah and Ethan walked well ahead of Will and me, poking at a tunnel system map between them.

"Derinkuyu had a ventilation shaft that was also used as a well," Dr. Massi said excitedly. "Most ventilation shafts are too tight for any of us to fit through, but one through which water is drawn should be wide enough. We may be able to use it to escape."

She hurried off, ducking into tiny doorways and whirling around columns, and the trickling sounds I'd heard since we entered the city grew louder as we followed her. The passage became a staircase that took us up and then back down again until it opened into a large cavern filled with water that gave off an eerie azure glow. The ceiling was two stories high at least and at the apex, a beam of daylight shone through a well shaft and hit the water.

"Oh, excellent," Ethan Stone said. "A way out. Good thing I was sure to be bitten by a radioactive spider so I can scale these walls and ceiling and shimmy my arse right out of here."

Will studied the well shaft for a long moment. "I don't think that would work," he murmured as Ethan's bad joke went right over his head. "I could fly up there. It's too narrow to fly all the way up, but I could climb. If I'm out, then I can find a rope, or look for another exit."

I nodded. "Good thinking. Maybe we can be out of here by dinnertime. I'm starved."

He shrugged off his T-shirt and handed it to me so I could keep it in my pack. He stepped over to the edge of the water and his wings spread with a slow grace to their full sixteen-foot breadth. Rebekah drew a sharp breath and whimpered, but she managed to hang on to her composure. Will jumped into the air, his wings beating a cloud of dust off the ground, and he rose through the center of the slant of golden sunlight. It only took him a single powerful wing-stroke to reach the shaft. His hands dug into grooves in the rock and he pulled his body into the narrow tunnel, the muscles in his arms and back twisting and straining with strength. His wings re-formed into his skin and his boots kicked into rock to push himself higher until he was out of my sight. My gut tightened for several long minutes as he scaled the well shaft and I held my breath when I couldn't hear him anymore.

Then something tumbled through the shaft, banging on rock, and a bucket tied at the end of a rope appeared and splashed into the water.

"Ellie!" Will's voice called from the surface. "Ellie, get the others to swim to the bucket and hang on. It should be strong enough to hold the weight while I hoist you all out one by one."

"There must be an active village built around this well," Rebekah said.

I dipped my fingers into the water to test the temperature. It was surprisingly chilly, but we'd warm up once we got to the surface and into the sunlight. "You two go first," I instructed.

Rebekah stepped into the water gingerly, moving slowly as her body adjusted to the sharp cold. She shivered a little once she began swimming, her head and backpack bobbing above the crystal-clear water. She reached the bucket and tried climbing into it, but it was so small. She accepted defeat and merely hung on with dear life. She gave the rope a couple of tugs and Will lifted her into the air slowly and smoothly with ease. Ethan's turn was next, and then at last it was time for me to get into the water. I made a little gasp at the chill, and I tried to keep my backpack from submerging with the Naphil's heart wrapped within. I reached the bucket, gently set my pack inside, and gripped the rope tight. I tugged once and looked up into the bright well shaft, wishing I could see Will's face. The bucket began to rise and my body rocked left and right as I rose high into the air. Determined not to look down, I stared at that hole until the sunlight practically burned my retinas out. The shaft was narrow and the rock walls clawed at my clothing as I was lifted through. I tried curling into a ball to keep my body from hitting the side as much as I could, but my hair still got caught on sharp pieces of stone jutting out.

As I reached the top, hands grabbed me and lifted me into blinding daylight. I stumbled over a rock ledge—the wall of the well, I realized, as my eyes adjusted to the bright light—and caught my balance before I hit the ground. They were Will's arms around me. I caught his scent before I could squint up into his face. I looked around him for the others. The well was situated in the center of a small, unusual village comprised of tall, cone-shaped houses made from mud and brick. Rebekah crouched over, talking to a small boy in dusty jeans. Ethan, cursing up a storm, wrestled his backpack straps from a few relentless sheep who really wanted whatever he had in there.

"Shirt?" Will asked.

It took me a moment to remember that I'd taken it for

safekeeping so his wings wouldn't rip the fabric. We had only brought so many changes of clothes with us. I dug the shirt out of my backpack, which was mostly soaked with water despite my attempt to keep it dry, and handed it to him. I also checked on the heart. The linen wrapping was still wet with blood, but it didn't look like the heart was damaged. The water even seemed to have washed away a lot of the blood. Now we just needed to worry about how we were getting out of the Middle of Nowhere, Syria.

Ethan Stone let out a triumphant roar when he won back his pack and, still dripping wet, stomped over to us. He pulled a plastic waterproof case from the bag and snapped it open to retrieve a satellite phone.

"You thought of everything, didn't you?" I asked him, bewildered and relieved to see that phone.

"Not everything," he replied as he fiddled with some buttons. "Satellite phone with GPS enabled, yes. However, I didn't bring towels." He put the phone to his ear. "Yusri? Hello? We're ready for pickup."

30

ETHAN STONE EXPLAINED TO US THAT THE RITE OF my ascension could only be performed on hallowed ground, and it was Will's idea to travel to Israel. The final showdown would be at Armageddon, at Har Megiddo, and I decided that I should ascend someplace very sacred. After all, there wasn't a better place for one to become an archangel than in the Kingdom of Heaven. I wanted to maximize what power we could draw from Earth into this spell. I needed to be as strong as I absolutely could.

After Yusri picked us up in a helicopter, Ethan offered us a room at a luxury hotel in Aleppo, but I only wanted to get out of there. We rented a Jeep to leave Syria and continue to Jerusalem. Even if I wanted to crash for the night, I'd never be able to fall asleep. I felt sick and restless over what had happened at Ain Dara. Something inside of me had changed, turned—like a piece of my humanity was now missing. I was used to having blood on my hands, but this was different.

Ethan Stone promised that he'd fly into Jerusalem at first light. Will and I packed our things into the Jeep and headed out. We also didn't want to run the chance of meeting any more of Sammael's goons. If he'd stationed one in Aleppo, then there were bound to be more. Will and I needed to keep moving to lessen our chances of being found.

The journey was over three hundred miles in pitch-dark night. I drove, partly in an attempt to cure my restlessness and give myself something to focus on. To my dismay, that left Will with nothing to focus on but his worry for me.

"You did what you had to do," he said gently.

I glanced at him before staring back onto the road. "I've been telling myself that a lot lately and I know it's true. I just don't like doing what I have to do."

"You're not the only one," he said.

I exhaled. "Will you be all right once I become an angel again?"

"I don't know," he answered. "I'm just following your lead here."

"If I do this, then we have a shot at beating Hell. That's all that matters."

He was quiet for a few seconds. "Not all." Before I could reply, he spoke first. "I won't stop your ascension. You're the one thing I can't be selfish about, but I am nevertheless. I finally understand why Michael forbade me to love you. In some ways it makes me a stronger Guardian, but in others I am crippled. I just never expected I'd have to give you up."

"When Michael asked you to become my Guardian, did you ever consider saying no?"

He slumped deeper into the seat, thoughtful. "Not even once. Instead, I wondered if I was willing to give up my life for you, to lay it down for you. I wondered if I was willing to become expendable and insignificant, to relinquish my own dreams and desires and to become a servant. When he asked me to be your Guardian, I considered only selfish thoughts, and I realized that they were things I could sacrifice. I knew that I wanted only to have you in my life, to protect you and to follow you, so that in the end, I wasn't losing anything at all. But now I'm going to lose you after I believed I would have you forever. This is the first time since I became your Guardian that I feel like I've ever given up anything, that I feel empty. You were a gift."

I glanced at him again only to find him watching me with those crystalline green eyes. "I believe there's a chance that I will be myself when I'm an archangel again, and that I will survive using the hallowed glaive."

"I will pray for it," he said.

We arrived in Jerusalem just before dawn. Will had taken over driving at about the halfway point, so I was able to get a little sleep, but it was nowhere near what I needed. We decided that we needed to rent a room somewhere and rest before we did anything else. The size of the city allowed us to disappear into the crowd and would make it hard for our enemies to track us, so we found an inconspicuous hole-in-the-wall inn that had vacancy. I texted our location to Ethan Stone. After a few hours of fitful sleep, we woke to a fierce rapping on the door. Will got up, rubbing his eyes, to let Ethan into the room. I pulled the covers over my head and hid, but kept one eye peeking over at him.

"Morning, morning," Stone sang so cheerfully that I wanted to break his kneecaps. He set two large brown paper bags on the little round dining table across from the bed. "Oh, don't look at me like that. I brought you breakfast!"

The smell of food lulled me out from my hiding place. I flipped the blanket over and crawled across the bed toward the bags of goodness. I grabbed one and tore it open. My stomach roared like I hadn't eaten in days. Inside was a plastic container of eggs and another filled with a salad and a big chunk of bread. "Aw, no bacon?" I asked.

Ethan gave me a reproachful look. "You're joking, right?"

"Yes, moron." I pulled out the eggs first. "Thanks for breakfast."

"It's good," Will said approvingly through a mouthful as he dipped his bread into some pasty stuff. "We don't have a plan of action yet. We just wanted to get here, to Jerusalem."

Ethan slapped a tourist brochure onto the table. "St. Anne's Church. That's where we're headed."

I slid it closer so I could take a look. The cover featured

a photograph of a beautiful and ancient Roman Catholic church built of gold and gray stone. "Why?"

"Because I paid a groundskeeper to leave a gate unlocked," he replied. "Also, it's nine centuries old and supposedly the basilica sits upon the birthplace of the Virgin Mary. *Also*, also, the acoustics are incredible. I've been dying to play AC/DC in there for years."

I chose to ignore that. "So, food now. What next?"

"Shopping for your ascension rite," he replied and handed me a sheet of paper. "Now don't go all schoolgirl squealy on me. We're buying herbs, not shoes. I have a list and you have a list. It'll be like a scavenger hunt. Now you can go all squealy."

I glared at him and read the list of ingredients he requested for the spell.

"Afterward, we'll meet at St. Anne's." He started toward the door but turned back before leaving. "Don't show up until after ten or eleven, okay? Everyone in Old City will be down at the Festival of Light, so we shouldn't be bothered. We don't want anyone wandering by while we're trying to shove an archangel into that skin of yours."

Then Stone was gone.

I sat on the bed, gazing blankly at the ingredients list in my hands. Will eased down beside me, took the sheet of paper from me, and set it aside. He took my hands and held them in his. My small, slender fingers fit perfectly through his callused ones, like puzzle pieces. My hands moved over his, my fingertips tracing the lines in his palm, and then I drew his hand to my cheek. I had a horrible thought that I wouldn't remember or care what his skin felt like against mine once I ascended. I wondered whether, if I touched him for as long as I could, the feeling would be burned into my memory and made permanent, with no force on Earth or in Heaven able to chip it away.

Will felt my sorrow through our bond and pulled me close. "We'll make it through this. We always do."

"We've never been through anything like this before," I whispered. "Never anything so uncertain."

He was quiet at first, thoughtful. "Facing the unknown is a part of life, something humans have done since their creation without any special powers. They've survived by sheer will and heart. You have both of those things, stronger than anyone I've ever known. We don't know what exactly will happen tonight, but you have the will and the heart to make it through anything, even through this. I believe in you."

"But why do I have to lose who I am in order to save the world?"

He lifted my chin so I couldn't avoid his firm but gentle gaze. "If you forget who you are, I will just have to wake you up again as I've always done."

I bit my lip and before I could say anything back, he kissed me and I wasn't afraid anymore.

* * *

By nightfall the light festival, which Ethan had mentioned would serve as a distraction for us, was in full swing. From the top of the Mount of Olives, music thrummed like thunder and laser lights danced across the low-hanging atmosphere. Thousands and thousands of people were in attendance, pouring through every street past imaginative displays of galloping horses made of light, shadow monsters playing behind trees, glowing figures of men climbing over stone walls . . . Old City was alive and surreal, and I longed to stop and enjoy the festivities, but there was no time for that.

St. Anne's was even more beautiful in person and at night. Golden spotlights lit up the stone walls, but our movements were safely cloaked within the Grim. We entered through a wooden door and passed through a small courtyard filled with incredible flowers. Ethan met us at the front entrance and allowed us in. Passing humans would never notice us as long as we stayed hidden in the Grim.

Ethan had already spread out our ingredients for the ritual on the cool stone floor, and Will helped me set out the herbs, oils, and incense to sort and measure. Just as I placed the grimoire among them, Ethan used his power to flip the book open and the pages settled to a passage written in Enochian.

"Is this the spell?" I asked Ethan.

He was fiddling inside a duffle bag on the altar when he replied, "It is. I'll need to speak the words. You can stand there and look pretty while Will assists me. I shall be your Frankenstein and Will shall be my—much larger than normal—Igor."

Will sighed as he lit the incense and candles and placed them, one by one, on the altar steps below Ethan. When I looked at Ethan again, he was pulling a battery-powered MP3 docking station out of a duffle bag. He set it onto the floor and plugged in his iPod.

"I didn't think you were serious," I called to him. "You can't play that in here."

"I am *always* serious," he replied. Suddenly AC/DC's "Highway to Hell" burst out of stark silence and echoed off the cathedral's vaulted ceiling.

"Are you kidding me?" I cried, struggling with myself not to chuck the book at his head.

"Oh, bloody hell," he said as he fumbled with the player and shut it off. The basilica fell quiet again. "That was inappropriate. Sorry!"

I looked across the book at Will for support, but he was grinning ear to ear, trying not to laugh. I shoved his shoulder so hard he almost toppled over. "Stop laughing!"

He caught his balance and put his hands up, unable to hold back his laughter anymore. "It was funny! You have to admit."

"It *wasn't* funny," I hissed. "It was horrible. *You* are horrible, Ethan."

"No," he said as he fiddled with the iPod. "Classy. Always classy."

Music blasted once more, this time "Thunderstruck." Seeing Will laugh made me realize we needed some kind of levity. I had to savor this moment of good spirits and fun, because I couldn't be sure when or if I'd ever have another one like it. I wasn't sure when the next time I'd see Will laugh would be.

I finished measuring out the oils and incense needed and placed them in small ceramic dishes. I unwrapped the Naphil heart, which was still as red and bright as when I had cut it from its owner's chest, as if no piece of it had even begun to decay yet. Ethan gave me a clay bowl to set the heart in and he instructed me to anoint the organ with the correct oils. Then it came time for me to stand in the basilica while Ethan dipped his thumb into three different oils and drew lines down my nose and over my lips. He drew the oil across my necklace as well and then he stepped back.

The music was gone and the only sounds I heard now were the distant cheers of spectators at the Festival of Light and the pounding of my heart. The candlelight on the steps below me cast a golden glow in the basilica, occasionally interrupted by beams of light from outside. Ethan lifted the book to read the angelic spell, his voice a haunting echo through the cathedral.

Fear, like ripples in reverse, growing stronger as it

spread, took fierce hold of me. I tried to look at Will, but when I did, I was struck by the memory of the first time I witnessed him double over in agony as my overwhelming guilt and grief spilled into him through the ink in his tattoos that bound us together. The angelic magic gave us a connection deeper than anything else in this world, and though its purpose was to alert him when I needed him the most, this magic was also very cruel. I tried to contain my fear, because I knew my emotions echoed into Will and made him feel everything that I did through physical pain. He felt my fear like knives in his gut, and I didn't want my last action as me—as Ellie—to be to cause him pain.

Will's gaze captured my own and held it tight. "Eyes on me," he said. "My face, Ellie. Eyes on me. Don't be afraid."

The green of his eyes was so bright and his breathing became more and more labored. Unbidden tears rolled down my cheeks and I watched him struggle to keep standing. He knew that I'd discovered how my suffering affected him physically, and it only crushed my heart more.

"Let me take it," he murmured. "It's okay. Let me have this. Let me do this for you."

I nodded, choking down a fearful swallow of air. I could feel the ancient words taking affect. A light grew inside of me, a warmth that was foreign, but still felt familiar. I could no longer watch Will's face. The light I felt inside me began to shine through my skin, giving me a glow of my own. I watched the light gather along the spider's web-work of veins in my skin, replacing my blood with bright gold until I gleamed like a beacon. I fumbled for my necklace, my fingers brushing past the leather cord carrying the Pentalpha, and I found my winged necklace and gripped it tight. I held it between my fingers as if it were my lifeline, my last link to my humanity, even though it contained the archangel grace that would strip my humanity from me like meat off my bones.

The light, my glory breaking free from its chains, was growing too bright and I could barely keep my eyes open. Ethan kept chanting even when I could no longer see him. My body seemed to take on a mind of its own; the magic lifted me off the floor as my hair whipped around my face as if I was trapped in a hurricane. I looked down, forcing my eyes open so I could see what was happening. Ethan lit a match and tossed it into the bowl with the Naphil heart, and the red organ sparked and went up in flames. My body lurched as the smoke from the burning heart and fragranced oils engulfed me. It smelled like cooked meat and flowers from a funeral.

"Ellie," Ethan called up to me, practically yelling over the rushing of wind through the church. "Ellie! Your necklace! Break it and free your grace!"

I yanked on the pendant, snapping the clasp apart, but I didn't get the chance to chuck it at the stone floor. It shattered on its own in my palm in a flash of light and instead of dispersing, that light—my grace—collected itself like a sentient thing and clung to me, my clothes, my hair, spreading over my body and sinking into my skin.

"Oh my God," I breathed. "Shut your eyes, Ethan. Shut your eyes!"

Something inside of me exploded and the erupting light was bright enough to fry human retinas from their sockets. My glory and grace devoured me, changed me, filled me with a sensation that I'd long forgotten. There was an intense warmth all around me and then it turned to heat, to a blinding heat that seared the edges of my clothing. Pieces burned off and were blown away. My hair was a tornado of fire around my body. My shoulder blades tingled and became numb and I swore I glimpsed a feather fall to the floor.

Then I felt nothing. Saw nothing. I wasn't sure how long I stayed like that in the whiteness, but that eternity ended in an instant. The fire and light vanished, and the candles blew out, drenching the cathedral in darkness. My toes touched the floor, boots silent on stone, and my hair settled around me. My shoulders were no longer numb, but they felt heavy with the weight of my wings.

"Her eyes," the human murmured as I passed him. "They're solid gold. She's ascended."

My Guardian stared at me, lips parted, and he took a step forward to follow me. "Ellie?"

I stopped. The feathers from my wings brushed the floor, lucent feathers the color of moonlight with just a breath of gold, and I picked them up, folding them against my back. "I am not Ellie."

His mouth clamped shut, his jaw clenching. I saw these things, recognized the pain on his face, but I felt nothing in return.

I continued walking toward the sanctuary doors. "I am Gabriel."

31

"ELLIE!" MY GUARDIAN SHOUTED AT ME, BUT I didn't stop. "Gabriel! Where are you going?"

I ignored him and continued through the crowds cele-brating the Festival of Light. Few humans failed to notice me, but I suspected that was because I had not yet with-drawn my wings. I would need to take to the air soon.

Jerusalem had changed since I'd last seen it with my archangel eyes. I remembered passing through here just this evening in my human form—I remembered everything—but experiencing these neon streets now was different. I remem-bered thinking the displays of light were beautiful, but now I asked myself what had made these lights beautiful? I wasn't sure I even understood what "beautiful" meant.

My Guardian made an angry sound as he pushed through the crowd to catch up with me. "Ellie, God damn it—"

"I accept your presence, Guardian," I told him as I watched several women wearing white dresses threaded with tubes of light whirl around us in the street. "But I am in no danger."

"You accept me?" he hissed. He grabbed my arm and yanked me around and into his chest.

I twisted my arm until his bent the wrong way and he cried out, but I grabbed his wrist with my free hand before he could let go. His knees buckled and hit the ground. "How *dare* you touch me, Earthling?" I snarled, baring teeth.

He gaped up at me. He did not seem to understand that he was only a reaper. I remembered . . . I remembered that he had touched me before, that I had let him, that I had . . . But I was an archangel now. I was not to be touched.

"Hey," said a meek voice to our right. It belonged to a young man who stared at my charred clothing and gigantic wings. He seemed to accept that I was part of the show. "Is there a problem here?"

I released my Guardian and waved a hand, shoving my power into the human's chest and blowing him away from me. He toppled through the crowd with a cry, taking down a light display with him.

"Ellie!" Will shouted at me in anger. When I looked at my Guardian, I saw the revulsion in his green eyes. "What are you doing?"

I continued on my way. He shouted my human name behind me as he fought to catch up. I scanned the tops of the buildings around me and spotted the Dome of the Rock. I spread my wings and they carried me into the air. I flew fast, moving as a ball of fire, a falling star, and I settled at the top of the golden dome and spread my wings to help keep my balance. I inhaled the cool night air alive with the heady scents of Jerusalem. I was not supposed to breathe. I had ascended and become an archangel, but this body . . . I was still partially human.

My Guardian dropped less gracefully onto the dome. His boots slipped and his wings folded into his back. "Ellie, what the hell? You just bolted. Are you okay? How do you feel?"

He caught my attention and I stared at him, my hair whipping around my head. "I do not understand your questions."

"Oh no," he said sorrowfully. "Don't let this be real."

"I empathize with your attachment—"

"You *what?*" His body rocked gently in the wind. "Who *are* you?"

"You know who I am."

He shook his head, his anger clear. "You are not my Ellie."

"No, I am not," I said. "Not in the way you knew me." I slid down the side of the dome and leaped onto the flat roof.

He followed me, jumping down to return to my side. "But she's in there. She's a part of you."

"That is true," I said. "I am Ellie, but I am also Gabriel. I'm not human. Not anymore."

He reached for me and I began to pull away, but I stopped

and allowed him to touch my cheek. "Have I lost you?"

His fingers against my skin were warm and not unpleasant. As much as I wanted to push him away, I didn't. "I'm right here."

"You don't understand, do you?" he asked, his tone heavy with sorrow. "You can't feel anything. You don't even know me."

Something instinctive and uncontrollable stirred in my chest, a flutter of heat and longing. "I can feel. I can feel your touch."

"That's not what I mean," he said. He drew in a short breath and bit his upper lip, a gesture that gave me more unwanted feelings. "It's more than that. Don't you remember me? Don't you know me?"

"I remember you," I said in a small voice. "Will."

He backed off and clenched his fists, his lips trembling. "You say my name like you don't know me."

It was then that I pulled away and the coldness returned. "I know you. You are my Guardian."

He stared at me, slack-jawed and pathetic. "That's it?"

I spread my wings and started to turn away from him. "I am sorry."

He shook his head. "You don't even know what sorry means. You've let yourself become just another heartless angel."

Over my shoulder, I narrowed my gaze at him. "And you are just a reaper."

He said nothing for several long moments, and just as I was about to leave, he drew a deep breath and spoke. "This . . . this is far more cruel than anything anyone has ever done to me. This is worse for me than if you had died. This is torture."

I studied, perplexed, as the agony on his face deepened. I knew the extent of his emotions for me and I knew how I had felt about him, but now I felt . . . nothing. I remembered, but the feelings were only memories, distant, fading things far out of my reach. Perhaps there was nothing after all. When I looked at my Guardian's face, at the sorrow and pain in his eyes, I felt regret for what I had said to him. That was nothing I had ever felt before in Heaven. Angels had been created to be perfect soldiers. We felt no regret, no mercy, and certainly no compassion. I was an archangel once again, but I had changed.

Something in my pocket vibrated. I slipped out a device, something my human memories recalled was a cell phone. I stared at it and Will took it from my hand. He took an instant to identify the caller on the screen and then pressed the phone to his ear.

"Hello?" he answered. "It's Will. Yeah. Sort of. Just meet us at the hotel." He recited the address and hung up. "That was Cadan."

"Ah," I said. "The demonic reaper."

"My brother," Will growled. "And your friend. You'd better not treat him the way you treat me."

I did not reply to that.

"I'm calling Ethan and telling him to clean up the evidence left behind in the church," he continued. "He can meet us at our hotel room where we'll regroup with Cadan. Do you remember where—?"

The rest of his question was lost to my ears. I'd already taken flight and left him.

I had to tuck away my wings when I returned to our hotel. The mortals of today weren't as welcoming of my presence as they were the last time I visited as an archangel. The times had changed. I'd lived all of them, and I was grateful for maintaining my human memories. I would have had a much harder time navigating this new world without them.

But the memories also made things more complicated. My Guardian . . . How I had allowed myself to have feelings for him—to *love* him—was beyond me, but I'd been human for so long. I was built to be a soldier, the perfect machine created to seek and destroy. I commanded my own legions of angels that devastated and banished the armies of Lucifer eons ago. When I was first told I would be sent to Earth to destroy the demonic reaper spawn of Lucifer's Fallen abominations, Sammael and Lilith, I had felt the first flicker of emotion since my creation. I was . . . uncertain. I'd seen the humans, watched them grow from languageless creatures into a species with ideas and ambitions, and I wasn't sure I would be able to walk among them. To feel as they do. To smile the way I'd seen them smile. I carried a dark secret in my heart: I wanted these things. When I become mortal, God gave me a human soul. He told me that His angels weren't as perfect as He had hoped we would be, that there was something missing in us, something that kept us from reaching our full potential as His creation. He told me that my human soul was a gift, that it would save me—save us all. And then I had felt the second emotion since my creation: doubt.

My time in Heaven was always so brief in between my mortal deaths and I remembered nothing the instant I returned to my human vessel. That had been frustrating. No matter how much I trained with my brothers and sisters in Heaven, or how much strength I gathered in my archangel power, it all went to waste the moment I returned to Earth.

When Michael had discovered Bastian's plans to release Sammael and Lilith, my orders were to remain in Heaven. On my next reincarnation, I had to be stronger, faster, and more certain to defeat the Fallen. We'd hoped that the longer I delayed my return to Earth, the likelier chance I'd retain my memories as my true self. Unfortunately, this had the opposite effect and I'd had an even more difficult time regaining even my human memories. I'd set myself even farther back and only made myself more human, a mewling little thing— a human teenage girl.

But now my power had returned to me. It surged through me like a torrential river waiting to be unleashed. Now that I had ascended, everything had proven worthwhile. Yet there was something inside of me that churned and whispered to me, something that had a different and immeasurable power of its own: my soul. It had stayed with me through my ascension, because it had become a part of me. My soul was who I was, the unique individual I had become.

And yet . . . That human version of me proved to be stronger than any previous incarnation. As a human girl, I had felt insurmountable fear, yet I had surmounted it. I had felt love, and I had fought harder for my friends and family because of it. I had faced enemies that should have defeated me, and yet I walked away alive. There had been strength in my human self that no one could have ever anticipated—or perhaps someone did and He had been right. Perhaps this human soul was a gift after all, just as God had promised me.

But would it save me? Save us all?

I found the key to my hotel room in my pocket. Once inside, I tossed my burned clothing in the trash and put on fresh jeans and a shirt. My stomach rumbled, surprising me. I hadn't expected to feel hunger now that I had ascended. This made me wonder how human I had remained.

The door burst open and my Guardian emerged, his face clenched with anger, and as soon as he saw me, relief poured over him. "Thank God you're here. Why would you take off like that?"

"You said that we would meet everyone back here," I said.

"You're supposed to wait for me!" he shouted. "We're supposed to stick together!"

I put my palm to my belly. "I'm hungry."

His eyes bulged. "You're—? What is wrong with you?"

"This form is strange to me."

"Strange?"

"I was human only minutes ago," I said. "Now I am an archangel." I held out my hands and tightened them into fists, watching tendons and joints move and contract. "There is blood in my veins. I'm not supposed to hunger, or feel tired, or need to breathe. In truth, I don't know what I've become. I am an archangel, but I am more than that."

He lifted both his hands and touched either sides of my face, letting his fingers spill into my hair. "You know exactly what you are."

I studied how the hard look on his face softened as he touched me, as if the feel of me did that to him, comforted him. "You are very peculiar."

"I'm just being me," he said. "You're the one acting weird."

"I remember everything," I told him, and I didn't push him away. "You loved me."

"I still do, even though you don't love me anymore. I promised you I would."

I couldn't look away from his face, no matter how hard I tried. "This is not permitted."

His gaze fell and he reached for one of my hands. He

drew it close to his lips. "What isn't?"

"You are not permitted to touch me."

"Then stop me." His eyes flashed brightly. His nose and lips brushed my palm, his breath warm on my skin, and that uncompelled sensation returned to me.

"I don't want to," I told him. "I'm not supposed to want you to touch me."

"You smell like jasmine," he said very softly. "It's the cream you put on your skin every morning after your shower. You still smell like the human girl you were minutes ago. You still *are* her. I know this body of yours as well as I know my own. You're still my Ellie."

His lips found my wrist and he closed his eyes as he kissed the tender skin there. I shivered and drew away from him, afraid of this feeling he gave me that was more than physical. I remembered too well the way he made me feel, but I didn't understand it. I knew what he felt and that I had felt the same, but those emotions were gone and never should have existed in the first place.

He looked at me with eyes full of a mixture of hurt and determination. "I'll bring you back to me."

I started to say something, but the door opened again and another reaper stepped through. This was the demonic reaper, the brother of my Guardian, and behind him, a second demonic reaper appeared.

"Hey, guys," Cadan greeted. "You remember Ronan, right?"

I recognized the tall vir's ginger-colored hair and candy-orange eyes. He wore a wary expression and his gaze shifted from Will to me. "Gabriel," he said, his tone careful.

Cadan watched me cautiously, studying me. As he grew closer, I sensed his demonic energy scratching at my own power like cat claws on a wall, digging through paint and plaster with an ear-splitting screech. I gritted my teeth hard and crushed my nails into my palm to keep myself grounded. I had called this demonic reaper my friend, this demonic reaper who had told me he loved me. The emotions in me now were so stirring, so conflicting, and I did not know what to do with myself. I was an archangel. What had I done to deserve the love of a demonic reaper? It was a strange thing.

"Are you okay?" he asked, watching my fists tighten as hard as they could. He took a step forward, but stopped himself. There was fear in his eyes as he gave Will a panicked look. "What did you mean by 'sort of' on the phone?"

"She's an archangel," Will confirmed. "But things are . . . complicated."

"How complicated? Is she dangerous?"

I glared at both of them. "I am still able to hear you."

"How do you feel?" Cadan asked. "Stronger?"

"I know I am stronger and I am ready to fight," I said. "We must gather our forces and meet the armies of Hell on Armageddon. Is Ronan your recruit?"

"I am, among others," Ronan replied stiffly.

"I have a little army of my own now," Cadan said. "Those

who have been loyal to me before are no longer afraid to stand against Sammael."

"Good," I said. "I'm grateful for your allegiance. I hold no ill will toward those demonic who will fight by my side."

He gave me an odd look. "Are you sure you're okay? Ellie, are you in there? You seem . . . off."

"She's still settling in," Will said pointedly, and crossed his arms.

I met his piercing green gaze. So much was stirring and unsaid in those hidden depths, and I remembered how I once comforted him when he looked like that. I shut my eyes tight. I remembered so much. I was weary with it all.

The hotel room door opened once more. Ethan Stone seemed out of breath and relieved. "You found her. Excellent. That'd be awkward if we handed out 'lost archangel' posters all over town. No one would take us seriously, for God's sake. They'd arrest us!"

"Ethan," Will mumbled disapprovingly.

"Well, they'd arrest you first," he continued, pointing at Will. "You're far more shady-looking than I. The tattoos. That's what it is."

I stepped up to him, having to crane my neck to look into his face. "Thank you for assisting in my ascension. You will be rewarded upon our victory."

His mouth twitched. "*Upon* our victory. Of course there's a catch. My men are willing to meet you on Har Megiddo, but I have no intention of taking command of them, or to stick around for the battle. I've had enough excitement with you to last me several lifetimes."

"You're leaving?" Will asked.

"Weep for me if you must," Ethan said. "*Adieu*, my reaper friends, and currently archangel friend. Look me up if you survive the apocalypse, yeah?"

After Ethan had gone, Cadan gave an update on the state of our army and that of Sammael. "I have a hundred or so recruited under my command. I've led in battle before and I'm willing to take more."

"Have you heard from Ava and Marcus?" Will asked.

Cadan nodded. "They have several thousand soldiers, perhaps enough to fill a legion, who will arrive tomorrow at dusk on the hill. All reapers have been anticipating this battle. They've been ready."

"Sammael knows we're in Jerusalem," Ronan said. "The battle on Armageddon has been long foretold. He will have his spies watching the hill."

"I will not wait for him," I said, gazing down at the Pentalpha around my finger. "I will call him to me."

Will watched me with a careful gaze. "Are you sure?"

"I have the power I need," I said. "It's time to fight. Do we have an estimation of our enemies' numbers?"

Cadan looked grim. "Ten thousand. Likely more. We're still outnumbered two to one, even with an archangel on our side."

"Do not forget how David defeated Goliath," I told him.

"Not with skill in warfare or large numbers, but with faith. You must believe that we can win, or we can*not* win. Have faith in me and in yourself."

"Always." He offered a small smile that lasted for only a moment and he turned toward the door. "The sun's coming up. We'll meet you on the hill at twilight."

The two demonic reapers left me alone with my Guardian once more. The stillness between us was eerily quiet and as tense as cracks in glass. Though he sat in a chair at the table and said nothing, Will seemed to be balancing on the edge of screaming at the top of his lungs. I did not know what to do. I was exhausted, not only from the journey and my ascension, but from the battle I waged against myself deep within. My humanity, my human soul, was not lost; it lingered like a stubborn piece of flesh left hanging from the cut of a sword and was just as agonizing. My archangel discipline wanted to yank it off and cast it aside, but I clung to it. I knew I was supposed to let go, but I didn't want to. I was afraid to. Acknowledging my fear had to be the first step of my undoing.

"Are you prepared?" Will asked. "We should sleep a few hours, eat, and head to the hill."

I refused to make the mistake of letting my thoughts show. "I have been preparing for this a very long time. I will evoke Azrael, claim the hallowed glaive, and I will defeat Sammael and Lilith."

He stood and eased toward me, but remained several feet

away. "It's okay if you're afraid. I know the angels are not supposed to feel emotion, but I know you do. I can still feel you through the link in my tattoos."

My heartbeat quickened as he neared me, no matter how calm I struggled to stay. "Emotion is a weakness."

"That's not what you've said, and believed."

"I was wrong."

"You're wrong now," he said. "You're lying about what you really think."

I glared at him. "How would you know what I think?"

His smile was small and secret. "Because I have loved you for five centuries and I know your heart. You've spent a lot of time teaching me to bend the rules and to follow my heart, and you know what? You were right. So there is no way I will ever believe that everything about you has changed in one night."

"I know better now," I told him. "Anything but obedience is wrong."

He shook his head, his gaze hardening. "You don't believe that."

"I am an archangel," I said. "I must obey—"

"And give up happiness?" he asked, cutting me off. "I know you remember what it felt like to be human. You can't deny that."

I took a deep breath, summoning my courage. "I don't deny it. My humanity haunts me."

"Then come back to me," he begged. "With every second

that passes I see a little more of Ellie in your eyes."

I tried not to look at him, words sputtering out of me like water. "We are not supposed to feel. To feel is to disobey."

"That isn't you talking," he said. "I want her back. I want Ellie back."

"This is who I am, Guardian."

"No. She's still in there." He grabbed me by the wrist and yanked me against him, startling me.

"Let go of me," I ordered. "What are you doing?"

His firefly eyes, all green flames and shadows, seared into mine. "I'm waking you up."

I gasped as he dipped his head and kissed me hard, opening his mouth against mine and crushing me into his body. I pressed my hands into his chest, feeling his hot skin beneath my fingertips, and I knew I should push him away, but I didn't want to. His kiss brought memories raging to the surface of my mind, thoughts I couldn't experience without . . . without *feeling* with a part of me that was deeper than my skin, a part of me that ached. I felt happiness and comfort and a wanting for him, every inch of him. I felt this human soul stir and cry out, beating at the walls that had caged it in when I'd become an archangel again. My human soul was the core of this body, my archangel power just an extension—something alien. I had to accept what I was now: an archangel with a human soul. I was happy, and that made me stronger, more determined. I was a puzzle made of pieces that didn't belong, but when he touched me, those pieces melded together with perfection, as if they'd always been meant to. As if he'd always been meant to touch me.

He pulled away with a deep breath, his eyes even brighter than they were moments ago. They scattered over every inch of my face and returned to linger on my lips before his gaze met mine, his fingers twining through my hair. "Say my name," he ordered, his voice low and husky.

I swallowed hard. "Will."

His jaw tightened and he shook his head. "No. Say my name like you know you love me. Like you remember what it feels like when I touch you. Like you remember what I feel like."

I shut my eyes and remembered the heat of his skin on mine, the sound of his voice in the darkness, the sound of my own name on his lips whispered into my ear like a prayer.

A human tear rolled down my cheek and I wasn't ashamed of it. "Will," I breathed.

He smiled that familiar smile that was only ever for me, and I once again understood what beautiful meant. *He* was beautiful. The love I felt for him was beautiful. Will. My Will. Then he kissed me again and I lost myself in him.

32

I WATCHED THE MOON RISE OVER HAR MEGIDDO from my perch on the hill overlooking an expansive valley of green farmland, rich dark soil, and rock. I sat atop an ancient stone wall built into a ledge, one leg dangling over the edge, and I leaned onto my other knee. The stone was still warm from the day's sun, and the ruins cast long, clawlike shadows in the silence. The scrub-covered hill was dotted with tall palms and fresh excavations uncovering layers upon layers of human civilization. Soon the hill would be dotted with blood as well.

Will came toward me, hopping over a low stone wall and jogging up a staircase carved into the rock. "They're here," he said.

I gazed ahead at a great shadow coming up the hill and I smiled, nodding in approval. Ava, Marcus, and Madeleine had returned, and with them, a legion of angelic reapers. My three friends came forward with the other angelic reapers serving as my generals, the elite. I recognized the faces of Berengar, Calix, and Evolet. A fiery-haired female staying close to Ava had to be Maeghan, her contact in Brussels.

"Ellie!" Marcus called. He looked tired and, in fact, they all did. "Did it work? Are you an angel?"

I answered by spreading my wings, tearing through the fabric of my shirt. Surprise lit their faces—some showing fear—their gazes running the length of my wings, spilling over the gleam of the feathers in the moonlight. Only Madeleine looked upon me with sadness.

"Thank you for joining us," I said to them.

Evolet flashed me a smile. "What can I say? You inspired me."

"My lady," Berengar murmured, and dropped to his knees. "Gabriel."

The army of angelic reapers knelt to the ground, folding over like a wave breaking the beach. I surveyed them, friends and strangers who'd come here to perhaps die for our cause, and I stood up from my spot on the ledge. We were outnumbered two to one, but I knew that more than ratios and ready swords mattered in this battle. These soldiers had faith in me as their leader, and faith was what we needed to win.

"Rise," I called out to them, and the sea of reapers returned to their feet, a thousand pairs of eyes like a rainbow of stars across the dark land. "I do not wish for tribute. I wish only for your faith in me. We have all come a long way to meet on this hill. Some of you may be afraid, and that is all right."

I looked at Will below me on the ground, whose smile was quiet as he watched me.

"It is natural to feel fear," I continued, "but tonight I offer you courage. It is all that I can offer you. I cannot guarantee victory or even your lives, but take of me my courage and glory will be yours. I thank you for fighting with me through the eons and for fighting with me tonight for possibly the last time."

A great energy rolling through the hills made me lift my gaze. I took in the sight of yet another army—this one led by Cadan. He had come through, just as I knew he would. I smiled, because I was no longer afraid of the emotions I felt. Among the demonic reapers who had turned their backs on Hell was a force of at least one hundred heavily armed humans. They had to be Ethan Stone's promised mercenaries, humans who had trained to combat the demonic reapers—yet tonight they submitted to the command of one.

I heard hissing and spit curses, the shuffling of boots and clinking of metal blades coming from the angelic reapers, who clearly weren't as accepting of the new arrivals as I was. The humans who had joined the demonic were battle scarred and seemed to be champing at the bit for action in the field. What they lacked in numbers and supernatural strength, they made up for in grit and passion.

"Gabriel," Cadan said when he stopped at Will's side and his opalescent eyes met mine.

My smile widened. "My friend." I lifted my head to address our growing army. "Tonight we are all friends. The world is not so black and white as we have believed for a very long time. Once our enemies, these reapers are now our friends, and we are united against a common enemy."

Ronan came forward, flanked by two demonic reapers, a male and a female. "This is Anders and Adara," he announced. "They will join Cadan and me in leading the demonic infantry."

I offered them a warm smile and withdrew my heavy wings. "Come with me," I said to my generals.

They followed me a little ways higher up the hill covered with the ruins of an ancient city along a path meant for tourists and excavators. I beckoned them to a bit of open ground where I'd been devising our main tactic. They studied my formations etched into the dirt. I marked our location on the hill and down into the valley where Hell's armies would come.

"Where did you learn all of this, Ell?" Cadan asked, marveling, his eyes following the path of our formations.

I frowned at him. "I am the archangel Gabriel, second only to Michael in Heaven. I led our armies to victory over Lucifer and then over the Nephilim. This is not my first battle."

His mouth twitched. "Oh, right."

"When the demonic armies come," I said, "they will

expect us to be defensive, stand our ground, and to defend the hill. I don't care about this hill. It's just rock and dirt. We will not wait here while they overwhelm us with their numbers. They will attempt to wrap around us, to charge our front and fold around us like wings on either side until we are crushed. We must do that to them first. We must take an offensive approach."

"We have to stay spread out," Will said.

"Yes," I agreed with a nod. "It will spread us thin and weaken our ranks, but if we surprise Sammael's armies, then we can even the odds, perhaps even gain the upper hand."

Madeleine studied the diagram in the sand. "But how? We are at the top of this hill and they can see everything."

"Not everything," I said. "They won't be able to see behind the hill and they won't expect us to charge at them. This is an infantry battle, but that doesn't mean we're limited to the ground. Our center—led by Will and Madeleine—will charge down the hill at the enemy center and catch them by surprise. They will certainly not expect that we have demonic reinforcements. Even *I* never expected so many. Thank you, Cadan. As our center charges, I want our wings—each led by Marcus and Ava—to fold around the enemy center, trapping them. I will need you to divide the human soldiers between our wings. Our demonic forces will come from overhead. We will trap them in the front, on the left and right, and from above. We will give them nowhere to run and we will annihilate them."

"And their leaders?" Berengar asked. "Lilith and Sammael?"

"Leave them to me," I said. "Do not attack them, because you will not survive. Keep the formation, keep driving. Wait for my signals to close the wings and to swarm from above. Does everyone understand? Cadan, Anders, Adara, get your infantry behind the hill. Do not engage until I tell you to. Ava, Marcus, the rest of you, prepare your forces."

Cadan nodded and took his captains with him to move the demonic troops, while Ava and Marcus went to divide the angelic troops into the wide, thin front with flanks that would—if successful—close on the armies of Sammael and Lilith.

Across the valley, a wall of space began to shimmer like heat rising from the pavement. Shadows moved through the darkness, headed directly for Har Megiddo. Their shapes crawled across the earth like the flames of an inferno licking across the ceiling of a burning room, only these flames were pitch-black in the night. The armies of Sammael began to pour through the Grim—five thousand demonic reapers, maybe ten.

"Madeleine," I called to her, catching her attention instantly. "Scout the edges of their forces. Find Lilith and Sammael and return to me with their locations."

She gave a curt nod, spread her wings, and lifted into the air. It was now time for me to summon Azrael and claim the hallowed glaive.

"Stay close to me," I said to Will and took his hand. "I need your strength now more than ever."

He shut his eyes and put his forehead to mine. "You have it."

When he stepped back, I clenched my right fist and spoke to the sky. "I am the Messenger, Gabriel, she who is set over all the powers. I evoke thee, Azrael, the Destroyer, lord of the shepherds of the dead."

I waited for that brilliant flash of light announcing the arrival of an angel, but there was none. My mouth opened in surprise and fear and I gaped at the ring on my finger. It grew warm when I used its power, but Azrael did not appear. Nothing happened.

"No, *no*," I moaned. "Why won't it work? I don't understand!"

"What's the matter?" Will asked, eyes bright with worry.

"The ring," I said. "It won't work. I did exactly what I did when I called Azrael last time. I don't understand why it fails now."

Will looked on toward the dark horizon. "Sammael's army is coming. What should we do?"

I took a deep breath to steady my nerves. "I will fight without Azrael's glaive."

Madeleine returned then, touching down from the sky and folding her wings back.

"Is Sammael down there?" I asked.

She shook her head. "Lilith leads them."

My jaw set and I searched the incoming army of Hellspawn. "Where is Sammael? He's the one I want."

"You can't defeat him without the hallowed glaive," Madeleine warned.

I gave her a sharp look. "Whether I have Azrael's glaive or not, I must fight. I have returned to Armageddon and now I must meet my brother in combat."

"Ellie," Will pleaded. "Sammael's armies are here. We can fight them first, then figure out why Azrael won't be summoned."

"No," I said firmly. "We must kill their leader and the demonic will scatter, confused and without orders. We must cut the head off the serpent and then deal with the rest. This is our best chance. Madeleine, take control of the front. When the demonic reach the edge of the hill, charge."

She left and I climbed to the crest of the stone wall once more. "God give me strength," I whispered to the stars.

The armies of Hell flooded into the valley to clash with the angelic and demonic reapers who fought for Heaven. Soon my ears would fill with battle cries, dying screams, and the clash of metal.

"I am the Messenger, Gabriel, she who is set over all the powers," I called out. "I evoke thee, Sammael, the Lord of Souls and Fallen angel of death. I am the Will of God and you shall come forth, incubus, the serpent with the lion's face, the Venom of God—"

"That is enough name calling," came a voice that sent

snakes through my belly. "I heard you the first time, little sister."

The sky flashed with blackness, impossibly darkening the night for an instant, and lightning cracked across the clouds. The blade of the scythe ripped through the sky first, encrusted with the eyes of the humans whose souls he'd devoured as if the dead eyes were jewels. Trophies dangled from the staff of the scythe—human and animal hair, bones, and teeth—and I stared into the face of the grinning skull mounted atop the enormous blade. Sammael, boasting his true Fallen form, emerged from the shadows, his charred, skeletal wings spread to a pitiful width, the joints cracking and burned tendons tearing. His armor gleamed like oil slicks in the moonlight, and the horns on his head cut through the failing light like spires twisting toward the heavens.

He touched the ground, settling light as a feather. Flanking him was his pair of pet leonine reapers that had come through the void when he was released from the sarcophagus. Their dark slate coats rippled over sleek, sinewy bodies, and when their eyes—as golden as Sammael's and mine—found my face, they snapped their powerful jaws and the bone spikes in their manes prickled. Will stepped close to me, shielding me as they circled us both.

"Gabriel, Gabriel," Sammael crooned. "Look at you, all grown up and come to Armageddon to sound your horn. I warned you what would happen if you stood against me."

I summoned my Khopesh swords and angelfire swallowed

them, the white light devouring the darkness. My wings burst free and I launched myself off the ground at him with a fierce cry. I lifted a sword—and then teeth clamped around my ankle and yanked me back to the earth. I fell onto my hands and knees, grinding rock into my skin, and before I could turn to see what had hold of me, it dragged me backward across stone. I whipped around, beating my wings to break free. One of the leonine reapers stepped in front of me and I turned my head to see the other had been the thing to chomp down on my ankle. I swore as the leonine in front of me moved in for the kill. A figure blurred above it and it looked up, hissing like a crocodile, as Will swung his sword through its neck. The leonine's head went spiraling through the air, its quilled mane scattering spikes across the ground.

With that threat gone, I shoved my free boot into the dirt and kicked off. I spun in the air, sweeping an angelfire-drenched sword toward the remaining leonine reaper's face. It was smarter than its brother; it dropped me and opened its jaws to roar as it backed off. My boots found the earth again and I stomped toward the reaper, wings wide and swords swinging. It sank onto its haunches, skeletal tail swaying left and right, talons kneading the rock, carving gouges into the surface. Then it sprang, claws questing for me, but exposing its unprotected chest. I stepped aside and slashed a sword, cutting deep into the leonine reaper's chest. It loosed a scream that was almost humanlike and it hit the ground, shredding earth with its claws as it slid to a stop. It whirled and came at me again. This time I stood firm and didn't give in as I slashed my sword again. My blade cut through the hard cage of bone and tore the tender organs within. The reaper's body burst into angelfire and ash, vaporizing around me.

I didn't wait for the flames to disperse before I burst through, looking for Sammael once more. But instead of him, I saw his army of demonic crawling toward the bottom of the hill.

"Madeleine!" I screamed, praying she would hear me. "Engage!"

Almost immediately, our army rushed forward. The demonic front line, confused as I'd hoped, halted their march. They lifted their swords, turning their offensive strike to defensive, as the angelic forces cascaded down the hill and collided with the demonic. There was a tremendous sound, almost unidentifiable. Voices grunting and bodies thudding and sword strikes and dying . . . There was so much of everything that it was like a relentless white noise. The overwhelming numbers of demonic reapers began to pour around the edges of our center and I glimpsed a few attempting to climb the hill.

I pointed at them and called to Will, "Take care of them! Don't let them find Cadan's forces!"

Will nodded and took off like a shot, cutting through the overflowing demonic reapers. As the enemy force began to weaken and thin its front, I looked for Ava and Marcus, who waited with their troops, watching the battle intently.

I hopped onto a rock ledge so that I could be seen and heard by my army. "Left and right flanks, engage!"

The answering battle cries were deafening; boots thudded the earth as the remainder of my front line swept both sides of the demonic forces and closed in. Amidst the metallic shrieks of clashing swords, the guns belong to Ethan Stone's mercenaries flashed and popped like hundreds of small fireworks. Bodies were cut down as the angelic reapers pushed and carved into the demonic troops, squeezing them tighter into one another.

With a manic grin, I turned around to signal for our sky infantry. "Cadan!" I called, letting the wind carry my cry. "Engage!"

My voice echoed into oblivion. There was no response of battle cries and rushing of soldiers. There was nothing. He didn't come.

Oh, God. Oh my God. Where was he? Where was Cadan?

My heart pounded faster and heavier, like a train rocketing toward me. I didn't want to believe that he'd abandoned me, *betrayed* me. Cadan, my friend. He told me that he loved me. I'd even . . . I'd even *what*? Had feelings for him? Loved him, maybe?

"Cadan!" I screamed. *"Cadan!"*

The demonic reapers I believed came to fight for me, believed could help us win this battle. . . .

They were gone.

I was wild with fear, spinning, looking in every direction,

staring up at the sky, hoping to see them diving down to engulf the enemy and finish them off.

My eyes returned to the battlefield. I could no longer see Marcus. I watched Berengar fall, crumbling to stone. Madeleine was taken down by an ursid reaper and then I lost her position. And Ava. Oh, Ava. A demonic reaper opened her throat and slashed again, taking her head with the second strike. I felt my human soul wither and tears came through my eyes, running into the blood on my cheeks. I looked for Will, but I couldn't see him. There were too many bodies struggling above more bodies on the ground.

I turned, unable to bear the sight of the carnage, and I turned right into Lilith. I took in a sharp, painful gasp.

"Oh, did someone leave you high and dry?" she asked as if speaking to a child with a skinned knee. Then she punched me right in the face, making my head snap back. "That can't possibly help your abandonment issues, can it?"

I snarled and sliced my fiery swords toward her. She flicked a wrist and my body went soaring through the air. My back slammed into a stone wall between a row of crumbling ruins. With another wave of her hand, I zipped through space again and the front of my body hit the wall opposite the narrow path. I moaned in pain as her power smashed my body into the rock and mortar. She flung me across the road again and this time *through* a wall. I landed in a heap of crumbling stone, dirt, and earth crushing my body. Lilith lifted me, every part of me shrieking in agony, through the mountain of debris covering me and I didn't realize my swords were missing until I was high in the air and frozen by her power coiling around my limbs. I thrashed as much as I could, but she held me too tightly. Then she hurled me over a rock ledge and into a pit. My body slammed into the enormous sacrificial altar so powerfully that the stone foundation erupted, leaving me in a crater of my own making and my broken wings sprawled out beneath me. It was all too much for me to even stop and notice the irony of my situation.

I was unarmed, beaten to a pulp, and abandoned by Azrael and Cadan. As I stared up into the black, starless sky, catching Lilith's silhouette at the top of the ledge she'd thrown me from, a tear slid down my cheek.

No. I couldn't feel defeated already. I'd come so far, through thousands of years of torment and war to get here. I couldn't give up, but I needed help.

"Azrael," I whispered as I slowly pushed myself off the ground, closing my fist around a handful of pebbles. Blood ran down my arm and dirt clung to my hair and clothing. "Azrael, *please.* I need you, Brother."

Lightning cracked across the sky, over and over, crisscrossing each strike and never fading. The atmosphere grew heavy and low, pulsing, hammering with thunder. I stared, perplexed, as the clouds parted as if a knife were being drawn through them, carving a gash a million miles long.

And then the angels poured in through the hole in the sky.

33

THEY WERE SO BEAUTIFUL, THE ANGELS, AS THEY dropped from the sky like pearls swinging off a broken necklace, bright and gleaming and tumbling through the air. The angels descended on the demonic reapers as Cadan's forces had been meant to do. One of them came straight toward me, shooting like a fireball. He slowed and I recognized him. His silvery wings reflected light off his armor and his dark skin was luminescent, russet eyes streaked with gold. I had to blink. He seemed a little human in his corporeal form.

"I apologize for my poor punctuality, Sister," Azrael said, smiling ear to ear, "but I brought some friends."

He offered me a hand and as soon as I took it, heat rocketed through my body to the tips of my wings, healing me instantly. "You came," I breathed, having to force the words out past my utter shock.

"We were at last given the orders to descend to Earth," he said happily. "Michael leads the legion. We will devastate the demonic Hellspawn. It's up to you to defeat Sammael."

"But not alone," came another voice. Antares settled to the ground beside Azrael, her gleaming auburn hair settling around shoulders and wings. She had returned to her former glory and was even more achingly beautiful than before. "I don't believe our bargain was entirely even," she said. "I'd like to amend that tonight, if you'll accept my assistance."

I held out a hand for her to shake. "Thank you."

Antares watched my hand curiously, and then I realized how human the gesture was. But she surprised me when she took my hand in both of hers and held it tight. "I'm honored to fight with you," she said.

"And I with you, but—" I turned to Azrael. "I lost my swords."

"You don't need them anymore." Azrael held out his arm and the hallowed glaive shimmered into existence. I stared at it, bathed in the beauty of the weapon, and I took the staff tenderly in both my hands. I closed my fingers around it, feeling the heat from its energy course into me and meld with my own, as if it were merely an extension of me—a fifth limb.

"Remember what I told you," Azrael said, voice grave, "about summoning the power to use the hallowed glaive."

I looked up to meet his gaze. "I know. I'm ready. Thank you, Brother."

Antares called a long, elegantly curved sword. "I will meet you on the battlefield. Good luck to you." Her wings carried her into the air, and she was gone.

"I must return to Michael now," Azrael said. "All of our brothers and sisters have come to fight and to bid you farewell."

I smiled at him. "I'm happy that I won't be alone when I lie down for the last time."

Azrael jumped into the sky, beat his wings once, and shot toward the battlefield so fast that he became a ball of fire once again. I squeezed the staff of the hallowed glaive again, testing its center of balance. I wasn't nearly as tall as Azrael, but the glaive, behaving like a sentient thing, seemed to adjust to exactly where I needed it.

"*Gabriel!*" Lilith screamed in rage from above.

I answered her call, leaping into the air, feeling rejuvenated by my healed body and new hope. The black eyes of the Demon Queen fixed on me as I dived for her, and the hallowed glaive lit up with angelfire from blade to pommel. She drew her own weapon, a thin blade nearly as long as she was tall. From above, I struck, swiping left and right with the glaive. Her sword glanced off each blow and she whipped her body out of the glaive's path when I thrust it right at her chest. This was my vulnerable point, I realized, when she sliced open my arm. I left myself open with every attack. I hissed in pain and spun my body, smashing the pole of my weapon into her back. She hit the dirt with a grunt and my boots found the earth.

"I hate you," she snarled. "You, and everything you stand for."

"The feeling is mutual, I assure you," I said in return.

We circled each other, searching for any sign of weakness. She wore no armor, so all I needed to do was get past her sword. The length of the glaive would help me do that, but I still felt a little clumsy and unused to such a small blade in proportion to the long helve. I charged at her again and her blade met my strike; left and right I sliced, cutting fabric and flesh as she cut mine. I launched off the ground and kicked her in the chest. As she staggered away, I flipped the glaive over my head and thrust. The blade plunged into her belly, just shy of her heart.

She bared her teeth at me, grabbed the helve, and yanked the blade from her body. She held fast and I refused to let go of my weapon. She dragged me toward her and slashed with her sword. When I ducked to avoid losing my head, she kicked me in the ribs and then again right under the chin. I flipped end over end through the air and hit the ground with a grunt, feeling my cracked ribs and jaw twisting and snapping back into place. The healing was even more agonizing than when they first broke. Lilith came toward me and I struggled to rise, flailing, and every muscle in my torso shrieked as the ribs healed. I reached for the glaive, but she crushed her boot into my wrist, shattering it as well. I screamed in pain, writhing.

"My favorite song!" Lilith said joyfully. "Though I do prefer the chorus to the verses. What shall I break next to get you to sing the bridge?"

"Ellie!"

My head fell to the side just in time to spot Cadan jetting toward us. Lilith snarled, having noticed him too. She cast a hand out, her power grabbing his body and hurling him over her head through the air. He hit the rocky ground with a thud and an earsplitting crack and then lay still.

With my good hand, I grabbed a fistful of dirt and pebbles, and just as Lilith looked back at me, I chucked the debris into her face. She screeched and clawed at her eyes, but she lost enough of her focus for me to roll free. I grabbed the pole on my way to my feet and shoved the blade with all of my strength right through her chest, punching through her body cavity, stopping her cold.

Lilith dropped to her knees and the glaive's magic killed her, sending lightning through her veins and crackling in her open mouth and eyes. I ripped the blade back out and she began to shudder violently, collapsing onto her back. Her death throes finally faded when her life did, and the lightning consumed her in angelfire flames. As the power of the hallowed glaive took the Demon Queen's life, I could feel it slowly taking mine with her. I'd used so much of my angelic energy to destroy her that I wasn't sure if I had enough left in me to battle Sammael. It was suddenly harder for me to breathe. My limbs felt heavier and a bit numb, as if they were full of sand.

I darted toward where Cadan had fallen, and I crumpled to the ground by his side. I checked him for injuries, which healed quickly, and I held his face, searching his opal eyes.

"Cadan," I said to him, turning his face to mine.

He grimaced with pain as he sat upright. "Did you get her?"

I nodded. "What happened?" I asked him. "Why didn't you move the forces? Where are Adara and Anders?"

"Anders killed Adara," he answered with a grunt of discomfort as bones cracked into their rightful positions. "The traitor tried to stop us from engaging."

Rage boiled through me. "Where is Anders?"

"Over there," he said with a gesture of his head in one direction and then in the other. "And over there. He's in a few pieces after he tried to kill me too. The *stupid* traitor."

I smiled at that, overjoyed that what I feared had happened wasn't the truth. "I worried that you had betrayed me."

His expression crushed with hurt. "No. Never."

"Thank God," I said, and hugged him close.

When I released him, he smiled up at me a little deliriously. "You're a beautiful angel. You glow. And you're badass. Just as I thought you'd be. You never disappoint."

"Hit on me later," I said with a grin. "We've got a war to win."

I took his hand and helped him to his feet. "Where are the demonic troops?"

"Still waiting," he said. "Anders distracted me from hearing your signal and I never sent them."

"That's okay. Heaven sent reinforcements. I give you my signal now to engage. Clean up what's left of Sammael's forces and I will find him and destroy him. My body is growing tired and I have to do this now before I'm too weak. I want to say good—"

Cadan took my hand and pulled me to his chest, making me gasp. He touched my cheek, thumb brushing my bottom lip. "No," he said gently. "That will not be the last thing you say to me."

His fire-opal eyes, hardened, impassioned, moved over my face, my throat, my shoulder, my wings. He opened his mouth and inhaled, but he said nothing. He just gave a nearly imperceptible shake of his head and gazed at me.

"I have no words," he told me.

I stared at him and swallowed, feeling my heart whirring in my chest. "That's a first."

He grinned sideways and drew my face to his. He kissed my cheek, pausing, lingering as if we had all the time in the world to just stay like that. He held me close, as if we'd just been dancing and I couldn't help closing my eyes and leaning into him. This kind of comfort was something I'd never experienced as an angel before, this human sort of love, a friendship.

He pulled away and I opened my eyes to his face. "Thank you," he said, all the humor gone from his expression. "For fixing me."

"You never needed redemption," I told him. I put my hand to his chest. "You had it in your soul all this time. I never would've made it this far without you."

"You'll make it farther," he promised. "Don't give up hope. Now go. Kill the Lord of Souls."

I didn't have it in me to tell him that I was already dying, but I understood that he knew. I just needed to find my strength and keep fighting. I squeezed the helve of the hallowed glaive in my hand. The staff was so solid that it gave not even a gasp under my strength.

Cadan turned and jogged toward the back of the hill where his forces waited. I stood, strung so tight I felt like I was about to snap, as I listened to the assembly of the legion of demonic reapers who'd pledged their loyalty to Heaven. There was a great rushing of wind as wings and talons took flight, blackening the crest of Armageddon with their shadows as they descended on the armies of Hell.

I raced through a path between crumbling buildings toward the top of a rock ledge to watch the demonic reapers descend on their kin. I searched for Sammael, but I couldn't see him. Where he had gone when his leonine reapers had distracted me was a mystery.

"Sammael!" I screamed. "Come and show your face, you coward! Sammael!"

A hand clasped around my throat from behind me, tightening around my windpipe until it creaked. "Here I am, Sister," he hissed, his ice-cold lips brushing my ear.

I cracked the back of my skull into his nose. He roared in anger and I twisted away, swiping the glaive through the air between us. The blade shrieked across his chest plate.

The Lord of Souls glanced down at the gleaming streak I'd put in his armor and frowned. "Azrael's glaive."

"Look familiar?" I taunted, circling him.

"When he and I last met," Sammael said, "Azrael fought me with that blade."

"He should have killed you with it," I growled. "But I supposed he's left that up to me."

I charged at him, slashing and thrusting the blade, forcing him to move backward. The staff of his scythe clanged off the staff of mine, the angelfire lighting the space between us, and his demonfire exploded, the flames dancing obsidian and midnight. I caught the scythe in the hook blades of the partisan. The demonfire blazing against my skin felt more like acid than flames. My wings beat once to launch my body into the air, dragging the scythe with me as I spiraled over Sammael's head. I forced his weapon to the ground and released it to thrust my blade toward his face. The metal ripped through his corpse-gray cheek, flinging blood. He stepped aside, scowling and wiping his cheek with the back of the obsidian gauntlet covering his hand.

I thrust with the blade again and he whirled out of its path, smashing his elbow into my face as he came around. I hit the ground on my back and I kicked him in the knee. He grunted and collapsed forward and I kicked him in the chin. His head snapped back and he staggered, falling to his knees. I scrambled away, jumped to my feet, and returned to my ward just as Madeleine had taught me. I tried not to think about her, for fear that she was dead along with Ava.

I gasped for breath. My body was buckling. This power—it was all too much for me. I'd remained in Heaven for decades to gain power, and now it was killing me. I had to call all of it in order to use the hallowed glaive and it was slowly destroying me.

Sammael was angry. With blood smeared across his face and golden eyes blazing, he launched himself at me, charred wings wide. He swung the burning scythe up high, towering over me, dangling bones and teeth clinking against each other, and he brought it down in a sweeping arc as I threw my weapon to parry his. The scythe hooked through one of the outer partisan blades and completely around the staff, and he pulled the glaive right out of my hands. It went soaring through the air behind him, landing nearly two dozen feet away from me, and my angelfire went out like a candle flame. Before I could dart around him to retrieve the weapon, his form vanished and reappeared in front of me, blocking my path. I ran the other way, but he blocked me again. I needed the glaive. Without a weapon I would die immediately. I raced directly for him, to his surprise, but instead of colliding with him, I hit the ground and slid across the pebbles and dirt and right through his legs. I stopped sliding and rolled to maintain my momentum, and I collected the glaive. My heart pounded. I felt my strength slipping.

He set the pommel of his scythe on the ground and lifted his hand. His power snaked off his form and slithered toward his palm, inky tendrils coiling around his armored limbs. Then his power rushed at me full-force, a black tsunami of electricity and Hellfire. I took it straight on, but it was so strong that I felt my boots slipping in the dirt and I was forced to fold my wings to protect them. Wind threw pebbles in my face, whipped my hair around like flames. I gripped the staff of the hallowed glaive tighter and I took a step, but I couldn't move anymore. Summoning the power just to keep myself standing was draining me.

I glimpsed a shadow passing behind Sammael's form and an enormous blade punched through his body, right through his armor. The sword slipped free and Sammael doubled over, and I could see Will at last. My Guardian raised his sword to strike again, but Sammael's power hurled into his chest, knocking him back, which lifted the force rocketing against me barely enough to free me. Will hit the ground and when his green eyes met mine, I knew. I wouldn't let the distraction go to waste.

Wings spread, I launched, my energy erupting like a bomb, and I raced full speed toward Sammael. I thrust the glaive, he knocked it aside with his hand, and I smacked the pommel into his ribs. As I slashed the blade, I studied his armor, searching for weaknesses that would allow me a killing blow. My best chance to kill him would be through his unprotected neck. The metal collars of his chest plate were high, but they didn't cover every inch of his vulnerable skin. When the scythe hooked in the outer partisan blades this time, I was prepared. I wrenched it from his grip and flung it across the ground. I spun the staff around my body and before he could retrieve his blade, I pressed the tip of the glaive directly into the hollow of his throat, freeing a trickle of blood from his soft skin. His golden eyes stared up into mine, his life firmly in my grip.

"It's over," I snarled.

The hardness in his expression did not falter, even though he knew he was about to die. "I am not the only lord in Hell. Others will rise to take my place. The Morningstar will crave revenge."

"Let them come."

I slashed one last time and opened his throat. He coughed and gagged, drowning in his own blood. I watched him suffer, feeling the wall my archangel discipline had built around my emotions crash down completely. I let my tears run as I stared into his face. He seemed beyond the pain now, and perplexed by my emotions. His mouth moved as if he would speak but was unable. Lightning flashed beneath his skin, once, twice, three times. And then his eyes rolled into the back of his head as his life's blood was spent, pooling in the dirt beneath us.

I turned away, gasping for breath, and gazed upon the battlefield, knowing I had friends among the dead. Still, our forces had devastated the armies of Hell. The bodies of the dead had turned to stone, and the valley looked more like a boulder field than farmland. There were human corpses lying bloodied and broken among the reaper remains. My heart felt sick and I was tired, so very tired. But I wasn't done yet.

"Ellie." Will's voice was quiet behind me. I closed my eyes as he stepped near and I sensed his heavy, gentle presence. He laid his hands on my arms, his touch soft and warm.

"Where are my friends?" I asked. "I want to see them."

He drew away, his fingertips lingering on my skin, and then he started down the hill. My grip on the hallowed glaive grew weak and I almost dropped it. Will called to Marcus, and they met among the ruins. Will dipped his head close to Marcus and said something I couldn't hear from this distance. Marcus put a hand on Will's shoulder, and I had to look away.

I glimpsed Cadan walking among the bodies. He moved toward a reaper lying in the rubble. I saw that the fallen vir was Ronan, still lingering. Cadan knelt beside him and took his hand. They exchanged words, and moments later, Ronan was gone. I wanted to call to Cadan, to comfort him as he grieved for his friend, but then I remembered that I did not want him to repeat so soon what he had just endured. I didn't want to make him watch me die. Our last words had been enough.

Will and Marcus made their way back to me through the

debris. Marcus offered me an encouraging and triumphant smile that still couldn't hide his sadness. His clothes were torn, filthy, and bloodied, and his skin was marred by still-healing wounds.

"We've won," Marcus said. "Ellie, you did it."

"No," I replied. "We all did it."

His gaze seemed to search for the injuries bringing me down, but he would find none. "The angels are helping our forces kill the last of the enemy. The demonic reapers who fought with Cadan are spared but the ones loyal to Hell are destroyed. There may be pockets of them somewhere in the world, but there's no way they can replenish their ranks before we find the last of them and wipe them out. The war is finished."

I felt a rush of relief and joy, and I smiled. "I never thought this day would come."

"Did our friends make it?" Will asked.

"Ava is dead," Marcus said, his voice grave. "She was taken down by a demonic vir. Cadan is helping the others look for survivors."

Will looked toward the now-quiet battlefield. "My mother?"

"Madeleine was injured badly, but she'll live. Evolet is with her now, making sure she heals."

"You've done so well, Marcus," I told him. "If you find Azrael, please thank him for me. And give Kate my love."

He hesitated before leaving, but then he yanked me into

him and gave me a strong hug, burying his face in my hair. The hallowed glaive slipped from my fingers and clattered to the ground as I wrapped my arms around him with the last of my strength. "You're the one who has done well," he whispered. "I'll be seeing you soon."

He pulled away, and I was sad to watch him leave. I wanted to follow him, to help Cadan find the survivors, to keep on going, but I was so tired. My breathing became even more ragged and I closed my eyes, feeling the wind on my skin, savoring it. My wings vanished back into my shoulders, unable to hold their form any longer. I was falling before I realized it, but strong arms looped around me, and I sensed him all over, took in his scent, felt his rough cheek against mine.

"I've got you," Will whispered, his voice so weak I wanted to cling to him and comfort him. He knew as well as I that I was finished. The endless power of the hallowed glaive would take one more life tonight.

He picked me up and carried me to a soft patch of grass at the top of Armageddon, and this was the place where I would die. The clouds had gone and the night sky had opened up with a cascade of bright stars. The air was cool on my skin and where Will touched me, I was warm. It wasn't so hard to breathe now that I was lying down, but breaths came slower and shorter. My heartbeat wasn't so fierce now, but it was pumping a sense of serenity through me that I didn't fear. For the first time in many, many lifetimes, I wasn't afraid to die.

But when I looked up into Will's face, everything changed. The sorrow in his green eyes was so terrible and so beautiful that I was overcome by it. I'd only seen his tears a handful of times in five hundred years, but still they shattered me every time.

"I can't do this," he said, trembling. "I can't say goodbye to you forever."

I offered him a smile as sweet and as big as I could summon, but I was so fragile. "It's all right. This was meant to be."

He bit his lip and said, "So were we."

Tears rolled over my cheeks and slipped into my hair as I gazed up at him. "I am so sorry. I love you. Please know that. It's the only thing that matters now."

He shook his head. "You can't leave me alone."

"But you're not alone," I told him. "You have your mother and your brother and your friends."

He touched my cheek and traced my lips. "I'm nothing without you."

"Do you remember the night you kissed me for the first time, when I told you that I wanted to live?"

He exhaled, the breath stolen from him, and he nodded. "Yes. Oh, God, Ell . . ."

I smiled at him. "I have. I have lived. Thank you."

He said nothing, but a tear fell from his eye and hit my cheek.

* * *

Time had passed, but I couldn't tell how much. Will held me in his arms and I curled my body into him, feeling the rise and fall of his chest as he breathed, listening to his heartbeat. My own heart slowed and I grew weaker as my body broke down, but I wouldn't untangle my fingers from around his shirt. I memorized him, his scent, the feel of him holding me, every contour of muscle beneath his skin, every rip and tear in his clothes from battle. . . . I wanted this moment to burn itself into my mind, into my soul, so that wherever I went once I closed my eyes this last time, I wouldn't forget him.

"Ellie," he whispered, breaking the silence between us.

I tightened my fingers around the cloth of his shirt. "Yes?" My voice was tiny, soft, barely anything more than beating butterfly wings.

His chest shuddered and I felt a warm drop of tear fall onto my hand. "You were quiet. I thought you'd gone."

"No," I told him. "But I'm so tired."

"Stay here, please," he whispered. "I'm begging you."

"I'll try to come back," I promised. "I'll find a way. Will you wait for me?"

"I'll wait forever." His lips pressed against my hair and he tilted my face up. "I swear to you that I will still be here. Even if you never come back, I'll keep waiting for you."

"I will fight all the way here if I have to," I said, clutching him tighter.

"I know you would. You're the fiercest girl I've ever met."

I moved my hand up his chest to cradle his face and

I pulled him down to me. I took a breath just as I kissed him. He kissed me back gently as his lips moved with mine. Then he broke away with a wretched, sorrowful sound and he kissed my cheek, my temple, my forehead, and my lips one last time.

"I'll be here," he said. "For however long it takes. A year, ten thousand. I will not leave this world until you return to me."

I brushed my hand over his cheek until I couldn't hold it up anymore. "I promise I'll come back to you. I won't forget your face. I'll come back."

And then Will's face faded away.

EPILOGUE

Will

THE ONLY REASON I WAS HELPING KATE MOVE INTO her dorm was because Marcus had made me. And because I liked Kate, though she still scared the hell out of me.

And because she told me I needed to be happy again.

I wasn't especially fond of the university life in East Lansing. It was manic, alcohol-and-study-crazed, and there were too many people for me to enjoy it. But it felt safe from reapers here. Since the battle on Armageddon, the numbers of demonic reapers loyal to Hell had been devastated. Reapers no longer prowled the Grim, hunting humans. There were some reapers out there, but so few they were hardly a threat as we picked them off, one by one. We and the angels had just about wiped them out. I was, to be honest, bored and unfocused. Marcus, however, was clearly thriving.

"I think I may enroll," he confessed.

Kate dropped a box of clothes onto the narrow twin bed on her side of the room. "You can't just enroll, moron. You have to be accepted."

He gave her a haughty grin. "Oh, they'll accept me. As soon as they hear I'm in town, they'll send their sexiest interns chasing me down the street, waving scholarship offers printed on fragranced paper smattered with lipstick smudges."

Kate promptly socked him in the gut and knocked the breath out of him. "Find my hangers so I can put my clothes away. It's after dark and I want to go party. All the fraternities heard I was moving in and I don't want to keep those hot frat boys waiting. Boys . . ." She sighed. "Their attention spans are so limited, you know."

Marcus grinned, grabbed her shirt and tugged her close, and he nipped her neck playfully. I sighed, shook my head, and set the television I'd just brought in for her on the desk. I'd tried so hard since we came up here not to look at the other side of the room, where Ellie was supposed to be moving in her own things today. I never realized how difficult it'd be for me to help Kate move in until I saw the empty bed and desk. My heart tried to break all over again. Everything was just too empty now.

It had been two and a half months. The university hadn't assigned a replacement roommate for Kate. Things would be easier if there was someone there to fill the void Ellie had left, but there wasn't. All I had left of her were her swords. I had wrapped them in cloth and put them away in my room. I couldn't even look at them anymore.

Ellie had died in my arms. Even as an archangel, she had felt so small and fragile. I had held her dying so many times before then, but that final time was different. We had come so far since we were reunited. We'd loved so fiercely. She had been mine if only for such a cruelly short time. A few months in five hundred years was not enough time. I'd do it all over again, though. I'd lose her forever all over again. I would never give back those few months even for a less-broken heart.

One by one the angels had come to the top of Har Megiddo where I sat, holding her body close to mine after she'd died. I'd fought alongside them in that battle, but up close, when they stood quietly watching us, they looked as beautiful as they looked unreal. The angels weren't supposed to feel emotion, but they were weeping. All of them. Their tears stained their flawless faces like rain running in rivulets across stone. Azrael was the only one of them who came to me, knelt in front of me, and took her from my arms. He was the angel of death come to carry his sister home. I didn't want to give her up, knowing it would be the last time I ever saw her face. I had died on that wretched hill with her.

I stayed with my mother for a few weeks afterward. I did as Ellie had told me, got to know my mother again, and during those weeks, I felt glimpses of what happiness used to be like. My brother hadn't been around for almost a month, but

Cadan had his own way of grieving, I supposed. Once our pain faded and every day seemed less difficult to endure, I wanted to know him like family, to know what it was like to have a brother. To feel less empty.

I wanted to move on, but my soul wouldn't let me. Every day I awoke with hope, but it was too early for Ellie to be reborn—*if* she would be reborn. There was no sign from the angels, no word on what had happened to her. I even took the Pentalpha and attempted to summon Azrael or Michael and beg them to tell me if they knew where she was, but the power had gone from the relic as she had from this world. There were no words for the hopelessness I felt after that.

But I prayed every day for her to come back to me, somehow, some way. I would never stop praying.

"Do you need anything else?" I asked Kate, trying to pretend she and Marcus weren't practically tearing each other's clothes off while I was still in the room.

"Mmm?" she asked, pulling herself from Marcus just enough to glance at me. "No. Thanks for everything, Will."

"Actually," Marcus said, untangling himself from her and peeling her hands off him. He eased toward me while she pouted. He dipped his head close to mine and said in a low voice, "Do you mind stepping out for like, two hours?"

Behind him, Kate guffawed. "*Two* hours? You wish!"

I slapped a hand on his shoulder. "Sure, man. You got it. I could use some fresh air."

I headed out of the dorm room, shutting the door behind

me, and I wandered toward the elevator. The hall was packed with students and parents who hadn't quite finished their moving in yet. I stuffed my hands in my pockets as I stepped into the elevator. It rumbled slowly to the main floor and then the doors whined open, allowing everyone to pour out ahead of me. I strolled through the lobby and out into the night. The air was crisp and the sky was clear and bright with stars, though they were a little difficult to see among the haze of city lights.

I meandered past the tall dorm buildings, through the parking lots, weaving around vehicles, and aimed for the field beyond the small woods. It was interesting how this bustling, sprawling city just ended so abruptly and became farmland. On one side of the road, it was a busy university campus and on the other, there were fields and trees and lots of deer.

A blinding flash of light above my head made me squint and shield my eyes. It was unlike anything I'd ever seen before: a falling star, hurtling toward the earth. I watched in awe, slack-jawed, and the hairs on my arms rose, tickling me. My mind raced with possibilities, but I had no answer for what I'd just witnessed. So I ran, unsure of exactly what I was following, but certain it was no natural phenomena. The energy erupting from this thing was enormous, and whatever it was, good or evil, it was dangerous.

The falling star disappeared over the tops of the trees and the ground gave a tremendous roar and shook like a quake so strong that I was knocked to the ground. I picked myself off the grass and kept going. I had to know what it was. I had to know. I was lost in a daze, blinded on every side of me but up ahead. Nothing mattered in the world but finding this fallen star.

I darted through the trees, my shirt catching on twigs, but I didn't stop. The woods began to thin and then I found myself in a clearing, gazing at a smoking, shallow crater in the earth.

I didn't know when I'd stopped breathing, but suddenly I gasped for air. Heat and energy rolled across the grass toward my feet. I crept forward, sliding down the gentle slope into the crater, staring at the thing in the center of it that emanated a brilliant light and slowly unfolded itself before me.

Wings the color of moonlight and gold unfurled themselves from around a small, crouched feminine figure. The light coming from her was blazingly bright, but I never squinted, only stared wide-eyed with an overwhelming hope and careful joy. The girl pushed herself off the ground, her strange white clothing luminous beneath her wings. She lifted her head to look at me from beneath a waterfall of hair the color of cherries and dark chocolate and flame, and I fell to my knees.

She smiled, a gesture so beautiful and sweet that I felt tears sting my eyes. "Hello, Will."

"Impossible," I breathed, unable to compose myself. I

was shaking all over as if I were freezing, but her light was warm and gentle.

She stepped close to me, folding her wings back. She lifted a hand and my body rose unbidden to my feet. I reached up with trembling hands to touch her face.

"You're real," I said, staring at her in wonder. "This isn't a dream. Gabriel, you've returned."

Her smile became something that was very human and held a thousand secrets.

"Just call me Ellie."